Earth

Weeps

Not

By: Don Tynan

EARTH WEEPS NOT—A Work of Science Fiction

By: Don Tynan

   DonTynan.com
   dtnapa@hotmail.com

Copyright © Don Tynan, 2013

Printed for distribution by: Don Tynan

ISBN:0615775845

Provenance

Ten thousand stories have shouted out in never ending permutations a pending doom for mankind. An untold number of eyes have descried such catastrophe approaching on the near horizon. The prophets of apocalypse for decades prior rang the bells of alarm. Sages, seers, and scientists alike time and again tried to warn us of an imminent tragedy if we didn't change our ways. These deafening cacophonies of overlapping voices did little but deaden our ears to the growing danger. We didn't listen. We didn't care to listen.

It is simple to say that as mortals we face demise daily—such is life—into tragedy born we are. Live fast, for tomorrow you may die, was our mantra. Back then, our craven souls, possessed with a thirst for an ever higher standard of living pushed us on without a care for ourselves, or for the planet we live on. Our style of life was likened to one of a freight train speeding out of control and down a steep slope. At any turn it may fly off track, and go a tumbling to a fateful end.

A person's life should be likened a loan. As each

day passes a tic is marked down in the ledger of perdition's bank denoting a debt due. Silently that debt grows. No one individual, no one country, knows the amount of credit to be drawn there upon. At his whim the grim reaper of fate will arrive one day with notice in hand yelling, "Your loan has been called, sir. All your debts are immediately due and payable." In a world void of certainty we tarried on, mindlessly, carelessly; we destroyed what we willed, we took what we wanted—and then that prophesied day arrived.

Our end came unbidden; neither did we initially take note of it as such; not in our frenzied state of mind. The year was 2007. It first appeared as a crash in American markets, and came on the heels of a huge run up of values, and thus perceived, albeit wrongly, as the bust end of a boom-and-bust cycle. "Just a natural retracement of markets," we thought. "We can borrow and grow ourselves out of it." Yet this economic downturn persisted in spite of remedies to fix it. Locally, people, then towns, filed for bankruptcy. Then we saw larger cites falter. Soon this monetary blight spread wider and deeper across the globe.

In the years to follow countries fell, their economies smashed by overspending and monumental debt. To prevent a deepening crisis faltering nations required and demanded immediate financial assistance. However, these economic afflictions resisted the injection of any curative measures, and year after year our woes continued to worsen. The modern world saw a continual decline in their standard of living. Out-of-work masses gathered to protest, and challenged their governments do something. But what could they do? We had borrowed too heavily, and invested little. We were out of time, our line of credit cancelled. Nature's dreadful harbinger was at the door and banging hard to din payment from our souls. She knew well the only collateral we had left to bargain with were our souls. Whole societies had lost hope. Normally peaceful civilizations turned to violence, and out of anger and ignorance immolated their own cities. The year was 2016, the world was aflame, and mankind was standing at the precipice.

Then like an understanding parent, the universe decided to intervene—or so we thought. A wondrous majesty dropped from the skies. One so magnificent and supreme we awed in its presence. "Could it be anything but a divine gift?" we asked, "or was it merely God's final taunt of us as punishment for our sins?"

My name is Dr. John Parker, survivor. I am the chronicler of Earth's encounter with an alien species called the Breen, and of the horrible tragedies which befell our species. Why fate thrust this bane upon me, I cannot say. Some speculate that it was only happenstance. Others believe that a hidden force, perhaps even the hand of god played a role in it. Personally, I considered it a bitter and unwelcome curse. Regardless, what follows is my recount of that momentous, yet ominous, First Encounter with a group of highly evolved Spacefarers who washed up on our shores those many years ago—they came, they saw, they partied.

When the Breen arrived our planet was in the midst of a horrible and deepening economic crisis. Crude oil shortages were fracturing commerce; other resources were in depletion mode. The costs to produce needed materials like fertilizer were skyrocketing. We were seeing a buildup of rioting in normally peaceful populations. Localized wars were becoming more common, and threatened to spread wider. Humanity was on the verge of slipping into another dark age. To say it was an inopportune time to have visitors drop in would've been an understatement. Our house was in a mess, and we were not in the mood to entertain.

We treated them poorly, at first, those emissaries from another planet. Their supremacy over us was immediate and obvious. Our military feared them for their superior technology, and we all trembled in awe before them. Eventually we warmed to their presence, and to quell our fears, the Breen made it clear that they had not come to conquer, that they came in peace, and only wanted to be friends. Some of our leaders saw the danger in that friendship—I did not. Even if I had, there would be no way for me to have prevented the scourge that ensued.

Perhaps their arrival was a curse, perhaps it was a god send? Perhaps it was the universe's way of offering us clues to our survival? Those are questions for philosophers of the future to ponder; that is if there are to be any? There has not been a baby born here on our planet since early 2018. Not that it matters now. The years of war following the Breen's visit have left Earth's civilizations in shambles. I must say now that we had no idea our civilization was so fragile. That we, the self-christened masters of the universe, could see our civilization fall so precipitously and totally, took us all by surprise. The horrid deaths of billions due to starvation, disease, and conflict have sadly taken mankind to the brink of extinction.

It is for history's sake that I have reported the following events which unfolded here so many years ago. I have taken great pains to see that these events have been portrayed truly and correctly. All Breen data have been converted into human equivalents. Most of their data were taken from my interviews with, and the experiences I shared with them during their stay. I was allowed unfettered access to their ship's logs, and their holographic data recording devices. This allowed me to reproduce in clear detail their journey to Earth, why they came here, and more importantly, why they did what they did to us.

Occasionally, I have interjected a note containing my own thoughts, and any other information I felt pertinent, in the hopes that future generations will find them of use. These are not scientific observations. No, they are, for the most part, merely behavioral and historical observations taking brief note of cause and effect. It is the state of our science and technology that determines how we deal with the situations we find ourselves embroiled in. However the cause and effect relationships that led up to it were precipitated by human involvement.

It is too late to second-guess the choices we made in generations past. This is not the time to play that game, for now we struggle each day just to stay alive. Was it fallible man himself who caused his final descent? To posit that question, should we not also ask, "Is man inherently evil, or simply stupid?" I hope the following chapters may lead you to an answer.

To those of us who are still alive, to those of us who still care, to those who may exist in the future, please, read the following, and learn…...

1:

Earth in a Balance

In The Beginning
September 17th

There I was, at home, and sitting on the couch. Laptop computer resting on my, well, lap. For background noise I had the television on and the volume turned down low. It was already late at night, and I had been working on my book for the better part of the day. Why I chose to write a book escapes me. Being out of work, I certainly had the time, yet the question remains. I could feign to those who ask that unseen forces manipulated my hands to type. The ideas, for sure, were mine. There is no mistaking my dysgraphia, or, for that matter, lack of writing skills—thank you mister work processor. But the courage, the brazenness to dare put forth what I thought was a cure for the human condition? That, would take some embarrassed explaining.

For about the tenth time I had to modify the books introduction. The burden of rewriting what you once thought was good enough frustrated me. I would've dumped the whole mess off on an editor if it weren't for the stack of bills flung into a heap on my kitchen table. By dogged persistence I suffered through one last reading before I quit for the night...

Introduction for Tipping Points

Man pays casual regard to the world in which he lives. We prefer to believe that we are not subject to Mother Nature's rule anymore. That through some twisted sense of manifest destiny we have the right to do as we please, regardless of possible outcomes. And we and the world suffer for our mistaken beliefs. I have oft heard it said of late, that we treat our planet the way we treat each other—poorly. And that now we are beginning to reap the rewards of our misuse—hinting that man's time here on Earth may be coming to a close.

We find ourselves now in the early years of a new century. A century which could have seen man attain great wonders. More likely, due to our mishandling of our planet, it will see us reach an apex, and then go tumbling down a dark side into oblivion. Many prophesy that we are already at the brink of extinction. That we are currently experiencing the opening stages of a worldwide collapse. Any peruse of recent headlines would confirm that theory

When we reach that proverbial tipping point; what would it look like? Would we notice the opening stages of this collapse for what they are? Might they not look somewhat similar to what we are experiencing today—worldwide economic and environmental stress? Is Mankind, the most intelligent species ever to evolve on Earth, on the verge of slipping back into a dark age?

I cannot think that we have traveled this far in

our evolutionary journey just to have our species die out. That there isn't a grander underlying process silently guiding our evolution, and that, aside from our protests, we will never be able to completely sever the universe's umbilical cord.

My name is Dr. John Parker. I hold two advanced degrees; one in economics, and the other in the natural sciences. After graduating college I found work at a large brokerage house, where I helped them make sound investment decisions based on natural trends. After years of employment I was laid off due to company downsizing in the wake of our current economic slump. Now, out of work, and unable to find suitable work, like many of you, I have decided to write a book hoping to explain the reasons for this economic reversal, and to offer solutions for a recovery. I have titled this book, *Tipping Points*. It is an economic treatise highly critical of our government's role in our current deepening crisis. In this book I spell out how our economic problems are due less to ineffective political avarice, lender greed, and Wall Street gambling, and more to the world having hit a tipping point with regard to population versus living status and resource depletion. Trying to instill urgency in you, my readers, it predicts certain global disaster if immediate steps are not taken….

Yeah, that sounds good enough. Now to clip some of the day's headlines into my notes. Let's see,

Thirty-five killed by suicide bomber in Iraq
Twelve killed in rioting in Greece
Former Russian protectorate demands freedom
Tenth grader in US shoots and kills three fellow students

Then, and thanks for the interruption, the phone rings. Caller ID says that it was my brother again. "Crap! Can't he call at an earlier hour?" ... "Hello Sam, How are you?"

"Just calling to see how you are getting along, John."

"I'm making my daily tallies from the headlines. It has been another rather bloody day."

"For the life of me I don't know why you do that."

"It's research for my book."

"Oh God, there you are, back on that book idea again."

"Haven't much else to do right now, Sam."

"You could shelve your degrees, and look for a job, say, in the services industry?"

"Dam it, Sam. I know what is going wrong with our world. What kind of person would I be if I sat by and did nothing, said nothing? What kind of a person would that make me?"

"Normal, brother. There is nothing wrong with being normal."

"So, I should just sit back in my Easy-chair, open another beer, and zone out on some mindless TV program? ... Sam the world is ablaze. Don't you give a damn about that?"

"There is nothing we can do about it John. Those are the facts."

"Well, you might feel that way, but I am going to at least put some words out there."

"I wish you well, by the way, how close is your book to being done?"

"I am putting the final touches on the last chapter."

"Oh, and what is the last chapter about?"

"It is about parenting."

"Parenting, I thought you were writing a book about world economics, not family values?"

"Yes, well, my experience suggests that what the world needs the most right now is parenting."

"Brother, I just don't understand you anymore."

"Sam, it's late. I'm hanging up now."

"Good-night, John."

"Good-night, Sam." … "Idiot."

"Now, let's see. Back to writing." Reaching for my writing pad on chapter notes for parenting I make some scribbles, "What the human race needs right now is parenting. Parenting, as from??? Nature, the cosmos, Gaia—WTF is Gaia anyway? Government interference—no, no, no! Who in the hell could the human race look to for parenting? … Ah, what the fuck. Sam is right; we're probably all screwed anyway." Weary from writing I put my book notes away and decided to surf the net. Someone told me about free e-publishing. Well, what's a broke economist to do?

A Month Later
I did it. Ignoring the nonbelievers, and struggling through a maze of publishing hurdles, I managed to get my book out there. Some of my ideas might be quite severe, but tough love is far better than codling the masses with more giveaways. When will politicians stop playing Santa Claus? Although, it could be argued that our current problems far overshadow national debt woes. You can pay off debt, but what do you do when you run out of food to eat?

As the months crawled on
I was just returning home from a short jog. It had

been three months since I first published my book, and till now sales have been scant and few. Perhaps I should have chosen a different genre to write about. Current events by an unknown author—not a big seller. My brother hasn't even bought a copy yet. Doubt he can read anyway? Walking into the kitchen, I notice the blinking red light on my phone. What's this? Someone has left me a message? That reminds me, "Note to self, remember to cancel land line." That's an expense I don't need anymore. … "So, who wants what?" I pushed the play button, a young sounding lady's voice melted into my ear, "Hello, Dr. Parker, my name is Sherry Lawson; I am the personal secretary to General Rudy Bradley. This phone call is to advise you that you will be receiving a letter from him in your mail today. The General wants to talk with you regarding your new book. You have a meeting with him already scheduled for here at the Pentagon. All of the details will be spelled out in the letter. We hope to see you then." I replayed that message five more times. "I must say, she has a sexy voice, but what kind of joke was this?"

Later that day, after the mailman had come and gone, I went out and opened my mailbox; and with some caution. I had received a crank call earlier, and was worried that pranksters might be targeting me. Inside was a clutch of junk mail, several bills, and one curiously official looking large envelope with a return address to the Pentagon. "Well, whoever it is, they are going to great lengths to mess with me."

Retiring inside, I tossed my boring mail onto the mound of others built-up on the kitchen countertop. I couldn't pay any bills at this time anyway. The official looking envelope hit the pile then slipped over the top and down onto the floor.

Bending over to pick it up I noticed it had been sent express delivery. "You don't do a hoax and waste money on express do you?" I thought to myself. … "Alright, let's open you up."

"Huh," was all I could say. Just as the sexy woman on the phone mentioned it was an invitation to the Pentagon; complete with travel orders, and a round trip plane ticket.

January 13th, 11:01 AM

This is something else, me walking around in the Pentagon. Two days ago I was just another nothing hiding out in my southern Arizona home. Now I have been invited to meet with an austere group of senior American leaders. But what is it they want of me? I agreed to the meeting, but I must say that I am worried that I might be hushed away to some frozen gulag. I wasn't kind in what I said about our government and their role in our deepening crises.

Shit, I'm going to be late. Seems I've been walking around this place for a fucking eternity. Good thing I thought to arrive thirty minutes early. If I knew this place was this big I would have bought a god damn plane ticket. Lost in the pentagon, good one, John. And what is it with this fifty's-ish architecture. Dooh dooh, doo doo, Dooh doo, doo doo, the fifties, wasn't that when the twilight zone came out? Geeze, here it is, and I'm only a minute late—whew.

"Good morning miss, I'm Doctor Parker, I have an appointment with General Bradley."

"Yes, we have been expecting you Dr. Parker. You sound a bit winded. Have any trouble getting here?"

"Let's just say I've caught up on my weeks' worth of exercise."

"Must be your first time here, let me buzz the General" ... "General, Dr. Parker is here."

"Please show him in Sherry." Hmm, Sherry, the voice on the phone message.   "Sherry, that is a pretty name," I said, and got nothing, not even a look up, or a little smile. Could be my not being in military attire.

"Dr. Parker, let me show you into the meeting room?" and she adds, "You better take off that hat." All business, I get it. There is a coat and hat rack just off to the side of the door opening into the meeting room. I see a nice assemblage of military jackets and perfect as new hats hanging from this rack, and my god, look at all that brass and brick-a-brack. And she wants me to put my old dusty Aussie next to them? Might be the one thing about the military I agree with—they wear hats.

I respond to the lovely young lady by saying, "Thank you, Sherry." I took off my hat, hung it, and followed. "Wherever you want to lead me you lovely thing you," thinking to myself, "Even if I blow this interview, maybe I can get a date later." Just as we entered the room I whispered to her, "I'm not doing anything later?" A stupid line I know, one that only works in the movies. Well, this time she did break a little smile.

"Ah, Mr. Parker, come on in and have a seat." I took it that that was the General speaking to me. He didn't rise, not for me anyway. And though he was seated, I could still tell that he wasn't a tall man, definitely overweight, and probably in his mid-sixties. "My aide will introduce us all once you are comfortable." Obviously, this General stood on little that could be called tradition. I took him to be coarse, to the point, and controlling, which was anathema to my freewheeling scientific mind. I couldn't but hate him instantly.

Present at the meeting:

> General Rudy Bradley, and two aides.
> Adjutant General to the National Sec. Council, and his aide,
> Adjutant to the US Undersecretary of Defense, and an aide,
> and an appointed liaison from the President's office.

After some introductions, "Parker," said General Bradley, and in his sharp and throaty tone, "we have read your book and quite frankly, someone higher up than anyone here felt pretty damn scared about your conclusions." I suspected the General was hinting at Presidential involvement. "So, what we want is for you to think for a moment, and then let us know if you would be interested in working for your government." Then he added, "We want to give you a chance to research further the ideas you put forth in your book. You will have the opportunity to select a group of other scientists and economists to work with you. We want to see if your ideas have any merit." and he went on to say, "You will be the commander of this group. You will decide who you want to work with, and where you all will meet. I want you to scour the world for its best economic minds. Gather together these minds, and do your research. Then, I want you to make reports of your findings to me, and I will pass them on to the President. So you can see we are very serious about this." Short, not so sweet, and just like that. My lips must have been turning up at the corners. What? A job, I am in need of one, but I didn't hear any mention of pay? Should I push it? I mean, I have them right where they want me.

General Bradley went on to say, "Remember, if you take this job, you will be working for the government. You are going to be given top-secret security clearance, but with that comes responsibility. Everything you do from then on is to be considered sub-rosa. All research belongs to the government; all papers you write will need to be given sensitivity checks before they are disseminated. Further, there will be no books about the work you do here for us." after a short pause, "Also; be careful if and when you talk with the media. We aren't going to put you in seclusion. Your having autonomy is very important, and will be helpful and necessary to your research, I am sure. Just use this freedom wisely."

While listening to the General, I am thinking to myself, "Can I possibly work in such an authoritarian environment?" But then that nagging little guy on my shoulder shouted out, "You are in serious need of a job, idiot."

"Mr. Carter, if you decide to take this job, I will assign one of my aides to assist you in getting started. You will need his help to teach you how to use the government system."

"General, Sir, what sort of time frame am I working with here?" Shit, just listen to me, General sir. Hah! I'm not enlisted.

"We want some damn good preliminary reports within three months," he said.

"Three months. I can do that, and I am excited about getting a chance to do research work for a change," was all I had to say.

"Good, then you will do it?" My book was not the huge money tree I thought it would be, and my two degrees weren't in big demand right then either. This was a chance to get on the map. So, I decided to suck up my pride, but talk about working for the enemy. "General, Sir, you have a deal," I said, and like that I enter the proverbial lion's den.

Some more small talk ensued, and went on for about fifteen minutes. Then General Bradley said, "Parker, welcome aboard. Put together best team you can." With that, the others present stood, shook my hand, and left. Thunderstruck, dumbfounded; the stupid little smile on my face said it all. I didn't know whether to go, or where to go. Talk about being a lost fish in a pool full of sharks.

"So Parker, why not stay and talk with me a little?" asked Gen. Bradley. There was a silent pause while the other attendees collected their wraps and disappeared from view. Then General Bradley said, "I see you have two degrees, one in economics and one in natural science. I don't see how the two mesh. What does animal behavior and the natural world have to do with economics?"

"Is this guy kidding?" I thought to myself. Not wanting to be rude I responded, "Well, actually there are many examples of economic principles hidden in nature, sir. Economics is not just about the interchange of money, as we are accustomed to thinking of, but actually, it is also about relationships. It is about the competition between species for food and survival. It is about the controls Mother Nature has built-in to help keep it all in balance."

"I see. Very good reply. In your book, you have a chapter titled *Growth, and Not Growth* where you hinted that man has tipped the balance, and that population pressures are to blame?"

"Yes, the population explosion. I may have laid it out too hard there? Everyone seems to treat any talk of population control as a taboo," I said.

"Yes, you may have been overly blunt. It is a sensitive topic. How did you arrive at these conclusions about population reduction?"

"Well, if you break our socio-economics down into three parts. Let's label them the trading markets (stocks, bonds, banking, etc.), the housing markets (which includes all forms of real estate), and population centers (labor forces and entitlement pools). As every grade-schooler knows, life and markets rise and fall in cycles. What we need to realize is that the law of cycles applies to populations also, only on a different time scale; say sixty years.

Trading markets seem to cycle every ten years. We just witnessed a cycle, or fall in the housing market, which has a slightly longer cycle than the trading markets. What I was getting at in *Tipping Points* is that there are varying time scales to each these three markets, population having the longest. That you can't just pick any one of them and think of it as separate from the others. They all crossover and interleave each other so much so that neither is independent of the others. That being said, it is populations turn to cycle. To me the only question is how far it will retrace, but it needs to if we are to save mankind."

"So in your mind, economic health is tied to population size, which, according to you, means we are headed for a worldwide collapse if populations are not reduced?"... "Most other economists I have talked to say we can use growth to get us out of this recession."

"Growth, as taken to mean growth in

population, forcing a need for more jobs, which would create more growth, and so forth," I said. "No sir. The fact that unbridled growth had the appearance of working for nearly fifty years, or over several economic cycles, is what lulled us into this worldwide problem. Growth is not the answer General, it is the problem. It is sort of like a Ponzi scheme, and at some point all will come crashing down, and it has. The point I tried to make in *Tipping Points*, is that every person exacts a toll on society. It is my claim that we have reached a point where there are too many people taking from the system, so much so that no amount of job growth can help. It is only our arrogance that won't allow us to admit that we too are vulnerable to catastrophic reversals of fortune. That population size can and should be kept in line with what is considered sustainable to prevent massive die offs."

"Yes, I see," he said. "Further in your book you stated, 'It is not a revitalization our economy needs, but a revamping.' How can you be sure revitalization won't work?"

"Revitalization, with what?" I responded. "You just can't revitalize a technological society with a more primitive agricultural one. One popular journalist recently suggested we revitalize our economy with the help of non-native labor forces; who would be picking strawberries and cabbages out in some field. This is preposterous of course. You just can't support a higher, or more cost heavy economy, with a lesser one. As the saying goes, "You can never go home again." Picking strawberries will not create enough income. The profit margin on farm produce is far too low compared to the costs associated with servicing our modern society. "It's a revamping which is needed here, or better yet entering into the next age. What I called: The Post-Technological Age."

"You think the technology age is over? I see people buying more gadgets than ever," he said.

"Yes, but the gadgets are getting cheaper and cheaper to make. Mass production means more products at cheaper prices, which means smaller profit margins. It also means more machines doing the work, which means fewer people employed. We cannot win this war the way it is being fought, General. It is time to look for a new strategy. We need to enter a new age."

"Now that is the kind of talk I can understand, Dr. Parker." He went on to ask, "Well then Parker, what, in your estimation, lies beyond the tech economy—what is next?"

"Well, General Bradley, I don't know. I have some suspects though, but more research is needed. I hope that is what you have hired me to figure out? And with things getting worse I better work fast."

"About how much time do we have, in your estimation, before things get really bad?"

"Personally, I feel the problems we have experienced in the past few years have been an indication of the onset of a winding down of the excessive growth of the past sixty years. What we are seeing now is a continuing erosion of our American standard of living; and this I feel will continue to worsen. We are not in a critical moment yet. There is still ample crude oil to feed our hungry world. However, if oil production decreases by even as little as 5 percent, we will experience serious supply disruptions."

"Parker, for all our sakes I hope you are wrong. A lot of what you say makes some sense to me, but slowing down or even reversing this worldwide population explosion, well, that would take some doing."... "I'm assigning my aide, Sgt. Mike Streblow, to assist you. He can get you set up, and will be at your side for as long as you need him. For now, I suggest we agree to meet every two or three days to see how you are progressing. Remember, time is of the essence." I took that as my cue to leave, but we were having such a nice one-sided conversation.

Just then Sgt. Mike Streblow mysteriously appeared at the door to the conference room. He ushered me out and down the hall to find an office. On the way out I made eyes at the secretary. I didn't get much from her. She did this little hoot owl thing with her lovely eyes and brought her lips together as she sat upright, but nothing more. Perhaps I was out of line making any advances to her in this work environment. I'll have to ask Mike for a copy of the military's rules of dating.

In General Bradley's office about five minutes later,
    "Sherry, would you come in here please?"
    "Yes, Rudy, I'll be right there."
Once she was in the privacy of his office, "That Parker, quite a charming character isn't he?"
    "Yes, he is different from most who pass through here."
    "You're not taken by the military type, are you Sherry?"
    "Well, let's just say I'm still playing the field."
    "No need to be diplomatic with me, over a year here as my secretary, and I can't remember you once dating any of the many available servicemen who have passed through these doors. It's alright. A serviceman's life isn't meant for everyone."

"Uncle Rudy, it's not that; it's the whole DC scene. I had enough of that growing up with my dad." She added.

"How about that man Parker, I saw him making eyes at you. As one man talking about another, I think he finds you attractive."

"Hmm, could be, he is a handsome man, and definitely not DC."

"No, he certainly is not a military man, and he is new in town. Why don't you take him out and show him around?"

"Why, Uncle Rudy, that almost sounds like an assignment?"

"Nonsense, just go out and have a fun time?"

"And then report back to you?" she quipped.

"Like they say, you are pretty and smart."

"If I am going to be on extended duty, shouldn't I get extra pay?"

"So then you'll do it?" asked the General.

"Boy, you are serious about this, aren't you?" She thought to herself, "I should say no to him, but I could use some casual fun, and that Parker is cute. That was about as close to an order an un-order can get. I got this position only because of my dad's long term friendship with Rudy. When dad died, Rudy treated me as a daughter. So I owe him that. The General is suspicious of Dr. Parker—why? What kind of threat could an economist from Arizona possibly be? But General Rudy's intuits were usually right."

"Oh, Alright, Uncle Rudy, I'll do it. I could use a night out."

2:

Serendipity

Earth Date: January 26th
The Breen
Outer space, that black canvas upon which our starry nights are painted, next each hanging point of light a possible world lie, and behind that point of light countless more worlds hide shinning, waiting to be found. We live on one tiny speck in that backdrop of shimmering starlight. We call it home, or planet Earth. We now know our home is not the center of the universe. That we live on a small planet, next to a rather small and unimpressive star, located on the outer reaches of our galaxy. Our galaxy alone contains so many stars, in fact hundreds of billions, that a lifetime spent could not count them all.

To suggest the Earth of being the only planet to contain complex life-forms would seem, on the face of it, ridiculous. Our nearest neighbor is no more than four light-years away. Within sixteen light-years of Earth, there are over sixty star systems, and within eighty light-years of Earth, there are over one thousand stars together with their many planets. Suppose one of them might contain life?

In a small nearby solar system lies a star designated as BSC 3687 (Breen Star Chart). This system is located in an area of our galaxy rich in older solar systems ranging on the average of 4.2 billion Earth years. The Breen, an ancient race of star travelers, charted this sector with probes over one hundred thousand years ago. At that time, their probes returned data showing this section of space to be rich older star systems, many of them containing planets showing signs life, or capable of being terraformed to support life. At that time, the Breen were still terraforming and colonizing planets much closer to their home world of Be'eerreen Prime.

Recently the Breen Senatorum has decided to terraform and colonize farther out from their home bases. Quad 68 is over three thousand light-years from Breen Prime. Their decision to travel so far out, and thereby bypassing many nearer quads for habitation, was done in part to avoid disputes and claims by other neighboring species that may arise on systems closer in. Apparently, the galaxy was still big enough for all.

Following a three-month trip, the crew of sixteen Breen were only moments from their destination. A planet located some 70 light-years from Earth. The existence of this planet is currently unknown by Earthlings. The ship's Captain's name is Here'eee, he would later refer to himself as Harry. Their targeted planet was charted by probes they sent through this quadrant of space one thousand centuries ago. Only a quick survey of the planet was done at that time as its atmosphere showed it to be incompatible for complex life. It was located in the so-called Goldilocks zone, a region not too close to, nor too far from the central star, and providing for enough light warmth to allow water to exist in all three of its phases. Although BSC3687-3 had all of the ingredients for life to have evolved, it was found to be lifeless—A mystery. The Breen love mysteries.

The most ancient species in their local group of species, the Breen preferred to be thought of primarily as Terraformers. Captain Harry and his crew, of course, wanted to be thought of as the best Terraformers, and now with their new designation of 'Deep Space Terra-Formers' they felt a push to prove it. Opening up an entirely new quad to habitation so far from their home world would, if successful, be for bragging rights for a century to come. This tiny crew was up to the challenge, but it was going to be a difficult task.

Adding to their difficulties, they were traveling in an older class of space cruiser they affectionately called the Val. She was a small spaceship by current standards. Faster certainly, than the newer galaxy class ships, which were more like traveling pleasure stops than serious work craft. So this wasn't going to be a pleasure cruise—just hard work as usual. Furthermore, the Val, and a few ships like her, are training vessels, and carry the usual compliment of three cadets among her crew of sixteen.

On approaching planet BSC3867-3, Captain Harry addressed his crew,

"Well, here we are crewmates, and welcome to the boonies."

Arlen, the ships second in command jumped in and said, "We are pretty far out."

"I have never been this far out," said Hippee, the ship's chief, "have any of you?"

"Nope, not me," said Arlen. "Uncharted territory it is, perhaps we will find space monsters here?"

"Space monsters, let's get serious," said Hippee.

"Yes, we are way off the beaten path. I kind of like it," said Harry.

"You like the boonies, Harry?" asked Arlen.

"Harry's up for Planetship," chimed Hippee.

"You, Harry, a country lover, a dreamer," quipped Arlen. "I never would have guessed it. Are you sure you want to be stuck farming for centuries on a little planet this far out?"

Hippee then went a bit further, "That's right, Harry. Planetship does come with some rather menial responsibilities. You'll first have to get married, and then have children. That means having to hang up your space spurs for centuries, or even longer." Planet-ship was one of the ultimate goals for terraformers. Just imagine having a planet named after you, plus the option to stay and settle down, raise a family. You also had the option to be planet governor and act as Planet Counsel to the Senatorum.

"Let's do all we can to help our friend get his planet," said Arlen. "Why I can hear Planet Prime's propaganda campaign now—there's a picture of Captain Harry sitting on top of his rustic farming tractor, and a caption reads— 'Another victory for Deep-Space Terraformers.'"

The cadets, now all at their stations, turned to face Arlen and broke out in belly laughs. "What's this?" asked Harry, sensing some sleight on the part of the cadets.

"Oh, Arlen is still trying to work on his sense of humor," remarked Hippee. "It seems an incident with a local girl back on that pleasure planet we just left hurt his feelings."

"Oh yeah, I remember. She called him a humorless machine."

"Yes, so he's been embellishing ever since." Arlen then walked over to have words with the cadets. Harry yelled out, "Alright, enough banter. We have work to do. Someone call down below and wake everyone else up." Arlen, as he walked off was heard mumbling, "That space trollop."

Harry started barking out more orders, "Cadets, set up to launch probes, I want a detailed survey of this planet."

"Probes being programmed, sir, and Captain a detailed survey will take about two days to complete."

"That's alright; rule book says we need a detailed survey. Might be some form of life down there. Remember rule six—respect all life."

"Yes, Captain," echoed the cadets, and in a patronizing tone.

"Lower departments checking in, sir," said Heenon. "I've got Dr. Sa'aarron in Planetary Ecology requesting permission to go outside in a god-suit, and Bennie and a couple of others in Terranomics want to know if they can take a skiff down to the surface?"

"Great Maker! They want to take a skiff down to the surface of this hell hole? It must be five hundred and some degrees down there." Harry then got on his quantcomm, level one, to address the whole crew at once. The Breen, though not true cyborgs, per se, are still composite beings. Beings which have reached the apex of personal development, and have some very interesting organic devices built into their bodies. One of these was a quantum telecommunications device, enabling instantaneous communication among any Breen, anywhere, and at any time. Each device has three levels of access: level one being public; level two more specific, and level three private.

"Alright, everybody listen up. There will be plenty of time for joy riding and other personal activities. First, I want us to get set up proper, and that means getting surveys started" The words "Yes Harry" could be heard to echo throughout the ship. Even a cuss word or two was whispered. It had been a long trip, and other than their holo cubes, and a cramped recreation deck, the Val offered little in the way of entertainment. Everyone wanted a leg stretcher.

Arlen couldn't help but remark on the echoing complaints, "You know, Hippee, this ship is constantly on the verge of chaos. I think that shows Harry's lack of experience being a captain?"

"No, I disagree. That's just Harry's style of command Arlen, freedom of expression to the point of anarchy."

"Yeah, so you are saying he has a friendly personality, and I don't. I get it."

"Come on Arlen. Forget about that girl back on Pleasure Planet. She probably says things like that to all visitors."

"You're right. I just don't like short lifers jabbing at me. They should show more respect to us." The Breen, having conquered life's mysteries, at least those which deal with the sciences, and being masters of genetics, have increased their own life spans a thousand fold. They referred to less advanced races as short lifers. Short lifers were sometimes looked at as inferior. This was one reason some Breen felt a need to think of themselves as more akin to gods, and wanted their due respect. Whether you call it arrogance, egotism, or even something actually deserved, this desire to want to be treated and a thought of as superior, plus their reluctance to share their genetic and technological prowess with other species, caused raspy relations on many planets they regularly visit. I found that for all their advances scientifically, that they still held on to and exhibited all the personality quirks that humans considered a nuisance. They were a dichotomy in action. One could even say they have vanity.

"Probes programmed and ready, sir," shouted the cadets.

"Very well, launch when ready." Sitting at their control stations, the cadets busily pushed buttons and touched icons on their computer screens.

"Probes away, Captain." With that, a flurry of survey probes, spheres about seven feet in diameter, emerged from the Val's hull, and shot off toward the planet below. Their purpose was to produce a detailed survey of the planet's surface. They would look for signs of current life and/or past life, assess the planets mineral resources, take current atmospheric measurements, analyze chemical composition of surface mater, and measure the total amount of water present. They would also check on magnetic fields, ascertain current geological activity, and also attempt to determine the planet's geological history. This information will become necessary to answer the question of whether or not this planet can be made habitable.

"Alright cadets, this is important. As probe data comes in, see to it that it is relayed to the proper departments down below." Part of their training is to learn the ropes of terraforming.

"Yes, sir." They echoed, responding in unison as though they were one.

"Any designation for this planet yet, Captain?" asked Heenon.

Hippee, who had been standing idle over beside Arlen at the opposite end of the control room jumped in to say, "Yes, let's name it. Anyone have any ideas?"

"Arlen, do you have any suggestions on what to name this planet?" asked Harry.

"What, a rock this remote?" said Arlen. ..."How about something like "My old country home." The cadets at hearing that again broke out in laughter. Harry, ever stoic, replied, "Sure, we usually pick just a one-word name, Arlen."

"Anyone else have an idea?" Ge'eenna, working a deck below in Planetary Genomics, chimed in, "How about naming it after your first son Harry?" Ge'eenna was the only female member of the crew; she worked in Doctor Sa'aarron's Planetary Genomics Department.

"I have no children as yet Ge'eenna."

"Yes, but what would you name him, once you do?"

"Hmm, we talked about that. It would have to be a name like Ga'alle'een, you know, a name with a strong historical significance."

"Then planet Ga'alle'een it is," confirmed Ge'eenna.

The trio of Cadets, unable to control themselves, shouted out, "It's a boy!" Laughter erupted all over the ship. Harry, un-phased by all the hilarity stated, "Well, I'll have to get a Planet-ship first." The Breen live by a very strict code regarding propagation. It is a sensible and obviously necessary rule if you live seemingly forever. In their minds, one

of the biggest sins a species can make is to over
populate. So population, and therefore, reproduction
are tied to ecological surroundings. i.e.: how many
people can a given planet sustain without infringing
on other life forms, or causing environmental
degradation. And this number, as it turns out, is
surprisingly low.

"Preliminary data coming in from the probes,
Captain."

"Let's have a look at it."

Heenon put a holograph of the planet below
showing what data were currently known, and
started a readout of the stats, "Average surface
temperature—350 degrees Fahrenheit, no traces of
any current life forms, atmosphere 20 percent
methane and 13 percent sulfur, 20 percent oxygen,
nitrogen at 45 percent. Normal volcanism for a
planet this size and age, strong magnetic field,
apparent age 4.2 billion years, and on and on. Just
like the data from the old survey sir."

"It is still a hell hole down there," said Harry.
"Normal volcanism, and yet there is an abnormal
amount of sulfur and methane in the atmosphere.
Well, that is a mystery." On the ship's intercom he
called down to Dr. Sa'anntee, leader of Solar System
Ecology, "Doctor, any ideas what happened here?"

"No, not enough data yet Harry."

"Isn't it unusual for a planet of this age and
orbit to have elemental sulfur and methane still in its
atmosphere?"

"Yes, you are right, it is quite odd. I suggest we
do a deep solar system analysis."

"Cadets, put up a holo of this solar system for
me." In the middle of the information and control
room, or ICC, a holographic representation of this
solar system appeared showing the central star and

all of the planets and debris fields—condensed from scale.

"Harry," said Sa'anntee, "Let's send out probes to analyze the outer solar system's evolution. I bet those two large gas planets in the next two orbital rings had something to do with this planet's mixed-up atmosphere."

"Cadets, spin up several more probes, and make sure they have AI capabilities," ordered Harry. "There is something odd going on here. Let's get to the bottom of it."

 After a few minutes the cadets called out, "Captain, special probes ready, sir."

"Then go ahead and launch when ready. Arlen, I want you and Hippee to go down to the launch bay, and make ready a skiff. You two might as well follow these probes to the outer reaches, and make some preliminary water availability assessments." Water is life's elixir, whether you are an alien or not, most all life depends on it. Water can normally be found in abundance at a solar systems outer reaches in what is called the comet belt.

Arlen and Hippee headed down to the launch bay to prepare a skiff for travel to the outer reaches of the solar system. Skiffs are small spaceships, or shuttles, similar in shape to the Val, yet sportier in design. As with the Val, they employ quantum wave pulse technology for propulsion, and are capable of hyper luminal velocities.

Back in the ICC, "Probes away, Captain."

"Very well," said Harry. "I am going down below to check on a few things in Planetary Genomics. While I'm gone you three have the con."

The trio of cadets remained sitting at their consoles. As planetary data continued to pour in from the probes they funneled it to the appropriate science departments below. Thirty minutes passed. Due to their incessant chatter, they were slow to notice a security alert. Heenon was first to notice and yelled, "Geerron, look at your board!" Immediately, the other two quickly peered at Geerron's control station. One small red light at the middle right side of his console was blinking. "Great Maker! Can it be?"

The trio took to a huddle and began whispering among themselves, "Should we tell him?" ; "It might be nothing." ; "Can't we keep it quiet for a while until we have something more concrete?" ; "Keep it quiet from Harry? U nuts?" ; "We'll still get credit for it."; "Damn; this could be huge!" ; "This is a once in a decacen event." ; "Yes, it's huge." ; "We'll all share in this equally, right?" ; "Definitely, and kudos to us all."; "Just wait until Arlen hears about this," and the drivel continued without stop.

Some twenty minutes later Captain Harry returned to the control room with Dr. Sa'aarron at his side. They were discussing some procedural matter. At his return to the ICC the cadets straightened up and turned forward. They each let their hands rest in front of them on top of their consoles. Their fingers were interlocked and a curious smug little smile was pasted on their faces. Noticing an abnormal quiet coming from the location of the usually boisterous cadets, Harry turned; three ashen faces stared blankly ahead.

"Heenon, what is it?"

"Sir, we are picking up some modulated E-band emissions."

"What, from this planet? It must be a mistake."

"No, they are not coming from this planet, they are too distant for that, and they are coming in askew of the solar plane, sir."… "Best coordinates we have been able to come up with are there." He pointed to a 3D viewer screen up on the side wall of the ICC. It currently showed a section of space. "But as you can see, sir, it is a big blank. There is nothing there."

Harry gazed over at the wall screen, pondered for a moment, then quickly realizing what this could mean; shot his gaze back over to the Cadets. "So Cadets, this is huge for all of us. Well done!"

Harry and Dr. Sa'aarron walked slowly over to the control station where the cadets were sitting. With smiles on their faces they peered across the panels and saw the blinking red light. They then looked at a plot of the transmissions on Geerron's screen. "Ok, here is what we will do, you three continue to monitor. Record the transmissions and set up a database. Then see if you can analyze the signals. You three will all get badges for this." Harry, commended his cadets, but this was a discovery the whole crew would share in. Mysterious emissions coming from a deep dark hole in space could mean only one thing, and the cadets knew this instinctively. Modulated E-band transmissions meant advanced intelligent life. The weak signal meant they were coming from a place far off, so they had been traveling for a long time; perhaps up to a century or more, which suggested that the sending civilization was currently even more advanced. Encountering new and previously unknown sentient beings was a stunning and meritorious event. The Breen have been terraforming for untold centuries, and have created many, many planets on which they and other species now inhabit. However, for all their vast networks of planets, naturally evolved and intelligent life still remained quite rare. So this new discovery was epic.

Harry using his quantcomm, level two, "Hippee, Arlen, the trio have detected far-off e-band transmissions."

"Oh, Great Maker," remarked Arlen, "now they will be even more unbearable. Good thing we are leaving the ship for a few days." Arlen actually enjoyed having the cadets onboard, but feigned not to in social situations.

"We can't get an exact fix on the transmissions," said Harry. "They are pretty far off. On your way to the outer reaches I want you two to set up an RF-grid?"… "Why not set it at about one AU to a corner?"

"OK, Harry, we'll set up the grid first, and then go rope a comet," said Arlen.

"Oh Boy, I sense a field trip coming up," said Hippee. "This discovery of new life is too important and exciting not to go and investigate."

"Yeah, well let's just see how far off they are first before we pact things in here?" … The two were making their final preparations to leave the ship when Hippee said, "Arlen, look over at the end wall."

"What is it Hippee?" Arlen turned his gaze over to the far wall, "Oh, you don't mean?"

"Absolutely, they need to be checked out anyway."

"Yeah, but we haven't been in-serviced on them yet."

"That's the beauty of it. We will be." The two finished loading up for their trip, boarded the skiff, and departed for the outer reaches of the solar system.

"Harry, we're off, see you all in a couple of days," said Arlen.

Back in the ICC, "Captain, my security monitor shows two god-suits missing from their station and now onboard the skiff," mentioned Heenon.
    "God-suits, what could those two be thinking of?" Harry mused quietly to himself, "Ah, of course, a snowball fight."….

3:

Cosmic Roulette

Day two at planet Ga'alle'een
 On board the skiff, and in deep space,

"Arlen, we are approaching the third and last point of the RF-Grid, we can go ahead and turn on Harry's radio triangulation device."

"Not sure we needed to make the corners so large Hippee. One AU to a side is huge."

"Well, why not, we got here in no time. I'm checking the grid's plane to see if this is the best spot. Yes, right here is perfect. Go ahead and launch the last probe here."

"Launching probe now. Would you check to see if all three have hooked up?"

"That could take a few minutes," said Hipp.

"Not too many I hope, I am anxious to get out to the Oort cloud region."

"Why do you want to travel so far?"

"We'll swing by the comet belt on the way out to make Harry's water estimates, but I want to head out to the Oort cloud. I don't know there is just something about the icy-blackness of space out there. It helps me to think."

"OK, the grid is up and running Arlen. We can leave at any time, and I didn't know you did that much thinking?"

"It's deep thinking I need to do. Now hold on tight Hipp, we might as well have some fun on the way out." The two were headed out to the rim of the solar system, and the beginning of the Oort cloud region, a place where monsters were rumored to exist. They each have a new design of a god-suit with them. This suggested they were going there for more than contemplation.

Back on the Val it is Day 2 in orbit around planet Ga'alle'een. The deep-space probes sent to investigate the outer planets are starting to return data. These data are just now being analyzed by the various departments on board the Val. A forensic investigation of the solar systems evolution is being attempted. This was thought necessary in order to figure out the puzzle on the planet below. An answer of the cause of the planet's anomalous atmosphere is necessary to determine whether or not it can be made habitable.

After a long break, Harry returned to the ICC,

"Captain, while you were away, the probes on the planet's surface returned data showing extensive ruins," said Geerron, one of the cadets.

"Seriously, this hell hole once had advanced life? Show me a holograph of the planet's surface, and layer these ruins you've found on it," snapped Harry.

"Putting them up now, Captain."

"That is just amazing. These ruins show a class G-4 civilization spread over much of the planet. How close are we to being done with the surveys?"

"Perhaps one more hour, sir."

"Get me Dr. Sa'aarron, down in Planetary Genomics."

"Tying you in to the Genomics Department."

Harry leaning over the cadets control station, "Doctor, this planet was inhabited once, and according to the data we have received as recently as one hundred thousand years ago. What do you make of all this?"

"Yes Harry, we have been looking over the raw data for a while now. It is all very interesting isn't it?" said Dr. Sa'aarron. "It appears to be just as I suspected. We are positing that an impact with a large asteroid wiped out all life on this planet."

"What do you base that on Doctor?"

"Some disturbing data from one of the probes we sent out to the fifth planet. Give us another couple of hours and we will have an answer for you," he said.

Space Monsters

Far out in the solar system's nether region, Arlen and Hippee have pulled their skiff up to a large comet. It was just a huge chunk of frozen ice which had been floating out there for an eternity. Comets are common throughout a solar system, but tend to congregate in certain zones or belts where they lie in wait for the gravity of some object to give them a boot from their orbit, and send them tumbling in toward the inner planets. Oort cloud comets, though large in number, lie at too great a distance to be of use in terraforming. However, if you just want a place to sit and be away from it all…

"There is your space monster, Arlen."

"Yep, that is a big one alright. I like the way our

lights glisten off its surface—that deep coal black sheen."

"Yeah, and that's about all we can see of it. Comets this far out are usually a little cleaner."

"Well, five billion years of dust build-up didn't help."

Back on the Val a call came up from below decks,

"Harry, it's Dr. Who. Have you heard anything from Arlen?" Dr. Who'een, also known as Dr. Who, leads up the Terranomics Division. He is well known for his terse mannerisms and adamant over stricture to what he perceived as proper protocol.

"Why no, can't you raise them on your quantcomm?"

"Since when is it my job to call him?"

Harry, somewhat aggrieved at Dr. Who's brusque attitude responded, "I got it doctor, your water assessments. I will call them and get back to you." He then shot a groaned look over to the cadets who heard everything. "Engineers and their egos," using his quantcomm, level two, "Arlen, I need you and Hippee to check in."

After a brief pause, "Yes Harry, we were just about to exit the skiff."

"Leave the ship, tracking shows you two out in the Oort cloud? Couldn't you find comets closer in?"

"Yes, we passed some big ones on the way out here."

"Have you finished your water assessment yet?" asked Harry.

"Not quite, it could take a few more hours to complete."

"What, a few more hours? Don't think I don't know what you two are up to, Arlen."

"Listen, I've got irate Terraformers gnawing at

me back here."

"We will try and hurry then, Harry."

"Sure you will Arlen! Don't forget to duck."

"Thank you Harry." … "Boy he sure let's Dr. Who get under his skin way too easily."

"See, I told you he'd know. Harry knows all," said Hipp.

"Yeah, and if he is such a smart captain, then why can't he learn not to be afraid of Dr. Who?"

"What? Harry afraid of Who? He's not afraid of Dr. Who, Arlen. Harry is a delegator, and as such he is just looking for someone else to do the dirty work. That way he can retain his higher sense of command."

"So what you are suggesting then is that shit runs downhill no matter where you are in the universe?"

"Yep, and I think Harry likes your abrupt, almost argumentative approach with the senior doctors. Even though I know you don't really mean anything by being short with them, you perhaps unwittingly have found a way to keep their bloated egos in check."

"Then I am a good second in command?"

"You're the best Arlen, the best."

"Let's get these suits on. I'm eager to try them out." Arlen and Hippee don their god suits, make a few quick checks, and exit the skiff.

"You know, Hippee, I'm going to hate taking advantage of you like this."

"Think again, big fella."

"Hey, these new suits have a different configuration on the control panel, even some colored lights. Mine are blinking, some red and some green. Perhaps we should've read the directions, heh?"

"Perhaps you should have. I downloaded the instructions when we first came on board the Val three months ago. Just touch the yellow button that is your mind link."

"Got it."

"You've pulled us up to a big one Arlen."

"Yeah, lots of water ice out here, but it is way too dark. I can't even see my toes."

"I got it. I'll have the skiff put out some flares," replied Hippee. A line of flares spewed out of the skiff and took up positions to form a matrix surrounding the mountainous block of ice.

"That's better, now that I can see I'll energize my suit."

"I'm already energized," Arlen, "and showing all green across the board. Now to try and move."

"So, as I understand, you don't have to grab on to anything to move. You just walk normally?"

"So I have heard." His suit already energized, Hippee starts to walk in empty space. "This is quite cool, Arlen, it's just like having a terra-deck to walk on. I'm going to try and run." With the use of negative energy, Hippee is able to walk and run in empty space, just as though he were on the surface of a planet with positive gravity. He takes off running in the direction of the comet while Arlen is still fiddling with his controls.

"Alright, my power pods are energized, Hip. Now I'm going to take some steps. Yeah, it is remarkably easy. I guess we won't need the tensor fields anymore?" Just as Arlen was taking his first steps a chunk of ice the size of a water melon smashed into him, "Oh, damn you, Hippee."

"Harry did tell you to duck." And the snow ball fight was on…

Back on the Val

"Cadets, you three have the con. I am going down to Planetary Genomics," and with that Harry left the ICC to meet with Dr. Sa'aarron about the planet below.

"Great, were alone again at last. Are we still getting that signal?" asked Heenon.

"Yes, and with the sensor array on line we have been able to capture some very strong signals. I have been collecting the data, and storing it in a side computer for easy analysis."

"Is there any analysis yet?"

"Yes, the computer suggests it is an archaic form of audio and video."

"Wow! In a couple of days we should have a reconstruct of the signals. Imagine seeing these aliens for the first time. Oops, the surveys have just completed. All data has been routed below."

"Do we need to retrieve the probes? No they auto-destructed."

Down in Planetary Genomics, Harry and Dr. Sa'aarron are pouring over the latest data.

"Harry, we have tied in our computers in with those in Solar, and are currently processing the data streams from the deep-space probes, and this is all being coordinated together with the planet's data we collected."

"Let's see what the computers have come up with."

Just then Dr. Sa'anntee, head of Solar System Ecology, yells out over the intercom, "Yes! I was right again. Look there, the fifth planet out. Its size makes it a huge gravity hole and a magnet for space junk. Perturbations in the orbits of several of its moons and the disruption of the ring structures coincides well time wise with the impact here on this planet."

"So you're suggesting what?" asked Harry.

"Indications are that a large asteroid or comet entered the fifth planets gravity well and knocked one of its small moons out of its orbit, and it then collided with another moon. This small moon probably had huge elemental sulfur deposits. The methane deposits probably came from the other one. When the two moons collided, their individual mater combined, and a large part of it broke off, and was kicked out of orbit. In fact, we have found many large remaining masses of these moons still in orbit around the fifth planet, and they have the exact chemical makeup that we find in the atmosphere here on Ga'alle'een."

"So large pieces of these two moons coalesced and were then ejected from orbit?"

"Yes, that appears to be so, portions of the two combined from the impact and were shot out of orbit, and later found their way here. That impact caused the total destruction of this planet's ecosystem."

"What a terrible way to go," said Harry. "There must have been a billion souls on this planet at that time."

"Not so good for the previous keepers of this planet, but better for us," said Dr. Sa'anntee.

"How so Doctor?"

"Everything we need to make this planet whole again is right here. It's a simple thing to do. All we need to do is remove the sulfur and methane from the atmosphere. Once that has been accomplished, the temperature will fall to livable levels. After that, and with perhaps a little more tweaking, this planet can be re-populated. You've got your planet Harry."

"Great Maker!"….

The Snow Ball Fight….

Arlen and Hippee have parked their skiff next to a mountain sized chunk of space ice. A comet five miles long which has been floating for eons in the solar systems outer reaches some 30,000 AU's from the central star. The two are wearing god-suits, a new design of (space-worker operation assist body suit) with some rather incredible features. One being the ability to walk, run, and jump in the cold dark empty reaches of outer space, quite a feat in a weightless environment. The two Breen have already donned their suits and have exited the ship. Arlen was just getting the hang of this new design, but Hippee with the advantage of having already being aware of the suits operation is already hurling comet balls. The snowball fight has begun and after Hipp got off the first shot,

"Oh, damn you, Hippee."…"Ok, you got in the first shot. Here, take this." The duo exchanged shot after shot at each other, all the while the distance between them on the comet's surface increased. Hippee, avoiding several volleys from Arlen, took cover behind an ice ridge two hundred yards off.

"I see you hiding over there Hipp," said Arlen. "I'm going to see what this suit can do, and turn it up a couple of notches." Arlen chose to enlarge his god suit to level five, but wasn't aware that there would be a time delay for the negative energy to rebuild. Hippee seeing this, and not being one to pass up an opportunity grabs the biggest chunk of ice he can, and fired it head-on at Arlen.

"I see what you are doing there Hipp, that's a wasted shot. I'll just move to the side." As the large ice cube zooms right at him, "Wait, wait. What's this? Hip, my suit won't move. Come on, mooove! Oh, Damn!" Unable to move out of the way, Arlen takes the full impact.

"Ha, Ha, Ha, you should've read the instructions Arlen. After you enlarge your suit it takes a few seconds for the negative energy to rebuild. Ha, Ha, Ha."

"That's very funny, Hipp." Angered, his ego bruised, he's forced to wait for revenge while his god-suit reenergizes. Seconds later, his suit now enlarged five steps to fifty feet tall, five times the size of Hippee's, he gets set to fire back. "Alright Hipp, you're in for it now. I see you running there." Hippee was spied running across the icy flat plain of this giant sooty black rock of ice. "Your energizer filaments all aglow make you stand out against this comet's black backdrop like a reverse silhouette. You make a juicy target."

"Take your best shot big guy."

"Alright, you asked for it." Hippee's ploy was to run to the far side of the comet, jump down the edge and then run as fast as he can across the bottom side. Then he would come up on Arlen's rear and let him have it. Arlen, seeking revenge, reached down and into the comet's icy makeup. Whit his giant hands made up of energy fields he grabbed a hold of a house sized chunk of ice, raised it up over his shoulder, drew back, took aim, and let fly. The massive yet weightless snowball hurtled at terrific speed directly at his friend. As Hipp reached the comet's far rim he jumped up into space, did a summersault, and then dropped down below the edge. Just as he disappeared from sight, Arlen's giant snowball impacted the comets surface right where he last standing, exploding tons of ice out into empty space.

"There, how'd you like that one?" Hippee gave no response. "Hipp, you ok? Hipp? Damn, Hippee, are you injured? Hipp, talk to me." Arlen, fearing his friend injured, ran over to the edge where he last saw him. "Hippee, c'mon, where did you go?" For all he knew, Hippee could've been blown into the consuming blackness of space never to be seen again.

Just as Arlen peered over the rim of the comet he heard Hippee contact him over his com unit, "Arlen, I'm right behind you."

"Huh?" Arlen straightened and turned around to lay eyes on his friend, then, Whaam! He took a torturous shot to the gut from another large snowball.

"Oops, damn!"

"Gotcha again, big guy."

"Yes, you sure did."

"I'm surprised you fell for that one Arlen?"

"I give you the win this time Hipp. Here, I'll turn my suit back to level one." The two friends, the snow-ball fight over, sat down on an icy ridge at the comet's edge.

"This has been fun. I've wanted to do this for quite a while," said Arlen. "These new suits are incredible."

"Yeah, I can't wait to do some real work in them."

"We haven't turned it up all of the way yet."

"No, just to level five. Supposedly, it goes up to one hundred. That would be large enough to easily move this entire comet, and push it on a course toward a planet."

"Yes it would, but not from out here. It is just too far out to be useful. There is much more water ice closer in. There's nothing out here, just black emptiness, even the central star is a mere point of light. No, nothing much out here, but it is nice to just sit here and ponder that we are nearly a quarter of the way to the next star system. From our perspective, space, I find, is getting smaller and smaller."

"Yes it is, and I have heard that on our research planet Derex'een they are working on a galaxy drive. Imagine terraforming in another galaxy?"

"Now that would be something. Ever faster, ever farther. Hey, that could be our new motto."

"I never took you for the thinking philosophical type, Arlen?"

"Oh? You haven't? Well, thanks for the compliment." … "You're a really good friend Hip— glad to have you on-board for this gig."

"Right back at ya, Arlen."

With the coal black glisten of the comet as there background the two officers peered off into the empty void of the interstellar medium and contemplated their future. The options of having a long life were plentiful and allowed them to accomplish many things, yet as their species traveled the path to immortality they were losing the things that gave life meaning. With no daily struggle to survive, with all their needs catered to, with no quest to drive them on, there was a tendency to grow apathetic, and as century after century ticked off the emptiness of the years weighed heavy on the Breen soul, the best respite for a jaded existence— space exploration.

"Geeze, look at this space suit, what a mess, these comets are a filthy lot."

"Yeah, no way we're going to be able to clean

these suits way out here. Let's get back to the Val, and give Harry his water estimates."

"I think Harry is going to be pissed."

Day four...

Crew briefing, Dr. Sa'aarron is speaking, "So we have resolved the cause and the problem with the planet's atmosphere. We have determined that this ecosystem is complete as demonstrated by the ruins on the surface. This planet once had bountiful life. Our next step is to find a way to remove the sulfur and methane from the atmosphere, and by so doing, curb its runaway greenhouse effect. Once we do that, the planet should cool down to habitable temperatures, and we can then introduce new species.

Rather than building and utilizing many huge machines to process the atmosphere, it would be far easier and faster to create a microbe to do the dirty work. We have a ready supply of bugs in my lab which we have used in similar situations before. Our focus for the next few days will be to adapt these bugs. We need to make them hungry. Very hungry. We will design one to eat sulfur, and another one will be engineered to dine on methane."

Before dismissing the crew to their tasks, Harry mentioned, "As you all know, to their credit, the cadets located signals coming from an alien intelligence. Our space array has determined that they are coming from a planet that isn't that far off, only about 70 light years distant. These transmissions continue to pour in, and the data is being analyzed. In another day we should have them deciphered, and I will inform you all of those results then." The crew gave the cadet's a hearty round of applauds.

Day Seven

It was mid-day on the Val. Harry was in the ICC along with the three cadets who were all sitting at their posts. Harry was standing out in the middle of this great room sipping on some noxious looking brew. So far, it was just another uneventful day. Dr. Sa'aarron's microbes were still being tinkered with. Then, just as he was taking a sip, an alert went off on Le'eennon's status panel. They all heard the sound of three short beeps, and then a white light began to blink. Harry shot a look over to the cadets' direction,

"Something of interest, Mr. Le'eennon?"

"Yes Captain, the computer has resolved the alien transmissions. We have figured out what they are and how to display them."

"What are they then?"

"A primitive form of audio and video, sir."

"Video?"

"Yes—so far we have captured two video clips, and many more radio voice transmissions."

"No kidding? That's incredible. We have video transmissions from a previously unknown race?" In some wonderment, "Well, who sent them, and what do they look like? I guess we should have a look at them then. This is momentous, let me address the rest of the crew, *Attention crew, the cadets have deciphered the alien signals. We have videos of them, and we will put them up on your wall screens now.* Select one of the transmissions Mr. Le'eennon, and put it up so we can all view it."

"Putting it up now, Captain." The entire crew fixed their eyes on any available monitor screen. "We have only two video broadcasts deciphered as yet." This was their first view of an alien race living on a small planet three thousand light years from their home word. Expectations were high. The transmission started out as a grainy black and white film, old style, not smooth, very bad resolution, and the gray black balance was terrible. The audio was even worse. Only a garbled static filled monotone could be made out.

"Is this the best you can get it?" asked Harry.

"No Captain, I can have the computer enhance the video. Here, let me tie in the ship's computers. The audio is very degraded. I can filter out the static, but it will still sound garbled, and as yet we do not have a grasp on their language." The computer enhanced video began to play. Everyone remained mute, not a word was spoken on board the ship as the movie played.

"It is really unimpressive." Arlen was the first to break the silence. "Looks like one person making a speech—what, this is the first video we get of a new race, one which has been traveling through space for light-years to reach us, and all we get is a political speech? It's almost comical."

"They are a Breenoid looking species though," mentioned one of the crew.

"I disagree. I see no resemblance to anything Breen at all. Just another bi-pedal short lifer species," said another.

"Look at the very odd way they dress."

"Yes, and look, they are still covered in fur." The commentary and speculation went on Breen style with one conversation overlapping another for some minutes. In my experience with the Breen they would often gibber-jabber so much no one knew who said what. The old film they were watching and commenting on was actually a transmission of President Roosevelt giving an opening speech at the

1930's world's fair.

"Where is this planet located?"

"It lies roughly seventy light-years away. We plotted its location against the old charts of this quad and came up with this planet. Our probes surveyed it over one hundred thousand years ago. It was not given a name, just coordinates."

"Do we have the data crystal for it," asked Harry.

"Yes, it was an older style survey, so there is not a lot of data, but it still shows quite a beautiful planet. There was no dominant species there at that time."

"We can check out the old survey later," said Harry. Disappointed by the crew's reaction to the video Le'eennon quickly stated, "We have another video, Captain, here I'll switch to it."

"Now that's interesting."

"It is a competition of some sort."

"Ah, it's a ball game, how sporting." The second video was a short broadcast of a baseball game being played in old Chicago. A game broadcast complete with sound.

"Now that is something I can get into." The crew members recognized the next video as a sports competition, and began to relate to our game of baseball. Of course, sports should be listed as a universal constant.

"Is that all we have to date Mr. Le'eennon?"

"We also have a number of audios, sir. Would you like to hear some?"

"No, not now, let's set up a time tonight when we can all meet together in the observation lounge."

Harry and most of the crew were not yet taken by our cinema. That would follow. Radio began to be widely broadcast around the turn of the 20th century. Television did not become popular until the late thirties. Early broadcasts were weak, far too weak not to be drowned out by natural processes found in the atmosphere and in space. Distance also becomes an obstacle as electromagnetic waves diminish with the inverse square law. Stronger radio transmissions began to creep out into space a few decades later. The Breen were looking at radio and television signals which had been traveling at the speed of light for over seventy years. Earth of that era was in the nascent stage of broadcasting. In the years to follow many changes were to arrive which would put hundreds, and then thousands, of transmissions out into the cosmos each and every day. Sadly, the Breen's introduction into earth's radio and TV was initially a big disappointment to them, but we were a freshly discovered race, and that commanded more investigation.

Day Nine—To Terraform, or not to Terraform
Planetary Genomics department had been working hard on adapting some microbes. Dr. Sa'aarron and his cadre of technicians were tinkering with the bugs DNA to make them stronger, change their diet, and enable them to reproduce more rapidly. They were building a supper bug, one that would feast on the atmospheric contaminants to produce metabolites that would fall to the surface and then be modified again in natural processes. This process was already underway in the air. The planet's atmosphere would heal itself, but at such a slow pace, it could take another ten thousand centuries to return the planet to a habitable state. The Breen were going to speed things up.

"Ge'eenna, let's give Harry a call and tell him we

are a go with the bugs," said Dr. Sa'aarron.

"Of course, we will need to coordinate with Terra for its dissemination," she said. Dr. Sa'aarron was a thoughtful Breen, one not given to nasty bouts of flippancy, or terse jabbering, unlike Dr. Who. The two doctors did not mix well, and Sa'aarron, though not timid, would rather delegate what he likened to needless exposure to Dr. Who, or any of his, as he has more than once been heard to say, caustic trio of technicians.

"Yes," said Dr. Sa'aarron, "and we will let Harry deal with that, our job is done for now."

Harry was notified that a strain of supper bug was ready to be introduced into the atmosphere below,

"Doctor, are you sure this bug is safe?" asked Harry.

"What? Of course it is not safe. If there were any life left down there they would get wiped out in a matter of days."

"What did you need to change in it to make it stronger?"

"Mostly we just made it hungrier. You know, if you get hungry, you eat more, and if you are a bug and you eat more, you multiply more, and so on."

"Your bug is that strong?"

"Yes it is, but I have built in the usual safeguards. It will, as it grows and multiplies, mutate back into its prior benign self," said Sa'aarron.

"Do you have estimates of a time line yet?"

"No, we just do genetics Harry, applications are for terra to figure out."

"Oh—and you want me to deal with Terranomics."

"Why, thank you for offering, Harry."

"I need a bigger ship," complained Harry.

Harry looking over in the direction of the trio of cadets, he was slowly tapping his breastplate with his fingers, "Well, let's get this done." Calling down below, "Dr. Who, I have a vial of death for you."

"Hah, a hidden message there from Sa'aarron, I gather. Ask him to send Be'nnee over with his deadly brew. We will disseminate it immediately down into the upper atmosphere. We can get a time line once we see how fast it gets to work." Dr. Who, head of Terra, was renowned galaxy wide for his terse mien, and was always straight to the point. Be'nnee, on the other hand, was well-liked by all the crew. He was just a friendly guy who refused to get caught up in the petty infighting.

Day 13, The Time Line

Dr. Who and his Terranomics Department, true to form took the super bugs and had them disseminated down into the planet's upper atmosphere at twelve equally separated locations. The most effective pattern I am sure. Right away, the microbes began to eat and multiply. Each generation a doubling in number than the previous and with a bug which split in two every thirteen minutes, within a day the number of microbes was beyond counting. This doubling would continue as long as there remained food to eat, and that was the estimate Harry was asking about—the time line.

Terranomics had as its responsibility, as the name implies, transforming a planet, which further implied its atmosphere. They were watching how the bugs grew and spread. This enabled them to arrive at the time line which in this case was...

"Harry, it's Dr. Who, we have your time line. It is going to be three months plus or minus two days."

As always, Dr. Who was short and to the point. Upon hearing that they had over three months of dead time coming up, a cacophony of voices full of groaning complaints, all overlapping, erupted on board the Val. The dead of space is just that—dead. After a three-month trip to BSC 3687-3, and another two weeks sitting in orbit while making pre-terraforming investigations, and now faced with at least another three months of sitting around with nothing to do, understandably the crew immediately reacted with great dissatisfaction. The Val was a confined space, and offered very little to keep active minds happy.

"Three months, sitting here in dead empty space," cried one.

"That is why the newer ships are so large," said another.

"Yeah, the floating pleasure stops."

"Seriously, we can't even go down to the planet's surface for fun."

"We could go out and have snow-ball fights?" offered Arlen.

"Snow-ball fights? What?" said someone from terra.

"Engineers, never mind," remarked Arlen. "How about rebellion?"

"Harry, you better get control of this."

"Well, there is one option that is nearby," he mentioned.

"Oh, and what is that?"

"And it has the added plus that I can justify it as paid leave," he said. Now that got some attention. "We have located a new species, and rule number 47 states all new sentient life forms must be investigated when deemed appropriate. So there it is—your paid vacation."

"You know, Harry is right about this. How far away was it, 70 light years? We can do that in twelve days. Get there, and still have plenty of time to relax on some sunny shore."

"Yes, plus my estimates show it will take another ten or so days after the bugs have eaten their fill before they have fully mutated back to normal. So we actually have an extra ten days of R and R."

"Great, let's go." A consensus was asked for on the subject, of course it was a unanimous vote. Now it was all up to Harry. As ship's Captain his decision reigned supreme. How would he vote?

The Sign Post....
The Breen have been using quantum communication techniques for several hundred thousand years. They now have it down to a fine art. Problem one, before you can communicate by quantum means, you first need to have a beginning point, and an end point. You just can't select any point of space and send a message to it unless, for lack of better words, you have a receiver at that location. To that end, the Breen build receiver stations whenever they reach a new place they may want to communicate with. These stations are called 'sign posts.'

An interesting choice of term—*sign posts*. Beyond being simply quantum communications portals, they also possess the ability to monitor, say, a planet, and can be instructed to send out worker-probes complete with specialized nanites capable of being programmed to perform just about any function. Talk about being able to turn on your lights from a cell phone, or start your car. How about while you are on vacation seventy light years away, calling your roombot and telling it to open up a can of cat food, or better yet mowing your lawn. Or, if you are an advanced race of spacefarers, monitor a planet being terraformed, and possibly, in some other situation watching or spying on someone. What better way to mark your territory, and keep the inhabitants under some sense of control.

Harry made a deal with the crew regarding the trip to earth, saying,

"I don't know. We are talking about a first contact here. They can be pretty complicated if not downright dangerous." But it was as though he was all alone and talking with himself for not a word for a change could be heard coming from the rest of the crew. Their minds were made up. Mutinies were not uncommon on Breen ships, and by the crew's dead silence he knew this subject was nothing to joke about.

"Well, alright, this is a rare opportunity. We will all go, but only after we build and install a sign post."

With that the silence broke, and once again there was constant and overlapping dialogue. Harry called down to Terra, "Dr. Who, we will need you to install a sign post in orbit around this planet."

"Very good idea, Harry, we will get on it immediately."

"What, did you just give me a compliment doctor?"

"It's not a compliment to agree with correct thinking, Harry."

"Oh. How long do you anticipate the construction to take?"

"Out here in this back water, could take a full day. First, we have to contact home world and download security codes and protocols. Second we need to coordinate with at least four other posts to get an exact space-time lock."

"You need to coordinate with at least four other posts?"

"Yes, we can't be off by as much as a nanosec with other posts, or it won't work, and all of these planets are moving at different rates of velocity, and also varying directions. It's a logistical nightmare."

"Well, pull from other departments if you need."

"No, we will handle it."

And the crew of sixteen Breen made their preparations to visit Earth….

4:

The Trip to Earth

On their fourteenth day in orbit around planet Ga'alle'een, Doctor Who's planetary sign-post was placed in orbit and activated. Completed in record time and it would now monitor and record progress of the changing atmosphere on the planed below. That information could be conveyed to the Val wherever she was in the galaxy. The crew were free to leave. There was no point in sitting around in cold empty space for ninety days or more, when you can run next door and have a cold beer with your neighbor.

"Stow your bags boys and girl; our next stop will be planet Earth. Dr. Who, is the sign post activated?"

"Yes Harry, my board shows all green—we're a go."

"Cadets, check your status screens. Are all crew members in their seats?"

"Screen all showing green, Captain."

Harry made a quick ship wide announcement,

"Attention all crew, engaging quantum-wave pulse generators. Cadets, lay in your course to the Human's system."

"Course laid in, Captain."

"Very well, deploy squibs."

"Squibs away, and tracking on course. Patching in data transfer now, sir. All three are online, and data shows course ahead clear."

"Ok, Mr. Heenon, engage main drive system."

"Main drive engaged, sir, velocity picking up. I estimate two minutes to space normal speed."

The Breen use a method of propulsion they call quantum pulse wave technology. This was a way of using the basic forces of nature against each other to propel a ship through space, and without the need for a fuel tank. All you needed were positive and negative energies, which are intrinsic to the fabric of space. The hull's fractal design was the secret to this technology. It was grown by nanobots and ranged from meter wide ribs down to the atomic scale. A wave of positive energy would be sent through a region of atoms. As the wave passed this area it would be pulsed with negative energy, giving a slight quantum push to the atoms inside of the hull material. Singly, each little pulse would amount to very little, but added together with the quadrillions of pulse nodes found along and inside of the entire length of the ship's hull the power amassed was enormous. With proper timing and varying the intensity of the pulses, the ship was driven forward, and its velocity could be increased to well beyond light speed.

"Alright Cadets, it is crucial that you continually monitor scanning data being sent from the squibs until we go into hyper."

"Aye, aye, sir."

Minutes later, "We're at space normal speed now, sir. Tracking ahead from squibs shows course is clear."

"Very well, increase pulse waves, push that throttle ahead Mr. Heenon, let's get up past light speed." The most dangerous time for a space-ship was accelerating beyond space normal, and until you reached and passed light speed. At such high speeds hitting even the smallest pebble would be catastrophic. Which is why the Breen utilize a method of space travel which employs the use of squibs, or small unmanned space ships used to lead the Val on her course. They would lead at a predetermined distance based on the ship's velocity, scan the area of space around them, and relay those findings back to the Val.

"Our velocity is picking up, Captain. I estimate we will be past light speed in three minutes."

And off sped the alien ship on its twelve-day journey to Earth to meet mankind.....

Journey to Earth, Day Two
It had been two weeks since the Breen first began receiving our old radio and TV transmissions, and they have begun to amass quite a library of our old radio shows and early television broadcasts. Harry was in the ICC, or ship's bridge. He spent most of his time there. He has just received a notification from the ship's genomics department.

"Harry, it's Doctor Sa'aarron."

"Yes Doctor. What is it?"

"We have been spending our free time analyzing the alien transmissions in an attempt to learn their language."

"Oh, and have your efforts paid off yet?"

"Yes Harry, our computer has been successful in learning the alien's language. I am placing language equivalents into the main computer for all of the crew to down-load into their individual internal computers. Ge'eenna is working on a genetic patch to allow our native nanites to adapt and modify our larynx so we will be able to speak their language."

"Excellent doctor, we all look forward to understanding what is being said in these shows." Harry then made an announcement, "Note to all crew, we now have language equivalents on the humans. Tonight's shows will be our first chance to understand what these aliens are saying, so everyone be sure to download Ge'eenna's vocal modifier." The fact that the Breen understood and could speak our language, and that they had the technology to make these adaptations and were willing to put them into play, was a clear demonstration of their dominion over less advanced races. We, on the other hand, have no way of understanding the Breen language. Half of the Breen vocabulary is vocalized beyond the range of our hearing capabilities, and the parts we could hear sounded like a cross between a whale and a dolphin—there was no way we could currently interpret that.

Journey to Earth, Day Three
Each night the crew got together to watch programs that had been received during that days travel through space, and due to the speed of the ship, through time as well. Aside from the entertainment value, the Breen were being shown how we have progressed through the years. By the time the transmissions had reached planet Ga'alle'een, they

had been traveling at the speed of light for nearly 70 years. Our cinema, of course, changes over the years. By the time the Breen arrive at earth our cinema will have evolved from the Silents to Talkies, from black-and-white TV into color, then into digital and high resolution clarity, and now 3D. Furthermore, the styles of production and acting have changed with our changing social mores, tastes, and current events. Think of the roaring 20s, the war years, the advent of the atomic age, another world war, the space age, through all these genres our transmissions would read like a road map of our civilizations' progress—westerns, sci-fi, TV dramas— all reflections of who and where we are in our development.

Roughly, six years will have passed on Earth for each day the Breen crew sped through space, plenty of time for major changes to be noticed nightly in their cinema viewings. Imagine being able to sit back in your armchair and casually watch as the generations passed by.

That evening Harry was enjoying some pre-show banter with several crewmen,

"It is very interesting to watch alien programming in this manner," he said. "It is giving me an Earth history lesson in a way. I wonder how much of this cinema is accurate and real."

"Obviously, much of it is just theater—a dramatization," said Dr. Sa'aarron.

"Yes, but even in their science fiction there are seeds of truth. A design perhaps of their hopes and aspirations, a reflection of their dreams and achievements," said Harry. "I have never watched a species evolve as we traverse time like this. It is really neat."

"Yes, and they do seem to be advancing rapidly, almost too rapidly," said Sa'aarron.

"What is on schedule for tonight cadets?" asked Arlen. He and Hippee were partial to our western movies.

"Let see, we have a western, something called Rawhide, and another war movie," said Heenon, who was in charge of today's movie selections.

"They do have a lot of war movies," noticed Hippee.

"And I've selected a science movie for you Captain; something titled, *It—The Terror From Beyond Space.*"

"Excellent, attention crew we will be assembling at the usual hour," said Harry. "Who is on refreshments for tonight?"

"I'll do it," said Arlen.

Later that night, as the movies began
"First up tonight we have another science fiction space movie," said Heenon.

"I like that," said Sa'aarron. "It shows the humans are already exploring space."

"Then, we have one of everybody's favorite, a western, and then something new called slapstick."

"Slapstick; is there a definition for that word?" asked Harry.

"Nearest guess we could come up with is comedy."

The classic sci-fi movie, 'It—The Terror From Space' began to play ... and commentary was soon to follow,

"What's this? They have built spaceships, looks like they are already exploring other planets?"

"Not in that thing they aren't. It's just a flying tin can with rockets for propulsion. It would never get off the ground."; "Perhaps they built it in orbit?" ; "But why build a tin can?"; "Yes, very primitive."

"Is that supposed to be a storage bay?" asked Dr. Who. "They are in the weightless void of outer space, on a ship moving at high velocity, and with loose crates lying about? Not likely."

"Oh, look, there's the monster," said Be'nnee.

"Great Maker!" exclaimed Sa'aarron. "If that is their take on what life looks like beyond their planet, they are going to be quite biased."

"Look, one of them is going to use explosives on the monster! They are going to use explosives inside a spaceship—that's crazy."

"This movie is really bad, much worse than many of the others we have seen. What else do we have?" asked Harry.

"Here is one you'll like. It's the western titled, Rawhide."

"Good let's get it and another movie up now."

"There's that monster again," said one of the crew. "It appears to have toes on its arms and its feet. Not an evolutionarily sound depiction of life."

"The monster looks pissed off," said Be'nnee. "Perhaps they should try to talk with it?" Fifteen perplexed heads turned and stared at him?

"That's enough, shut that one off, and roll the western and the comedy," barked Harry.

"Now that is more like it," said Arlen. "I don't know why, but I find these westerns relaxing." The Breen would often watch three movies at a time. It made for entertaining viewing for them, but it did make the commentary hard to follow.

Day Four
Questions begin to Arise. Just how much can you glean about a people form watching only television

transmissions? What kind of picture of our world and society can one build from these shows? Are they accurate enough to draw conclusions from? What if you make a mistake and misinterpret what you see? Just before the nightly shows a conversation between Arlen and Doctor Sa'aarron took the usual mien.

"I find it amazing," mentioned Arlen, "that these beings who developed on a planet three thousand light-years from Breen prime look so much like us."

"It is an example of convergent evolution," Sa'aarron quipped.

"Evolution, we evolved on entirely separate planets." Arlen fired back, and Sa'aarron responded, "Call it an interplanetary dictum that drives evolution everywhere in one direction."

"Nonsense, doctor."

"Then why are all prime species Breenoid?"

"Simple, it's just circumstances, not some grander underlying God process connecting us all."

"Splitting semantics atom thin aren't you Arlen?"

"We have another western tonight Arlen," mentioned Hippee. "It's cowboys and Indians."

"Well, yippee kayay!" yelled Arlen.

Sa'aarron winced, and worrying that his shipmate might be experiencing a form of space madness asked, "What's that Arlen?"

"I'm not sure. We understand and can speak what they call English, but some of their words don't make any sense to me as yet."

"But you like saying them anyway?"

"Huh? Well, guess I'm just getting into the spirit of it, and here's another one for you, Heeeehaaw!"

"You boys may have watched a bit too much TV," scoffed Dr. Sa'aarron, who then ran off to the sanity of his lab.

I found it interesting that the crew of the Val were taking up sides over us based on our cinema. With little else to judge us by their reaction was somewhat understandable, but with prejudices growing our future fate could hang at the end of a long string of barely intelligible theatre from generations passed which goes to the point Harry made about 'First Contacts' being inherently dangerous and difficult. Suspicion and misinformation always rules that day. And contrary to old sci-fi lore, I doubt an alien's first words would be, "I come in peace, take me to your leader." That just isn't what evolution has my subconscious expecting from such a frightening sight as a UFO hovering overhead. We would initially have two options, fight or flight. Understanding and acceptance would come later, much later, but at what cost?

Day Five—Tour of the Ship

It is early morning on the Val. Harry has just entered the ICC to find Heenon alone and hard at work at his control station. The following is an excerpt from Harry's personal log.

"My goodness, Heenon, have you been here all night?"

"Yes, Dr. Sa'anntee asked me to help coordinate some work he is doing with the archeological computer."

"The good doctor is obsessing again is he? Well, it's time for my routine weekly inspection of the ship. I'll stop by Solar first to see what he's up to."

I really admire that cadet. He is always willing to help out with any task, and he is even tempered unlike many of the bloated egos on board. After leaving the ICC I went directly to visit with Dr. Sa'anntee in his lab two decks below.

"Good morning doctor, I hear you've been up all night again, what have you got?"

"Yes Harry, we've been filling up our time with more research. Now that we understand the human language, we have been going back over these transmissions. There is much knowledge of earth interweaved into their theater, we are trying to sort it all out. I am working on extracting geographical data; names of places, land masses, and the like. Heenon is helping us to overlay it with the survey data collected by the probe survey done one hundred centuries ago."

"So you're trying to build up a patchwork of data on the planet Earth?"

"Yes, and I have Ge'eenna here working on historical references; their leader's names, important happenings, wars, and the like. Bennie is analyzing their technological capabilities, trying to separate out science fact from fiction."

"Sounds very exciting, I look forward to seeing your review."

"Where you off to next Harry?" asked Dr. Sa'anntee.

"Thought I might drop in on Doctor Who." Suddenly I heard a rush of sneers resonate across the Solar departments laboratory. This was more than interdepartmental distain. Dr. Who was known for his argumentative style which at times rubbed off on his techs.

"Careful Harry," said Sa'anntee, "they will be in a bad mood down there in Terranomics, and have been for several days now, nothing much for them to do out here in empty space."

"I'll watch my step."

I left Solar, my next stop, the Terranomics department, one deck below. Terranomics is the largest department on the ship, and occupies two whole decks. That is an awful lot of space for only one doctor and his three technicians. The word TERRANOMICS is prominently etched above the door headway. Right below it is a small sign that reads, *ALWAYS KEEP DOOR CLOSED*. Put there by one of the engineers no doubt. Not exactly saying stay out, but certainly implied. I cautiously poked my head inside but didn't see a soul. "Hello, is anybody in here?" It's a huge room, and oddly silent, all I can hear are my own words echoing back. "OK, I'll snoop around a little. Ah, there they are." Terranomics has its own holoroom. A sign over its door said, *busy, room in use*. "Looks like Who and his techs all in there together, but what are they watching?" … After more careful thought, I don't know, and I don't think I want to know? Deciding that things are normal as normal can be for engineers I leave Terranomics and continue my tour. "It would be nice to have some company this morning," I thought.

"Arlen would you and Hippee join me, I'm headed for Planetary Genomics?"

"Sure, is there anything we can help with?"

"Yes, I need to complete my weekly inspection of the ship's outer spaces, and just thought it might be nice to have some company."

"We'll meet you there in about five, Harry."

Upon entering Planetary Genomics I noticed this room was also very quiet. The only person in here is Doctor Sa'aarron. He was sitting alone with his back resting on the front of one of his gene typing machines.

"So Doctor, I hear you are lending out your helpers again?"

"Yes, Harry, Sa'anntee is an obsessive sort, and there's not much for me or my techs to do down here right now."

"That will all change when we get to Earth."

"Oh, so this is going to be a working vacation?"

"We'll find something for you to do."

Sa'anntee then turned to me and blurted out, "Harry, Arlen and Hippee are coming down the hallway." The matter of fact way he said it startled me.

"Now, how could you know that?"

"I can smell them."

"Funny, seriously though, sometimes your knack for prescience scares me." Just then Arlen and Hippee walked in.

Perhaps it was the scorn on Sa'anntee's face, but Arlen sensing something said, "Are you talking about me again doctor?"

"Nothing like a nice argument to start the day, hey Arlen?" Sa'anntee shot back.

"It's like a morgue in here," said Arlen. "Your techs mutiny again doctor?"

Dr. Sa'aarron, not wishing to get into a protracted diatribe said nothing more to Arlen. He then rubbed his restive eyes and said, "If you three are off for a walk, may I join you?"

"Certainly, I would enjoy the company of all three of you." My thankless inspection has now turned into a morning constitutional. This ship has many extraneous places not to mention the navigation pods, and each small and confining hold needs periodic inspection.

"I always enjoy going down into the pods on these inspection tours," said Dr. Sa'aarron. "There is something about being in such a small enclosed space; you can really feel of the power of the pulse waves as they build inside the hull."

"Really, I think I know what you mean, Doctor," said Arlen. "I also like the small confining spaces; it's like being inside the womb of the ship." ... "By the way, either of you know what the entertainment is going to be tonight?"...

While I was pondering through the ships logs to chronicle the Breen's journey to Earth, it was this little exchange between Arlen and Dr. Sa'aarron which caught my eye. I had also noticed on several other occasions the Breen being abrasive with one another one moment, and best of friends the next, acting as though an argument had never occurred. Was this a clue into the Breen psyche, or just an example of alien behavior? The answer to that question is still unresolved.

Day Five—At the Movies
The Breen have been viewing earth transmissions for over a week now. With their trip through time they are now watching signals which were sent out into space back in our sixties era. Popular shows of that time were the TV Westerns, The Twilight Zone, and of course, a modern classic, Star Trek. That night as the crew gathered together in the observation lounge which doubled as a movie theater, the usual banter broke out.

"Captain," said Heenon, "I am noticing an increase in short films. What they call promo movies. Colloquially, the humans call them ads, or commercials."

"What does that name imply?"

"It is an industry. These humans are very capitalistic."

"Huh, that could be useful," said Harry.

"Capitalism is the most sensible form of economy for a planet in their stage of development."

"Yes, even today we use a pseudo form of capitalistic trade," mentioned Booh'raan, one of Dr. Who' techs.

"Yes, but mostly with only the offshoot planets. You know, like Breen'nerra," argued Hippee.

Not all Breen shared the same desire to be complex beings with machines coursing through their blood, or to live the life immortal. Some preferred to live a natural life, to be born, experience a life unaltered, have a family, grow old, and then to die someday. The average lifespan on Breen'nerra is 350 years. There are many offshoot planets among the Breen collective, each with a variety of beliefs about how best to exist. None of these offshoot civilizations are shunned. In fact, they and their beliefs are embraced and celebrated. Any Breen could visit and live on any planet within the collective, and many do, using them as retirement planets.

"Yes, it is nice that they have trade, but why must we watch these promos?" stated Harry. "Note to the cadets, no more promos."

"I don't know," shot Dr. Sa'anntee. "They do give us a window into their daily life's goings on. Take this one; it is about some sort of food stuff. They seem to prefer to eat it while watching movies like we are."

"Really, what is this food stuff called?"

"It is called popcorn."

"When we get to earth we will have to try some of this popcorn."

"I think that is the purpose of the promo ads, Captain, to get you to buy the popcorn."

"Alright, I'm putting up tonight's picks," said Heenon. "We have something called … The Twilight

Zone."

"What more poetry?" asked Arlen.

"No, it is more like a psycho-drama. We also have a western called, Bonanza, and a new sci-fi. I'll put the three of them all up together." The three movies began, and this was the Breen crew's first introduction to Star Trek.

"Hey, look, they now have a ship kind' a like the Val."

"What is this show called," asked Harry?

"It is a weekly serial show called Star Trek."

"Are you kidding me?" snapped Harry. "So, in less than ten years' time earthlings have gone from tin can spaceships to starships with warp drive. What is going on here? Doctor, how long is normal for this type of technological jump."

"Generally three centuries," said Sa'aarron.

"Maybe they had help?"

"Maybe they stole the technology. Remember that Roswell Incident?"

"That's right Hippee," said Arlen, "and the alien autopsy. Now we must suspect that they killed the aliens to steal their technology."

"Huh, well let's be quiet and finish watching the show," said Harry. "They call it Star Trek, a story about a strong-minded captain of a futuristic spaceship on a five-year mission to explore outer space—what's not to like?"

The Breen are very imitative, and in the near future Harry will on occasion ape himself into the role of Captain Kirk, and it will become immediately obvious to the rest of the crew. That action is what earned him the nick name Captain Kirk. In fact, all of the crew had favorites they liked to emulate to some extent. They enjoyed mimicking other cultures, much the way we might use an Italian or French word like ciao, or bon jour in our conversations. This was not so much flattery as it was a stroking of their egos. Plus it provided entertainment, and gave them something to break up the boredom of a long trip. Nine days into their journey, and only three days until First Contact, it was time to build up a consensus of who and what we earthlings were. This was creating rifts between the crew. Who were we? Given the huge spectrum of human beliefs, our religious and practiced socialisms, our psychological states, health and personality traits, differing education and experiential levels, left questions unanswered. Knowing something about your next door neighbors is an important consideration when accepting an invite to dinner. The Breen were just about to commit themselves to a three months stay with seven billion neighbors; roughly 200 different countries of varying levels of development, and they would become the focus of the sum total of all of it. I never thought to ask, but they must have their own version of a Murphy's Law. It would only take one bellicose potentate to ruin your day, and Earth has many Generals of War; all eager to ply their trade.

Going up to a new neighbor's door for the first time I always felt a mix of hope and fear. It was no different for the Breen. After having watched a multitude of various transmissions; everything ranging from TV commercials to attacks by Space aliens from Mars; from I Love Lucy programs to epic war sagas, Captain Harry and his crew were struggling to gain a perspective on how they would be received by us. The Breen live by a galactic code of procedures honed over many millennia. Procedures designed to preserve order and safety of all intra-galactic civilizations. These were accepted rules which outlined courses of action against hostile species, real and perceived; current and future. Would we be considered a hostile species? Not that the Breen were a police force, they weren't. This was more of a loosely interpreted treaty requirement signed to by all in their interplanetary community. A community we would soon be forced to join.

After the evening's entertainment, a conversation erupted between the crew. The showings that night were particularly controversial, and even shocking to watch.

"Well, they do look a little like us," said Hippee.

"They are much more violent though. In fact, I sense a trend in them toward more and more violence," said Arlen.

"Yes, I to have noticed a turn toward more violence in them, and it is also of a more personalized form," said Sa'aarron. "Our own early per-space history had very little intra-species conflict. That is all they seem to do: wage war on others of their own kind."

"I wonder what spurs it on in them?" asked Harry.

"I would advise caution on this first contact Harry," said Sa'aarron. "We now know they have entered an atomic age."

"Yes, and with their ever more powerful weapons, they could be a threat."

"I don't want to have my life extinguished while on vacation," added Arlen.

"Who does?" said Hip.

"Where is the rule book on emerging species?"

"Oh—stop it Arlen, I know what you are getting at," said Harry.

"Well, what is it then?" asked Be'nnee.

Dr. Sa'aarron blurted out, "He's talking about

Rule 37—No violent species may be allowed to spread beyond their own planet."

"Strange we should let then exist at all," said Arlen.

"We don't yet know they are violent beyond control."

"No, but if they are, then what do we do?"

"Can't let them spread their violent ways out into space."

"Many of the dominant species that would be within reach of their early space age are unarmed pacifists to the extreme. No match for a militant race bent on domination and exploitation."

"Then they will have to be removed as the dominant species on their planet." And the debate continued on into the late of night. Whose will be the voice of calm detached reason, of cool objectivity?

By the twelfth day of their journey to Earth Harry had reasoned a profile of human behavior. The following is from his Captain's Log…"We are faced with a species which has evolved rapidly; perhaps too rapidly. They are a very intelligent and creative species capable of great compassion, but also often exhibiting great hate bordering on evil. The strides they have been able to make within the past two centuries are remarkable among their peers. If their hatred and fears can be removed, they would make a wonderful addition to our community. What they lack, and must be taught, is a perspective on how they fit into the galactic community. Once they learn they are not alone in this universe, it is hoped they will cast off their penchant for violence, and peacefully join us."

As the time of First Contact neared, tensions grew

among the crew. Following is an accounting of
conversations recorded on that last day of the trip.

"Personally I think they have grown out of their
primitive need for war," said Harry.

"That is not how I see it Harry," said Arlen.

"Harry, you are basing your interplanetary
policy on hope of change, and pity for the human
condition," said Sa'aarron. "Foreign policy should be
based on mutual respect, and a desire to advance
peacefully among friends, not on hope and pity."

"One should not overlook their violent past
either, and need I point out they have murdered
more of their own kind in the past century than in
the preceding millennia." said Arlen.

As pointed out by Dr. Sa'aarron, certainly man has
killed enough of his own kind in the last century to
earn the scorn and distrust of any sane thinking
species. All of us know of the six million or more
lives exterminated by the Germans in World War II,
but somehow glossed over in our history classes are
the thirty-five or so million killed by Stalin in the
Russian Pogroms, and the sixty-five million killed in
China in its own cultural revolution. These facts are
often omitted from our discourses, what, for political
correctness? One does not know the answer to these
questions, and that alone is troubling. Further, has
China, or Russia, or Germany, or Japan, for that
matter, ever apologized for their war atrocities?
Have we for our belief in Manifest Destiny, which saw
the murder of countless early American natives?
Many find it comforting that today they can go out
right now, and after a short walk or drive purchase a
guiltless chocolate malted in any American city. I say
guiltless, but are we? Have not the deaths, the
killings, the wars, made murderers of us all?

However, we conveniently compartmentalize or rationalize our evil deeds. We shelve them until time and memory can no longer recall. Is the pain of our guilt too great to bear? I have read accounts of the Russian pogroms. Nothing could ever bring more tears to a person's eyes than to hear such pointless cruelty to even one's own kin. As far as the Chinese revolution goes, we have what, children murdering their parents and grand-parents, students killing teachers—how do we define insanity? Had the Breen known the full extent of our murderous ways they may not have been so quick to show us any mercy, and we may have seen earth passed on to our heirs— the Apes. Earth would now truly be the Planet of the Apes.

   "I'm giving them the benefit of a doubt doctor," Harry added. "They have made the jump into space, and that requires remarkable technological growth, and also a commitment to cooperation among the many groups needed to accomplish that great feat. To that they are due some respect."
   "OK, Harry, as ship's Captain, which course of action we take is ultimately your call."

During the twelve-day trip to Earth, the crew, after having viewed hundreds of our broadcasts, began to develop strong feelings toward us. Some saw us as worthy of a curious respect, and wanted further contact; others felt contempt towards us for our perceived violent ways. To half of the crew, we were likened to vicious animals to avoid at all cost. Many of the crew members said they would prefer to spend their whole three months leave on some remote little corner of our planet, as far away from man as they could get.

The crew were split evenly, half seeing a potential friend in us. The other half wanted nothing to do with humans. They deemed us too savage a species. Several crewmen were heard to suggest, "Eradication of the human infestation of the planet Earth would be best for all." But time to build a dominating consensus had now passed as planet Earth lie within sight. First contact was but a handful of hours away. How would this historic first encounter between two species with such differing views on life turn out?...

5:

First Contact, part 1

Washington, DC
Tuesday, February 22

Five weeks ago our government hired me to put my
keen intellect to work, and to delve deep into our
current economic problems in search of a solution.
For that I needed a team of economists and
mathematicians. Selecting the finest minds required
me to look far and abroad. It took weeks to
assemble a team and to locate a place for us to
meet. I picked a top economist and mathematician
from India, and another from Japan. There were also
a couple Nobel Laureates from the Netherlands.
Counting these experts together with their assistants
I had amassed a rather large group of individuals.
The logistics of gathering them all together was
daunting. To simplify things we decided we would all
meet at a central location. Resorting to a globe the
best strategic place to convene turned out to be Rio
de Janeiro. I love solutions with dual purposes. Every

other week we would collect in Rio for a week of work and…. The rest of my time is spent back home in DC correlating data and making reports to the General.

I am an intellectual. I accept that. People often mistake my intellect for arrogance. Tough. If I am labeled arrogant for being smart, then it is a good tradeoff. As part of my genius process I talk things over in my head. Yes, I talk to myself. It is usually just mindless chatter, but there is an incessant conversation going on inside my mind. As a result it may appear at times that I am ignoring others. This disregard is not by choice. If I were a generation younger I might be thought of as a cool geek. Instead I have now aged into some sort of a no man's land. They used to call it maturity; not social isolation. Though I will admit to being a bit of a bigot, my intolerance is aimed at ignorance; race, age, or sexual orientation has nothing to do with it.

Tuesday is my day off. Outside it is brisk, clear, and a perfect day for an invigorating walk. I am new to Washington and its winters. Doubt I will stay and live here after my job ends, but we'll see. In need of supplies I decide to walk the three short blocks to the food mart. We Americans just don't walk enough anymore. Stepping outside, I zipped up, and trod off. My feet were punching through the little ice pockets frozen over the sidewalk spall. Their crunching sound amuses me.

This older part of town has some sidewalks with real character. The technical term is deferred maintenance—cracks, tree root uplifts, chuck holes—trip hazards all. I have to watch my step so that I don't slip, slide, or stumble. Looking ahead I spied a few locals out in their yard a few doors down.

"Good Morning," I said as I walked by their front

yard.

"Hello," the young lady replied. She looked to be in her late twenties (and already fat). "You're the new guy we've been hearing about." What, people are talking about me? Curious to learn more I stopped to chat a while.

"Yes, I've just moved here from Arizona. I've been here for little more than a month, and working six days a week I haven't gotten to know many of my neighbors as yet."

"We hear you're some kind of scientist or something." They must be part of a gossip network.

"I'm an economist actually. I just got a job working for the fed. That's why I had to move here to DC." I had to make a mental note that people here is DC are quite different than people back in Arizona. They talk differently, for one. Plus, people in Arizona have a slimmer, tanner, and more weathered look. Partly, I guess, due to the dry heat. Here, with this cold, you are cooped up for five months each year. The lady went on to say,

"Gossip has it that you wrote some book?"

"Why … thank you, it's nice to hear that someone has actually heard of it," I said. "By the way, my first name is John."

"I'm Tina, John, and that lump on the porch is my husband, Mike. Get up Mike and shake hands with our new neighbor." Mike mumbled something and got up. We shook and shared a bit of small talk.

"Well, it's been nice to meet both of you. I was just on my way to the store."

"We won't keep you any longer John, and by the way—nice hat. You don't see any like that around here." Again people are making remarks about my hat. They are more common in Ariz. I've come to think of it as a signature. Suppose if I wanted to be more DC I should bare the head, and get a black trench coat? That'll be the day.

Before I got to the store I passed a few more locals. Damn—when I was young, you just didn't see much of that. Seriously, though, obesity is not funny. My book *Tipping Points* has two chapters devoted to overeating as it relates to the economies of collapse. After all, health issues exact a heavy toll on our dollars, both personally and collectively. Believe it or not, the huge growth spurt in world food production was a leading contributor to our current economic woes. Victims of our own success we are.

It was my book that got me this DC gig. It was a short, not too well written book. Written in all too simple language, that no one really read, and yet here I am. Actually, the one person that did read it was some big mucky-muck at the Pentagon. He apparently found it more of a horror story than actual hard science, but it scared him, at least enough to mention it to higher ups. So they called me in, sat me down, and offered me a job. Their spiel to me was, and in deep military gargle, "We don't think your conclusions were right Parker, but if there is the slightest chance that they are, and then we want to know how those scenarios might play out. We want all bases covered." That was the General talking. Talk about a strange combination of conflicting personalities, or is it just the universe playing games. Me working with the military, the military actually seeking sage advice—wake me when it's over.

Shit it's cold here in February. With only a block left to go I sped it up a little. For this new job, I had to move from my sunny and warm home in southern Arizona to Alton, a suburb of DC. I picked Alton as it was cheaper to live here a little outside to downtown, but still close enough to keep the commute time down. Alton was actually a small town all to its own, which found itself absorbed by DC expansion. They used to call it urban sprawl. Curiously, you don't hear that term used anymore. Alton is an older area, but I like older, you know that quaint sort of obsolescent charm. A throw back to my childhood I guess, back to a time when we all had fenced yards, and a stronger sense of individuality. One could sense that I am not a big fan of current housing trends, whole areas of lovely older houses being razed to make way for huge ugly multi-story apt complexes, multi-generation housing, and condos. It might be the scientist in me, but I notice trends, and this one is a symptom of a bigger disease.

Finally I arrived at the food mart. Freezing, I entered the store and shook the icicles out of myself, grabbed a shopping cart, and it was off to isle two—potato chips, then around to isle four—frozen foods where I picked up a few TV dinners. Then to the produce section to get some apples. Let's see—apples— red and delicious. $2.89 a pound! For frik'n apples!? Shit! In the old days, I could just pick one off grannies tree. Inflation, what a terrible concept. Maybe the communist's had it right? Just then an old tune popped into my head, "Oh, Country Boys Can Survive."

Now that's an idea. Country boys can survive. Who could argue with such simplicity? Let's see, isle six—beer—no, too expensive. Continuing my thought—country boys would do better today in this economic downturn. Why, I asked myself? Simple. Apples, yes apples, but not just apples. Country boys could grow their own eggs and ham, er uh, chickens and pigs, and vegetables too, just as my grandparents did. Anyway, if we all had-say, an acre of land?

It was nice to reminisce, but the somber realization is that we are living in a different time. We have shifted from the earlier agricultural and industrial economies. Now we are in what I call a post technological economy. Poets think in terms of eras, for historians its ages, but for economists, the ages and eras translate into economies. They are all the same, but with just a slightly different bent. As we pass from one economic age to another, we lose much of what we knew in the former. And today I fear we have lost a connection to the land that was an important buffer for our survival. And what have we gotten for it, a faster and faster pace of life, high-rise apartments, overpopulation, and environmental degradation; the list goes on. We certainly have not been a friend to mother earth either. At some point might she not fight back? Force us to slow down, show some respect to her and the other organisms we share this fish bowl Earth with? But as the saying goes, "You can never return home again—can't go backwards."

Damn—back to isle 4, forgot to get some jerky, all the while singing in my head that tune, "Oh, Country Boys Can Survive." As a naturalist/economist I know the dangers of letting one organism grow beyond the bounds of its natural controls. Is that what we have here? Are humans becoming an invasive species? Have we actually grown past that prophetic tipping point? Or are there hidden controls? Ones that nature, or the universe, has in store for us? Jerky—into the basket with you. We have built an amazing and beautiful thing, this human techno-society—and in such a short stretch of time—only about one hundred years. What lies beyond our today, and for whom, or what? These were some biting questions. The ones General Bradley hired me to try to find answers to.

Passing isle 6 again—beer —cold and beckoning—alright, alright, I reached down and grabbed a six-pack of cold ones; into the basket with you. After all, why face a worldwide economic collapse sober?

That's enough groceries for a few days. Now to get out of here. I scanned down the check stands— ah, there's checker Becky. What a looker, and I think she's single. I hurried to get in her line. Old man Powel was already there, and standing in front of me. He is sort of a local lifer; one of the few lifers left in Alton.

"Nice to meet you again, Mr. Powel."

"Right back at you John, are you out for some exercise?"

"Me? Yeah, why waste a day off?"

"You get Tuesdays off?"

"Yeah, well, it was about the only compromise could be made with what we are doing."

"More secret stuff, I'll bet?"

"Not so secret and actually I'd like to explain it all to you some time." Just then the General's warning popped into my brain. "Everything you do here is sub-rosa?" Yeah, well, sub-rosa this General.

Right then we heard an extraordinarily loud— kabooom! … kabooom! Then the building actually shook. Mr. Powel jumped. Shaking he asked, "What the heck was that?"

"Sounded like a sonic boom. You know, I saw the space shuttle come in at Edwards twice, and it made that same sound as it entered the atmosphere."… "Only I remember the Shuttle's booms seemed to be much more distant. That one was right up on us."

"I thought planes were banned anywhere near the city?" Powel asked.

"Yes, that is what I heard also."

"A sonic boom. You're probably right. You're a pretty smart guy." Powel, visibly shaken, paid for his groceries, and we said good-bye. "Hope to see you again soon," he said.

"Alright Mr. Powel—hope to see you again soon, too." I didn't see him leave the store. My attention was now focused on Becky.

"That Mr. Powel seemed a little upset by the sonic booms. People are a lot shakier these days, especially after 9/11."

"Yeah, He'll be OK." We made a few more mindless intercourses as I put my meager acquisitions on the counter.

"Looks like you are eating light again."

"Yes, job is taking me out of town in a few days. No need to buy too much."

"Oh-where to this time?"

"In two days I'm off to a conference in Brazil on global economics."

"That pretty heady stuff," she said, "but Rio. It sounds more like a vacation you're going on."

"You wouldn't think so if you knew how nerdy the group of people I'm going to be with are."

She gave me a little smile and said, "Suppose I should feel sorry for you then." We made some more small talk, and shortly I'm all bagged up and get ready to turn away and head out of the store. Then there's that little devil on my shoulder whispering, "Close the deal stupid. Ask Her Out!" I never could quite, well, I find it hard to ask women out.

"There you go, John. See you when you get

back?"

Stumbling for something to say, I said, "Certainly, I'll only be gone for five days." I thought to myself as I left—"Geeze, you idiot scientist, can't you ever act normal?"

Grub in tow, tail between my legs, I exited the store, when it hit me—that bitter chill of February in DC. Zipping up, I looked over and noticed old man Powel, and a small group of people standing out at the curb and looking toward downtown. "Might as well go over and see what's up……"

* * * * * *

Earlier— In Deep Space

Out way past the orbit of Uranus, out farther than our Solar System's Thermo-Pause, the Breen ship is speeding towards our home. Their twelve-day journey to Earth from terraforming on BSC 3687-3, or planet Ga'alle'een, some 70 light-years distant, is almost over.

"Captain, we are approaching the Human's solar system."

"Good, show me a hologram of it."

A holographic representation of our solar system appears out in the middle of the ICC room. "Cadets, plot an 80 degree polar entry course to planet Earth. We don't want to hit any space rocks when we come out of hyper." The Breen have been using hyper velocities for millennia, and have perfected it to a fine art, yet the many dangers of such a high speed still exist. Any impact at such a velocity would be catastrophic. Collisions with space debris are currently the leading cause of Breen deaths. So the utmost care must be taken to avoid collisions. Most of the matter in our system, asteroid belts and planets, lies along the ecliptic, which is why Harry chose a polar entry.

"Yes sir, making course changes now." A linear representation of their course to Earth appeared in the holo as a red line arching on a collision course to our planet.

"Scan ahead Cadets, how does the course you have plotted look?"

"Course ahead looks clear, Captain. Squibs are tracking on new course," replied Heenon.

"Let's wait until we are two AU's out before we drop out of hyper," said Harry.

"That will take about another four hours at this distance and velocity, sir."

"I understand." … "Arlen, is your first contact presentation ready?"

"Yes, done it is. We will give them quite a show." On hearing that, the trio of cadets started chattering amongst themselves. The cadets often talked and acted as one, and with their drivel overlapping it was hard to distinguish who had said what. "Wonder what he has cooked up this time?" ; "We'll find out soon enough." ; "Perhaps too soon." ; "I've seen parts of it. It's just bits and pieces of the transmissions we recorded on our way here." ; "How is that an introduction?" A little laughter ensued.

Four hours later
The cadets were still sitting at their stations,

"We are approaching two astronomical units distant from Earth, sir."

"Alright, rescan ahead," said Harry. "You just can't be too safe."

The cadets made another sensor sweep, "Sensors and squib data shows all clear ahead, sir."

"Fine, take us out of hyper. Let me know when we reach space-normal speed."

Harry seemed edgy and was being more cautious than usual. The gleaming jewel they all had traveled so far and so long to reach now lies but a few hours ahead. This young captain was with some trepidation facing a personal demon—inexperience. This would be his first First Encounter—poor fellow. The Breen, for all their advanced technology, and eons of experience, still feared the uncertainty of daily life.

"At space normal speed now, sir. Setting scanning to automatic," said the cadets.

"Mr. Heenon, first have the squibs do an end run to Earth, and let me know when they are done with that scan."

"Programming squibs to do a detailed scan, sir. This will take a few minutes." Sensing a growing unease in their Captain, Heenon glanced over to his two comrades. For a moment they all made eye contact. Harry's uncertainty was palpable, and as his grasp of command appeared to lessen the three cadets began to get a taste of their own apprehension.

"Scans complete, Captain. No hazards noted ahead," said Heenon, and after clearing his throat, "At this speed, it will take another six hours to reach planet orbit, sir."

"Fine, reprogram squibs to remain in orbit around Earth. Allow them to make non-intrusive scans only. … We don't want to be charged with spying, at least not yet." Harry's reassuring witticism brought smiles back to their faces.

"Reprogramming squibs, sir. I am entering changes now."

"Good, place all data they collect directly into

the computer and correlate it with the archival footage we have of this planet. Now, let's spend some time at space normal to have a first look at this planet."

Two astronomical units out from earth is still, by our standards, very far away. That's twice the distance of the earth from the sun. At that distance no one on earth would have noticed the small ship suddenly appear in space. The Breen's arrival will be a complete surprise.

"Captain, should we plot a course to set us into orbit around their planet first? Check it out?"

"No, that would be like some peeper criminal casing your home. Let's show them the respect they are due and go right to the front door. We will blast straight down through the atmosphere and into their capital city, what was it called again, oh, yeah; they called it Washington DC. We'll give them a real show. I think that is a better approach," said Harry, always eager to go boldly. His mood had changed, and now the crew members were getting into the mood. They had traveled for nearly two weeks to get to Earth, and excitement was mounting regardless of the possible dangers ahead. We were a new species, an alien species, and when two species alien to each other meet for the first time it creates the perfect recipe for disaster.

The Breen decision to blast straight into Earth's lower atmosphere, and right to our nation's capital might sound sensible from their point of view, remember they think, due to our sci-fi cinema, that we earthlings are much more advanced that we actually were. Plus they have been making interplanetary visits with other civilizations for centuries. From our point of view—well, it scared the hell out of us.

Harry using his quantcomm, level 1, "Doctor Sa'anntee, the squibs are in orbit around planet earth, you and Be'nnee can now start gathering up the data they find. Please coordinate your findings with Arlen, he will be running the first contact greeting message." He got no response. He then turned to Arlen,

"Arlen, do we know where their capital is located?"

"Well, most of the films we have watched, and according to Dr. Sa'anntee's work with extracting useful data from them, indicated their capital building was located on the north American continent, in a city called Washington DC."

"Show me what we know about this planet?"

Arlen went on to say, "Doctor Sa'anntee was able to build up a representation of planet earth off of the many programs we intercepted on our way here. It shows what we believe to be an accurate representation of their planet currently. I'll put it up as a holo, here take a look." A three foot in diameter holographic sphere came up out in the middle of the room. It was a holographic globe of our planet showing major land masses and oceans, some national borders, and places data, but was far less than a complete picture of earth, the one that every fifth grader has all burned into our heads.

"And that is all we have?"

"Yes, that is all we have?"

"Where is Doctor Sa'anntee, he won't answer my calls?" asked Harry.

"Haven't seen him," said Arlen. "Now, let me show you a quad-sphere of the North American continent," Arlen pointed to a map of the US, but other than the location of a few cities, and some mountains and lakes, there was nothing else to look at.

"We need much more data. Get me Solar System Ecology on the main com line. Has anyone seen Sa'anntee?" Hippee then answered over the ship's intercom system, "He's is sequestered in his lab Harry. He's working on some new project." Just then Sa'anntee replied, "Harry, you need to come down here and see this. It's remarkable."

"What is it Doctor, we need to be making landing preparations right now?"

"It's the amount of data feeds the squibs are getting from the planet, and what they are showing us. Furthermore, I found out why their transmissions started to go dark a couple days ago."

"I'll come right down. Cadets you have the con. Let's hold it here for now, and bring us to full stop." He then hurried off to Solar

"OK Doctor, let's see what you have."

"Just look at it Harry," pointing to one of his signal receivers, "we now have hundreds, and at times thousands of transmissions coming from earth each second. We couldn't detect them before as they were weaker signals, but more directed, and they have gone digital, a truly remarkable achievement."

"But you predicted this would happen. Isn't digital a natural progression?"

"Yes, but I did not expect it to happen so quickly. To make this jump usually takes a species a century or two—not only thirty years."

"Are you able to understand any of these transmissions?"

"Only a few of them. They are encrypted, and with quite sophisticated codes. Some are obliviously military, other's just common everyday talk.

However, the wealth of data coming in, it is just astounding. We have decoded some of it. I have basic data like talk and causal communication; there is global positioning data, weather data, and scientific data, which are coming from satellites in orbit, and we even have intercepted hundreds of movie shows. Also, of interest, there are at least three satellites sending real-time visual and sensor data. And look, they also appear to have a global access information web—quite civilized of them. We aren't able to access it as yet. Ge'eenna is still trying to work out their transmission protocols, but we can pick up what is being transmitted, and store it for later. We are overwhelmed down here Harry; I am calling in help from Terranomics and Planetary Genomics."

"We are running some of the data though the computers to produce a clearer picture of this planet, but we are going to need some additional time. We should stop and wait here for a day, Harry. It could take that much time to get a handle on their transmission codes."

"No Doctor, we're going in today, in just a few hours. You can work on deciphering their codes and all later. However, it is interesting to note that they have advanced so far. Just give me the planetary data you have so we can precisely locate their capital city."

The Harry's decision not to spend adequate time gathering data on our planet, and then allowing time to decipher it, proved to be disastrous. More time would have shown them that we were not as technologically, or socially, advanced as they had thought. Further, they might have gained some insight into our always paranoid reactions to sudden change. He might have learned of our intense fear of having our cities over-flown by UFO's. But now, thanks to the squib data, they had a detailed description of Earth, and of our capital city, their prime target, and Harry was ever more driven to make contact with us, today!

He quickly left Sa'aarron's lab and hurried back up to the ICC. "Cadets, re-engage engines, set course to Earth at space normal, and then take us directly into their capital city. Once there we will hover at two hundred feet and start our greeting. Remember, and this is important, there will be a huge build-up of static electricity from blasting through the atmosphere. At only two hundred feet the discharges could be deadly. You will need to disburse the static buildup before we get below one thousand feet. We don't want to electrocute any of our new friends."

"We're making preparations now, Captain. Estimate we will reach planet Earth in four hours."

"Coming in at that high a velocity, and dumping off our electrical build-up in an air burst just before ground contact will really be a spectacular show," added Arlen. "I like it, kind of gets your excitement level way up. It's a brilliant idea Harry."

It is just an observation of mine about Captain Harry, Arlen, and Hippee. And I would never have said this to their faces, but they were leaders who were blinded by their mission, and they chose not to listen to the advice of the brilliant scientists around them. This was most curious considering their supposedly advanced brains. Also, from my personal experiences with these three, well, all I can say is that they were by far the biggest of the thrill seekers. The other Breen in the crew actually seemed tame, or even timid, next to Harry and Arlen. Perhaps the best leaders are at times the most brazen and unabashed in personality. Our human corollary might be General Bradley; he was just as brash and always gung ho; like I said, it's just an observation.

Four Hours Later
Now only minutes away from Earth, the Breen ship was on final approach,

"We are on final approach to planet Earth, sir."

"O.K., switch to your navigational hologram of the planet. I want to see just a quad-hemi showing our entry course to their capital."

"Coming up, sir." The holograph of Earth hovering out in the middle of the ICC switched back to a view of only the northern hemisphere, "Their, that's everything we currently know of the North American continent, sir."

"Now, can you show me a three dimensional display of their capital city on the side wall."

"Yes captain, we now have a street map of their central city." On the starboard wall up popped a large pictorial map of the city of Washington DC. It showed everything; street names, buildings, monuments, etc.; all thanks to our internet.

"Now. Ah—there, that's the city they call Washington. Take us right into the heart of it, Mr. Heenon."

"Course plotted, sir. Landing procedures entered, and we are starting our descent."

"Sound inertial warning. Attention crew, we are at planet Earth, commencing landing procedures. Everyone take you seats." As the Val slowed down the ship and crew would be exposed to excessive G-forces. All loose objects needed to be securely restrained. The crew had landing seats rise up below them. They literally grew right up out of the deck. More of a bed than a chair they were designed to encapsulate an entire body. A crewman would reclined down inside, then all of his appendages, arms, hands, legs, feet, and head, had a shock absorbent foam expand against them.

"The crew are all seated, and my board is showing all green, Captain."

"Good, take us on in." Charging into Earth's upper atmosphere the ship's hull began to heat and glow red. Diving straight for Washington left no room for maneuvering. The crew experienced dreadful forces of rapid deceleration and a violent buffeting of the ship as it burnt through the atmosphere and slowed down.

"The city is coming into view now, Captain. I'm making slight adjustments to course; we should head for those taller buildings there in the center of the city."

"Agreed."

During the last ten miles of her descent the view to observers on the ground was spectacular. With her body angled slightly upward she looked like a huge whale surfing down through the sky.

At fifty thousand feet in altitude shock waves began ripping the air apart causing huge swirling vapor clouds to spread out and behind. A sonic boom rocked the city streets for miles in every direction. At fifteen thousand feet the slowing ship started to shed her static buildup. Bolts of lightning were seen zapping all along the sides of the space ship. This massive release of energy heated the vapor clouds into bright iridescent pink and blue plasma. Observers directly beneath the UFO said the show was too eye popping not to watch.

The Val then leveled off and began to hover, but the blast of hot air around her continued on to the surface knocking bystanders below it to the ground. Those who didn't look on in astonishment screamed and ran for any available protection. At ground zero cars crashed and many were left abandoned by their fleeing occupants. Our military wasn't aware of this invasion until people started overloading emergency phone lines. Then the real show began.

6:

First Contact, Part 2

Tuesday, February 22, 11:15 AM

I had just left the grocery store when the bitter cold of winter hit me. The chill freezing at my unprotected neck and chest went deep to the bone as I paused to swiftly zip up my coat. Out by the curb I noticed Mr. Powel. He had joined a small group of people who had gathered. They were all looking toward downtown, and seemed captivated by something. ... Out of curiosity I decided to walk over to see what was going on.

"Hi guys, what's up?" I'm ignored. They didn't utter a word. I'm thinking it must be me—the outsider. They're all just standing and looking down Fairfax as if mesmerized. Then one of the men raised an arm, and pointed toward downtown. As I turned to let my eyes follow his arm, Mr. Powel said, "That's your sonic boom, John."

"Sonic boom?" ... "Oh yeah." As I focused my eye's town ward, there appeared to be a large object in the sky, and maybe half a mile away. "That looks like a blimp," I blurted out.

"It's no blimp," one of the other men spoke up. "I heard the booms, turned, and saw it come right down out of the sky. It's like the sky just split open. There was this huge thunderous roar, and a whoosh as it leveled off, and then a fireworks show of lightning zapping all around it."… "That's an alien spaceship. I'm getting out of here. C'mon Honey." They turned and rapidly walked away.

"Boy, they sure looked scarred Mr. Powel. People really are skittish these days. But to conger up a spaceship from a blimp?"

"Well John, if it isn't a spaceship, then what is it?" I looked to Mr. Powel, "You're shivering, is it the cold?"

"No, it's not the cold, after 30 years living here in Washington, I'm used to that. It's that damn spaceship thing."

"Now come on Mr. Powel. Let me give you my scientist opinion on it." Trying to put some calm sanity back into the afternoon, I strained my eyes to scan the huge air machine. "To me, it looks like a dirigible, you know, a blimp, and a big one at that."

"You're the scientist John. I can't say, but Mike there said he saw the damn thing come down blasting right out of the sky, and I have never known Mike to be anything but a straight talker."

Patronizing a little I offered up, "Yes, they sure were scarred. And whatever that thing is, it is making quite a commotion downtown." The sky machine was headed for us, but still about half a mile away. I scoffed, "Spaceship indeed?"… "Listen. Above the clatter going on below it, can you hear it? Sounds like old TV commercials," I said.

"Let me see if I can make them out? …Yes, since

you mentioned it, I can hear it now. That is if I block out all the screeching tires and blaring horns. You have good ears, John. " We both listened for a bit, then Powel said, "Look John, it's turning east down Sutter. Odd shape for a blimp, don't you think?"

I put my 20-15 vision to work. "And look; now I think I can see what looks like a large movie screen on its side."… "Yes, it's a Jumbotron, like out at the Ballpark, and they're playing scenes from old movies. This is looking more and more like an advertising gimmick."…I then turned to look at Mr. Powel, and said, "You're still shivering. Are you going to be alright?"

"I can't say. I just have a bad feeling about that thing. It scares me."

"That is an odd shape for a blimp," I said. "And I have never seen one with large projections coming off it like this one. And listen to all the commotion going on below it." We hear more of what sound like car accidents. "Whatever it is, ad campaign, or whatever, it is one big mistake. I can't wait to see whose head goes for this one."

"John, this is getting to be more than I can take. I think Mike Jones was right." Mr. Powel seemed close to panic, I thought that if I could engage him in some chatter it might calm him down?

"What, that this is a spaceship. Nah, it's just a big blimp with a TV screen." …"Listen, there—hear that—that's a James Bond theme. Those are all old movies and commercial themes being played on a giant TV screen. Who ever heard of invading aliens playing movie trivia anyway?" That's it, use logic on him John. Personally, my calm objectivism was giving way, and a twinge of doubt began to well up from the lower portion of my scrotum.

"It just turned down Exeter," said Powel, "and

it's heading right for us now. Tell me John, how's a blimp turn like that—huh?"

"Those three bottom projections." I explained. "The two down in front and the other one below and behind—they're probably pusher fans." Actually, he's right about the odd shape, and listen to me, am I losing it too? "C'mon, Mr. Powel, all blimps have fans for control and navigation. This one just has an odd shape, and a large television, and I've seen hot-air balloons of all shapes."

"Let's say that you are right, that this is just some sort of publicity stunt. Then it has to be the biggest blunder of all time. Can't say how many car accidents we have heard. There, there's another one. Gonna be a price to pay for all that."

Minutes passed, and the great machine in the sky drew nearer to us. I began to question my own resolve about the planet of origin of this monstrous aircraft. I was shivering, and not sure if it were the cold, or the shot of adrenaline pumped into my veins. Trying to keep it together, I resorted to rational thought as a means to keep my fears at bay.

"Look at the scenes playing on that big screen." I said. "That's a clip from a John Wayne *Western*, and I know I heard an *I love Lucy* theme before it."…We tried to switch our attention to the television show and away from the alien craft, but it didn't calm down Mr. Powel, or me. "It's all random as far as production years go," I said. "You have an oldie, then a modern movie, then oldies again. Can't figure out what they might be advertising?"…"Perhaps it's a new game show, one on say, movie trivia." Then I asked Mr. Powel, "Have you heard of any new game shows coming out this season?"

"No, I have not, John. That ship looks even

bigger and scarier as it gets closer. This thing really is huge. How something like that can float, and move about like it does is a mystery to me."

"It's only a block away now, and if it keeps going straight it will pass right by us." I said. "And listen, I know that theme. That's the Star Trek theme from the original TV show. You know the opening shot where the enterprise goes swoosh across the screen. … that brings back some old memories."

"Yes, I hear it. The giant screen is side away from us at the moment so I can barely make it out, but I remember that scene well. That's the original star trek show alright." said Mr. Powel

"This has got to be an ad stunt for a trivia show. There, that's another theme from another old science fiction movie. This one is from the original movie *Day the Earth Stood Still.* However, that came out way before *Star Trek*, which was in the sixties? *Earth Stood Still,* I think, was released in the mid-fifties? It is all just a jumble of old cinema. There doesn't appear to be any logic to it at all."

As the huge floating machine neared us, the scenes playing out on its screen became clearer. Possibly, for a moment, I entertained the thought that this might actually be an alien craft? But these are our movies, Earth movies, not scenes of alien beings or scenes of some other world—this was nothing but confusing? Vacillating back—no, I thought, this is only a very large blimp—with a very odd shape.

"You might be right about this being an ad campaign, John, but the quality of their Jumbotron is amazing, it sort of jumps right out at you. How did they get those old shows to look 3-D. The clarity and depth in them is way beyond anything in high-def that I have ever seen."

"Are you still worrying about space invaders, Mr. Powel?"

"Don't tell me that you've ever seen anything like this?" Mr. Powel was trying to wake me out of my scientific disbelief. "I'm shaking in my boots here, John."

"Hold on for just a little longer, Mr. Powel." I said. "It's just half a block away now.""..."Listen, what's that I hear—LSMFT? What the fuck is LSMFT?"

"I can help you with that piece of trivia, John, and I'm not surprised you don't know it. Let's see, you must be in about your late thirties."

"Yes, I'm 38."

"So that little ditty came out well before you were born. That's from a TV commercial from the fifties. They used to advertise those cancer sticks on TV you know. LSMFT, that stands for *lucky strike means fine tobacco*. Maybe this is all just about advertising some trivia show, as you say." Powel quips.

"Glad to have you back with me, Mr. Powel." Feeling reassured that this UFO is merely a big blimp my heart beat slowed some. "You know, it might be interesting to have a trivia show pitting us younger folk against you older folk. Are you up for the challenge?" That's it, John, keep our minds occupied. Focus on something familiar.

"You're on, John—if we live through this, you're on. It will be right in front of us very soon. Geeze, there's another accident. Why do you suppose there are so many accidents?"

"People looking up, and you see, that's proof positive."

"What's that you're saying?"

"That just proves that you can't talk on the

phone, drive a car, and look up at the alien spaceship all at the same time."

"You do have a wry, witty side about you, John. Ever want to do stand up?"

"Yes, then I could add comedian to my resume. That might open up some doors."

I tried making scientific observations to calm myself. I noticed the blimp was moving again. It was close enough now that I could see its skin, or hull, clearly. If it was a blimp, or hot-air balloon, we should see that its skin is made of some sort of fabric. There are what look to be ribs built into it; these are annular ribs running up and down its length. They look to be perhaps three feet wide, and show a depth to them of about a foot. It appears like they go all the way around circling the body—perhaps they are for strength. Those three pods which stretch below also appear to have ribs circling their bodies. I have no idea as to what the skin is made of, you can't see through it, and it possesses a depth or texture that is unknown to me. Other than that huge TV screen, which appears as a holograph projected over the hull, I can't see any other identifying features. There are no port holes, no cockpit, no antennae sticking out. Aside from the rings, and if you turned off the movie show, this thing would look like nothing more than a giant cigar with three pods for legs to rest on jutting out below. … I shared my observations with Mr. Powel, and then added,

"Actually, this thing looks just like a toy you would give a child to play with in the tub."

"There's that wit of yours again, John."…"And what if it is a spaceship, what would its skin look like then?"

"Ha, Ha, you got me there, Mr. Powel. Yeah, it

looks like a big toy, or maybe a giant maraca. Actually, it resembles more a ribbed percussion instrument called a Mexican Guiro." I didn't know where this flippancy was coming from. Sure I was nervous, but these involuntary actions scared me, and the levity didn't ease my fears any.

"John, what the fuck is a Guiro?"

"It's a Maraca with ribs along its length. You must have seen one once, they make a unique rasping sound?" I added.

"More humor again, John?" Mr. Powel then added a few observations of his own, "John, aren't all air ships supposed to have numbers painted on their sides, and how about those red and green lights, you always see them on planes?"

"Yeah, I do find its apparent exterior sterility interesting and odd." And as the hulk of that giant airship drew closer, "Mr. Powel, are you feeling this?"

"What's that?"

"The hairs on my arms and the back of my neck, they're standing straight up. That thing is building up a lot of static."

"Yes, I'm feeling it, but my hair has been standing up ever since I first heard those sonic booms," he said. "What do you think the static buildup means?"

"Can't say, Mr. Powel, but I just saw that blimp just jump ahead. I mean it's not moving smoothly like you'd expect a blimp to, at times, it just jumps ahead, it stops for a moment as it hovers in one spot, and then it shoots ahead. Never seen a blimp move like that, and further, other than the din of those old movie themes and the crashing cars, horns, and sirens, I can't hear anything. I mean there is no pusher fan noise; I hear no engines, nothing."…"Should be some loud engine noises.

There's gotta be to move something that large."

"Christ, John, now you are starting to sound like me. I thought we agreed it was just a blimp?"

I shot a quick look over to Mr. Powel. I just stared at him, wondering; my stomach muscles were clenching, and I had pulled my shoulders in. My arms were just hanging at my side and shaking inside my heavy coat. Could he be right, could this actually be? Putting my body's reactions aside, the realization that this thing was other-worldly was tearing away at my scientific sensibilities. I didn't know what scared me more, that fact that I was actually starting to think of this beastly contraption as a spaceship, or that I was starting to lose it along with Mr. Powel.

"Don't look at me like that John," he said. "It scares me. I was relying on your calm scientific analysis for support."

As we were standing there, the craft of unknown origin practically upon us, we heard an ominous warning from a race of invading space aliens—albeit from a fifties sci-fi flick—"*Peoples of Earth, Look to Your Sun for a Warning*." At any other time I would have laughed at that garbled threat. Powel and I both heard those prophetic words. Shaking in terror, we looked straight at the blimp/spaceship when all of a sudden it jumped again. This time it lurched nearly one hundred yards forward, and was hovering right over us. If that alone didn't get me to jump right out of my socks, just then a scene from that old sci-fi movie came to life on the giant TV screen. It was a clip of that old film, the scene where the alien space saucer fires its death ray beams. Only this time we saw the death rays quite literally shoot forth right out of the holographic image of that space saucer.

The special effects, the sights, the sounds, seemed so real. We watched as the rays sprayed out and made a sweep through the parking lot. Then, as if controlled by some demonic force, the evil ray projector beneath the image of the saucer turned and pointed its reflector dish straight at us. Immediately we were pelted with a spray of death rays. Our bodies were pierced through and through.

We weren't vaporized, but that was all Old Man Power could take. He collapsed right in front of me, poor guy. I had partially grabbed on to his limp body, and bent down with him to ease his fall. As I knelt over him, I looked up again at the giant screen. Then, once more, death rays shot-out at us. They looked real; I swear I actually felt them as warm penetrating arrows.

Just then gang bangers driving an old caddy sped into the store's parking lot where their car came to a screeching halt. Out popped two men, each with guns. One of the men took a shot gun, aimed it at the machine which hovered in the sky only one hundred feet above us, and shot at it. If this wasn't all happening fast enough, now a police car ripped to a stop below the airship behind the bangers caddy. Their cruiser doors flew open. Two officers quickly got out, jumped behind their car's open doors. Drawing their weapons, they ordered the two bangers to drop their guns. Holy shit!— Hollywood could certainly never have dreamt this up. This was all too real, all too weird.

As odd as this all was, it got worse. Then I heard what seemed to be a voice coming from inside of the airship. The voice said, "Alright, that's enough, shut it down." And then I heard, "Aye, Captain." With that the TV screen went blank. "Aye, Captain?"…I'm hearing English? Do space aliens speak perfect English—I think not?

Again, from inside of the airship, I heard—
"Enable two way external viewer." … "Two way
viewer on, sir." Then the screen came alive again.
What I saw was, to borrow a phrase, just out of this
world. Inside of the ship, I'm assuming I'm seeing
the interior of the machine, there were three people
sitting at, and behind, some control panel, which was
located at the end of a large room. Another person
was standing out in the middle of this same room. At
first blush, they appeared to be human, but on closer
examination, they most obviously were not. At this
point, everyone, cops, bangers, all of us, stood
motionless as we looked up and listened to the
discourse going on inside the airship.

The Captain, or what I believed to be the
Captain, a tall, rather well looking individual, simply
stared down at us. There was a quizzical look on his
face, almost as though he was as confused as us. I
changed my gaze from him to the three sitting at the
end of the room. One of the three individuals kind of
gave me a little half wave, not knowing if it was
permitted or not by his Captain, I guess.
Instinctually, I half waved back at him. What were
we dealing with here? My brain shuts down. Not
really knowing how to explain, well there must be a
psychological block built into our brains that won't let
us accept what we are seeing, if it is say, way out of
the ordinary, and thereby not able to explain in
detail. Think—does not compute.

From inside, one of the three sitting behind the
control panel called out, "Slow moving air ships
coming in our direction, Captain."…"Let me see it,"
said the Captain. With that the Captain switched his
attention to a small screen on a wall, at the far end
of the room in which he was standing. On it, I could

clearly see three of our large helicopters. They were flying in a V-formation, and headed towards the alien ship. I don't know the exact type of helicopter, military of course. On the small screen, they were encircled by orange lines—just an observation.

The Captain then looked back at me, and then shot a knowing look over to one of the three who had waved a moment ago. The being, sitting behind the control panel, gives me another half wave. I waved back, not knowing if we are waving hello, or good-bye, or whatever?

Next I heard their Captain say, "Cadets, two way viewer off, and take us up to greet these primitive flying machines."

Cadets? Aliens speaking English—perfectly? My brain is on tilt. I noticed the large screen disappear, and with hardly a sound, the great beast hovering over us sped up and away to the southeast, presumably to confront the helicopters. My thinking—blimps don't speed off.

The chaos here on the ground turned to mass stupefaction. The police apparently got orders to be elsewhere, and left. The bangers got back into their caddy, and followed. I looked over to the grocery store entrance. There I saw a crowd of people huddled inside the doors. They had been taking in all the action outside. Then I saw Becky. I motion to her. I mouthed—"I need help with Mr. Powel." She and some of the people in the store came out. A pharmacy worker tended to Powel, who had fainted. People were gathering in small clumps here and there, and then a larger crowd formed across the street. People were sharing their cell phones and Tablet devices. I guess the show was continuing off in the distance. Boy things hit the web fast.

I slowly rose to my feet, and not having a cell phone with internet access, decided to join the crowd across the street. I could see the giant spaceship again as it is hovering perhaps a thousand feet in the air about five miles off. The helicopters, all three of them, were splayed out in front of the spaceship. It looked like a Mexican standoff. The four air ships sat there facing each other for perhaps two minutes— just eyeing each other. Someone in the crowd help up a larger video device. A network news group was airing the event live from a location right below. I could clearly see the military helicopters hovering in front of the great alien sky ship. Then, why we could not tell, but one of the helicopters shot at the space ship. We actually opened fire on space aliens. The same aliens who only moments earlier waved to us. Why?

What followed also seemed uncharacteristic of a confrontation. The alien ship did not return fire. You'd have expected some phaser fire, or a photon torpedo, or two. It simply hovered in place for another minute, while the helicopter unloaded another round of 50 caliber bullets. Then we saw the alien spaceship rise up, and pull away from the engagement with the helicopters. Higher and higher it rose. Then it changed course to due west all the while continuing to rise up, and out of sight. That's it? As quickly as they had arrived, they were gone. "Okay, where are my groceries? I'm going home to have some beers."

Still in a daze, I couldn't collect my wits. I gazed over to see Becky. She was pointing me out to some media reporter whom I hadn't noticed had pulled into the parking lot. I walked over to share my thoughts. I remember the reporter saying to me,

"You're John Parker, the John Parker?"

"Huh, what?" My brain was still elsewhere.

"I'm sorry," she said, "let me introduce myself. I'm Julie Nunez of Headline News. Our department has been following your work with the military with great interest. That is how I know who you are."

Oh great, just how do people find out about such things? Nothing is kept secret here in Washington. "Sorry, Julie," I replied. "I'm still sorting out what I just saw."

"Yes, the young lady said you were here and witnessed the alien craft up close?" "Is that true?"

"Yes, I did."

"What can you tell us about the encounter?" she said. I hadn't yet realized that I was speaking right into a microphone, and that we were being not just videotaped, but this transmission was also being aired live.

"I'm still putting it all together." I said. "They waved at me, you know?"

"What? You mean you saw them, the aliens that is?"

"Yes. I saw them, and the interior of their ship."

"Can you describe them for us?" the reporter begged.

I went on to describe the whole ordeal Mr. Powel and I suffered through. Every detail I could remember that is. I had no idea the whole world would soon be listening to my every word.

Back at the Pentagon, "General, you have to see this. It's Dr. Parker. He's on TV news talking about the alien encounter," said Sherry, the General's secretary.

"What, Parker, damn! Get me Harris on the line," Bradley barked. "We're under attack, and

Parker is pussy foot'n it with the enemy, damn, double damn."

After my interview with the reporter was over, somehow I managed to find my groceries and head home—what a day. At home, out of curiosity, I turned on the television. I thought that I might be able to catch something on the news channels. I was concerned as to why we had fired on the aliens. What greeted me had me shrinking down into my recliner. "Dear God!" I explained. "What the fuck'n hell have I done?" There's my mug on just about every channel. "What the, … and why did my hat have to fall off?"

It was now only mid-afternoon. Too early for drinks, but I didn't care. I twisted the top off a beer and poured it over some ice cubes in a tall glass. With my hands still shaking I pondered catching the next red eye back to Tucson. I just wanted to disappear. A loud knock at the front door shocked me back to the present. I answered; it was Lieutenant Harris, one of General Rudy's aides.

"The General sent me to collect you, sir. He insists on seeing you immediately."

I asked Harris, "Should I make a run for it?" hopping that some levity might sooth over my frayed nerve endings.

"I don't think that will help, sir. It's about the aliens, Dr. Parker. The General considers this a matter of national security. He just wants to debrief you." Just wants to debrief me? A rendition is more likely. Well, there goes a good job…..

7:

Harry's Island

Day One

Captain Harry's First Contact attempt was a horrible failure. Our capital city had been ruthlessly invaded, or so we thought. People on the ground, and in tall buildings, were frightened out of their wits. We suffered scores of injuries, most resulting from car accidents. Emergency services were stressed. Military defenses were put on high alert. Our government did what it thought right to protect us, and attacked the alien UFO. The bullets fired at the Val did no damage, and were not a threat to it, but we didn't know that at the time.

Harry, looking a bit distraught, with his left arm extended he was leaning up against the viewer at the end of the ICC. The primitive flying machine hovering only two hundred yards away shot at the Val with another salvo of fifty caliber bullets. "Cadets, I see no reason to linger where they we aren't wanted. Take the Val up and away from this place." The Breen ship pulled away from the engagement and rose up into the clear blue sky and out of the sight of the spectators and cameras on the ground.

"Course heading, Captain?"

"What? Oh, yes, thank you Mr. Heenon. Make your course west, and level off at one hundred thousand feet." The Val, flying at an extreme altitude, floated effortlessly through our atmosphere on a heading west of DC, and out across central US. Our government ordered war planes to engage the alien craft, but couldn't keep up with it, and had to call off their pursuit. The spaceship was too high, and traveling at too high a rate of speed for our best jets to follow it.

"This is a truly beautiful planet," mentioned Harry. "Too bad it's already occupied. Let's change course and head more toward their equatorial zones." The cadets entered the course changes and angled the Val south and out over the Pacific Ocean. Harry, still in a pensive mood, understood now that we earthlings were not as advanced as he had hoped.

"This is nice," said Harry, "I just need a moment to think. Let's just coast and sightsee for a while longer." Onboard the Val reactions of the crew varied. Arlen exclaimed relief that he wasn't destroyed earlier. Be'nnee and Hippee who had been observing the show from a rest area off to the side of the ICC exclaimed how happy they were just to be done with it all. Dr. Who, down in Terra, grumbled something unintelligible, but two of his techs mentioned they thought Harry's response timid, and argued that one slap deserved another. On the back of all their minds though was a burning desire to put down and exit the ship. This trip was first and foremost a vacation, and interaction with a new race secondary.

"Captain, at this speed, we will reach the equatorial zone in two hours."

Harry didn't reply. Still in a funk he was fretting over how to save the First Contact, and his face. Looking around, the ICC room appeared sterile and empty; this was no place of solace. He didn't want the company of his crew right now, mental and physical suffering worked best to help him think. Walking over to a side wall he called out, "Chair" and a captain's chair grew right up from the deck below him. There he sat for the better part of an hour.

The Val and her crew of sixteen were casually drifting through Earth's atmosphere. No longer over territorial US, they were now out over the ocean and international waters. Perhaps safe from pursuit and attack, they did not know for sure. This course will take them south out into the pacific basin and toward a future unknown...

Two hours later
"We are now over equatorial waters, Captain," stated the cadets who had shown the utmost quiet while remaining at their stations. Hearing that, Harry rose from his perch and stepped out toward the middle of the ICC. The chair immediately disappeared back into the floor.

"Then let's turn, and head west along the equatorial line. Put up a tactical map." A 3D holograph of our planet appeared out in the middle of the ICC. "Now, show me our position and tracking." Shaking off his pensiveness, Harry was getting back into the mood.

"That's it. Zoom in some, all I want to see just a quad-hemi." The projection changes to a sectional map of Earth from only between the two tropics, and what we call latitudes of 140 degrees west, and 150 degrees east. "Look at those many small islands," mused Harry. "Move us over there."

"Changing course to south by south west, sir."

"We're too high, Mr. Heenon. Take us down to twenty thousand feet. If we are going to be here for a while, we might as well get comfortable. Let's find us a nice little unoccupied island and make it our home." stated Harry. The pacific basin is home to over twenty thousand islands of various sizes, eighty-three percent of them absent of man. The south pacific is also quite remote, and certainly out of the reach of the casual observer, and hopefully humans hungry for a fight.

Hippee, who had been down below decks aiding Dr. Sa'aarron, upon re-entering the ICC exclaimed, "Great Maker, I love field trips." Everyone on board was now well aware that their captain was in search of a temporary residence. In this case a tropical South Seas isle. Thoughts of the earlier encounter were fading, and hopes for a long overdue shore leave raised their spirits.

"We are scanning this section of the planet, Captain," said Heenon. "What we are seeing are many islands ahead, and most appear to be void of human habitation. This part of earth is a vast ocean with few large inhabited lands."

"Good, select a few of these islands and let's have a closer look."

"Putting up ten of them on the side wall now, sir." Ten overhead views of south pacific islands appeared on the side wall—all in stunning detail.

"I always enjoyed house shopping," quipped Hippee.

"Look there Hippee?" said Arlen. "Look at that one!"

"Yeah, looks quite familiar, It's a lot like that island back on Pleasure Planet."

Now, more and more of the crew were taking an interest in selecting their new home. Conversations were breaking out all over the ship. Everyone was looking to their monitors to have a look at what Earth had to offer.

"You're right, Arlen," said Harry. "Cadets, separate that one out, let's have a closer look at it."

All the projections on the side wall disappear except the one, now much larger and clearer.

"Nice, I see a large lagoon, sandy beaches, high volcanic peak. And no humans?"

"Double checking, sir. Nope, it's clear."

"Boys, I think we have found our new home."

"Are you getting all excited like I am," asked Hippee of Arlen.

"I'll be happy just to get my feet on solid land once again." Arlen shot back.

The entire crew has been confined inside the ship for over four months. Like any sailor, they relish dry land for a change.

"Cadets move us closer to that island, and set to hover at about 5,000 feet."

"Island coming into view, sir. Preparing to hover."

"Terranomics are you getting this," asked Harry.

"Dr. Who here. Yes Harry, we have been watching, and I must say we are all getting a little bored down here."

"Well, we have an island resort for you guys to design and build."

"An island? How much time do you plan on spending here Harry?"

"Doctor, we have just short of three months left before we need to get back to terra-forming planet Ga'alle'een. I think we will spend it here."

"Harry, it's your call, but can't you just dust these earthlings off, so we can get on with a real Breen sized job?"

"Terranomics types aren't known for their patience," argued Arlen.

"Sorry Doctor, regulations require me to find a way to save this race in spite of themselves."

"Great maker's patience!" quipped Dr. Who.

"Typical of an engineer," said Arlen. "A total lack of Breenanity. Ever wonder what the galaxy would be like if we let the engineers to have their way?"

"We're over the island now, Captain." Heenon and the other two cadets made ready for landing.

"Dr. Who, have your group design us up a plan for this island," ordered Harry. "As we are going to be here for a while, I want to see some creature comforts built in. Let's make sure our new island home is upscale. Wouldn't be much of a vacation if we had to camp out in tents for three months on a deserted island?"

"Fine Harry, we will have a plan up to you in thirty minutes." Harry switched on his ship-wide intercom, "All crew members, Terranomics is designing us a temporary home here on this island. Send any housing, or other requests, you might have down to terra. We are going to be here three months, no reason this trip can't be the best shore leave we have ever had."

Harry motioned to his two senior officers, Arlen and Hippee, "Let's huddle up. Come over here by the cadet's so we can all put our brains together for a moment. I have a plan to discuss with you." The six of them gathered together while Harry explained the idea he had reasoned out.

After a short talk, "That's textbook, Harry," said Arlen. "Just like the Hoosenine submission on planet BSC58."

"Yes, as we recall from studies at the academy, a quite similar situation," offered up the cadets.

"Brilliant!" said Hippee. "I like it."

"We'll first need to confirm my suspicions with a survey," said Harry.

Harry then called down to Dr. Who, "Doctor, we will need guest quarters. Put them next to the tarmac."

"Guest quarters? ... For whom?"

"Earthlings, of course."

"Great Maker, you're not going to invite them here are you?"

"That's the plan Dr." Grumbles echoed all the way up to the ICC.

"That's pretty typical of terra people," said Arlen. "Their only concern is to use their little bugs to grow things."

Hippee added, "Yeah, the engineer type; devoid of tact and feeling."

"It's like that on all ships," said Arlen.

"Yeah, like the little gods they think they are," and Hippee went on to say, "They would just wipe out an entire race of billions of souls for their own uncaring needs." The Cadets sat quietly, taking in and trying to make sense of all the growing discord between departments.

"Alright enough banter, let's get to it," barked Harry.

"Captain should we put up a defense grid?" asked Heenon.

"Yes, not very friendly have they been?" added Hippee.

"Their reaction to first contact could have been some kind of misunderstanding. Why should we expect them to try and attack to us again?" wondered Arlen.

"First Contact Protocol, they always do. They fear what they don't know. I have studied the reports of many first contacts. The few that do go well are usually from pacifist species. I suspect earthlings are more of an aggressor type. They probably have devised a list of protocols for possible alien attach."

"But we haven't attached them?" rejoined Arlen.

"Typically they don't see it that way, and I wouldn't either if I were them," said Harry. "We do pose a real threat to their way of life. Especially if this is an H-7 population. So let us not take the chance. We'll set up a defense grid."

"An orbital array then?" asked Heenon.

"No—their weapons systems are very primitive. We won't need an orbital array. Just set up a security net, out to say, eighty miles, and let's get it up now." Heenon and his clique of cadets got busy preparing to put up the security array.

About thirty minutes later
"Harry, it's Doctor Who, your preliminary plans are ready for you to view, and you'll be happy to know we are calling this project the Island of Captain Harry." The three cadets snapped a look at each other. They knew that Dr. Who rarely gave out praise or endorsements, and that this was neither, but a sort of chiding, and aimed at Harry.

"Let's see it then," ordered Harry. When in his captain's mode he was a rather focused man—or Breen that is, and never showed to be phased by the snipping and chiding from the crew.

The Cadets arranged the plans from Terra to be displayed as a holograph out in the middle of the ICC. A realistic display of the island appeared together with the modifications the Terranomics department dreamt up.

"Check it out. Those guys work fast don't they?"

"Interesting take Doctor," said Harry, "But the water slide? Where did that come from?"

"Planetary Genomics, Harry. They originally wanted a ski slope, but I convinced them that that would be somewhat confusing in the tropics. So we compromised on the slide."

"Well, why not. Imagine greater I always say?" quipped Arlen.

"I see the tarmac, guest quarters, and there is only a short walk from the ship to the swimming lagoon and a beach where we can lay and tan, all very nice."

"I see that hugely tall water slide flows down into the lagoon, it looks just like the one back on Pleasure Planet, only this one is a lot taller," said Hippee.

"How do you get up to the top of the slide?"

"There, down below, and off to the side of the beach, we will put in a rapid elevator."

"Ah—and there is a walkway down to the ocean. All of that tropical water reminds me of home planet," said Arlen.

"What, no environmental controls?" asked Harry.

"We can add some, how about a sky-dome?" said Dr. Who.

"Excellent, then we would have active weather control, plus have our activities hidden from prying eyes above. Now, these humans, when they come to visit, may have certain other needs. Let's leave some room next to the guest quarters for future expansion; we want them comfortable and happy while they visit. Also, I can see we are going to need to have a go between; someone who can advise us on all things human, an ally, a friend, and chronicler."

"Yes, that is right Harry, in the Hoosenine submission the Captain in charge of that mission used an influential person from their own population."

"Hmm." Harry broke off for a moment to think, and then said, "It all looks great Dr. Who, when can you get started?"

"We can start now."

"Why not start on the tarmac first, so we can set the Val down?"

"Good idea."

"Give me a time estimate for completion," Harry asked.

"A job this small should take no more than two days to complete."

"Very well Doctor, and dare I say, make it so?" Harry was really getting into the moment by copying a line from a popular sci-fi show. This got a good laugh from the cadets as well as a groan or two from the rest of the crew.

"We have the security grid ready for launch, Captain."

"Then make it so, mister."
Heenon, at his console, touched an icon. Suddenly, a series of probes erupted from the ship's hull and sped off to their predetermined positions. The security grid was simply an array of evenly spaced sensor probes. In this case, the probes would be positioned at a distance of eighty miles from the

island. Each probe was set to hover in the air at an altitude of fifty thousand feet forming a giant circle of safety.

"Sensor probes away, sir."

With a steaming cup of brew in his hand, Arlen approached his captain, "Here, Harry, this is for you."

"Why that's nice Arlen, I didn't ask for anything, what is it?"

"Earl gray tea, I thought you might like a cup." Their laughter could not be denied and the entire crew shared in it. Harry had picked up a liking for Star Trek, and was quick to emulate Captains Kirk and Piccard's distinctive command lines. Furthermore, the Breen rarely missed an opportunity for prank or levity, and this one was too juicy to ignore.

"Clever Arlen, by the way, whose responsible of tonight's programming?"

"It's Heenon's turn."

"Ah—great, I can't wait to see your choices, Mr. Heenon."

"Thank you sir, any requests?"

Before he could speak, Arlen erupted in and said, "How about a sci-fi movie where a vastly superior and powerful race comes to Earth to enslave its people, and make it their new home."

"Interesting, I'll check to see if there is something like that in our limited library," said Heenon, pretending he didn't get it.

"Security net coming on-line, sir. Probes are hooking up together, and it is done."

"Let me see it on the big screen," said Harry. A tactical representation of the security web showed up on the sidewall screen.

"Looks good cadets, set it on automatic. Once

we get settled in we can start our surveys."

"Harry, if your plan is to work, we will need to learn much more about them, their languages, customs, capabilities, etc." said Hippee. "Coming in to this planet we scanned quite a number of communications satellites in orbit. Let's send out some probes to see if we can hijack their data."

"What? Spy on them? That's not neighborly."

"No, but a necessary prelude to invasion," said Arlen.

"Yes, before we go vaporizing entire populations we should at least learn about their mating rituals," added Hippee.

Doctor Sa'aarron was just entering the control room, and overheard the duo, "You two are certainly making light of their situation. Remember our main mission statement, to find and provide for new life whenever possible. Both of you know that 68.5 % of all tech emergent species extinguish their natural resources and die out."

"Really Doctor, they are but one species on a planet with several million. Why should we favor one species over so many others?"

"Such lack of compassion coming from a number two," he retorted.

"Not so at all doctor, what we have here I suspect is a prime example of an H7 society," argued Arlen.

"We don't know that yet," said Dr. Sa'aarron. "We won't know that until after you have made your surveys. And Harry, need I remind you of your orders regarding H7 civilizations?"

"Please Doctor, I am on your side here." The Breen classify civilizations by combining two scales. One using a letter denoting the most advanced society's apparent level of knowledge, the other a number code denoting how all of a planet's societies combined relate to and impact their environment. An H-7 classification denoted an end phase. That a society had reached an ecological pivot point, and was creating a destructive and increasingly unsustainable use of resources leading to an inevitable collapse. The Breen and all other member planets have set up rules regarding H-7 planets, but still, the course of action to be chosen falls on the shoulders of the captain involved.

"Doctor, why don't you stay and help the cadets get your survey started?" said Harry. Arlen and Hippee took that as their cue to exit the control room, and they headed down to a storage bay to sort out their thoughts. Verbal confrontations between Breen were rare and physical ones even rarer. Disagreements will inevitably crop up in any society, which is partly why we have devised laws to live by. The Breen were no different, and stresses were beginning to show between the crew members. If Captain Harry is going to salvage this first contact, and possibly gain a Planetship, he will have to find a way to keep everyone working together smoothly and willingly. Can this recently promoted Captain rise to the challenge?

Getting Settled

Down in a cargo bay, Arlen and Hippee are in the process of locating some basic creature comforts they will want to take outside,

"You don't like Dr. Sa'aarron much do you Arlen?"

"Actually I like him a lot. He is a revered geneticist, and oldest member of our crew. I just don't see letting one species dominate on a planet to the detriment of all others. And that's the way it almost always is on these H7 planets. We always bow to the prime species."

"Yes, I'm with you. I'm not sure why planetary ecologists always prefer the dominant species either? However, those are the rules. My main concern is for Harry. I would like to see him get his Planetship. That would be good for him, and good for the service. You know, promote from within."

"Yes, he gets his Planetship, and then I move into the number-one spot."

"Why Arlen, I didn't know you were anxious to be a captain?"

"I'm not really, but I don't know, as I look ahead, what do I see? Nothing as yet. It might be nice to achieve the next step, or just retire from the service for a millennia or two, move to some small planet for a where I would have the option to take a wife and have a child."

"Yes, and that might be what makes us Breen superior to these short-lifers."

"What's that, Hippee?"

"Options and choices. We have time on our side. The short-lives burn it all up so fast. What, with merely a hundred or fewer years to live, they have to act fast, and as almost always is the case they act irrationally. They rarely have time to develop a thinking mind."

"Yes, I get your point. Of course, this was all covered at the academy in exo-planet theory class. Remember?"

"Ah—that's where I heard it before," said Hippee grinning as they both shared a chuckle or two.

"Ok, I suspect we will need a skiff shortly. Let's spin one up."

Back in ICC a call came up from Terra— "Harry, It's

Dr. Who, your tarmac is ready. If you would put us down, I could use a leg stretcher." Dr. Who, the penultimate engineer with an attitude, always exhibited a sense of formality in his speech, which many mistook for arrogance.

"Got it, Doctor," said Harry. "Cadets, take us down—gently." Landing wasn't a difficult process for such a sophisticated ship as the Val, yet to Harry, and to all Breen captains, the skill was found in the finesse, and the gentleness of a landing was the judge.

"Roger, Captain, putting us down—gently, sir." Heenon with a look of apprehension on his face turned to his mates and said, "Ready." The Val began to lose altitude. "Le'eennon, give me a count, "three, two, one, and were down. Pulse engine off."

"I didn't feel a thing," commended Harry, "good job boys."

"Great Maker, I love training missions," quipped Dr. Sa'aarron, who was still in the ICC room. "What's that word I'm looking for—oh yes—nostalgia? My cadetship was quite some time ago. This brings back memories."

"Good, we are settled. Doctor, now that we are down would you stay with the cadets and get your survey started? I want to go and join Dr. Who, and the rest of the crew on his leg stretcher."

"Certainly Harry."

"Captain, before you go, would that be a standard survey?" asked Heenon.

"Standard survey—no, a standard survey contains way too much data. Let's just do a basic eco-survey. Do you agree doctor?"

"Yes—that's fine. I'll see to it Harry. Go and stretch your legs."

Harry, using his quantcom, "Arlen, are you and Hipp

still down in the storage bays?

"Yes we are."

"Why don't you two join us outside? We are going to walk this island and breathe some real air for a change."

"What, are we down already?" asked Arlen. "That was smooth. We didn't feel a thing down here. Sure, we'll be right out."

"Doctor, just a few more adjustments, and the survey probes will be ready," mentioned the cadets.

"I must say, you three, are some of the most skilled cadets I have ever worked with."

"Thank you, doctor," the trio echoed.

"Heenon, you are what, 350?" Dr. Sa'aarron was inquiring about his age.

"Actually I am 358 years old, sir. Geerron here is the oldest at 442, and Le'eennon is the baby at only 278. Doctor, I heard that you just recently rejoined terraforming section?"

"Yes, I had served in the corps four times before coming back this time. On my last respite, I spent over 4,200 years on a little planet called Spinneea."

"Wow, I have read about Spinneea," remarked Heenon. "It was a naturally evolved planet, was it not?"

"Yes, and it was a very lush and lovely world. Somewhat like Earth here, and before we discovered it, it had been inhabited by a prime species. They disappeared some tens of centuries earlier."

"Oh—so there was no prime species alive on Spinneea when it was discovered? What happened to them?"

"The usual. We found many ruins they had left. Did extensive excavations, and found the people there had achieved quite a high degree of advancement. However, in the end, their population exploded. Once they'd burnt through their natural energy resources there was nowhere for them to go but down. Their social structure began to fail. With not enough energy available to service their huge population, starvation and war set in. Our findings indicate that a super virus then emerged, and decimated the remaining population even further. After that, a dark age ensued, and they finally just died out."

"Sad," added Heenon.

"Yes, and that is what we need to prevent from happening here on earth. They are headed, I suspect, right down that same path."

"Ok—survey probes programmed and ready, Doctor."

"Then, make it so, cadets." The trio broke a quick smile at that one. Apparently, no one in the crew, including department leaders, were immune from imitating lines from our cinema. Heenon touched a button on his command console and a small number of probes emerged from the Val's hull.

"This survey will take roughly 24 hours to complete, Doctor."

"Yes, I understand. Why don't we put the ship on auto, and go out to join the rest of the crew, and explore this new world?" And with that, sixteen weary travelers, from thousands of light-years distant, exited their ship-home, and for the first time in months, put their feet on the soil of a new world, an alien world. Truly one of the greatest joys Breenkind can experience—walking the surface of a newly discovered planet.

The Breen Survey
Imagine witnessing a horizon wide string of fiery white balls all traveling at the speed of a jet airplane

as they blaze a trail across the sky above you. Possibly, as you are sitting inside an airplane, one of those glowing balls shoots through your cabin. Perhaps as you noshed on your salad course inside a fine restaurant atop a New York skyscraper, one of these fiery orbs rocketed through the building only inches above your table. These were just a few of thousands of reports hitting the news air waves as the Breen probes circled our planet. Every country, nation, and municipality; every mountain, desert, forest, or steppe; every sea, lake, or ocean was traversed. Every square inch of this planet was examined in detail. If there were any doubt in our minds that there was an alien presence on Earth, there was no more. This event brought the matter to home. People en mass that witnessed it, or saw it on endlessly repeated news reports grew scared. Scared enough to want to run, to hide, but where? This was no neighborhood dispute; there was no nearby border to cross to safety. No foreign power across an ocean was going to be come running to the rescue this time. No, this was a power threatening us from right here at home. A power that had unequaled controlled of the high ground; outer-space. There was nowhere to run. "Checkmate," read one Newspaper headline, and another, "kismet!" The press did little but fuel the fears of many.

The probes themselves caused no harm. They simply collected data about our environment, and transmitted it back to computers on the Va. However, it was an effective, if unplanned show of force. Though the probes, being only a controlled form of energy, passed effortlessly through ordinary matter, and left no physical effect, psychologically it was quite a different thing entirely. It gave us all a sense that we, the human race, were being examined against our will. This was an unacceptable invasion of our privacy—something we all guard and defend ferociously. This fearsome feat was obviously the work of superior beings with powers and capabilities and knowledge far beyond our understanding. Beings we knew nothing about. Was this act a prelude to attack? Should we fight back? Could we fight back?

To the Breen, the survey itself was a simple matter. The probes were programmed to do all of the work. It was nothing more than an array of sensor spheres which lined up from pole to pole. The initial probes traveled to a predetermined location. There they would each fission into two exact copies. In this manner they divided, and spread, and aligned themselves along a north south line. Once evenly spaced at roughly half a mile in distance they rose up to an altitude of one thousand feet above the surface below them and began to circumnavigate the globe in a coordinated line.

Harry ordered a basic eco-survey. This meant collect data on human populations. Discover the current health of our environment; make a tally on Earth's extant species, take atmospheric analysis, assess global energy usage and reserves. This was in essence a snap shot of man's impact on the natural world, how we interact with other life forms, and a determination of what these matrices predict for the future of our planet, and its prime species. Once the data were collected and analyzed, their computer would present them with an accurate picture of the state of affairs here on planet Earth. Would these results paint mankind as the best of caretaker for this planet?

Meanwhile, mankind experienced a future shock of sorts. As fearsome ripples spread across the globe and populations cowered, government leaders threatened reprisal, and military generals gathered and planned clandestinely to do just that. We were faced for the first time with the fact that not only are we not alone in the universe, not only are we not the most advanced species around, but we are being studied by a superior race with an unknown purpose…..

8:

The ARC Group

Washington, DC
Day One—after first contact

Call it an irony, call it a mystery, or call it just a universal coincidence, but what strange nexus brought the Breen to Washington, and directly into the hands of the one man in charge of protecting the air space above DC, who was also the man in charge of America's old and nearly mothballed Alien Response Committee, or ARC. Immediately following First Contact, Bradley called together this select group of senior military brass. This meeting was classified Top Secret, and only he and ranking members were allowed to attend. There would be no aides to help with regnum, no secretaries to take notes. Just four military men would be present, and of course, the President, who would be teleconferenced in.

The ARC group consisted of:

> General Stevenson, Commander 3rd Air Wing
> Admiral Arnie Johnson, Ret.
> Army Gen. Urev Breshinsky, Ret.
> General Rudy Bradley, COMM. NS and ARC group

The meeting convened, General Bradley speaking, "Gentlemen, obviously our worst fears have come true. We are under attack by an alien force. How and what we do next could very well determine the future of mankind. Arnie, please pass out a copy of *The Plan* to everyone here. We all know this plan by heart, but let's go over it once again together, and step by step. We can't afford to get anything wrong."

"Rudy, I can't believe this is all happening," said Gen. Urev Breshinsky. "We wrote these plans over fifty years ago, and they haven't been touched since then. Are you sure they still apply?"

"Yes, they are old, but the reasoning behind them is still sound and never more urgent. Is there anyone here that thinks that these aliens don't pose a serious threat to our world? As *The Plan* mentions even if they have come in peace, the probable outcome would still be disastrous to our world."

"Yes, I suppose you are right."

"We must get the President involved with this, and right away."

"I already have been in contact with the President. He didn't even know the ARC group existed."

"Well, it did all start out as a kind of joke."

"Yeah, well, it isn't so funny now is it? I informed the President of the existence of the ARC Group, and what we are charged with. There is a copy of *The Plan* at the White House, so he and his staff have been reading it over for the past hour. We will contact him back soon, but for now we need to follow protocol and get out memos to all branches of the Armed Forces, CIA, and the FBI. Oh, and we now need to add a new name to the list, Cyber Security. Make sure that they are informed to notify us directly of any unusual occurrences."

ARC—Some Background

Late in the nineteen forties, with all the hysteria surrounding the Roswell Incident, and other ET scares, our government felt it necessary to establish a committee to investigate a possible alien attack, and to make recommendations on how to handle it. Thus was born the Alien Response Committee.

It was tasked with setting up, and exploring possible alien invasion scenarios; what to do if and when ET's attacked. They would dream up and play out attack scenarios, or mental war game plans. These game plans were drawn up over fifty years ago, during a time when kids were being instructed to duck and cover under a desk in the event of nuclear attack. We lived, at that time, in an age of fear, and that is what came out of the original Committee's recommendations, a work of defense strategies born out of fear, poor judgment, and lack of any real knowledge on the subject.

The Plan, as it is called, was a thick binder containing military stratagems, numerous what-if scenarios. Most of them were taken right out of Hollywood movies about alien invasions. Bottom line—the appearance of aliens, whether during an invasion, or not, posed great danger to our way of life. Recommendation—destroy all aliens. This one-sided approach was never questioned, neither were the recommendations ever up-dated. Why bother, no one in the military ever took the possibility of an alien invasion seriously? It was just another cover your ass, just in case of, program. If some curious reporter ever happened to ask, "what if," you simply say we have already researched the possibilities, and then you mention the name of the committee, and point to the binder containing *The Plan*. Because of this, the General and his group's members were living in the past, and were feeding the President of the United States outdated information. Could disaster but follow? …

The original ARC members have already passed away. General Rudy didn't join the panel until 1977 at the age of thirty. Other than General Stevenson, Bradley was the only current member not retired.

A synthesis of all the scenarios led to the Alien Contact Protocol, a very narrow set of actions to take, which would apply to each and every situation. *The Plan* left no room to maneuver in. There were no colors to their rules of engagement, not even shades of gray—just black and white, attack, or die.

Alien Contact Protocol—some of their original notes and findings.

1. This is your Planet, protect it at all cost.
2. To show weakness in the face of superior powers would be a mistake. If aliens arrive, destroy them immediately.
3. If you can't destroy them, find a way to balance the equation; abduct part of their crew as bargaining chips.
4. The allure of the alien's advanced technology will be destructive. For this reason, you must eventually

destroy the aliens, and erase any evidence of their presence, at the earliest possible time.

Day Two
General Bradley's ARC group was activated. Their first endeavor was to inform every military sector of the monumental first contact, advise them that the ARC group was in charge, and that they were to be apprised of any alien sightings, or unusual activities anywhere across the globe.

We failed to destroy the Alien craft and its occupants at First Contact. That was step one. If General Bradley adheres religiously to the ARC protocol, and if the President falls for it, his next step will be to find a way to abduct one of the aliens. Our military wasn't totally impotent in the face of their advanced foes. We still had satellites in orbit constantly watching everything and anything. We had no way to track the Val. She didn't show up on radar, and soared at an altitude too high to follow visually. However a line of fiery white probes stretching from pole to pole were easy to notice from orbit. Then it was a simple thing to backtrack them to their source—a small island secluded by a thousand mile expanse of Blue Ocean. Having triangulated the alien's location, a spy satellite was tasked to fly directly over Harry's Island and snoop on the Breen from above.

General Bradley was in open conference with Admiral Arnie Johnson, Ret., and several aides. They are passing around satellite photos taken last night, island time, of Harry's Island.

"We are all in awe over how fast these aliens have been able to transform that island, sir," said an aide. "They must have access to some kind of fantastic energy or something."

"Let me see that photo," barked Bradley ... "This dome that covers about half of the island, and hides every square inch except for the very top of the hill and that long southern hook of land, you say it was all built in a day?"

"Yes sir, in fact, most of what we can see was done in less than a day."

"Scary. What is that I see at the top of the hill?"

"Our reconnaissance photo experts say it is the top of a water slide, sir."

"What's that?"

"It is a water slide, sir, you know, the kind you might find at an amusement park."

"I know what a fucking waterslide is, damn it!"..."Why the FUCK would they build a waterslide?"

"We don't know, sir. What's more, there is a large tarmac where the alien's spaceship sits, there are some large buildings, and something is being done around the lagoon. We just can't say exactly what with that cover over all of it."

"You say we can't see anything below this covering?"

"No, not in the visual, but we are able to get through in infrared wavelengths, which doesn't allow for much detail."

"So they have found a way to hide their actions from us. To be sure, Mr. Undersecretary, they are up to no good. Waterslide my ass. The sooner we strike the better."

"Rudy, if you have a plan I'm all ears."

The General went on to outline his ideas, which were taken right out of the Alien Contact Protocol book. General Bradley outlined a plan which would under normal circumstances would be considered nefarious. No treaty existed between the Breen and any country. So technically the General's plan was not against international laws, unless you consider that the basis of our law is fairness, equity, and above all—a universal form of human rights.

"Go ahead Rudy, get your plans in motion," said the Undersecretary. "I'll pass them along to the President for final approval."

9:

The Hoosenine Submission

In The Year 2058

It was day two on Earth for the aliens. Harry was on board the Val and standing out in the middle of the ICC. I noticed that, in my opinion, he spent an inordinate amount of time in his command room, or you could call it the ship's bridge. But, I guess that is what captains do. The trio of cadets were again all at their stations. Several other members of the crew were below decks mulling around in their departments choosing not join crewmates outside enjoying the tropics. This was some curious behavior, and I decided to coin a name for it— spaceship lag. Their actions had been so imprinted on their brains they found it difficult to let go and relax.

"Captain, the results of your eco-survey has just been collimated by the computer," said Heenon. "Would you like to see the results?"

"Yes, but let's get Dr. Sa'aarron involved also.

Doctor, the survey results are in, would you come up to the ICC, so we can go over them?"

"Yes Harry, I'll be right up."

A minute later, "OK, let's pour over some of this data," said Harry, "what did the computer come up with?"

"Yep, there it is," said Sa'aarron, "and just as I worried. No doubt about it now. Nope, definitely an H7 civilization, and one of the worst I have ever seen. Our computer projects a complete societal collapse by their year 2058. And it won't be an easy ride from now until then either. Before the end there will be at least two major collapses caused by resource shock and wide spread economic downturns, all followed by disease, famine, war—all of the rewards of living way beyond your means. Further, I have never seen such a fractured species either. Aside from the main H7 body, we have huge populations living at D5 level, and even scattered B2 populations."

"Are the D5 populations sustainable?" asked Harry.

"No, certainly not. They pose just as great a threat to the existing environment as the H7 does. There are just too many of them. Look how their numbers have grown, and then look at the environmental destruction coinciding with it. If anything, in this situation, the D5 populations are worse than the H7's"

"What has the computer suggested as a planet sustainability level?"

"It is right here Harry, given the amount of fossil fuels available, planet size, land masses, and percentage of the planet needed to sustain other life forms, you get a number around 500 million humans."

"And they currently have how many."

"There are just over 7 billion, fourteen times too many to survive according to our standards. But not only that, just seventy years ago, about the time they first started sending out radio transmissions into space, the population here on earth was only about 1.5 billion souls."

"You mean that is a mere seventy years they have increased their population by five and a half billion souls?"

"Yes they have. And the trend is projected to continue to grow. They will overpopulate themselves right out of existence if someone or something doesn't interfere."

"What causes such huge population explosions?" asked the cadets.

"Yes, if we knew the answer to that question we would be Gods. For now the only answer I can offer up is perturbation theory. You know, shit happens. There is only one thing we can be sure of, and that is they are not likely to accept any form of interference. They will go kicking and screaming all the way to their planet's destruction before they allow anyone to challenge their reproductive habits."

"Even to their death you say?"

"To be sure, Harry, even to their death!"

Arlen was in the ICC's anteroom and had been eavesdropping, He was quick to say, "So we wait sixty years and then come back and take over. No one could fault us for letting nature take its course, and in return we get this beautiful planet. I can't wait to plant the Breen flag in orbit." On hearing that, Heenon quickly covered his mouth as his face ran florid, but he couldn't hide his smirk.

"Seriously Arlen, as a second in command you shouldn't be making jokes about a race of people trapped in unfortunate circumstance, and facing oblivion."

"We didn't cause their problems, doctor, they did. I say let them, for their stupidity, die out."

"He does have a point there," said Harry. "And I can't get over their reproductive proclivities. We Breen have a population growth rate of close to one child every one thousand years. Why should we kowtow to a species that breeds like vermin?"

"Harry! You can't be serious?"

"Why not!? Natural planets capable of supporting life are all too rare not to be exploited. Further, this little gem would make a perfect base for us in this new sector. What's more, we could all move here and have more children of our own. Start an empire, of sorts."

"Exquisite thinking, Harry," mentioned Arlen. "Quick, someone take a photo of him grabbing his lapel with his hands."

"Awh, shit!" exclaimed Sa'aarron, realizing he had been had. "You guys make jokes about anything. Really poor form. Billions of people on this planet are going to die needlessly of starvation and disease if we don't act, and act immediately."

"Well, we can't let that happen, Doctor. So, we need a plan, and put it into play."

"Don't you mean, make it so, Captain?"

"Yes, thank you for correcting me Hippee."
The results were in. Planet earth is in dire straits. Our civilization is headed for certain and total collapse due to resource depletion and runaway greenhouse heating, caused by our addiction to fossil fuels, and our inability to control our reproduction. The extinction of an untold number of species, including us, the dominant species, cannot be stopped without intervention. At this point you have

to step back and remove yourself from the picture. Then rise up, so that you can look down on planet Earth from a higher perspective and ask yourself, if I were given the knowledge that my species was about to go extinct, what would I do?

We are helpless in the face of our own demise? It has been intimated that everyone has a sense that all is not well with planet Earth. That we are headed in an unfavorable direction, however, and for whatever reason, and irrespective of this knowledge, we either are not willing, or cannot affect the changes needed to save ourselves.

The Hoosenine Submission

Ages ago, the Hoosen, a breenoid species, lived and evolved on a small planet in the Breen's home quad. Their planet being only two hundred light-years from Breen prime put them square in the grasp of their superior neighbors. For centuries the Breen watched them from a distance as they matured.

The Hoosen lived then much as we do today. Their species climbed up through their social ages: they had their Iron Age, agricultural age, and industrial age, same as we. They had their bloody wars too, or their savage years. All the while, the Breen sat by and watched without intervening. During that time the Hoosen had no idea the Breen even existed. Their mythos included no tale of gods above. There were no legends of blue tinted aliens anywhere in their collative sagas. Neither were there any tales of thunder bolts being shot down from above to punish misdeeds. As stealthy spies, the Breen kept any and all knowledge of themselves hidden from the Hoosen. They simply watched from a distance and let evolution happen as the centuries ticked away.

Once the Hoosen reached the end of their industrial age, they discovered their planet had crude oil reserves. Quick to utilize the magic that oil and gas could work, their civilization boomed. As it is typical at this juncture their populations exploded. By the time they reached their tech age, a necessary evolutionary step, they began to expend their resources way beyond what would be considered prudent. Their population growth in overdrive, they began to strip their lands bare. They denuded forests, fished their ocean's fisheries to decline, and mercilessly exterminated lesser species in their need for food and space.

Their planet's biosphere was headed for certain destruction. The Breen being ecologically sensitive could not tolerate this cavalier attitude anymore, and they decided to act. A First Contact was set up where the Breen introduced themselves to the Hoosen. They explained how they had been watching them for centuries as they developed, and that now they had reached a point where action was necessary to save them, and their planet. Once the Hoosen got over the initial awe of their voyeur's godlike status, they grew angry at being told to change by an outside power. They held to ancient beliefs which told them that only their life was divine and spirited. And that provenance demanded they allow their population numbers to grow unchecked—it was gods will.

Frustrated by the Hoosen's intransigence, the Breen captain formulated a plan of action. He first located a common man among them, took him to Breen prime, and let him marvel at the sights of a society living in perfect harmony with itself, and with the environment. This man was asked to chronicle his experiences so his own people could see and learn from them. The hope was that he would return to his planet, and guide his people down a different path.

Of course this approach didn't work, and the Breen now surmised that they would never change. It was not in their psyches' makeup. As conditions on the Hoosen planet worsened, the Breen captain thought up another tactic. Trying to awaken a sense of global awareness in the Hoosen, he ran a detailed ecological survey and showed them the results, the conclusions of which predicated a total collapse within a generation. Yet again they would not respond to his pleas.

Here the Breen, relatively unknowledgeable in the psychology of short-lifers, reasoned that, short of violence, nothing could be done to stop the death of an ecosystem and a prime species. In a last ditch effort, they proffered the idea to use an engineered virus to lower their populations growth rate. This was met with dismay and anger. These words were taken as blasphemous, decrying the Breen as irreverent the Hoosen populace revolted, and violent protests broke out. Disgusted by the impasse, the Breen captain made a worldwide speech scolding the Hoosen, saying their time was short—but they would not listen.

This was early in the Breen eon, and as yet no interspecies consortium of planets existed. There were no treaties to obey. No protocols had been devised to prevent the spread of violent species out into space. Loss of life on a planetary scale, though tragic, wasn't regarded as necessary to prevent. As an experiment, the Breen backed off, and decided to just watch to learn how the catastrophe played out.

They didn't have to wait long. Less than a decade had passed when one key oil field went dry and precipitated a severe economic collapse. However, this was about more than economics. Without oil, transportation slowed, food production fell, bloated populations use to surplus now experienced resource shortages and hunger— starvation can be a strong motivator. Seizing the opportunity, the Breen again approached the Hoosen with a plan. They would use their technology to help locate and produce several new oil fields that would provide enough energy resources to avert a planet wide collapse, thereby preventing the starvation and the death of billions. But this help came at a cost, the Hoosen had to allow the Breen to use the sterility virus, and allow for a natural drop in population size by attrition. With no real choice, the Hoosen agreed.

With new oil fields located and on line, and mass starvation was averted, the ensuing years saw a reduction in population size. It took generations, but attrition eventually brought the Hoosen population down to planet sustainable size. This gave them the time needed to develop alternative and sustainable energies. They also gained a healthy respect for their environment, and even today, thousands of years later, they live in an ecological balance, but now on numerous other planets. Thus, the use of the virus became known as the Hoosenine submission.

Of note…. "Our planet has been relying on one huge oil field for the majority of its crude oil production for over sixty years now. The giant Ghawar Field in Saudi Arabia came on-line in 1951. Earth has not yet experienced the failure of this huge field, however estimates are that it is in serious decline. If production in this one field is lost, we will be the ones experiencing a severe crude oil shortage, and right at a time when the largest population ever depends on it for survival. One should contemplate which fate is better? Would you prefer a planet-wide species death spiral caused by resource depletion, or acting as adults for a change and reduce our own population to a level where we all can all live a sustainable twenty-first century lifestyle?" ….JP….

Excerpt from Harry's Captain's log: "We cannot give them our advanced technology as they have not learned yet to manage their own affairs. We can make alterations to aide them along the way, such as clean up their environment, and reduce their greenhouse gases, but that would not be ameliorative to the bigger problems. It is not likely that we can gain their help in any plan we choose. We will show our survey findings to them, and make them aware of the dangerous path they are on, but I suspect it will not help. In the end, we will need to adjust the size of their population down to sustainable levels. I will discuss the plan with the senior doctors, and have them prepare the virus."

10:

Getting Settled

With remarkable speed, the Breen were able to transform their new home, Harry's Island, into a world-class resort, complete with swimming lagoon, guest quarters, and of course, a water slide. And, most marvelously, an island-wide cover intended for weather control. All of this work did not go unnoticed. The US Military, with the aide of their spy satellites now tasked directly overhead were relaying real time intell to the ARC group and General Bradley. Bigger minds than mine looked on in wonder at what was taking shape on that island.

Airbase X
Putting ARC's recommended plan into action, General Bradley has given instructions to the Commander of a small, obsolete, and soon to be abandoned army airbase in a southern California. Their radio shack was tasked with a satellite transponder now positioned directly over Harry's Island, and are commencing to open up

communications with the aliens. Harry and the cadets were still holed up in the ICC,

"Captain, hate to interrupt what you are doing, but we are receiving a transmission."

"What?" He asked. It had been a long day and he was feeling its effects. "What is it?"

"Looks like, well, it's in the FM band, and here I'll let us all listen to it." With that Heenon played the transmissions aloud, *"Earth to Aliens, Earth to Aliens, let's talk. Please respond to on this frequency."* And it keeps repeating sir, over and over. I think they want us to call on them."

"Curious," said Harry. "What is the response protocol to use?"

"In their language, I think it is, hello."

"Huh, well, respond at that frequency with a, *hello*."

"The signal is coming straight down from a satellite in orbit, sir. We determined that that was the American's spy satellite."

"Yes, I have been expecting them to make a call. It's obviously an obfuscation leading to a trap. They are pretty stupid if they think this is our first experience with belligerent races."

"I can direct a reply signal back to it." Heenon sent out a return signal—*"Hello to you."*

Back at Airbase X in southern California—for half a day several radio technicians had been sitting and listening for any possible response to their "phone call."

"How long have we been sending out live now?"

"Twelve hours, sir. I wonder if we should change our message?" Just then Heenon's *"Hello to you"* is heard loudly and plainly in the small radio shack.

"Dear god. Someone is responding. Quick,

check the source."

"It is coming from the island, sir."

"God, now what?"

"Here sir, we have the instructions from General Bradley."

With his teeth chattering, "Ah, yes. OK, send this, *"This is Corporal Blakely speaking. I am a representative of the US government, with whom am I speaking?"* The corporal's words rang out loud in the ICC,

"They are trying to communicate with us, Captain."

"Good, we have been waiting and wondering who would be first."

"Should we go on to reply?"

"Yes, yes …let's keep it short, say this … tell them your name, and ask how you may be of help?"

Heenon calmly made his reply, *"My mane is Heenon, Corporal Blakely, how may I help you?"* Back at airbase X they heard his reply— "Heenon, is that a name? Perhaps we heard it wrong?"

"I can't say. He said it was his name. … OK, what's next?"

Say this, corporal, "We want to meet with you."

"Just that?" … "Shouldn't we include the name, Heenon?"

"No, just that?"

"OK, I'll send it now, but I think we are keeping it awful simple stupid. …*"We want to meet with you."* In the ICC, Harry mused over this suspicious invitation. "Huh, funny they want to meet with us now. They didn't want to talk much two days ago. Respond with, "We agree to meet, say when, and send coordinates."

"Sounds a little informal, Captain."

"Eh, it's a start."

Airbase X received the reply, "Sir, their reply is …
*"We agree to meet with you, say when, and send
coordinates."*… "Sir, sounds like we are talking with a
machine."

"Might be, we don't know who or what they are.
… Just send this…" And tacitly a meeting had been
set up between the Human race and the Breen. It
was agreed that two representatives of Breen would
meet with a Human contingent at Airbase X the
following day at eleven in the morning pacific
standard time.

The internet
After setting up the rather questionable meeting,
Harry was standing out in the middle of the ICC with
his fingers clasped over his chest. In his usual
pensive look, he turned to the cadets and said, "Let's
get on with figuring out this information database.
Tell me what you have already."

"From what I gather, Captain, it is more than
just data. It is a communications network, and also
an entire barter and exchange medium. You can buy
anything."

"Anything? Show me Mr. Heenon, buy
something."
Going to a web site he located a book on world
history. "Here captain, watch while I buy this book."
Then he clicked on the buy icon and immediately got
a new accounts warning, "New account, … what is
that?"

"We need to set up an account," mentioned
Geerron. "Look, it is prompting you to fill in this new
account's page—name, address, email address, and
account number."

"If it is an exchange medium, you will need
something of value to exchange?"

"Yes, of course. Captain, give us some more time to figure this out … do we even have an address?"

"You three can continue to explore the use of the internet to purchase items. That is quite interesting. We are going to need a lot of items and soon, but your primary focus should be to continue to download as much data from their information system as possible."

"Yes sir." The three cadets spend the rest of the day investigating and getting acquainted with not just internet resources, but also the ins and outs of internet commerce.

U. S. Cyber Security Department

All of this internet activity did not go unnoticed. The Breen were in essence, burning up the airwaves by down loading so much data. At a secret location, somewhere in the state of Virginia, alarm bells were ringing.

"Sir, we have a new hot spot."

"Yes, I see it showing up on the traffic board." A large wall sized screen showing worldwide internet usage. "Where is it coming from?"

"A place located near something called Vanuatu."

"Vanuatu; that is a group of islands out in the south pacific. I didn't think there were any ground stations located there which could handle that much data?"

"There is nothing showing on the board either. Nothing for a thousand miles away in Australia do you find those capabilities."

"Is it an error?"

"No sir. It appears to be streaming straight from a satellite."

"Whose satellite is it? We will need to give them a call."

"It is owned by Pan Asian Internet Service's"

Cyber Security officer McGee then made contact with a Pan Asian internet service's representatives, owners of the satellite being hijacked by the Breen for internet downloads. A Mr. Hamatsu responded,

"Yes Commander, we are quite aware of this unauthorized traffic. Our satellite has been hacked, and we can't figure out how, or by who, or how to stop it."

"Have you tried to shut it down?"

"Shut it down, the whole satellite, are you nuts? That would cause a worldwide crash. We will just have to eat this one. I pity those guys over at InterTech though."

Back at cyber security— "Get me the Pentagon on the phone, no wait, that memo that came through yesterday regarding the aliens. We were supposed to call some General if we suspected anything unusual."

"It was a General Bradley, sir."

"Yes that's it. Get him on the line now. I want to have a talk with him."

"Busted,"... the charge, satellite and internet site hacking. General Bradley was informed of the unusual internet activity over the south pacific. Our military were already well aware of where the aliens were residing, but this information came on top of the other goings on by the Breen, and now taking over our internet. And truly, a shutdown of internet access would be calamitous given our reliance on it for everything now days. This knowledge, that the Breen were taking control of satellites and threatening to interfere with our everyday life bolstered Gen. Bradley's belief that urgent and severe action was called for.

Alien Contact Protocol

Airbase X informed General Bradley regarding positive contact with the aliens. His plan to sucker them into a trap was successful. As a general of war he now had a chance to ply his trade. He eagerly arranged an impromptu at his office. These so-called open conference meetings were pro forma only; just for cover and possible diversion, and the dissemination of misinformation. The true Plan was already agreed upon, and secretly put in motion.

Ordered to be present:
>   General Rudy Bradley
>   General Stevenson, COMM. 3rd air wing
>   A Joint Chiefs Liaison
>   John Parker, economist/naturalist
>   Several aides and security personnel

I was still in Washington, but scheduled to return to Rio the next day to meet with my elite group of economists. However, after the incident with the alien craft I was a bit shook up, and hoping to take a few days off. Then General Bradley called and said, "Parker, it's General Bradley. I want you in my office today at two PM. We are meeting to discuss the alien's situation, and I want you in on it."

"Yes sir, two PM, I can do that, see you then." He was as brusque as always. And how is it that he always knows when I am in town? Must be some spies in my laundry.

Later that day at two o'clock the meeting began, but late again, they had to start without me, "Alright gentlemen," said Gen. Bradley, "I have asked you all here to discuss this alien invasion. They have been here on our planet for two days now. Our President wants us to give him some options and plans. So let's talk it out."

"Do we know where they are at present?"

"Yes," said Bradley, "they have settled on a small island in the south-central pacific. Here, I'll put up a map of the area."

"Looks like there are no substantial human developments anywhere near them."

"No, they are about as far from anyone as you can get on this planet; that alone scares me. Further, our spy satellites are showing incredible changes going on. Gentlemen, need I state how serious a threat these aliens pose to our way of life?"

Usually a bit tardy, I finally showed up, "Ah, Parker, come right in."

"Sorry if I am a few minutes late sir. Just can't get used to the Washington traffic."

"It's alright Parker. You didn't miss much. I'll keep it short. We have reached out to the aliens, and have set up a meeting with two of them. It will all take place tomorrow at an airbase in California. I can't give you the exact location given your current affection with the media. Let me say this as strongly as I can, and this applies to all of you. Everything about this meeting is to be kept secret. I want you there at that meeting Parker. You are that friendly face they saw two days ago, and that is what we want, to be taken as friendly. Lieutenant Harris has your exact travel orders. We will all be there, including my secretary, Miss Lawson. So if you would go pact your bag, we are going to California ... our plane leaves at 8 PM tonight."

As I exited the conference room some thoughts

crept in, "He was a lot shorter with me than usual. Perhaps he is pissed at my tardiness? Perhaps he knows about my kissing his secretary? That could complicate things." I didn't salute and left without saying a word. Passing by his secretary on the way out my left hand dropped down and I tapped on her desk with my fingers. She and I had decided on codes to use when we were in the presence of possible military spies on our relationship. After all, you can't kiss in the Pentagon, and certainly not in the presence of General Bradley. Three taps meant— call you soon—a bit hokey, but we felt it best to keep our true relationship a secret for now."

The meeting was adjourned soon after I had gone. Everyone left except for General Stevenson, one of Bradley's longtime friends, "So that's your scientist Rudy, the one doing world collapse scenarios?"

"Yep, he's quite the guy, too."

"Quite the guy, a civ? Why you practically ... Oh, I get it, so you don't trust him, and you're trying to keep him close?"

"Yep."

"Are you having him watched?" Like a poor poker player, the General gives away a tell by an almost involuntary, yet however brief, glance up in the secretary's direction. General Stevenson noticing said, "Oh, you don't mean? I've known you a long-time Rudy, you are almost always right in your suspicions, but I can't help but think this time you are playing with fire. Careful you don't get burnt."

"I'm always careful. Now, let's get on with planning our real reception for these aliens."

11:

First Meeting

Friday, February 25ᵗʰ
Early Morning Hours of Day Three

Excerpt from Harry's Captain's Log: "This is going to be a busy day us. Before shore leave can get into full swing more improvements need to be made to the island, but more importantly, today a meeting has been set up with the humans. This meeting is scheduled for 11:00 AM pacific standard time at an airbase located in a place the humans call the southern California desert. I am sending in two of my best officers. They both know full well how dangerous this mission is, and will be wearing personal protection devices. Though I suspect it is a trap, it is a necessary first step."

It was just past 4:00 AM. Before they leave Harry reminds Arlen and Hippee to wear their PPDs for this meeting saying, "This is a primitive and possibly paranoid culture, take every precaution."

"Yes master," chortled Arlen. That got a chuckle

from the cadets who were already at their stations, and will be throughout all of this second contact.

Arlen and Hippee then exited the confines of the Val, and went over to where the skiff was parked. The island now secure, their toys could be left out in the open. Both Breen officer's hopped aboard and made preparations for their flight. Harry, still remembering last minute procedures, announced on his quantcomm, level two, "and Arlen, I want full recording on this mission. Send in a surveillance probe when you get a chance." Surveillance probes were quite small and stealthy. Measuring only 2 inches in diameter, and not built of anything solid, they possessed the ability to pass into and through ordinary matter, and could be maneuvered into common objects such as windows or walls. We are all voyeurs at heart; the Breen simply had better spy toys.

"Best of luck to you two," said Harry, "we will be watching." Arlen and Hipp took off and left the protection of their island behind them—into the wild unknown for the duo. After a botched first contact, and subsequent attach by our helicopters, this meeting, the Breen hoped, would open up some form of talks with us. Was the attack by our military originally a mistake? Were we now truly willing to put aside differences and act friendly, or was this meeting only some ruse to gain an advantage against a foe? We Americans had, as far as the Breen thought, attached without provocation, and the potential for danger still remained. Who knew what lie only a few hours' time ahead, so caution was advised?

"Hippee our destination is located some seven thousand miles away. We are supposed to arrive at eleven in the morning their time. Making time adjustments … so we have 45 minutes to get there. I'll let you fly."

"So no sightseeing? asked Hippee.

"No, there is too little time, and just so we don't scare any natives let's fly in stealth mode, and take us up into the ionosphere." The skiff, a ship capable of space travel, could reach fantastic speeds even in a thick atmosphere, but to travel the seven thousand miles in only forty-five minutes would require a velocity faster than a bullet. That would create a deafening noise. To keep their noise footprint to a minimum they will shoot up into space and back.

Forty Minutes Later
The morning of the meeting we all watched as the alien craft approached the airbase from the southwest. It appeared to have come in straight from the island. It arrived rapidly, and stopped just as quickly. It then hovered motionless in the air and at a low altitude. On the roof where we were waiting not a sound was uttered. Not one person raised a hand to wave and signal to our guests that it was alright to land. Someone had the forethought to paint a big red X on the roofs covering. That was the only thing festive that morning.

Ten minutes earlier I had followed the General and our small group Earth's representatives up to the roof. Why we had planned for our guests to land on the roof when there was a perfectly good tarmac all around us, was beyond me. Perhaps it had something to do with the four foot tall false wall that rimmed the entire roof to secrete our activities. I had expected to see a rather large group of greeters already waiting, but the rooftop was strangely vacant. What, no celebration? Why were there so few of us, and why the total lack of preparations? No color guard, no waving banners proclaiming *Welcome to Earth*. No red carpet. Where was the greeting due these otherworld ambassadors? Just a sloppily painted red X, and a short line of only seven humans? This reception stunk, and what was I getting into? I had some serious doubts welling up and that feeling in my crotch, the one I felt the day of First Contact, was back.

For the American public, or for the rest of the world for that matter, this meeting would never happen. A dark pallium was drawn over this usually sunny California site. Classified as beyond secret, only a hand full of people would ever know it had taken place. There would be no huge mob of reporters waiting to snap photos of the aliens and their spacecraft. No lookieloos peering out across the desert with spyglasses in hopes of catching sight of otherworldly beings. No other nations had been invited to attend, nor were they notified of this momentous event.

After about 30 seconds the skiff, still hovering silent and motionless in the sky, then sidled directly over us. I had seen helicopters make that same sideways move, but this ship had no rotor blades to provide lift, and it made no noise. It was like moving a chess piece across an invisible game board in the sky. The alien machine's presence was mysterious and it scared me.

"Nice of these people to give us such precise coordinates, Arlen."

"Yes Hippee, look there, on top of that building, that's the reception committee—looks rather small. I would have thought perchance a few more humans would be in attendance?"

"You would think they have aliens dropping in

on them all the time?"

"Remember what we were told regarding first contact scenarios?"

"You mean back at the academy in that exo-theory class?"

"Yes, in particular, the theory about the size of first contact reception committees. Might be just a caution, but I think we are about to walk into a trap."

"Well, looks like Harry was right again. Let's be sure to get a surveillance probe programmed right now while we hover for a sec."

The Alien Ship Lands

I watched as the skiff came in at about 100 feet up, hovered momentarily right above us, and then just settled down and onto the building's roof. Amazing! There was hardly any sound, no rocket noise, no whine of a jet engine, but again as they approached there was a lot of static electricity crackling all about. My hair was standing up, but then as old man Powel had said, it had been ever since I got picked to attend this meeting.

The craft they were traveling in was quite similar in design to the larger ship I had seen at first contact. Only this one had a bulge on the top front that looked like a cockpit, but the entire hull was opaque allowing us no preview of our guests. Again on the bottom of the craft, two small pods extended down and out in front, and one pod in the rear—possibly for landing, who knows for sure? I noticed the same ribbing structures all around. No idea yet as to their function, and as for propulsion, that's anybody's guess.

After they landed, all was quiet for the longest of moments. The only discernable noise was a warming desert breeze whispering in my ear. I was standing at the far left; General Bradley took up the opposite flank. Sneaking a look down the line, I noticed everyone's face, even my lovely Sherry's was drawn down long and frozen as stone. Flushed with fear they stood firm at attention, motionless, anticipating what was coming.

I returned my gaze to the ship and was making a mental note that there were no obvious cuts in the hull for a door or window when suddenly a door shape did appear on its side facing us. Not knowing what to do, I froze with the others. Then the door opened and swung up and out of the way. Straightaway out came the two beings from outer space. Emissaries of another world stood just twenty feet in front of us. I think someone farther down the line just shit their pants.

From my peripheral vision I noticed as Sherry Lawson, and one of Bradley's aides, took a step backward. I know I wanted to, but somehow I found the courage not to. An awkward pause ensued. It seemed like forever, but in reality it was only a few seconds. The suspense was frightening; someone had to break the ice.

The two aliens were standing shoulder to shoulder in front of us. They were much taller than any of us, and by a lot. I put the taller one on the left at well over seven feet; his pal was about six inches shorter. They cut quite a shape, but oddly enough, given their height, their body form didn't look out of proportion. I was impressed by their stature, and in a curious remembrance of preconceived alien stereotypes exposed a stupid smile. Watching movies and cartoons as a child I learned that aliens were either short and green, or tall and wispy, or bodiless except for an oddly huge bulbous shaped brain-head—and every kid knows aliens are always naked. This was not so.

After a long moment, the tall one decided to break the ice, and in a completely human way, he simply said, "Hello." It was his perfect sounding English that took me by surprise.

Then he added, "This is my crewmate, Hippee, and I am called Arlen."

The Brass appeared unable to move or speak. I couldn't take it anymore. Someone had to stand up, "Welcome, welcome to Earth," I said. Scared, I introduced myself, and stretched out a shaking hand. I mean after all, who could have guessed if these aliens even knew to shake hands as a greeting; it could have been an insulting gesture to them. What, stick out my filthy primitive ape hand? Our rituals could mean something entirely different to an alien civilization.

It was Hippee who was first to meet my hand with his. "Nice to meet you, John," he said. Having insinuated myself into an extra-terrestrial situation, I offered to introduce the others gathered with me. It certainly wasn't going to be General Bradley, or any of his cohorts. They couldn't move let alone speak at that moment. Of course, I introduced the General first, and then went down the line. After I finished, Arlen, who had been standing back watching, stepped in and said, "Nice to meet you all."'

First steps, it was awkward, but what was it with the Brass? Their reticence was palpable. There was certainly no ease at this meeting. The military men looked and acted as though they were facing off with a bitter enemy.

While Bradley stayed back, his two aides came forward and shook hands with the aliens. The guards were next. Finally, the General ushered forth, with his hand behind the secretaries back as he led her up, and the two of them shook and said hello. With his newfound courage he was loosening up, and suggested we all get off the roof and go inside to the conference room.

Having to land on a building roof, at an obscure airbase in the seeming middle of who knows where, then being ushered through a small door leading down a narrow staircase and into the cramped conference room, with only a handful of people in attendance. I don't know if it is just me, but if I had traveled across light-years to visit I might have expected something bigger. Maybe not the red-carpet treatment, but you know, perhaps a more open meeting with a few more dignitaries present, but that, like I say, is just me, and I am new to all this. Hippee and Arlen must have felt the same way, but we never talked about it again after that day.

After we entered the conference room, the two aliens took up a position at the end of two tables which had been pushed together into a tee. The rest of us were sited at the big end of the tee with our backs against the opposite wall. The two armed guards took up positions on either side of us. I might have felt uncomfortable, even apprehensible if I were sitting alone in a room, seemingly unarmed, and there were armed guards bracketing me against a wall and blocking my escape. However, at that moment Arlen and Hippee appeared quite relaxed. This was odd, I thought.

I had no planned speech, no planed set of questions to ask. Oh, I had plenty of questions, just no idea where to take the discussion. Fortunately, we had a General with us, and I relied on his direction. Why this had to be a strictly military affair,

I didn't know? It always turned out that way in the movies though.

Once we were all seated, the General's aides handed him a folder, opening it, he took out a ruled pad—apparently it had his talking points on it. He then led off with some questions, and his secretary, Sherry Lawson, wrote down every word. There was no recording device which again felt a little odd—a General renowned for his planning—huh? As the Bradley rattled off a question, I noticed an odd ticking sound coming from the wall behind him. While everyone else focused on the Q and A, I turned and saw what looked to be a small ball of buzzing static discharge halfway emerge from the wall. Then as quickly as it appeared, it disappeared back into the wall. Not sure I wasn't imagining things I looked away to rejoin the questioning. Hippee was answering some rather mundane question asked by the General when Arlen broke in and said,

"General Bradley, you are with your country's military. We get that. The lovely lady is here to chronicle this meeting, and these other two are here for you as your aides, and the guards are here for our security—yes?"

"Uh, yes, that is right," said General Bradley.

"So, then you Doctor John Parker, what do you do? Why are you here?" Doctor, I didn't remember introducing myself as a Doctor? This was a sensible shift in tactic; they had answered a few questions, now it was our turn to answer some. "Who, me?" I said. Then as if asking for permission to speak, I shot a glance at the General.

"Go ahead Parker, you take the floor for a few minutes, and gentlemen, if you will excuse me, I have to see to something, but I'll be back promptly." Gen. Bradley got up and left the room, and I now had a chance to engage these special visitors, "You don't remember me," I said, "but I was there on the ground the day you first came to town, your first contact with us."

"Actually, we do remember you John," said Arlen. "The older man with you that day, how is he?"

"Oh, Old man Powel, he's fine. He had just fainted from all the excitement."

"Yes, that is good to hear that he is alright, but John, you must be of some importance to your government, or you would not have been invited to be here? Mind if we ask what is it you do?" A very cogent observation on his part I thought.

"Yes, Arlen, you are right, I was invited here partly as I was there on first contact, but also because I head up a group of economists and scientists working on a special project for our government under General Bradley. Earth's many populations have been experiencing a long-term socio-economic downturn, and I was hired to investigate and to find some solutions to this problem."

"Then you are a scientist also, John," asked Arlen? He spoke almost as if he already knew I was.

"A scientist of sorts, actually I am an economist slash naturalist, two advanced degrees of not great importance at this time." I replied. "Actually, I have a question for you if you don't mind?"

"Of course not John, ask away."

"Let me preface my question by saying that you're almost perfect usage of our language is remarkable. A teller at my local bank, who has lived in America her whole life, can barely be understood. Yet you say that you all learned English in the past two weeks on your trip here. How did you accomplish this?"

"Computers, John. We captured your language from all of the transmissions we intercepted on our journey to your planet. Our computer was then able to analyze and translate it for us. Then it was a simple thing to transcribe your speech into our mental implants. It is all programmed in, if you will. We know your science is now toying with melding machine and brain. We have already taken that step. That is how we can speak your language so well."

"Fascinating, I suspect there is much we can learn from you?"

"Excuse me a second, John." With that Arlen turned to look at Hippee. Down the hall in a nearby room, the General was in a heated discussion with two men dressed in white lab coats. "I don't care what you two think," he said. "We already know that they are probably much more intelligent than we are; we know we have much to learn from them, but this is the way we are going to go about it. Now follow my orders and fill the syringes and load them into the guns, or someone else will, and you two will spend years in the brig."

"Yes sir," they replied.

At this point I still had no idea that the Breen had a spy probe in place, and were able to not only hear what was being said by the General, but were also capable of watching it in real time. They were privy to all of his shenanigans which had been relayed directly into their internal quantcomm devices. The proceedings were also being watched back on the Val by Harry and the trio of cadets. Shortly, General Bradley returned,

"Excuse me again, Gentlemen, please continue with your discussion."

Arlen, now looking a bit edgy, continued his explanation of Breen technology, "John, we have our computers as you call them with us, or in fact, inside of us. Call it a sort of organic machine-organ that is a computer which is interfaced with our brains. In addition to our built-in computer, we have internal communications devices, which connect all of us to each other."

Immediately, General Bradley burst in, "That fancy looking bracelet device you wear on your wrists, is that some sort of weapon?"

Arlen with a deadpan reply, "No." There was a marked change in Arlen and Hippee's mood since the General's return.

General Bradley went on to ask, "Why didn't your ship's Captain come to this meeting?"

"Oh, Harry," Arlen replied, "he's what you call old hat at this kind of thing, and he probably knew it was going to be a trap, and decided to use this opportunity to get rid of both of us."

"Uh—What?" Thinking to myself, "Where did all that come from? Have I been sleeping?"

"So you two are considered expendable?" shot back Bradley.

"We are just soldiers, sir," replied Arlen, and then he added, "General you don't have to do this?"

"Sorry Mr. Alien, but actually, I do," said General Bradley. Not using their names, and showing no respect for our guests at all. Fucking military. I knew General Bradley was totally wrong for this type of event. I was not sure why the discussion took this strange turn though.

"General Bradley, might I ask what are you up to?"

"Don't interfere, Mr. Parker."

"You see, we just can't have dangerous aliens popping around the planet causing chaos. It's your technology, can't let it get into some other country's possession." … "Again, I am sorry to have to do this to you."

"Do what!?" I asked.

General Bradley motioned to the guards who stepped forward. Just then into the room came two guys in white lab coats who handed two dart guns to the guards. The guards took the guns and immediately aimed them at Hippee and Arlen. "Gentlemen, I have to do this for the sake of our country, Guards."

"What?" I couldn't believe this was happening. "General, stop! You fucking idiot. You have no right to do this." My protests went unheard.

Bradley nodded to the guards. They fired at Hippee first. I jumped up, flung my hand's up in the air, and yelled nooo! Then I tried to move in front of the dart before it was fired, but way too late. The pistol went off, and a dart filled with who knows what noxious poison sped on its way right for Hippee—poor fellow.

"Good thing we wore our worker safety devices, Hippee," said Arlen, using his quantcomm, "and thank you Harry for insisting on it." Always capable of being in contact with each other wherever they are through the use of their quantcomms, the Breen back at the island were all watching and listening as the events played out.

Their bracelets were in actuality personal safety devices. Working in space carries many hazards, and the Breen, over millennia, have perfected devices to protect them when outside. There was quite a variety of threats they could sense, and then choose a course of action to protect the wearer. In this instance, the device chose to speed up Hippee and Arlen's reaction time. They were now able to react one hundred times faster than usual—much like receiving a shot of adrenalin.

The Breen's devices activated a microsecond after detecting the threat. Their activation made a heartbeat seem like an eternity to Hippee and Arlen. The dart's speed slowed to a crawl from their perspective, ample time for the duo to move out of its path. A fraction of a second later in real time the other gun went off. The two Breen watched as the dart meant for Arlen erupted in slow motion from the gun's barrel.

"Shades of alien autopsy," quipped Hippee.

"That's not funny," said Arlen, as he watched the dart slowly travel in his direction. Hippee's dart went past him, and impacted the far wall.

"Harry, are you getting any of this?"

"Yes we are, Arlen. Can you put some of that liquid on your analyzer pad?"

Arlen wrested the dart from the wall, and took a drop of the liquid from the tranc dart, and dabbed it onto an analyzer pad built into the bracelet. The device chemically broke down the poison, and transmitted this information to the cadet's control panel.

Arlen's dart was still traveling on its way right for him. "Arlen," said Harry, "we should make some sort of statement to the humans for being so rude."

"You mean as punishment, Harry?"… "This whole drama has been orchestrated at the behest of the one they call the General," said Arlen. "None of the others were acting of free will, just foot soldiers."

"Yes, then make sure that the General gets the point," said Harry.

"Ah," good idea, and with that Arlen moved to the dart. Even though from his point of view, the dart appeared to almost hover in air, it still had a lot of momentum, and would require great effort to alter its path. "Slowly Arlen," said Hipp, "Just push on the rear little by little. That's it; let it arc out and around, a little more, a little more. There you've got it." The dart was now on a path directed toward General Bradley's chest. Whatever poison he had intended for the Breen, he would now have to endure—a fitting punishment.

"By the use of their internet, we have now downloaded a lot of data into our computers," said Harry. "We must have something on the liquid in the dart. Give us a moment and let's see what the computer can find out about this compound."

The Seeds of Doom
Dr. Sa'aarron had been watching the event, and using his quantcomm called up to the ICC, "Harry, it's Dr. Sa'aarron."

"Yes doctor? I am kind of busy. What is it?"

"I hear you are planning a Hoosenine Submission. Just a reminder, we will need some of their DNA, and from both sexes, for your plan to work."

"Certainly Doctor, I will see to it."

"Arlen, computer results say the liquid in the darts is primarily a substance called ketamine. Looking up Ketamine, says here it is a drug used to tranquilize horses. Looking up horses, Horses— Jeesh,— Arlen they think you and Hippee are some sort of huge four-legged beast called a horse, you know, that is the animal they ride in the westerns."

"How very disrespectful," said Arlen.

"You two go ahead and get back here."

"Yeah, we were just leaving."

"Oh, and Dr. Sa'aarron says he needs a sample of human DNA for his virus, both male and female."

"I'll get it now before we leave." … "Horses, horses Hippee, they relate us to horses."… "I mean just look at that short, fat, and overly hairy human who calls himself a General. Now which one of us looks more like a beast, him or me? I ask you?"

"Arlen, I will get a DNA sample from the secretary. I'll just put my analyzer up to her thigh."

"Alright, and I will pluck a hair from the arm of the General. This attempt at our lives pisses me off. Let's get the hell out of here and get back to the island, and a warm and friendly beach."

From the point of view of the others in the room, the darts had just been fired. And no sooner had the guards fired them than we saw the first dart impact on the far wall, and the other had somehow turned in mid-air and ripped into the General's chest. The aliens were gone. Vanished! Bradley, with a very stunned look, slumped over in his chair, and then fell to the floor. Sherry Lawson screamed. I turned around not once, but twice, looking for evidence of the aliens, but in an instant, they were gone.

The white coats that had brought in the darts, tended to the General. I tended to Sherry. Well, any damsel in distress, I always say. The chaos in the meeting room took some time to subside. General Bradley was the most senior Brass present and he was on his way to the infirmary with a tranquilizer dart in his chest. Base military personnel alerted their Captain who rushed over to investigate, but really, what could be said? There was no evidence the aliens were ever here, no videos, no pictures, only some scribbles on Sherry's note pad—it was supposed to be kept all hush hush, you know. I was still hugging Sherry when he came into the room.

He looked at me and demanded, "Doctor Parker,

what the hell happened in here?" Well give me a field promotion of something. "Sir, uh," and before I could utter a word, one of the General's aides broke in, and ordered me not to say anything. Just a Lieutenant, he and the base Captain got into an argument over who was in charge. The lieutenant quoted some sort of order giving him the command if General Bradley were incapacitated. While they argued, I saw Sherry reach down to put a hand on her left thigh.

"Something wrong," I asked.

"Ouch, now how did that happen?" I looked down where she was touching and saw what looked like a small puncture, and there was a dab of fresh blood on it.

"It itches, damn, must be fleas in here," she said.

The dust was not going to settle on this meeting for some time, but I was moving on. I hated what had just happened. Sherry said she was going to go over to check up on her, what she called, Uncle Rudy. I told her I was catching a plane back to DC with one of the General's aides. I learned later that the chemical, and the shock of being darted, nearly killed General Bradley. Yeah, too bad. Idiot.

This despicable act, wrought in murky ignorance, surprised me. General Bradley, a lifelong military man, surely knows that you never attack an enemy who controls the high ground. From my perspective this meeting was of greatest importance. We all had questions, clearly, and aside from the shocking first contact, we knew nothing about each other. Who were these aliens, and where had they come from? And why? We needed to try to communicate at length with them, and would have if it hadn't been for military's lack of imagination. From their perspective anyone or anything possessing knowledge and powers beyond their own was a threat and to be resisted and destroyed. Where I saw the hope to gain clues to a brighter future, they feared the changes advanced technology would bring. Where I saw the potential for friendship with a new race, they saw only the danger of enslavement to superiors.

A debriefing, or an after-action meeting, was held the next day at the Pentagon—with me present. Testimony showed that no one saw the aliens or their ship leave. There were no radar traces of it as it approached, and nothing when it left. Some discussion as how to proceed ensued. My advice was to humbly apologize, but knowing the military that won't happen. I related the events that unfolded as best I could remember them. A few questions were asked of me for my opinions on the aliens' intent and capabilities, and then I was dismissed, and I thought that would be the end of it, and went back to my place in DC to rest. What the Fuck could happen next?"

12:

Seeds of Doom

Late Morning of Day Three, Island Time

Upon his return to the island, Arlen, still miffed at being attacked, entered the Planetary Genomics department, "Doctor Sa'aarron, here is the human DNA you requested."

"No, I didn't request it. Harry requested it. He needs it for his plan to work."

"Yeah, either way, there it is. And why did you need DNA from both males and females?"

"Well, we are going to have to, in effect, sterilize both sexes, and not that it is fairer that way. Human science being where it is, they could easily find a way around our sterilizing only men, and probably with a little work, women also. So I need to examine the reproductive genes of both sexes to build-in a control." ... "Oh, Harry is on his way down now, and wants to discuss the virus with me."

"What, how do you know that?" scoffed Arlen, a few seconds later Harry walked into Sa'aarron's department.

"Ah, Doctor, glad you are in. I want to talk to you regarding your virus."

"See, told you so."

"Has the doctor been foretelling events again, Arlen?"

"That's a scary ability, Sa'aarron. I think I am needed on some beach." Arlen, still peeved with General Bradley's attempt to alien-nap him, headed off for some much needed R and R.

"So, Harry, you wanted to see it?"

"Sure, is it ready?"

"Not yet, but I keep a supply of the basic molecular virus on hand. All we need to do is to adapt them to the human DNA. Here, I'll put them under a microscope so you can view them on this screen."

"So, those are they, just tiny little orange spheres."

"Yes, they are very tiny, but packed with some of our most sophisticated technology. These little guys have been many millennia in the making."

"How long will it take you to adapt them to human DNA?"

"Not long Harry, give me a day or two, and I'll have your bugs ready for you."

"Are they going to be spread by air?"

"No, primarily contact only. They have an affinity for flesh, and will spread easily by casual contact. An airborne virus would be too difficult to control."

"If it spreads only by contact, there is a chance that not all humans will get infected."

"Yes, but the isolated groups of humans aren't causing earth any harm. It is the largest population centers which are doing all the harm. Once we introduce it into the general populations it will spread by contact. It might take a full year for all mankind to become infected, but it will happen."

"What about safeguards?"

"I will built-in full safeguards. The virus will be effective only in the human population. Once it has been taken inside a body it will modify and adapt to that new environment. As long as it remains sequestered inside its host it will remain viable, but once shed, or expelled from a body, it will self-destruct within 20 seconds. That should also prevent any smart human scientist from separating them out for experimentation and analysis."

"If it is that fragile, how will it survive long enough to infect?"

"There is a capsid covering surrounding all of them. This covering will protect them for about one year out in the elements. Once inside a body, and once they have reproduced this capsid layer will disappear."

"How effective is it going to be?"

"Oh, it is going to be one hundred percent effective. Once this little bug is in you, that's it, no pregnancy at all."

"And what about those who are already pregnant?"

"Depends on the weakness or strength of the embedded embryo, but I would say that it will abort most pregnancies of one month or less. After that it is all up to nature."

"But the sterility is reversible, and will not go on forever?"

"That is right. The virus will time out over a period of fifty years, and it will time out at differing rates in different people. It's all going to be a baby lottery. Some humans will be fertile again in ten years, in others; the virus will run the full fifty-year course. That way, the Human race will not die out, but they will be given time to reach a sustainable population level."

"That is what they need most, time. Time to step back and examine the choices they have made. After that, whether they go forward with us as a space culture, or …?"

"Yes, will they have learned by then? Or? … At any rate, now that I have the human DNA I will begin work tailoring your virus."

"Thank you Doctor. I will see Dr. Who next, and have him ready a delivery protocol."

Harry then went to the Terranomics department to have a conversation with Dr. Who,

"You are playing god again, Harry."

"And that bothers you Doctor?"

"How can getting involved with these primitives ever lead to any good?"

"Wish you, that I should just let them die off?"

"That would be the natural end of it for them."

"Well, that is the debate. We are all just about split even, with half of the crew wanting to save mankind, and half wanting to let nature take its course. In the absence of any clear consensus let us at least try to save them."

"As you wish, Harry. Our plan for delivery is to target transportation hubs, airports, and most major metropolitan areas. Your virus will then spread out by contact. It might take a full year, but this method should infect them all, except the remotest. That is unless they catch on to our plan and set up isolation centers."

"What, these people cooperate in order to isolate whole populations from infection? That is not going to happen."

"We can have our small stealth probes equipped to carry the virus, and then disburse it. It is a very simple thing for us to do, and we can have it ready within a couple of hours once you get me the virus."

That Afternoon in the ICC
The cadets have been at it since three in the morning, have finally cracked our internet security protocols. They managed to hack into a bank owner's computer. Then, with a smidgeon of serendipity, they were able to create a fraudulent account for internet purchases.

DLW Holdings Bank, NYC.
Bank operations and security office. Mr. Wiedersheen, the banks owner, has fallen asleep while surfing online. His computers firewall has been breached, and its security codes compromised.

"Hey Janis, Mr. Wiedersheen is online again."

"What, I hope he isn't surfing porn sites again? I mean, he is ninety-two?"

"No, looks like he is attempting to create an internet account."

"Jesus! At his age, he might need some help with it   ."

"He does seem to be fumbling a little."

"Oh, yeah, that is right. I just remembered, his wife's birthday is next week. He probably wants to buy her something online. How much credit is he asking for?"

"It's for five Million."

"Wow, she is going to be blown away."

"Yeah, but what do I do?"

"I'm not going up there to question him. You better just authorize it."

"Your right, it is his bank after all." It couldn't have been any easier.

Once they had their fraudulent account activated, Heenon called Harry on his quantcomm, requesting he return to the ICC,

"Captain, I think we have figured it out. First off, we have been scanning this internet. It is a whole world unto itself. There isn't anything we can't get."

"You said that yesterday, Mr. Heenon."

"Yes sir, but we have learned a lot more. The humans use an exchange medium called web cash."

"And how do we get some web cash?"

"You need to set up what is called an account. It took us a while to figure out the questions they were asking, but our research paid off. We don't have what they call a physical address, so we used someone else's."

"You can do that?"

"We employed a technique we learned about on line called hacking."

"Explain this hacking to me?"

"Well, we needed, as you said, something to barter with. The humans also have an exchange medium called money. We found that money comes in many forms. Some are called hard cash. Some are called credit, also, barter, swap, and trade. So we went to a bank, it is a place where they keep money."

"They just gave you this money?"

"No, not at first. Earlier, we tried opening up an account for money. We tried putting in our names for a credit account. That didn't work. So then we found out the name of the owner of this bank. We put his name and personal information on our account, and it was approved."

"How much money did you get?"

"Yes, again we weren't sure how much. It would depend on how much things cost. We used the internet again to research average costs and incomes. There is a wealth term they use called a millionaire. This seemed to be an adequate amount, so we put in for a charge account with a balance of $5,000,000.00."

"Is that a lot?"

"Let's find out, we will purchase something's. Who wants what?"

13:

Old Fears

Feb. 26th
Day Four

On the morning of day four, I was back in Washington DC, and on the phone with Sherry. General Bradley was still in the hospital in California. He was OK, but given his age, and lack of physicality, or more likely, due to an overabundance of it, they decided it best to keep him overnight. I rued the events which occurred the previous day at first meeting. It turned out to be more of a military operation than a sit down with your local aliens social I thought it was going to be. There was enough confused purpose, and poor judgment by all parties in attendance, but I did let my emotions get the best of me, and I swore at the General. Not being that familiar with military law I worry that I might be guilty of a crime befitting a court-martial, and what about my position and future employment with the government?

"I don't know if I even have a job anymore?"

"Oh, of course you do, dear. What are your plans for the rest of the week?"

"I'm staying in DC for the near future. Actually, I would like to find a cave somewhere and hide. I have insulted my boss, and the press and onlookers have staked out my home."

"Oh, come on now. Stop worrying. Your fifteen minutes of fame are over. Soon they will find someone else to harass, and you will be alone again. And Rudy will be out of the hospital later today, and back in his office tomorrow. Why don't you stop by then and talk with him then?"

"After what I said to him? What if I get renditioned to some gulag in the far north, then I will never get to see you again?"

"I have known Rudy a long time. He is not as much of an ogre as you think; besides, I have an extra 30 for lunch."

"So you really just want to see me?"

"Of course, dear."

"Fine, I'll be sure to wear my best black tie outfit. It's the closest thing I have to military attire. That should impress him. Besides, if we are going out to lunch in a military mess, I should look important, for your sake."

"Aren't you always the thoughtful one?" she cooed. "Then I will see you tomorrow." I'm holed up in my house with the shades closed. The press know that I am locked up in here. They have come to the door several times, but I refuse to answer. Moving over to the blinds, I gently push one slat aside to peer out. Sherry is right; there are fewer news vans today. I can only see two out front at the moment. Why do they have to pester you so much? Haven't I already said all that could be said? God I tire of this.

I better go into the bedroom and get out my black suit. Best to put it on and make sure it still fits. Thanks to my recent good fortune I have been eating well, and have put on a few. I put on my dress suit, shirt, and coat—they fit well. "Black on black, that should impress him," I thought to myself, "and if not, they have the added benefit of doubling as a funerary wrap, just in case."

Alien Contact Protocol

According to the Alien Response Committee, or ARC, and *The Plan*, a collection of war game's scenarios designed for an eventual alien invasion, it was now time to implement step three. Step one; destroy the aliens at first contact, failed. Step two, abduct the aliens and use them as bargaining chips, failed. Step three was their last option. The original committee never made provisions for a Step four.

Having failed to destroy the aliens twice, and before resorting to a further and more drastic strategy, a cautious person might take some time to reassess his position, but not 'Ole' Rootten Tootten' Bradley. To him, *The Plan* was gospel. Time might have allowed for cooler heads to reason out a saner approach, but Bradley wasn't going to hear of it. We were going ahead no matter what. Forget, for the moment, that this was a unilateral plan of attack void any declaration of war. Forget that the aliens were now settled in international waters. Forget that there are some 195 other sovereign nations here on planet Earth who might be entitled to equity in the alien's presence. This is where General Bradley's thinking comes into question. He was an older man now, mid-sixties, an experienced old-school military lifer, with no plans to retire. His ARC group wielded too much power, and its only oversight rested with the President. War powers aside, too few brains, with too much power, do tragedy make.

Perhaps it was due to the Breen Survey, and the worldwide chaos it has caused, or fear and anger over the happenings of First Meeting, but our military was now more scared than ever, and bends to pressure from Bradley to attack the aliens. A nuclear attack submarine was ordered into the tropical south pacific waters. It would approach Harry's Island by stealth. No warning would be given. There would be no time hide or take cover. When they were within twenty miles, they were ordered to launch their weapon of mass destruction. A four megaton nuclear weapon would be detonated directly overhead. Thereby hoping to end once and for all the supposed danger the aliens posed.

An emergency meeting of the ARC group, and the President of the United States, had been called. General Bradley was being teleconferenced in from his hospital bed,

"Mr. President, have you any questions, sir?"

"Yes, this is a bold plan, how can we be certain this type of strong action is necessary? What is this contamination you fear so much?"

"Rudy here, sir. Think of it this way. Let me recount one of many examples given to us by history. When European sailors in their tall ships began to sweep across the pacific in search of Spice Islands, they had no idea that casual contact would negatively impact native peoples. But it did. The islanders saw their populations ravaged by deadly diseases. Those who survived found that they had been infected with syphilis and gonorrhea. For the first time in their history they experienced venereal disease. An infection they could not control nor did they even have any idea what it was. Further, not only did the sailors leave death and disease in their wake, they also brought the rats. These destructive animals had stowed away on their boats and escaped to become an invasive plague. Entire ecosystems were stressed—many were destroyed."

"Putting pestilence aside, perhaps the bigger curse we brought them was culture shock. The appearance of new technologies forever changed these ancient cultures. Their old ways were supplanted. Customs were abandoned. Some natives were enslaved, most were proselytized and forced to convert to foreign religions, and all were treated poorly and with gross disrespect. And as I say, this is but one example. Our past is replete with stories of lesser populations being overrun by a more advanced one. That is why the ARC plan was devised. To prevent us from becoming the next example of a generation lost, and of a people enslaved."

"Yes, I understand, Rudy. Christ! Has anyone had any contact with the aliens since they took the island?"

"Not that we can tell, sir. They all still appear to be on the island though."

"You're certain of that?"

"Yes sir. We have a satellite on constant lookout, right on top of them."

"How many of them are there anyway?"

"We don't know how many there are, sir. However, on a ship that size there could be several thousand. Each one of them a ticking time bomb threatening to spread their alien contamination across the globe."

"Damn, I hate to lose a shot at their advanced technology."

"Access to their technology is partly what we are attempting to prevent, sir."

"Yes, I understand."

"If you all think you can pull it off, then I will advise a go ahead. Have any of your brilliant military minds considered what, if any, defenses they might have, or what kind of reprisal we could be in for if they survive?"

"Survive a four megaton blast. Fat chance. Plus the sub won't launch until twenty miles out. Even if they did detect the launch, they would have at best only a five-minute warning."

"Yes, I see. Jesus Rudy, do you need to use such a big bomb?"

"Yes sir, as spelled out in *The Plan*, we must obliterate any sign they have been here. And that means completely destroying everything they have. That spaceship included. With a four megaton blast, all that will be left is a water-filled crater half a mile wide and one hundred feet deep."

"Doesn't sound like they have a prayer does it?"

"No, not at all, sir."

"Do you have a time line?"

"Four days, sir."

"Then let's make it so. Rudy, how long are you going to be in the hospital?"

"I'm being discharged in the morning, sir. I will be back in my office at the Pentagon bright and early tomorrow."

"I admire your dedication, sir."

"Thank you, Mr. President." And that was it. No consideration was ever given to the lives being extinguished—albeit alien lives.

Arlen and Hippee were cued to General Bradley's plan to kidnap them partly through the capabilities of a spy probe they surreptitiously installed into the meeting room walls. This probe was controlled by the cadets back at the island, and used it to spy on the proceedings.

The intell was immediately shared between the Breen. This spybot was not your typical CIA type bug, or even a robot as we would think of. It was more like a controlled electrical virus than anything of physical wires and electronic parts. This gave it the capability to move through and into objects, perhaps a wall, possibly a window, or any other inanimate object. Plus it could be repositioned anytime, and just about anywhere, truly, the nth word in spy devices.

Harry ordered the cadets to move the spybot out of the meeting room after First Meeting was over. He was ultimately interested in those who made the decisions. At that time, it seemed that General Bradley was calling all the shots, so where Rudy went, the spybot went. That meant the Breen were listening in on the plan to nuke them, and would be ready…

"Seems our choice to follow the General was a good one cadets. Geerron, what is the status of our defense grid?"

"Up and running perfectly, sir."

"He said four days. Let's not rely on that. They could try to strike at us anytime now. So let's be vigilant. Keep our defense grid on automatic, and I want someone here at the consoles at all times until we sort this out. I am going to make an example of General Bradley, and anyone else who is behind these belligerences."

"Yes, Captain," snapped the cadets. Harry was beginning to anger over the hostile intent of the Americans. Not that the Breen were in any real danger from an attack, but even a small dog barking at your heels grows tiresome.

Sunday, February 27, 11:15 A.M., Day Five
It was Sunday morning. I had just arrived back at the Pentagon. With my tail between my legs I am going to enter the Generals' office, and hoping to keep my job, make apologies for insulting him,

"Ah, Parker, come on in here." said Bradley in his usual sharp deep tone garbled by age.

"Glad to see you are OK sir."

"That was quite an event we had. They were ready for us Parker, that's for sure. It won't happen again. I promise you."

"General, if there was something I …"

"Stop right there, Parker. You just broke under pressure. This kind of thing happens to even the best of men. We were all pretty damn nervous that day, so don't think any more of it. Now let's put your regular duties on hold."

"Gulp!"

"This alien thing has the world on edge, and I want my best men available on hand, and that also means you."

"What? Why, thank you sir."

"Stay close for the next couple of days. We may have to act fast. Consider yourself on call, and keep your cell phone on your person. With that said, any plans for today?"

"Well, yes, sir. If you don't mind I would like to take your secretary to lunch?"

"No problem, why don't you two go and have good time." Whew, I survive.
As I turn to leave the office, "Oh, and Parker, Need I remind you to be careful what you say to the media?"

"No, sir. I mean, I will, sir." Thinking to myself—Now what the hell is happening here? I am no longer angered by his dropping of my title. I feel comfortable calling him sir. I am being indoctrinated. That is what is happening. As I approach the secretary's desk, I do a little tip of the hat routine and say, "Ma'am, may I buy you lunch?"...

* * * * * *

On the Afternoon of Day 5

Harry was in Planetary Genomics meeting with Dr. Sa'aarron regarding progress on his plan to save mankind.

"Harry, thanks for coming in, your bugs are ready for mass production."

"Should we go ahead and produce them all now?"

"Certainly, they have a long shelf life. I would ask you to reconsider your plan, but for the life of me, I can't think of another way in which we can interfere with this population within the terms of our treaties with the consortium. Your plan does work according to our computer simulations. That is provided their economic calamities don't side-rail them into all-out war."

"Well, war with them has become a way of life. One handed down to them by a long history of their heirs."

"If they do turn to war, they might exterminate themselves."

"We will just have to take that chance."

"Have you a time line for dispersal?" asked Dr. Sa'aarron.

"Soon, sometime in the next week, I think," said Harry. "We have enough to keep us busy for a few days, so let's wait for a while and get better established on our island first."

14:

The Invitation

Day Seven

It was late at night. I had been holed up in my house since early afternoon. This past week it has been one grueling day after another. Television interviews, military interrogations, and having to sit in conference with the General, all of this was quite enough. My home has been staked out by media and their news vans. My privacy invaded, I exist under a microscope. Everything about my life is now under full scrutiny.

I'm beat and entreat just sleeping for an entire day. I have been relying on the TV to put me to sleep. The late night news channels used to zonk me out. Now I can't even enjoy them. Damn! There I am, on jus about every channel, and again, why didn't I have my hat on. … Shit! Every channel I surf I see more shocking sights of my balding head. God, give me an old movie, or a nightly sportscast. Now that I am thrown into the public spotlight—well, I just don't like it—I want my boring anonymity back.

As I lamented my new-found celebrity, back on Harry's Island, the Breen were scheming, and I would soon come into their focus. Hours earlier on the island, Harry was in the ICC. The cadets at their station gazed on at him as he played over and over a recording of the First Meeting. Then he ordered,

"Arlen, you and Hippee come here."

"Yes sir, right away sir." They echoed, trying to imitate some of our military speak, no doubt gleaned from one of our old movies. The Breen were generally playful and imitative, and not above chiding one of their own. Even Captain Harry wasn't immune from insult. Something not allowed in our armed forces. The rules in the Terraformer corps were quite different from our military traditions. They don't salute, and their makeup was more of a loose amalgam of personalities and interests. No one was conscripted to a term, and could opt out, or quit the service, at any time. Harry held the rank of captain. That was so long as there were no mutiny, which did happen on occasion. Further, I found that most Breen detested being put into positions of authority over others, which made for an interesting command structure, but it worked for them, and that was all that mattered.

"Harry, you asked for us?"

"Yes, I have been going over a replay of your meeting with the General from yesterday. There is something I want you two to see. Here, I'll run it again. … There. Do you see it? Watch, there—the economist—see?"

"Oh yeah, that is Dr. Parker, we met him on our day of first contact, and again at the meeting with the General." said Arlen.

"Yes, but it is his actions that I am interested in," said Harry. "He appears to be trying to prevent you two from being shot with the tranc darts."

"Oh yeah. Seriously," said Arlen, "in the heat of the moment, I hadn't noticed it, but I see it now."

"Well, we were rather occupied at the time." adds Hippee.

"So he was going to take one for the team?"

"Yes, and here again at first contact. Let me play that sequence for you two. … Right there, just as Arlen's death ray strikes the two humans?"

"I'm not following you Harry?" said Hippee.

"Watch, I'll play it again. There, just as the old man slumps to the ground, Parker bends down to break his fall. You see, instead of running in fear like all the others, he stays to aid his friend. Boys, I think we have found a thoughtful and compassionate human."

"If so, he's a rare breed," mentioned Arlen.

"Perhaps they are not all alien haters Arlen," said Hippee.

"Now listen up, for my plan to work we need an intermediary, someone who can come here, get to know us, and work out things between our two species. Additionally, we need someone who can chronicle the events that are going to happen to their species. My intention is to have everything recorded for their world's future reference, and I think Mr. John Parker is just the one we have been looking for."

"You mean someone who thinks he is being smart and caring, but in reality, is being naïvely trusting?" said Arlen.

"That's the definition of a term I heard in that old movie last night. It was to be buffaloed," added Hippee.

"If you two can put your sarcasms aside, I have a task for you? Here is what I want you two to do. The cadets have located Dr. Parker. He lives in a house at these coordinates in Washington DC. I want you two to take a skiff, and go to visit him privately at his house. He knows you two from the meeting. Talk with him alone and see if you can gain his confidence. Get him to come here to the island, and once he is here I will explain further to him what we would like him to do. I think it best if you contact him late at night. That is the time of day when these humans revert to their caves. So you two better get going."

"So I am going to make him an offer he can't refuse," said Arlen. That one drew a bunch of laughs.

Commandeering a skiff, the duo again left the safety of the island and shot off into near space, some sixty miles high.

"Arlen, do you think this is a good idea? I mean heading back into alien territory? And I don't get their hostilities toward us. We simply came to talk and be friends. These alien beings are so far behind us, well, they are more like pets than talking thinking beings."

"Well Hipp, we originally came over to be friends, but what we have to do to them before we leave isn't going to be friendly at all. Perhaps some of them, like the General, sense the danger we pose? Anyway, let's do this for Harry's benefit. If he can pull it off, he might still be able to get his much hoped-for Planetship. Besides, it might be fun to capture and torture one of these humans. After that meeting, I feel we owe it to them."

"So then, we would call it, the Human Autopsy?" asked Hipp.

Arlen, shook his head in some disbelief, "I was just joking, Hipp."

"Oh."

Harry broke in on his quantcomm to say, "You two have a fun time, see you when you return."

"Have a fun time—that could mean just about anything, right?" asked Hippee.

"Yeah, let's get this Parker guy," said Arlen, "and show him a fun time Breen style. That might be punishment enough?"

"Hippee put up a navigation screen with the destination coordinates."

"It's on the other side of the planet."

"Yeah, there is no way we can get there, show this short-lifer a good time, and return before the sun is down. This day is shot."

"Well then, let's do some sightseeing."

"OK, powering up. What do you say we zoom on up to the ionosphere and then make a power dive down to DC?"

"Anything you want Arlen, you're driving. We are invisible to their current detection methods. Just don't make too much noise and we can have all the fun we want."

"Good—let's punch it."… "If this shore leave is going to be rewarding, Harry's plan to befriend the humans will have to work."

"Yes, I am hungry for some of the local cuisine. These humans can't all be like the General."

"Give it some time, we will find some party spots."

"I wonder what this Carter guy is really like?"

After the speedy trip up into outer space, and then a power dive down to Washington DC,

"Approaching the coordinates Harry gave us that he got off of their internet. Do we have a tactical layout?" asked Arlen.

"You kidding, their internet has just about every kind of map you can ask for. I'll overlay a map of Parker's neighborhood on your tactical screen."

"Well there it is, this is like using their own intelligence against them, I really like it. I'm slowing us down, a little farther, and there it is. Let's hover over his residence while you do a sensor sweep of the area?"

Before turning in I made a late night call to Sherry. There was something about the sound of her voice. I found it soothing, and loved hearing it. Strange, must be love. We hadn't made our relationship anything serious, but I do feel nature urging me to settle down. Time, what an enemy—far greater threat than any space alien could be. Forget the frown lines and wrinkles, what I wouldn't give just to have a full head of hair again.

"John love, I know it has just been quite a day for you. I'm worried that you are stressing too much. Is there anything I can do to help you to calm down?"

"No, not for tonight. I just need to rest. General Bradley said he wants to meet with me about something in the morning, and after that I have no plans—perhaps we can meet at the cafeteria for lunch?"

"Sounds like you are asking me out on a date mister?"

"If you can overlook that it is a military mess I'm taking you to?"

"Well, you are the only gentleman to have ever escorted me to that mess."

"Great, so noon then. Oh, damn."

"John, what is it?"

"Oh—the hair on my arms is standing on end again, just like it did the other day at first contact, I just can't seem to shake this funny feeling."

"Oh, you poor dear. Why don't you relax? Go and have a hot soak in the tub, and then get some sleep—I'll see you mañana." After a little more woo-speak we said goodnight. For a nightcap, I walked over to the fridge hoping to grab a cold one. As I reached for the door handle, Zap. Geeze! There is a lot of static in the air, must be a storm brewing? Damn, look at the hairs on my arm, they're standing straight up; god, my nerves? Popping open a cold one, "Let's see if I can catch the late-night sports wrap?"

Two hundred feet straight above, "There is only one human present in that house, it must be Parker. There is another one sitting alone in a vehicle parked across the street."

"Why would a person be just sitting in a vehicle this late at night, and in the dark?"

"My guess—surveillance," said Arlen.

"Are they watching Parker? For what?"

"They are a primitive and paranoid species."

"Yes, I heard that in a movie, but why watch Parker?" asked Hippee.

"Huh. I can think of only two reasons: one, they don't trust him; two, they don't trust us."

"Ah, you mean a Wheenaan's warning."

"What?"

"A Wheenaan's warning. Remember from back in your academy days in exo class, there was a Dr. Wheenaan who had devised a short list of things to be wary of."

"Oh yeah, he said, "Beware of the paranoia of certain species who are just intelligent enough to be dangerous." … And I thought that was all just hype."

"Well, we actually are going to abduct Parker, at least abduct him from their point of view," mentioned Arlen. "Harry, are you getting all of this?"

"Yes, I have been listening in; they're not trusting Parker certainly adds more intrigue."

"The General not trusting Parker is spooky, is it precognition on his part, something like Dr. Sa'aarron's eerie talent for prescience?" asked Arlen.

"The General may have some suspects," said Harry. "He is a very leery type. Here's what we can do." He then laid out a plan to smoke out the General's spying.

"Arlen, once we shut down we will be visible again. Let's put down in the rear yard where the skiff will be hidden behind the fencing. There appears to be an entrance at the back of the house. We can enter there."

"OK, putting us down."

"All is quiet outside, let's get out." Exiting their craft, the duo walked over to my rear patio door.

"What is a common greeting to humans, Arlen? How do we get his attention without being shot at?"

"I think they do a knock at the wall."

"A knock at the wall?"

"Yes, you've seen it in many of their movies. You just rap your hand on the wall, like this." Arlen raised his arm, and with his fist clenched he moves to knock on the back house wall.

"Wait," said Hipp, "I have an idea. I saw this in an old movie we watched during the trip coming over. In an unnerving tone you call out his name, like this, "Paaarkerr, John Paaarkerr. We're out here,

John Parker. No, you can't see us. We are not really there."

"Of course he can see us."

"I know that, it's from the movie."

"Very strange. Couldn't we just knock? Seriously, I think all this alien movie crap has gotten to our heads."

"Fine, I'll bang on the glass door." Rap rap rap.

Weary from days on end of being in the media spotlight, and stressing about things beyond my control, I was finally in wind down mode, and blessed sleep was only moments away. However, the universe had other plans in mind. I heard a loud rapping at my patio door,

"What the fuck. Who in the hell?" I snapped. … "If that is a TV crew in my back yard? God, enough already!" There was another, Rap, rap, rap. "Who's there?" I shouted loudly this time, and in an angry tone.

"John, it's Arlen and Hippee."

"Who?"

"It is Arlen and Hippee"

"Great Maker!" exclaimed Hippee. "Now I'm feeling scared. Arlen, he sounds mad, maybe we should go."

"No—wait—John, sorry to bother you at home, we just want to talk with you, could you let us in?"

I put on a face of rage and opened the curtains. I was ready to bark at someone, and there, just feet in front of me stood two seven foot tall slightly blue skinned aliens.

"What the?" Both of their faces lit up with this stupid little smile, and they gave me that little half wave. How very odd it seemed, but I was too weary to faint. Why struggle with the insanity of the situation, What, aliens in my back yard? So opening the slider I said, "Welcome, and of course, come right in," and keeping it quite human, "So what keeps you two up so late?"

"I'm detecting an attitude. John, if we came at a bad time?"

"Oh no, couldn't be better. So, what, let me guess, you're stuck on a small island, and have nothing to do at night?"

"Yes, you're right," said Hippee, "and I am also sensing quite an attitude."

"That was a bit surly," said Arlen. "Dr. Parker."

"Please, call me, John."

"OK, John, actually Harry, our Captain, sent us here to have a chat with you. We noticed your actions seemed to be those of a thoughtful person. Not like those of the General. We have a need for someone like you who understands your race, and can work together with us. We really just want to be friends."

"You mean, even after the meeting that went so bad, you are still willing to talk? After all we did attack you two. I think the General wanted to see you two on a dissection table. And how did you get away so fast? Can you bend time?"

The duo took a moment to look at each other, as though in private conversation. "Those are a lot of questions. Yes, we still want to get to know your species better, and we should not let the General's actions destroy any chance we have at becoming good friends. Up to the point we got shot at, we felt the talks were proceeding well. We would prefer to continue them, but on our terms, and on safe ground."

"I am not sure of what you are proposing, Arlen, where on Earth can we find safe ground?"

"Again, there are many questions looking for an answer. What we suggest is that you come and join us on our island for a few days. There we can talk, get to know each other better, and possibly formulate a plan to get our two species talking together."

"You want me to go with you to your island? Why me, I'm not a diplomat?"

"No, we don't want a diplomat. Politics would just slow down and confuse any talks. What we need is an intelligent and caring human, and Harry thinks that is you. You are a man we can trust, and I think that our meeting was a sort of cosmic kismet."

"Huh, interesting choice of words."

"Plus, you are currently world famous. Your people want to talk with you about your experiences. That access to international media is useful."

"So you need a go between, someone who knows the territory. I can understand that, and if this weren't all so sudden?"

"You do not trust us, do you John?" asked Arlen.

"Frankly, this entire course of events scares me. And you are right. I don't understand you well enough to trust you."

"If you don't mind my saying so, I feel that we, what you Earthlings call aliens, have been unfairly stereotyped by your species. You have built up suspicions regarding space races by watching sci-fi flicks, and have imprinted these fears into your collective conscience. You always portray ET's as evil doers. We aliens aren't all bad."

"No, I suppose not, but wouldn't more bad, than good come from exposure to Aliens advanced akin to say—God?" Perhaps unwittingly, I hit upon a most salient point and the underlying reason behind our military's decision to treat the Breen as Hostiles that even with the best of intentions, and knowing the human belief that power corrupts, as has been proven time and again; having such a disparity between species will lead to one of them ultimately being supplanted. Too bad I did not let it sink in.

"To your many questions, we would be willing to answer them all—given time, but not here, and not now. We are inviting you to meet and socialize with us on our island. Imagine being given a chance to meet with a race alien to you. One advanced far beyond your dreams and imagination. Should you not show some respect to their wishes?"

Arlen spoke direct and yet thoughtful. I was beginning to like him. So, I pretend to mull it over. I will miss the General's meeting tomorrow, wonder what he wants from me anyway and my lunch with Sherry? Well, perhaps they have cell phone coverage on that island?

"Thank you for appealing to my sentient side," I said, "I will go with you."

Then he said, "You see Hippee; there is a little Breen in them after all."

"Huh?" I was electrified over my good fortune in being the only human so far to interact one on one with extraterrestrials, a childhood dream, for many, come true. Yet, when he said *there is a little Breen in them after all*, a shiver ran from the top of my head and down the back of my neck, and I didn't know why. "Just let me put together a few things I will need." I learned from working with the military to always have a hot bag set aside for emergencies— this qualifies.

"John, mind if I take a picture of your home?" Arlen, careful not to hit the ceiling, puts a little device up in the air.

"A picture? Do you need some more light?" I

asked.

"Need some light?—accessing." And at not getting an acceptable response from his built-in organic computer, "John, we can speak your language, but I see there is still much we need to learn about your use of it. Could you explain needing some more light?"

"I meant, better lighting so you can take a clearer picture."

Hippee seeing some humor in my confusion broke out in a laugh. Then Arlen went on to explain, "Oh, no John, I, well, no. This is, well, you were thinking of a camera, yes?"

"Yes." I reply.

"No, this is a portable imaging device. Picture was a poor choice of words on my part. This is more than a picture camera, it will make a complete design of your house. Here let me show you." Arlen activated his imaging device. A second later he lowered his arm. "Here, take a look at this. I will put it on holo." A small holographic representation of my homes layout appears floating in the air above the device. In perfect detail, I might add.

"Wow, that is wow—I'm at a loss."
"I will upload this data into our computer. Then I will instruct it to have an identical representation of your house built for you back on our island. Your new home will be ready by the time we arrive there."

"Wow-OK," I think I will just sit back and let these guys drive—they seem to know what they are doing.

Hot bag in hand, holo of the house taken, I was led out to my backyard where there was a small flying craft waiting. It was the same one they arrived in at first meeting, and it was sitting square in my back yard—this was all just hilarious. As we approached the skiff, a doorway opened up and we climbed in, but I noticed it was only a two-seater.

"Oops," said Arlen. "We forgot to add a seat for John."

"I got it," said Hippee. He played with a few control buttons. Beneath my feet I felt the ship grow. It actually lengthened at the push of a button, and then up popped another seat, which appeared to have grown right out of the ship's deck. I had already seen that trick in a movie or two, so I wasn't shocked, but clearly awed, and if that was an example of the toys these creatures have, I am in for one hell of a good time.

"Have a seat John," mentioned Hippee. I sat down—it was more of a fall and slip down into—this was a full body-form seat (head, shoulders, torso, legs, feet and all). It felt comfortable and roomy.

"Now, John," Arlen warned, "this is no pleasure craft, so you will have to be seated in tightly. We don't have any inertial buffers either; you could be in for a bumpy ride." I look around but don't see any restraining devices, but I did see a smile form on Hippie's face. "What do these two have in store for me now?" I wondered.

"Once the door closes, your seat will engage and form a tight seal around you."
Hippee shut the door and suddenly I saw foam appear and expand to fill in the voids around me. I was encapsulated and couldn't move—had I just been trapped? To say the fit was a bit snug would be an understatement, I could hardly breathe. Then Arlen reassured me saying, "John, the foam is for your protection. It will tighten and relax with the G-forces we experience. You will notice that fast moves are restricted, but if you need to scratch an itch you

can stick a hand out by moving it slowly. However, you don't want to have your arms flopping about while we make quick maneuvers, or you could lose them."

"Lose them? My arms?" I asked. He just smiled. Was that meant to be an airline preflight safety speech? "So, Arlen, if we crash into the ocean, does this plane float?"

Quizzically he answered, "Does it float? … Why, yes, it does. John, just relax this is going to be fun."

How we were going to fly anywhere was beyond me. The ship had no wings, and the pods below the body looked more like skids designed for water landings. One other thing, there were no windows. There is a console in front, but I see none of the customary dials and gauges, just cryptic symbols. Without saying a word, Hippee touched one of them and a holographic image appeared in front of them on the forward hull. It looked to be a tactical screen; it was just a simple plot map of my neighborhood out to say three blocks. "Yep, seen that trick too, just a fancy Garmin type viewer," I thought. We were looking at an empty sketch; a couple streets were shown, lots with houses on them were outlined. There was also an image of an auto parked across the street from my house. It was tagged with a blinking yellow dot? I asked, "Are you guys going to drive like this with the windows up?" They gave each other a questioning look, as if they had no idea what to say. Then Arlen said, "Alright John here we go." I feel us rise up from the ground. "We will turn on the windows in a minute," said Hippee. Turn on the windows—now that one I haven't seen yet.

The ship began to rise up and then it stopped and hovered in place. If we hadn't changed direction, we would be oriented toward the south. I heard them talking to themselves. Arlen said to Hippee, "Let's wait until we are a couple miles out to turn on stealth mode." They had purposely left stealth mode off. Did I even know what stealth mode was?

Then they said laughing, "Ok John, turning on some windows now."

Note—"The Breen possess a remarkable intellect. We suspected that. They also possess a technology, or technologies far beyond ours. We also suspected that, but they also have a devilishly playful side to their normal stoic behaviors, and are not above pulling a fast one at any time, or for any reason. Plus they all have, from my human point of view, a hideous and sinister sounding laugh. I often found their playfulness disconcerting, and it usually came at inappropriate times."— JP…

Hippee mentioned the windows were turning on? At that the skin, or hull, of the skiff just disappeared. I mean it quite literally vanished from my sight. We could see right through it in all directions. I could still see Arlen and Hippee, and the holograph hanging over the control panel, but everything else just evaporated. It was fantastic! I was startled at first. I had the feeling that I might fall straight to my death. This was a scary mental reaction. Physically I was quite safe, but a bit woozy.

"Windows open enough for you, John?" asked Arlen. What got to me the most was the way they talked straight to you, as though we had been acquaintances forever. There was no alien upon alien social gap in their discourse.

"Yes, quite a view." I replied. I wasn't going to let on that I had nearly pissed my pants. "I have flown a lot, but this flight is to be a real treat."

"Oh, you haven't seen anything yet," mentioned Arlen.

"What? Was that meant to scare me?" I quipped. Then the skiff took off across town, and gained a little altitude. We were still moving slowly, perhaps only a hundred miles an hour. Slow enough to take in the sights. I knew the territory below, and was picking out places I had been to.

Across the street from my house a man got out of his car. No lights came on inside when he opened his door and exited. His dark visage melded into the blackness of midnight to conceal his presence. Looking toward my house, he noticed the small craft rise up off the ground and then bear to the south. Taking out his cell phone he placed a late night call, "General, this is Lieutenant Jones. It seems you were right sir. Good thing we kept an eye on Parker. I just saw what looked like a smaller version of the alien's ship rise up out of his back yard. It then took off towards the south. Using our new M-ray detector, I could see that Parker and two of the aliens were in it."

"Damn that Parker. Good work Jones. Go home and get some rest. I want you in my office first thing in the morning so you can give me your full report."

"Yes sir, General, sir. Thank you, sir."

Onboard the skiff—I noticed that a small holo above the control panel hadn't changed, it still showed my neighborhood. Further, the yellow dot on the car had turned red and was blinking. In a moment of spooky synchronicity, Arlen and Hippee turned and made eye contact. At that same moment back on the island inside the Val's ICC, Harry's eyes rose and opened wide to make eye contact with the trio of cadets. I would learn later that this was all part of Harry's plan. They were monitoring the car for any transmissions, and were rewarded. They now knew I was being watched by the General. Why was I being watched, and to what purpose I did not know? I hadn't reported in to the General about my leaving with the aliens, but I am not in the military. Should I have called and left a message? Was I required to? In retrospect it might have been a good idea. I left without his blessing or support, and I didn't have my passport with me, nor did I have a visa for where we were going, but somehow I don't think I will need them. Was the General cooking up some new plot against the aliens—probably? Hippee reached over, touched an icon, and the holo disappeared.

"John, mind if we do a little sightseeing?"

"Why no, not at all, I have never been in a small plane made of all windows. This is going to be a real joyride."

"Accessing—joyride. Ah. John wants to joyride Hippee. Shall we show him a good time?"

Just below us we were passing over an amusement park. "Arlen look that looks like a ride we have been on, the one on Schribneer's amusement planet."

"Why John, your people have amusement parks like we do. I'm starting to like earth even more."

Amusement parks? Aha, a light just went off in my head. I am beginning to understand now Arlen's point about our stereo typing aliens. Who ever thought of extra-terrestrial beings of having amusement parks? Or, for that matter: homes, schools, jobs, families, and the like. When asked what we think aliens look like my first thought might be one of an eight eyed, ten legged caterpillar sitting in a dark and smoky bar playing a guitar. Perhaps they are more like us than *Star Wars* had us believe.

"Hippee, I have an idea," said Arlen. "Scan that roller-coaster ride from the park down below, and input the data into the navigation computer."

"I see where you are going with this, Arlen."

"Now we will show you a real joy ride, John. I am going to turn the skiff here into a roller coaster car. We'll show you some serious Gs."

"John, how much g-force can you take?" asked Hippee.

"Well, I have heard pilot's pass out at about 7 g's."

"I think with the aid of our aero-gel body seats you can easily handle up to ten G's." Let's start there; I'll program a limit of ten into the NAV computer. … OK, have you ever been weightless?"

"No."

"Never been into space?"

"No."

"Then we will increase the length of our run to give you a longer-lasting speed induced weightless condition." The data for a stratospheric roller-coaster ride were entered into the ship's navigation controls, and with stress parameters set, we started off on *John Parker's Wild Ride.*

The skiff blasted off nearly vertical, and must have gone from our five hundred foot elevation to about fifty thousand feet in the blink of an eye. Then it leveled off briefly, then started to roll, we peeled over and began to descend down and down. At the bottom, the craft still rolling around, pulled up sharply and spiraled on its way up to the stratosphere. At the top of this loop we experience weightlessness as we fell along with the craft back down to earth. As the ship gained velocity my body was forced back into my seat, and the foam around me grew ever tighter. At the bottom of our run there was another sharp jagging maneuver and we shot back up again. The course changes were gruesome. As the force of acceleration grew the skin on my face pulled back We did a twist this time at the top of the run, and went into another weightless moment. Then we powered back to the surface upside down. We essentially mirrored the ride's design, only miles up in the sky.

"Was that wild enough for you?" asked Arlen.

Actually, I hate coaster rides, but in an attempt to humor my new friends I feigned liking it. Arlen said it seemed a bit tame to him, and he wanted to do it again at double the length and double the speed.

"Let's take it up a notch," he said. "This time we'll travel farther, and faster than before." I didn't protest. The entire experience got stretched out. Suppressing the screams, my body was jerked, turned, and flung into weightlessness. I was ready to lose my cookies and begged god to let it end.

The ride finally ended and we leveled off at about ten thousand feet, and my stomach muscles relaxed. "That was a much better run," said Arlen. Hippee, noticing my discomfort said, "He's turning Breen blue Arlen. I think our guest is more of a sightseer than a thrill seeker."

"John, you do look a bit blue."

"I'm ok."

"John, how about a deadfall or two?" I didn't dare to ask?

"Oh, you are going to love the deadfall, John," said Hipp. "Let's hit it." With that, the skiff shot up vertical, my chair foam evermore tightly around me. I had no idea how many Gs we hit, but it felt like my eyeballs would burst out through the back of my skull. We exploded up through the atmosphere, and this time out into the thermopause. I was now actually in outer space—WOW, and if I could find my stomach. Then Arlen killed the engine, so to speak, and we coasted until our forward motion slowed, and we began to fall due to gravity. And fall we did, and at an ever increasing speed. The skiff, and us inside it, started to turn, then twist, and then tumbled down through Earth's upper atmosphere. "The Breen find this exciting?" I thought to myself. Actually, they were right. Any thrill seeker would have been ecstatic. The conditions outside were hostile and dangerous, inside they weren't much better. We were still in windows open mode, and the visibility was unlimited. The brilliant blue horizon of Earth against the stark black of space was spellbinding. As we fell, we gathered speed, soon the ships outer hull began to glow crimson from friction. The cabin filled with a fiery glow. It was beautiful to watch. And then, Wham! As we re-entered the lower atmosphere the ride turned violent. We hit the air too fast, and bounced like a rock skipping on a pond. The sudden shock and crushing g-forces frightened me. I became drunk on adrenaline and a giddy euphoria had me happy to have survived, and strangely begging for more.

Arlen took the controls, and without slowing down, leveled off the ship to change our momentum, and then we veered upward again. Gaining velocity, this time he was going to pull out all of the stops. Like a mad man he pushed his ship faster and faster, until we broke free of Earth's restraining gravity, and squirted out into empty space.

That was enough for me. I had thought my body was going to come apart several times and entertained pleading with my captors to end my torture, but to my surprise, having lived through the experiences, I became trusting and comfortable with my new Breen friends, and began to relax. We were now somewhere over Baja California, but still many miles from the island, and look, I'm in outer space, and this ship's hull is invisible. I can see everywhere and everything. My hosts were oddly quiet for a change and taking in the beauty of Earth below. Suddenly, my thoughts changed to a consideration of just how intoxicating drugs can be. Certainly, the allure of such advanced technology can be likened to a drug. Then I pondered the fate of the Amerindian natives when first they met the Spaniards. Surely, they had desires for Spanish steel and horses. Sadly, for those natives, they had nothing intrinsic of value to save their lives, and in the end—Slaughter! Or is it more like showing fire to a Neanderthal for the first time—Irresistible! Would it be like that for us? What have we of any value to bargain with? I cannot imagine what the Breen could possibly ever need from us primitive humans? Will our fate equal that of the Incas?

"John, how was it?" asked Hippee. My seat relaxed, and I could talk. Feeling brave for the ordeal I said, "Is that all this thing has got?" Arlen and Hippee looked to one another, a little smile formed on their faces. "I think he liked it Hippee?"

"Yes, we will make a Breen out of him yet," said Arlen.

(Huh? A Breen of him yet?) I passed that one off to perhaps a difference in cultures.

What a vista Earth from space. I had lost all sense of time. I never noticed our return from orbit, or that we had arrived at the island. Still in some drugged out stupor I was, or was I simply so tired from too many long days. Later, I found myself in an exact copy of my home in DC, all thanks to the Breen picture. The rest of the night, or I should say early morning, was a blank, yet I couldn't shake that feeling inside. Like a little guy on your shoulder yelling, "Run you idiot, run as fast as you can…"

15:

A Fateful Mistake

March 2cd, day 8

This is my first day on the island after being alien-napped in the early hours from the comfort of my home in Washington DC. Will I wind up prisoner, subject of weird alien experiments, get my body cavities probed, or will my jailers turn out to be my greatest benefactors, or more likely, am I just to be taken away, to become part of a galactic zoo; part of some human animal exhibit—perhaps part of a breeding pair—Hmm?

There was a faint and respectful, knock, knock, at the door. Then I hear, "John, are you up yet?" Am I up yet?—who's he kidding? I went to answer the door. It was Arlen. It was only 6:00 AM. "Geeze these aliens get up early," I thought. With not a moments sleep, last night was truly shitty. Right now, I have that, "I'm tired, but I'm not tired," feeling. Adrenaline still coursed through my body. I was too wired to get any sleep, though I tried. Do I look forward to this day? Let's see, "What am I feeling right now—fear, anxiety, fear and anxiety?" Once, as a child, I caught a small mouse. I know now how that little mouse felt, being snatched up by some giant flesh eating ogre, and put into a shoe box? How cruel I was.

"Good morning, Arlen." I couldn't believe I had just said good morning to an over seven foot tall alien. And yes, even if he were human, his stature would have shocked me.

"Good morning, John. How did you find your house?" It was actually more of a condo stuck inside a hotel.

"Well, just fine," I replied, "after all it is exactly like my home in DC."

"Glad you like it. If you need to make any changes just let me know."

"Oh, am I going to be here long?"

"That is what Harry wants to talk to you about this morning."

At least they were willing to talk. I could ask them to surrender now to save themselves the embarrassment. I was trying to make light of my situation thinking that to do so might ease my apprehensions.

"Harry is on board the Val, when you are ready we can walk over to the ship and meet with him."

"So, I am actually going to be going into a spaceship?" I asked. Arlen, with a look of minor confusion then said, "Would you rather he came here?" Alright, call my psychologist. This is truly going to be a day of days.

"No," I said, "just let me splash some water on my face, and we can go."

We left my new house. I hadn't been outside yet

to look around. I was assuming we were still on planet Earth. The sun was just coming up, and it was getting light, not light enough to see clearly, but I did get a sense that this place was like any upscale Hawaiian resort. We passed through an atria. Looking out and across a sandy expanse to the southwest I spied what looked like a large pool or lagoon. So they had fresh water. We made a turn around the corner of the building I was housed in—I call it the Towers Hotel. Looking back and up at the side of the building I count, one, two, … six floors. And I'm on the ground floor—that would have to change.

"Arlen, you all have been on this island what, a week, and you have managed to construct all this in that short amount of time?"

"Yes John, the tarmac came first, then the overhead weather shield. The many amenities came next, but we are not done yet; the water slide is proving to be a challenge.

"And you plan on being here for how long?" I asked.

"We have only three months to stay here, and then we have to get back to work on our terraforming job."

"Oh, yes, I recall you mentioning that at first meeting."

"Is this building large enough to house all of your crew?"

"No, this building isn't for us. We all have quarters onboard the Val. We built this hotel for the comfort of future visitors."

"Oh, when are you planning to have visitors?"

"That all has to do with you. We, in part, want you to invite people from all parts of your world to come here to meet with us, but we need an emissary, a go-between, someone from your planet. That is what Harry wants to talk to you about, but I will let him explain it to you." I'm starting to feel better about being here. As we walked the sun crept up to peek over the horizon, and brought more of the island into focus—Wow—I didn't know who these aliens were, but they sure could cook. They took a paradise and made it a storybook paradise. We passed by another small building, turned a corner, and headed out onto the tarmac. It was just one big flat piece of, … well, it looks like cement? Scanning up and out, there it was, looming large was the spaceship from first contact. I had to pause for a moment. It was all catching up to me. Perhaps this was too much too soon—I got a queasy feeling in my gut, and bent forward.

"Are you OK, John?" asked Arlen.

"Yes, just give me a second." Was this more than I could take? Unable to come to terms with the enormity of my situation, my cognitive mind shut down, and my primitive brain took over. I became like a zombie, a walking brain dead zombie. To close down was the only way I could precede. Imagine you're a caveman, and you are suddenly transported forward in time, and deposited on a present-day New York City street. How would you feel at that moment? Doubled over in fear I would imagine. Perhaps it was my rational brain telling my primitive mind that its *Fight or Flight* response won't work in this situation. That I was trapped, and there will be no escape. Then a gentle and caring hand touched me on the middle my back. Empathy, human type empathy, from beings from another world?

"John, you're going to be alright," he said. "This must be a lot for you take in." An understatement on his part. Then Arlen related to me, "On our way here to your planet, we had made the mistake of thinking your race was more advanced than you are. We only had your transmissions to rely on." Some truth was coming through now. "If we had known?" Then he stopped talking. Not wanting to consider what I had just heard, I put it in the vault—I'll deal with it later.

The enormity of my situation was getting to me, humans and aliens together; they seem so similar to us of thought and action? Unlike Vulcan's, they do appear to have emotions? After a long moment, I straightened up, and we continued our walk over to the Val. It wasn't far, only about two hundred yards farther.

At the ship, I noticed that her hull had a slight blue tinge. I hadn't noticed that before. There are no noticeable cuts in the skin for doors or windows—as before nothing."

"How do we get in, Arlen?"

"Let's take what you would call an elevator. I'll call it down." From the left side of the belly of the of the great ship, and towards the middle, a circular cut took shape. It opened up, and a section of the hull dropped down in front of us. What waited in front of me was a small five foot in diameter elevator. It was suspended by four solid strands or cables which looked to be made of clear plastic. Only three of its sides were enclosed by a cross bar to provide safety."

"Shall we get on?"

Arlen led the way. I followed. Once we were on the lift, it began to rise. I wondered if Jonah was this nervous. Momentarily, we would be swallowed by the great beast—gulp. As we entered I noticed ships outer skin, or hull, and remarked, "It is a rather thick hull, is it not?" I'd never been a geek trekkie, so I didn't know about hull thickness. The hull looked to be three feet thick.

"It looks thick to you?" asked Arlen. Clearly, we were not yet on the same page.

The lift continued up, and didn't stop in the first room, but continued right on through one room, or deck, and then through another two, before stopping in a large room, which seemed to me to be near the center to the ship. Odd, when we got there, there was no lift to exit, its supports and cross bars simply lowered to dissolve and become part of the floor. "That was a neat trick," I thought. I recognized this huge room; I had seen the aliens in it on first contact.

I scanned around the room, and there he was, the man, or uh, alien, I met on first contact. He was standing over by the same three aliens I had seen before, and there is the one who half waved at me. Their captain had an imposing air about him. He was perhaps a few inches shorter that Arlen, but by his manner seemed more serious and threatening. I could tell this alien meant business. He turned to face me and said,

"Good morning, John, I'm Captain Harry." Then the cadets, as they were called, followed suit, only in chorus—"morning John."

"Uh, yes. Good morning to you all." Was all I could utter. Now that I have a better sense of the perspective of them, and their ship, I can see that they are much larger and taller than in my first assessment, and that slightly blue hue to their skin was unmistakable—yes, aliens all—no doubt about it. Ok brain, calm, calm. I don't know if I am to peruse around, don't want to get zapped for seeing anything secret, not that I could possibly understand any of this.

Then Harry mentioned, "John, you look tired, up all night were you? Perhaps Arlen's driving last night is to blame? Why don't you join us in our morning ritual? … We like to have a drink each morning. I find it a real pick-me-up. Here, I'll get you a cup." Harry moved over to what looked to be a wet bar area off to the right side of the consoled end of this large room and picked up some cups which are full of? … "This is what you might call a mixture of fruits blended into a liquid with a few nutrients added in," he said.

"Nutrients?"

"Yes, we Breen find it quite stimulating. Here, drink up."

Thinking to myself, "Drink up? Is this it for me? Well, at least it wasn't grape colored."

Took a quick sip, then a couple of gulps, "Wow, this is quite tasty." And it was. Way better that cool-aid. I immediately felt my energy coming back, even after a long night without sleep. That liquid must've been full of cocaine?

"That was very good Harry, thank you. May I call you Harry?"

"We are pretty much all on a first-name basis around here, John. I like it better that way. … This is what we call the situation room. This is where you saw us last week at our two species' first contact. You might say it is the ship's bridge. We call it the ICC." The room looked more like an empty hall with a broad desk-shaped control center shoved at one end. I made it to be twenty feet tall and wide, and forty feet long. The walls were blank—well not blank, just unadorned. There were no pictures, no windows, no furniture, or other furnishings that would scream of anything humanly recognizable. But they did appear to be covered in something hi-tech. They looked to be alive in a way, like being inside of a high tech computer screen with a brilliant blue wavy screensaver raining down all around.

"Mr. Harry?"

"Just, Harry, will do."

"Harry, I don't see much in the way of controls—you know, flashing lights, beeping noises, and all? How do you run the ship from in here?"

"Ah, you mean like on the bridge of the Enterprise. Beautiful ship, by the way. We thought it was an actual functioning spaceship you built—silly us. No—it's not like the enterprise. We run most functions here through interactive holograms. The cadets here have the job of bringing up holograms, or other screen types, like the one you saw last week. Cadets." Harry called to the cadets, they touched something on their console, and up came the large TV screen at the other end of the room. The one on which I saw the helicopters. "There, that is one type of screen, and depending on the situation, we can get quite a few of them going at one time. If you decide to stick around, you may get to see some of them in action?" The ICC would be some trekkies wet dream, but I had never been into such, plus this was all way above my science quotient. Mulling my situation over in my head I thought they might have kidnapped the wrong man.

"Harry," I uttered, "let me tell all of you how sorry and ashamed I am for our government's actions last week."

"We got off to a poor start didn't we?"

"And if there is something I can do, I don't know what, but if there is anything I can do to ease things over?"

Harry cuts my spiel short to say, "Perhaps so, John. Arlen explained to you that we would like to have you be our emissary. We can talk about what all that will entail, plus, contrary to the headlines of many of your world's newspapers, and yes, we do read them, we won't be staying here on your planet for more than three months. We are not conquerors. We have a schedule to keep..." Before he could finish his thought all hell broke out in the ICC. A loud alarm sounded, and I saw several red lights at the cadet's control stations begin blinking. Suddenly a large video screen appeared on the side wall right in front of us.

"Captain, we have a contact," yelled Heenon. "Submerged vessel on a direct course. She is carrying nuclear weapons, sir."

"Let me see it." On the side wall screen was an overlay map of the island and surrounding seas out to about two hundred miles. To the north and west of the island I saw something being tracked, and its track led directly to the island. The object was outlined in red? I would learn later this signified a threat level; with red being of serious concern. I guess the color red is a universal danger sign.

Harry called out, "Give me a closer look." Now all I saw on the screen was a half-mile of level empty ocean. Then Harry turned and stared coldly at the cadets, his hands were held close over his chest with fingers splayed as he meshed them together several times. His lips were pursed, and he had a bit of an angry look on his face.

Then the cadets in chorus murmured, "Oops, switching to 3D tactical, sir." So they make mistakes? Huh. The bland ocean surface view on the screen changed into a tactical representation, a slice through the ocean if you will, showing the object of concern. Spectacular graphics resolution, I might add. A submarine was clearly visible, and it appeared as though it were floating in air—I could even see its propellers moving. This was a real time representation of the submarine carrying nuclear weapons, and it caused quite an urgency on the Val.

Harry yelled, "Kill the alarms, please! Heenon, prepare a probe." Heenon was the cadet who had waved at me on first contact.

"Probe already prepared, Captain."

"Very well, send it on its way then."

I hear an unusual sound like something being launched or fired from the ship. At the far end of the room another screen popped up. It was an external view of the Val sitting on the tarmac. What I just saw was a small ball of white fire, perhaps three feet in diameter, erupt from the ship's hull. The view on the main sidewall screen widened, and we watched as the probe tracked on course toward the sub. Somehow they were able to visually follow their probe to its target. Its speed was fantastic. Mere seconds passed before it entered the waters near the sub, which was still some two hundred miles away. It made a surprisingly small splash on hitting the water's surface. At that speed any solid object should have blown apart. I watched as it continued on and appeared to impact the vessel up front on the nose. There was no explosion. I was expecting to see some fireworks. What had just happened?

The Shark—an attach class sub, was currently running at a depth of 450 feet, and was on a mission approved by the President of the United States, and the Pentagon. As part of a top-secret mission, the sub's name, her home port, and the names of the captain and crew were left unlisted—an extraordinary move given the annals of our military's history. The Shark carried SLBM cruise missiles, in this case special—which meant nuclear. The Pentagon, following General Bradley's Alien Contact Protocol, had cracked up this idea to nuke the aliens, and sold it to the President. They wanted to get them while they were all together on the island. "Did they even know, or care, that I was here also?"

Their plan, approach the island stealthily, and without notice, launch a cruise missile loaded with a nuclear warhead to be detonated over the island killing all the aliens. One should question why our military felt it necessary to destroy the aliens in the first place. Was this paranoia on our part? Who felt so threatened, they felt it right to take such drastic action? And now I was stuck smack in the middle of it. Without knowing it, the stealthy sub was being tracked by the Breen, who had just launched a probe to intercept the sub and determine her capabilities— or so I thought.

Sonar tracking officer—"Bridge, Sonar, object in the water—its cavitating—no, that's, that's impossible."

"Sonar, Captain, what is it?"

"There is no time, sir. Contact in three, two, one" Not knowing what the object was the sonar officer only reported what he heard, which was an object entering the water, and heading at an extremely high rate of speed on a collision course with the sub. Such an event would frighten any submariner. Even torpedoes, the usual sub-killer, only travel at best 60 miles per hour. An object traveling at hundreds of miles per hour under water was, until recently, unheard of.

The sonar feed was piped aloud on the bridge. There was the terrifying sound of a high speed object vaporizing water in front of it as it traveled on a collision course. And then it hit. Nothing, no explosion, not even a thump. But something did happen, an electrical discharge swept from the sub's nose through to the rear, shocking anyone in contact with the hull. Stumped, the ship's captain ordered,

"All stop. Sonar what the hell was that?"

"I have no idea, sir."

"That's not good enough mister. Get me answers."

"Yes, sir."

"All stations, report in. COB-get a detail together and sweep the boat for damage."

"Bridge, Sonar?"

"Sonar, aye?"

"Captain, plotting the object's course backwards, it appears to have come straight from the island, sir."

"So they fired at us. But what? And they know we are here—the surprise is lost."

"Stations throughout the ship are reporting to have experienced slight electrical shocks, sir." Perplexed, the subs captain ordered, "Forget the usual channels, get me the Pentagon directly. I want to talk with Admiral Givens." The sub's commander had no idea that his vessel was just infected with a Breen probe, and that currently the entire ship was being scanned, and each and every detail, including what was being said, was being passed on to the aliens back on Harry's Island.

Back on the Val

"Data on the sub is starting to come through, Captain. I'll put it up on the sidewall screen. Vessel is an attack class submarine, American flag. All vital data have been acquired. I'm putting up a schematic view. Oh, there, look." said Heenon. The schematic view of the sub clearly shows all the decks and rooms of the ship. In particular, in the missile room, four missile tubes were outlined, two were flashing in red.

"Nuclear weapons confirmed, Captain. Mega-ton range. Scanning her computers for additional information. This could take a while."

"Our overhead security web will protect us from any weapons launch, but I don't want them getting closer," said Harry reassuringly. "I'm going over there. Let's have a talk with their Captain, and I want to have a good look at that ship. I love museum artifacts."

"What the hell does he mean he's going over there?" I asked myself. Arlen, who had been standing behind me and to my left in an entry room area, stepped over to me, and forgetting that I was a human, whispered, "John. You are really going to enjoy what is coming next." There were other crew members coming into the ICC now. I could sense their excitement building, but I am surrounded by Breen. I'm standing deep inside enemy controlled territory, and I have never felt so short. "Is it too late to go back to the comfort of my desk job?"

Harry moved to the center of the room. Heenon touched an icon on his control panel, and what looked to be some sort of, well, I want to say a body suit began to grow on him. Starting at the floor it continued to grow all the way up to cover his entire body. Once he was completely covered, it started to glow—like the way an induction field makes a fluorescent tube glow. Then I heard Harry say, "Ready." The cadets tapped some icons on their consoles. All of the walls in this large room came alive. It was like being sucked inside the glass panel of a television screen when it is on. Harry was glowing; the blue rain screensaver walls of the ICC were crawling with energy. Then I heard Heenon say, "Turning on now, captain." There was a bright flash. The next thing I know, I was standing on the bridge of the submarine. At that moment the meaning and purpose of this entire room donned on me. It was all one giant hologram projector, and the Breen can interact with it. However, I wasn't a participant, just a spectator, and I wasn't really on the bridge of the other ship, neither was Harry. The images were being transmitted, real time, from the probe on the submarine, and it was Harry, dressed in some sort of interactivity suit, for want of a better name, who was directing it. A two way self-guided holographic projector—fascinating.

I could clearly see Harry, or the image of him, standing on the bridge of the sub. It was startling and confusing, and took some getting used to in order to separate out what or where I, or he, actually was. His avatar on the sub at first glance looked so real. On second inspection you could make out the ghostly glow hanging off it like a saint with a halo. He was standing still, for the moment, with his hands crossed. Then a crewman on the sub, sensing something, turned, we heard him yell out, "Captain, look!" At that, all eyes on the sub's bridge turned. Harry, or the projection of Harry, faced the sub's Captain, and in an act of Breen solicitude asked, "Permission to come aboard, sir." Obviously, the Captain and his crew didn't find that funny, but back at the Val my alien friends were in stitches. I could see the humor in it, but still I was a bit confused as to his purpose? Was he mocking the Captain, or truly showing respect?

    The Captain of the sub ordered, "No one move, keep to your stations." After a brief pause, and having gathered the courage, he asked, "What, and who are you?"

    "My name is Harry. I am the Captain of what you call the alien spaceship."

    "You are not really here. This is some sort of visual representation?"

    "Yes, your science calls it a holographic projection."

    "But you are able to interact with us?"

    "Yes, I can see, hear, and touch; and what I touch I can sense the same as if I were actually there."

    "But that is not possible."

    "Well it is, this may be hard for you to accept now, but I assure you someday your scientists will discover how to achieve it. Shall we talk Captain?" One could not help feeling for the sub's personnel, being thrown into a situation far beyond their control, and having no choice but to yield to an alien's wishes.

    "What is it you wish to discuss?"

    "First, let me say you have a magnificent vessel. I have a fascination for all things old. We Breen are explorers like you. This vessel explores your planet's oceans much in the way we explore the cosmos. Kindred spirits we are Captain. I would appreciate a quick tour of your vessel?" Harry didn't need the tour, with the probe's data he could virtually recreate it here on the Val, but seeing something, touching something real has far greater appeal.

    "By all means Mr? How should I address you?"

    "Simply, Harry, will do."

    "Alright then, Harry, please follow me." From the bridge up front to the aft torpedo room, they toured the vessel for twenty tense minutes.

"Captain, I much appreciate the chance to talk with you, and to tour your magnificent ship. I hope in the following weeks you will come and join me as my guest on our Island. I would appreciate the opportunity to return the favor and let you have an inspection of our ship. However, first, let's be honest with each other. This is not just a ship of exploration is it? This is designed to primarily be a ship of war."

"Yes, we are primarily a ship of war."

"And we are aware that you were sent on a mission to destroy us with your nuclear weapons."

"I will not lie to you, Harry. I was given orders by my superiors. They expect me to follow them, or they will get someone else to do it."

"I respect your honesty, Captain. We know of your General Bradley's plot to have us blown up, as you say it. We came to Earth only to visit as friends, but we realize that at times first contacts between alien species can be dangerous, fraught with uncertainties and misconceptions. Why, take your Native American Indians and your early settlers, or the raiding bands of Goths as they swept across Europe. Your history is full of examples of bloody clashes between cultures. Fortunately, for you and I, no one has to die today. We can choose not to be hostile, to allow for time for our two species to get to know each other. Obviously, we are not going to let you bomb us, and I ask you to reverse your course, do not approach our Island."

"Harry, if our military feels you Aliens are a risk to our nation and to our world, then who am I, a lowly captain, to second guess them. I have been tasked by the President himself, and I have no choice but to follow orders."

"I had thought we could become friends rather

than foes Captain. Back at the island all of my crew, and Dr. Parker, are watching and listening to this intercourse. They are wondering why you want to kill them?"

"Could you fault a soldier for following orders?"

"Captain, I asked, and I think politely. If you do not turn around I will make an example of you and your President. Then the whole world will see the duplicity of your leaders. Your America will be shammed and shunned by the two hundred or so other nations on this planet. Many of this planet's leaders don't fear us, and are eager to make contact with us."

"Frankly, Harry, that is probably what scares America's leaders the most."

After a short pause Harry said, "I understand" …. then another pause while he thought a course of action, "Captain, tell your President this, we are going to be here on Earth for not longer than three months, and then we will be gone. Do not approach our island again with ships of war of any kind. To do so will have grave results."

A Lesson to Remember

"Heenon." The Breen were expecting the Americans to try an attack and had prepared a response. By simply uttering just his name, Heenon needed no further information, and touching one icon on his console he launched four large spheres. Off they sped directed at the submarine. Their speed again was fantastic. In only minutes they traversed the two hundred miles to the sub. I watched on the sidewall screen as they entered the ocean. The screen then turned to a tactical representation showing the probes track through the water, and then their impact with the submarine.

"Bridge, Sonar—tracking several large objects in the water, sir. One thousand yards, they are on a collision course, and closing extremely fast.

"I thought you said you were not here to destroy us, Harry? I thought you said you came in peace?"

"We did come in peace. Your actions alone are what lead to this, not ours."

"You're killing us won't help you make friends with Earth."

"Captain, a moment ago you were the one who was going to destroy us. At least meet your fate with a soldier's honor," said Harry. "Heenon, I'm going to disengage" And with that, the visage of Harry vanished from the sub commanders view.

"Bridge—Sonar, Contact in three, two, one..."

The submarine was in no danger of being destroyed. The Breen sent four unmanned probes called power pods. They attached themselves magnetically to the ship's hull. Two pods took up position aft, and two at the bow, and on either side. Harry wanted to make a statement of Breen superiority, and make an example of General Bradley; this was the perfect opportunity for both.

The lifting thrust of the power pods was nothing short of phenomenal. The sub was, in essence, grabbed by the four probes which took a hold, and slowly at first, drove it up from the ocean deep. Shortly the submarine broke the ocean's surface, and then it continued to be flown up into the sky. Their course was directly toward Washington DC, and back to the man who originally sent her on her mission to destroy the Breen. Inside the sub's crew were safe. At no time did the acceleration exceed safe levels for human beings, but it did get a little toasty inside. Due to the fantastic velocity the ships outer hull began to heat.

Like land based raids, which are watched and managed by military spy drones, this operation was being watched by satellites above. The Pentagon was expecting to see a mushroom cloud sprout over Harry's Island. They didn't. Our military was alerted that something had gone very wrong with the mission shortly after the sub broke the surface of the ocean. There was long range radar tracking, and it picked up the sub as it soared up into the sky. Its track was determined to be on a straight line to DC. As a precaution all government adjuncts were rushed into bomb shelters. Once the sub began to slow down it was surmised that the White House was the intended target, and the president was hurriedly ushered down to his bunker. The General, who refused to head to a bunker, heard about the crash via channels, and then the news feeds picked up on it. The story went viral around the world within a minute of the crash.

Harry ordered the submarine flown to Washington. There it was smashed into the White House; America's greatest symbol of freedom and stability. Photos of the nuclear attack sub sitting on top of a crumpled White House circulated worldwide. To other nations and peoples, the scene drew some laughs. For us here in the US the feeling was somewhat less humorous. This incident brought the secret and unilateral actions of the United States' attempt to use nuclear weapons to destroy the aliens to worldwide awareness. The failed attempt, now made public, drew the scorn of the whole world. Many leaders of governments and industry hoped for an opportunity to garner support and technology from the aliens. Aside from the obscene profits to be

made, Earth was in desperate need of new forms of
energy and food production. Dead, the aliens would
be of little help to anyone. It was just this rush to
gain advanced technology that General Bradley and
his ARC fought to prevent.

Because of this brutish action, the World would
now have to wait for the dust to settle, so to speak.
They all knew now where the aliens were. A UN
consortium surmised it best just let them alone for a
stretch of days. A wait and see strategy was put in
place. All nations were cautioned not to approach the
aliens or their island. After a while a dialogue would
be set up, and then our world's leaders and scientists
would have a chance to discuss peaceful relations
with them.

I don't know, how did your day go? Perhaps General
Bradley didn't know I was on the island. He wouldn't
have let me be vaporized, would he? I was awed by
my surroundings and the events which played out
right in front of me. The word stupefied doesn't even
come close to telling how I felt, and it would be
some time before I came down off my high. Inside
the ICC the Breen were all high fiveing each other.
As yet, I didn't fit in here, in apprehension I shrank
back against a wall. Shortly my eyes peered up to
see Arlen staring straight over at me. He slowly
approached and said, "John, didn't I tell you this was
going to be fun." I wasn't feeling the fun right then.
Sensing I was in some discomfort he suggested we
exit the ship and sit out beside the lagoon.
"Anything," I thought, "just get me the hell out of
here."

Arlen walked me out to the lagoon, and let me
sit alone on the beach for a while to sort things out.
Harry's Island contained a paradox. It was a place of

beauty and solitude, and at the same time, a place of great confusion. It was obvious that there was no way out of this. My own government wanted me dead. Even if I did go home I would surely be labeled a traitor for my involvement with the Breen, and either imprisoned for life, or better for me, hung. No, there was no way to step back, only to go forward. I sat alone brooding for about twenty minutes, then Harry walked over and sat next to me. We talked for a while about various things of not great importance, then both Arlen and Hippee came over and joined us. The four of us just sat and yakked. Just regular chit chat among friends and with no obvious social gap. Then Arlen said he'd offer me a cold beer, but that the island had none, and that that was a problem. I agreed. "Perhaps we should make a run to the store," I suggested.

"That is part of what we want to talk to you about, John," said Harry. "We will go to the store, as you say, if you will go along with us?" That is when I got it. They needed me. When you are alone in a hostile territory, and everyone wants you dead, any friend will do. They truly needed my help. We were all castaways trapped on a small island in an alien and hostile world. Together, if we helped each other, we would survive. So, right then I made my commitment to these beings from outer space, "If you guys fly, I'll buy."

16:

Paradise, Not

Day nine, March 3rd

My second day in paradise started well. Like being on vacation, I woke when I wanted to, then showered, got dressed, and casually exited my new home to meet the day. Strangely, my mind was a blank; no thoughts remained of the previous day's calamity, or of my unearthly captors. I was all alone. The morning was warm, as warm as it had been all night. During the day, the sun's ample rays heat the ocean waters. Then as the sun's orange glow fades down into the darkest blue of night this trend reverses, and the heated waters then give up their gentle warmth till the morrow when this convivial dance will repeat. Outside I feel no wind on my skin, and all I can hear is the gentle lapping of waves on the shore, their echo so hypnotic that to languor here is to lose all earthly cares. There is a half-mile stretch of shoreline to the south of the island that is not under the protective weather dome. Before having breakfast I decided to stroll there. So far this morning I haven't seen any other people, or Breen that is. Looking, searching, up and down the shore, I see no one. I explored for perhaps an hour, just walking barefoot on warming sands with only washed up coconuts and hermit crabs for company. "Am I all alone here on this Isle?" I ask myself, pretending in my mind to be John Crusoe, castaway, lost for many years on some deserted isle. Then reality yelled out, "John, we've been looking for you. Come and join us for breakfast." It was Hippee inviting me to eat. Damn, damn, damn, I was having such a nice dream.

"So, Hippee, where is everyone?"

"We had an early crew meeting this morning. You were invited. Did you forget?"

"Oh, sorry, it did slip my mind. Hope I didn't miss anything important?"

"Nothing we can't go over with you. Come on let's get you some food."

There were no cafes here on the island. No small French patisseries. That would have to change. For now there was only the mess on the Val where I had gone to eat yesterday, which is where we all ate. Hippee had a menu translated into human for me. Interesting looking food if you can call it that. The Breen have been eating something they call synthfood. That is primarily what they eat when off world and out in the deeps of space. I learned that they had fresh food stores when they started out to planet Ga'alle'een, but they ran out two months into their trip. So the Breen are either poor planners, or big eaters. From what I have seen so far I am going with big eaters. Now, all that they had left to eat was the synthfood. It was not bad tasting, but a far cry from the good-looking *Star Trek* type food.

We entered the ship's mess. Only Harry and Arlen were still in here eating.

"Ah, John, come on over and let's talk." said Harry. "Here, I have something for you."
Harry hands me this little device hanging on a chain. I don't know, kind 'a looked like a religious charm. "What is it?"

"If you will put this around your neck, and keep it with you? Remember the recording device I gave you yesterday, the one that you said looked like a clipboard computer? Well, if that is too cumbersome to carry around with you all the time, this little device will record everything for you, and send it into the other device automatically."

"So it is a tracking device?"

"Tracking device? No, just a convenience. You can wear it anywhere. In the ocean, take it down the water slide, wherever you want to go."

"And right now it is recording what we are saying?"

"All that and more. You will see. Go ahead and have your breakfast now. By the way, John, any ideas what you want to do first today?"

"A tour of this spaceship would be nice."

"Certainly, we were just headed outside, but I will ask a couple of my crewmen to come in and help guide you on your tour. Then we can talk some more later."

I always found Harry to be firm and tactful with subordinates, but friendly. In fact, I was beginning to gain a sense of group think with all the Breen. You didn't get that with General Bradley. He barked orders, and you were expected to follow them. With the Breen, there was more of an esprit de corps.

Tour of the Val

As I finished with my morning meal, Booh'raan and Le'eennon came in and said they would accompany me a tour of the Val. Booh'raan was a tech in Dr. Who's Terra Division, and Le'eennon was a cadet, one of the trio. They became my shadows. Never for a moment did they leave me alone. There was very little conversation between us as I snooped around going from one deck to another, walking down each hallway, poking my head into every door. Many days later I would learn that my escorts weren't so much trying to keep me from escaping, no, my tagalongs were just bored, and looking for new companionship and enjoying the curiosity of walking a new pet. My recon of the Val was vital. I thought the intell I gathered might be of use to the General, if I were to ever escape.

Wanting to get a feel for her, I started my tour in the ICC. Most of the crew were outside enjoying the tropical sun. Except for my two shadows, the rooms and halls were empty and echoed our footfalls. Leaving the ICC, I then went upstairs. Booh'raan had mentioned that there was a meeting place up top known as the observation lounge, and that this was where the crew met to watch our old movies on their trip to Earth. Curious, I wanted to see it, but when we got there the lounge/movie theatre was just a void. By the curvature of the ceiling it was obvious that we were at the upper most part of the hull, which in my opinion hung way too low. It was not a large room, perhaps the size of a tennis court, and like all other rooms I had seen so far, this one had plain flat unadorned walls. I further noticed it contained no windows with which to look out from. I had half expected to find a wet-bar here, perhaps tended to by robot mixologists, and windows all about offering a superb view and perspective of the island, but there was no bar and no robots. Disappointed, I pressed on.

To regain my bearings I decided to return to the ICC? The best I could make of the ship so far was that the ICC is centrally located, with the science and engineering departments located below it. Other than a few blinking lights the ICC was dead quiet. With my escorts in tow, I headed below decks to have a look into the science departments. Rooms on the Val like any modern earth room have doors that open and shut, but these slide sideways, and to open them you press a wall plate. Entering, I found Planetary Genomics and Solar System Ecology likewise devoid of Breen. Fantastic places to visit, I guess, if you're into science fiction. I'm not, and had no idea what I was looking at. "Just science labs with high-tech tools," I thought. We then left and walked on. A deck below I came across the Terranomics Department. When I reached to open the entry door, my two escorts grabbed me on the shoulder and suggested that I not go in there. In a jocular tone I said, "Why, be there some vicious ogre inside?" The two Breen made quick eye contact with each other, then uttered in unison, "Yes, an ogre there is. That is Dr. Who's department. Few wish to enter. Especially not short-lifers." Huh. Short-lifers, now that was a new term I hadn't heard before.

Next, down into the belly of the beast, I went. The aft half of the bottommost floor is devoted entirely to recreation. Half of it was divided up into other rooms, or stalls, each about fifteen feet to a dimension, and all of them open to the hallway that ran down the middle. Their walls did not reach to the ceiling, but stopped halfway. The ceiling here was at least thirty feet tall. I asked Booh'raan what these cubicles were used for, "They are individual holo rooms. We can show you how to use them later, if you like." The other half of this great room was left open. The floor space was filled with many different and interesting looking gym apparati, that I would just have to return here and give them all personal inspection.

The Val was a huge ship, full of a maze of turns, a confusion of floors, and blind hallways. There was no way one person could explore this ship in one day, or a week, for that matter. I had been on several large cruise ships. The last one had a crew of one thousand and over two thousand passengers. The Val is every bit as large, but has a crew of only sixteen? Why so few? Where had all the others gone? At about nine hundred feet long and well over two hundred feet in diameter I worried that I might be nothing more than an irritant to this leviathan, causing her to spasm and suck me farther into her bowels, there to die, and my decomposing corpse to become her food?

There were many mysteries surrounding this ship. Her size for one, how could something of that bulk fly, and the Breen feel this behemoth is too small? Does not compute, and what is it with the interior sterility. What, my Spartan friends don't like to hang art? What about pictures of where they have been, or tributes to friends, family, and home worlds? Then I remembered, I was on a spaceship, one that traveled the cosmos, and at fantastic velocities. Nothing loose and hanging would survive. But what about high-tech pictures built right into the bulkheads? Something else, for sure, was going on here.

My tour of the Val so far has left me more confused than when I started. I asked Booh'raan about letting me see the engine room. He replied,

"There is no engine-room, John. At least not like in your *Star Trek* movie. Our mode of propulsion is built into the ship's hull." Not what I had expected to hear. I needed time to think about that one, and now, not only confused, but profoundly lost, I asked my Breen pals to lead me on out of there. Booh'raan sensing my confusion said, "John, if you are sincerely interested in the Val's design, I can get you a holo cube of her for you to study." Seeing how there weren't any arrows or exit signs hanging in the halls, I told him that would be a great help. I decided to put my tour of the ship on hold for now and exited the Val.

The most striking feature of this island and its many improvements is the weather dome—an architectural wonder. As I stepped outside the Val I looked up to see its sky high spars stretching across the expanse of our island home. This tiny spec in the ocean is only about a mile in diameter, and is shaped like a giant comma. The dome, looking like a huge oblong tortoise shell, covers the dot of the comma. Spaced along the northern shore, and starting several hundred yards in from the ocean, five giant fingers rise out of the sands. They shoot straight up perhaps five hundred feet then arch to meet up in the middle with their counter parts from the south. The cover is open at two ends; to the east, where the tarmac begins, the opening is large enough for a plane to fly through. My visage west is framed by the mountainous high volcanic cinder cone turned water slide which juts up just past the top of the end of the dome—all in all, it is quite striking, and I am awed. The Val, even with all her marvels, pales in comparison to the scale of the weather shield above my head. And they built this in a day?

The fingerlike supports of the dome are tied

together by five lateral beams on either side. Translucent webbing fills the interstices of the frame, and allows plenty of the sun's radiance to filter through to heat and light our play land. The protective cover continues down to stop just short of the tops of the palm trees which engrove this island. The shields simple design wouldn't be out of the ordinary, if it weren't for the immensity of it all. Inside this giant shell I felt safe and secure. Like returning to the womb, I was enclosed in warmth and kept safe from all out-world dangers, and eager to join my friends in their reverie.

"Booh'raan, what type of material is the dome made of."

"Primarily carbon taken from the air, John."

"That is fantastic. And you turned that there volcano into a waterslide. Is there a way to get to the top of it? I would like to have a look around from above."

"Of course. We have a rapid rise elevator there at the base beside the lagoon. Do you want to go and grab your shorts first?"

"Shorts? I'm not coming down that slide. No way!" My two guides just stood silent for a moment, staring at me, childishly blinking their naked eyelids. Not wanting to totally insult my hosts, I said, "Well, it does sound like fun. I will try it, but not today." By their expressions I don't think my tagalongs believed me.

"Come along, John," said Booh'raan, "let's take the elevator to the top, if you like, you can take it back down." He sounded like he was trying to guilt me into going down the waterslide.

I took the Breen to be much the same as us emotion wise, as though feelings are universal. Well, even lesser animals, in particular, dogs, seem to share emotions with us. But as for their childish looks? I am beginning to suspect a ruse is being played upon me. They all look alike. I don't mean they are clones, they just appear the same. Putting their totally hairless looks aside, and giving the differences in height, body structure, and head shape, and facial expressions, my Breen friends all appear to be the same age, about thirty-five years old. You have a thirty-five year old cadet, a thirty-five year old captain, and thirty-five year old senior scientists. Their similarity in age has to be due to more than diet and exercise. Had they found the holy grail of genetic research—eternal youth?

The sands of the lagoon beach lay only two hundred yards in front of us. Judging by the noise coming from that direction many of the crew are there and frolicking about. Just then, I hear a loud swhoosh. I count one, two, three, four, five, and then hear a body breaking kasplash. Someone had just come down the slide, caught air for five seconds, and then splashed into the cool waters of the lagoon. How these beings can take that kind of punishment is beyond me.

We approached the lagoon, it was just past mid-day. The sun was high up, shining through, and even with the protection of the dome I could feel it heating my skin. The smell of tropical flowers and hot sand seasoned with a salty ocean spray floated in the air. Arlen and Hippee and several others of the crew were sitting in lawn chairs beachside. They peered straight ahead as though zoned out on something. Near continual use of the waterslide provided entertainment. The last two hundred feet of the slide was a straight run down to the lagoon, but the slide ended some twenty feet in the air and with a slight upward bend. The faster you barreled down, the farther and higher you shot up and out into the lagoon. And the harder you smashed into the water. They made a competition on who could sail the farthest.

The rubble at the base of the volcano that faces the Towers Hotel has been cleared away, or transformed, into a rock outcrop, or low cliff, which runs along the west side of the beach area for several hundred yards. The lagoon, shaped somewhat like a long peanut abuts up to this cliff, and just off to the right where it ends, Dr. Who, had an elevator shaft built into the hillside. The Breen do nothing halfhearted, but to excavitate an elevator shaft inside solid rock, in but a few days, not to minimize the other reformations here is in a word, mysterious.

The three of us got into the lift, and as spacious inside as any modern convenience to be found in any tall skyscraper, we rapidly ascended through the dark tube hollowed from ancient basalt. The speedy ride up would have been worth paying admission for, but the view at the top of this hopefully extinct volcano left me dizzy and gasping for air. We were standing on the pinhead sized top, and well above the sky dome. At the top there were no safety ropes or restraining devices of any sort. I could see forever, but one fainting miss step and you would either tumble down the treacherous eroded west slope, and to your death in the ocean below, or, and no safer choice, slip and fall into the half pipe of the water slide.

I managed to find the exact center of this hilltop platform for no other reason than fear. Straining to stand, first I stretched my head skyward to sneak a view across the dome. I didn't feel secure enough to stand erect. Hiding my terror, I hobbled over to the slides entry port. There I steadied myself against the top edge of the tube. Before I could reassure myself that fear of heights is natural, Booh'raan and Le'eennon pushed past me nearly knocking me over. They boarded the slide and begged me to join them. My chattering teeth bid them goodbye. I watched as they zipped down the chute before hitting the first wicked twist and then disappeared. Now utterly alone and too scared to hear their yells of joy, the reality of my situation loomed heavy in the pit of my gut. There were only two ways back down—take the slide, or return in the elevator.

From my perch I could follow their yells as they zigged and zagged down and around. I had watched crew members zipping and yelling as they flowed down the slide from the vantage point of the lagoon beach. How safe it appeared from down there. The slide wends its way back and forth down the hills face. On three of the sharp turns the water dumps into a large pool etched into the hillside. Steam bubbles up from holes in the bottoms which amass into artificial clouds that hang on the mountainside. These hot tubs were a really fantastic addition, and in the weeks to follow became great places for me to soak and socialize. But right now I was still green. My problem, once you start down on the slide, there is no turning back. There are no easy slopes home. This slide ends with a death run and a twenty foot drop. I had to get down from here. Doubled over from adrenaline shock, I slowly, surely, shuffle my feet over to the elevator, got in, and descend down to the safety of the beach. That was the end of my island exploration for that day.

For the rest of the afternoon I was satisfied to socialize lagoon side where I discussed getting supplies to the island with Harry and Arlen. Harry's grand design was to turn the island into a destination resort, a place where Earth's leaders could come and visit. This intrigued me, and I agreed to help. Later in the afternoon the three of us met in the ICC. Heenon had found something of interest on the internet that he wanted to show us.

He found a store in northern Australia called Jungle Jim's Outback Trading Post and Cargo Shipping. It was the perfect solution. This was a whole emporium, all in one town, and only one thousand miles away. Though his stock on hand was mostly clothing, camping, and mining gear, he could pick up supplies from elsewhere, and then deliver them to our island. We arranged to fly there the next day. And I thought, "Wow, a trip to Australia. A place I had always wanted to go. What's better, there would be no airfare expense, no hassle in getting a rental car. We would fly right in, pick up what we wanted, and then leave promptly. The only snag in the plan, I would be traveling with aliens who were quite tall, and had a slight blue tinge to their skin. Perhaps they can be disguised as tourists?"

Next I mentioned to Harry that if he was going to have guests, he would need to have a restaurant.

"You are right John," he said. "So let's build a restaurant. Let's go and see Dr. Who right now."

"What, me, go into Terranomics? After all the rumors I have heard of his temper?"

"You'll be alright. Just don't ask boring questions."

Finally I had a chance to tour Terranomics. Upon entering, fearful I might get my head barked off; I hid behind Harry's tall physique. What I encountered inside was a baffling array of sci-fi fantasy machines I couldn't begin to describe. Terra was vast. It occupied two decks and stretched the full length and width of each. However its true mystery lies with Dr. Who and his small band of techs that ran this entire department. Dr. Who was standing at a work counter, and beckoned us over.

"So you boys need a restaurant," he said. "Here, look in this catalogue and show me what you want." He showed us this flat clip board sized device. Harry touched a button turning it on. A holographic representation of an actual restaurant appeared above the device. "Dear god," I exclaimed, "it is a virtual catalogue with holograms for pages." Harry scrolled through checking out the options. This was remarkable, there were hundreds of layouts of different types of restaurants to choose from. The astonishing high-tech toys these people have just won't end.

"Yes it is," said Dr. Who, "and for this trip I brought catalogues like this one on just about everything. These eateries are from various planets, and quite similar to those you would find here on earth, and of course, many are found on Pleasure Planet. Just select what you think you are going to need, and I can have it built."

After thumbing through the holographic catalogue for a while, Harry and I decided on two different restaurant styles. One offered formal dining and one was a fast food court style eatery. "Excellent choices," said Dr. Who. "They will be built out beside the Towers close to the lagoon, but not until tomorrow. It will take that long to produce and program the nanites."

"Fascinating," I said, "constructing, or growing things, with nanites. How is that possible?"

"Do you have a question, John?" asked Dr. Who. Remembering Harry's earlier warning not to ask dumb questions, I wasn't sure if I should continue. I sensed that Dr. Who was trying to engage me in conversation, but with only two days under my belt, I didn't feel I had earned the right to pry, so I begged off. "No, no, I'm just flabbergasted. This will be something to see. I can hardly wait."

"Fine then," he said, "if you two will leave, I have work to do."

Task accomplished, we hurriedly left Terra, and spent the late afternoon hours lolling about the lagoon beach. The sun filled day kept us entertained, but at dusk the harmony died. Something was missing. The pulse of my fellow castaways was not upbeat. The joyous levity which hours earlier had echoed across the sands went silent. Precious shore leave was being squandered. It pained me to see my friends so dour. I suggested a twilight lighting ceremony to pick things up. I suggested we light some fires and in a rash built some Tiki Torches and planted them around the lagoon. We all gathered and lit the torches, but they didn't have the desired effect, and the party died as soon as it had begun. "That was it," I protested. "Enough already, we cannot go on like this without adult beverages and real food. Tomorrow we are going shopping."

As members of the crew filtered off to their quarters for the night, Harry stopped me and asked how my experience with the Breen had been so far, when it hit me, crap. I hadn't called Sherry in days. With all the excitement, I just forgot. She must be going out of her mind with worry. Does she know the General tried to blow me up?

"Harry, I just remembered that I haven't been in touch with my lover in days. She must be quite worried?"

"John, have you tried your cell phone."

"No, but I doubt I could get reception way out here."

"That's OK," he said. "Heenon has a way to hook you up over the internet. Something he calls a VoIP. In the morning I will have him install an application so you can use VoIP on your cell phone. You are not a prisoner here John, feel free to call anyone at any time."

What?—call anyone? Say anything? Are the Breen that cavalier? Are they that certain about their situation, or am I not smart enough, not important enough to be considered a threat? I slept on those words of Harry's and the possible options they could mean. Probably should check the box at the bottom on this one—all of the above.

With the beauty for this island, and strangeness of the situation, I had forgotten there was still intergalactic brinksmanship going on, and that I was just a pawn on a much larger game board. However, neither Harry, nor any of the Breen were insensitive to personal matters, and like brothers, they would find ways to assist me in my love affair.

* * * * * *

Back in Washington DC
With the utter failure of step three of *The Plan*, General Bradley was in a meeting with his old friend, Admiral Arnie Johnson, a member of the soon to be defunct Alien Response committee,

"I tell you Arnie, I hear what these aliens are selling, but I am not buy'n it. They are up to something. Don't know what yet, but my nose keeps twitching."

"You always did have a nose for things Rudy. Why don't you give the President a call and see if he can put us back in the loop?"

Still spying on Bradley, Heenon made a private call to Harry, "Harry, you wanted me to let you know when the General made contact with his President."... Harry, one deck below said, "I'll be right there."

Bradley put his call in to the President, "Yes Rudy, how can I help you?"

"Sir, how is your new home?"

"Deplorable."

"Ah, Camp David can't be that bad. How soon will the White House be done?"

"The White House, not a chance, and with my numbers in the toilet, I'll be out of here in just a few short months. Perhaps the White House will be done in time for the next president to take office."

"Sir, I just have a bad feeling in my gut about these aliens. I know they are up to something, we just can't tell what"

"Are we on a secure line, Rudy?"

"Yes sir, and I have my office swept daily, and this is a secure and scrambled line. Couldn't be safer."

"I understand that you don't trust these aliens, Rudy. A lot of us don't, but what can I do? My butt is still in a sling after the submarine incident. Even a president must answer to someone."

"We need to keep on top of this, sir."

"You mean, get someone inside? How about that Parker fellow?"

"No, not Parker, he is too much of an anarchist. I sensed that about him first time we met. What's more, I fear he has gone over to the alien's side now. I have someone else in mind who could gain an easier access to the situation."

"Oh, do you have a name for me?"

"Sherry Lawson, sir."

"What, your secretary?"

"Longtime family friend and I put her to keeping an eye on Parker a month ago."

"God damn, Rudy. You're asking her to spy on her lover?"

"National security trumps puppy love in my book, sir."

"Rudy, I have the National Security Director here in my office. Let me put you on hold for a moment."

"Well, Dave, you heard him, what do you think?"

"The General does have a sense about things, and now because of our actions, we will most likely be cut out of access to any alien technology."

"Yes, you are right, but it was Bradley's fouled up sixth sense that got us into this problem to begin with."

"Nevertheless, having someone on the inside is always a good idea."

"One more incident and there's not a chance of my getting re-elected. Might be better if I sack the General, and come out saying the whole submarine incident was just a misunderstanding."

"What? Sack Bradley? He has longtime deep ties through multiple administrations, and remember he has headed up the ARC group for twenty years."

"And I'm a newbie. Yeah, you're right."

"Rudy, thanks for holding on the line. I appreciate your wanting to stay on top of things. I'll approve your plan to proceed with surveillance, and formulate some more options for me, but that's it. Take no overt actions against the aliens."

"Yes, sir. I understand, sir. Thank you for your

time."

"Tacit approvals only, take no overt action. Bloody damn politician worried only about his re-election. Couldn't give a damn about this country, only his own ass."

"Those are the times we are in Rudy. Take it, or leave it."

"I want to set up a full meeting of the ARC next Tuesday right here in my office."

Meanwhile, back onboard the Val, Harry and the Cadets were keen to Gen. Bradley's renewed attempts to harass them.

"Shouldn't we tell John about his lady friend spying on him?" asked Heenon.

"Tell him what, that humans can be duplicitous? No need to tell him something he already knows. No, let's keep quiet about this and just see where it leads. Good work Cadets. Keep monitoring the General."

* * * * * *

Earlier that morning in DC

Sherry Lawson, as well as the rest of the world, was quick to put it all together. While watching the television broadcasts of an American White House smashed by an American nuclear-armed submarine, well, it didn't take that much imagination to see who was behind it, and what their intentions were. She knew John had been taken by the aliens, and was on the island with them. Being kept out of the loop about the plan to use nuclear weapons, she felt cheated—as though she and John were being played.

Sherry confronted General Bradley in his office. "Uncle Rudy, how could you? You knew that John was on that island. What, you were just going to blow him up?" Then she stormed out of his office, left the Pentagon building, and went home. Shortly after she left, General Bradley had his aide drive him to her house where he apologized saying,

"I am sorry, Sherry, but national security is more important than any one person. You must understand that."

"Yes, I know, but there just has to be a better way?"

Always one to take full advantage, "Perhaps there is, the UN is setting up a committee to be prepared to meet with the aliens if and when they decide to talk again. I have no idea yet as to where the offices will be located, but some rumor has it that Rio is top of the list. I think that I could get you placed inside. There is a Professor Tynan who is to head it up, and he is an old friend of mine."

"Why Rudy, you never give up, do you?"

"Well, if the aliens do decide to talk with someone, we need to be apprised of who it is, and remember that Parker will probably be with them."

"Rudy, that's playing dirty."

"Sherry, this event is historic. Your country needs someone on the inside. The best person for that job right now is you."

"Rio, you say?"…..

17:

The Contamination

Friday, March 4th
Day 10

This is my third day as prisoner in paradise. I should
not feign being a captive though, for no bars prevent
me from leaving; only a thousand miles of shark
infested water. My jailers allow me to roam free, why
not, I am no threat to them. Yet, why should I
protest? A grander prison there could not be. All is
provided, the accommodations are lavish, the
scenery is profound, no curfew need I obey, and
there is no Ogreian cellmate to demand sexual
favors. I should yell loudly, "I have never been so
free." Thoughtfully, I contemplate that we
incarcerate all criminals on some far away tropical
isle, with guards as mates tending to the inmates
every imagined whim. But even paradise can become
a prison as Crusoe found out. In that respect, my
Breen friends are prisoners too. Which is curious,
with a spaceship at your disposal one would think

you could go anywhere; I sense a growing edginess'
in them. They long to spread out across our planet is
search of—they, we, are all explorers at heart.
Regardless, whether island, continent, or planet, the
restrictions of being Alien have forced us into exile,
but hopefully that will change today.

I was up early. The morning air today was warm
and laced with the perfume of the tropics. The sun
rose golden, freeing itself from its horizon-wide blue
captor. After breakfast I swam briefly in the lagoon
where the water is now kept hot-tub warm. The
island is a work in progress as each day these
master world-builders seek improvements and make
upgrades. Feeling a bit inferior, I need to find a way
to make my presence valuable to them.

Today I am going to lead my unearthly friends
on an away mission, one fraught with unusual and
intriguing problems. Our island home lacked modern
human niceties. Those things you might expect at
any travel stop—food and drink. In addition, we
needed maid service, a wait staff, cooks, etc.
Everything you need to make this world-class resort
operational. After pinpointing our tiny island on a
world map, we noticed the closest bastion of
civilization was Australia. For obvious reasons, we
couldn't pull into the local Wally Mart parking lot. We
chose a small town in the Northern Territories called
Brawley for no other reason than I liked the name.
With the use of the internet, Heenon was able to
locate a local store there. A place called Jungle Jim's,
which caught my eye. The store's proprietor, JJ also
ran an air cargo service—perfect. We will go to JJ's,
grab some of whatever we could, and then set up a
supply pipeline with him. All we lacked was a cover
story. Just before noon, the three of us, Arlen,
Hippee, and I, commandeered a skiff, and took off

for the land down under.

* * * * * *

With my prying eyes off the island Harry decided to give his Hoosenine Plan the go ahead. Everything to that end had already been prepared. Doctor Who was waiting in his lab. All Harry had to do was give him the final OK. Harry entered Terranomics,

"Well, Harry, do you still want to play god?" asked Dr. Who.

"It's not god I am playing doctor. We aren't exterminating this species, just giving them time and a chance to come to grips with living responsibly and sustainably."

"Yes, still I wonder if the universe meant for them to have a future? Shouldn't they have to struggle for survival like every other creature in the cosmos? You are playing favorites, of a sorts, now aren't you?"

"I concede to your point. However, I could equally say that our serendipitous meeting with these creatures was the universe's way of asking us to intervene."

"Very well, Harry. What about your new friend? Are you going to advise him of your actions?"

"No, I doubt he is ready for the truth, and I don't want to take the chance of alienating him. We'll wait for his trust in us to build further, then I will have to tell him." Commanders aren't supposed to show a lot of emotion, and neither did Harry. Whether he was troubled over his course of action or not, it didn't show, and up to this point he never mentioned having any misgivings about it to the crew.

Dr. Who, with the use of one of his futuristic

machines was able to produce a seeming never ending flow of baseball sized stealth probes—tens of thousands of them—inside each a vial full of Breen virus. The probes were programmed to fly to airports and large transportation hubs located around the world. They would also travel to our major population centers. There, undetected, they would release their payload—a few grams of liquid. The liquid with the virus in it would disburse to fall and make contact with common everyday things we touch. Our populations have never been more interconnected, and the virus was designed to take advantage of this. Once infected, travelers would surreptitiously spread it worldwide within a few days. We go out to eat, to shop, to socialize; and the virus spreads. We touch door knobs and toilet seats. We shake hands with our friends. We hug and kiss our lovers and family members; and the virus spreads. With every casual touch, a new person would be infected.

Outwardly, the virus caused no symptoms. You would never know you were infected, or that you were a carrier of a sinister and synthetic invader. Inwardly, it caused infertility in both sexes, and a lessening of the sex drive, especially in men. The Breen scientists did their math. They knew it would take roughly one year for the virus to reach 99.8 per cent of Earth's population, but this wasn't a common cold. You wouldn't catch it, ail for a week, and then get better. No, this bug was going to last 50 years, or more. Next year there will be few human babies born on our planet, and the year after that, none. From then on, there will not be a baby born on Earth for fifteen years.

Harry then advised Dr. Who to go ahead and unleash his virus. The probes were sent on their course. The sum total of this unparalleled action took him no more than two hours to complete. If we did question the Breen's mastery over us, this one contemnible act, so simple from their perspective, settled the matter. On the game board of life Mankind's stature tottered lower than that of a pawn—we had no move, no ploy, no en passant maneuver to even the match. Harry deigned to be doing humankind a favor; would the Hoosen ghosts imagine that favorably?

* * * * * *

Down in Australia

Jungle Jim's Outback Trading Post and Cargo Shipping. That name alone got me all excited. Heenon located JJ's over the internet. It was close by in Australia. We could buy just about anything through JJ's on line, but the problem still remained— who is going to pick it up and bring it back to the island. Right now, the sight of an alien ship landing in a shopping center would create pandemonium. Solution: Jungle Jim's Cargo Delivery Service.

Arlen piloted the skiff to within half a mile of the town. Brawley itself was hardly a town. One of those don't blink twice, or you'll miss it types. The town was located about twenty miles in on a mostly dirt road, and well over one hundred miles from the nearest city. We hoped its remoteness would be a safe advantage. Our plan was to act like tourists. We would park the ship outside of town, and walk the last half mile. Just go right to the store like nobody's business, work out a deal with Jungle Jim, then hightail it back before anybody could ask questions. We couldn't disguise Arlen or Hippee's height, but from a distance, they looked human enough. That is if they kept their ball caps on top their slick bald heads. I suggested they wear their pull over uniforms; the DST logo on them made for a normal punk rocker's look. Their bald and pasty white-blue appearance actually added to that look. They wore pants that looked like they came off any rack. Aside from their tallness, I felt we could pull this off.

Actually, we had no idea what to expect about the town, or its people. I knew northern Australia was isolated, but I was in for a shock as to how remote. We set down as planned outside of town in a wooded area hoping no one would discover the craft. After a quick security sweep, we exited the craft and started to walk to town. My excitement grew as we walked the bush. The sights and smells of the woodlands evoked memories in me. Visiting JJ's and Australia was like a page right out of a Tarzan film. As a child I was always intrigued by movies of Great White Hunters visiting some faraway place, either the jungles of the Amazon, or Africa's wild plains. What it must have been like to hack through jungle vegetation, to see monkeys swing through the trees on vines, or see a charging Rhino in real life. A visit to Jungle Jim's brought all that to mind for me.

As we approached the dusty outback town, which consisted of two bars, a grocery slash hardware store, filling station, JJ's, an eatery, and a seasonal Inn. I was taken aback by the rustic frontier look of the buildings. There was nothing modern about Brawley—I really liked it.

"There's the town, John, is this what you call quaint?"

"No, this is what I call rustic, but I like it. Kind of makes me feel like I'm on a safari."

"Reminds me of an old west town, like in your western movies. Arlen, perhaps we can get some cowboy hats, and I want one of those Clint Eastwood tops. You know the colored one," said Hippee.

"You mean a Mexican serape," I said.

"Yes, and some boots."

"Boots, what is your shoe size?

"I don't know."

"Well, big fella, you'll just have to try some on. There's JJ's, let's go on in."

"The store appears empty, John."

"Sign says open," I said. "The owner could be just out, or next door at the bar." As we entered the store my eyes took notice of the newspaper rack. There were some issues left, and two days old of course. The headline reads, Aliens Attack Washington, World Waits in Horror! This back water place has no idea that the aliens are on an island only a thousand miles away, or that Arlen and Hippee are the aliens.

Once inside, Arlen couldn't help but yell out, "Wow, look at all this stuff, Hippee."

"Yeah, John, what do you call these?"

"Those are called dungarees."

"Don't think they have anything in our size, Arlen?"

"No, how about these beach shorts. Let's try some on." Arlen picked out some shorts and went off to the dressing room.

"Hey Arlen," cried Hippee, and in a too loud a voice, drawing attention to us, "go ahead and try on one of these shirts, they have a nice print."

"Those are called Hawaiian shirts," I said. "Why don't you two enjoy yourselves? I am going over there to check on some shoes, and could you two exercise an indoor voice?" They were as excited as children. My one pair of sneakers were shot. The sandy beach play, walking on coral rocks, and wading in the warm ocean water have left them in shreds. Doubt I will be going home for a few days so I better buy two pair.

As I'm eyeing some sandals, Arlen again yelled out, "Hey, John, look here, some hats, just like yours," and he put one on. Who would have thought I would be on a shopping spree with extra-terrestrials in the Australian Outback? It does kind of blow my mind to think that aliens shop in stores like we do. We just aren't programmed to think that in some ways ETs could be very much like us. "That looks good on you, Arlen," I said.

Just then a man walked in, I took him to be the owner. He was your stereotypical Aussie who sported a ten-day growth, and an unlit stub of a cigar that appeared attached to the corner of his mouth. He was wearing nothing more than khaki shorts and a striped shirt—untucked and unbuttoned—of course. What is it about Australian's not wanting to wear their damn clothes? He was short and stocky, I put him to be about 5' 9" tall, and headed straight over toward Arlen, who was bent forward, and away from him. Approaching Arlen from behind, he said, "That shirt and shorts look good on you mate." This was a critical moment, so I froze. I spied on them as I bent down and out of sight. I was trying on a pair of sandals. Arlen straightened up and turned around to face the man. If you could have seen his expression right then. Here is a seven foot five person donned in only Bermuda's, an unbuttoned Hawaiian shirt, and an Aussie hat,

I hear a loud, "Krykie … Y'er a tall one."

Then a, "Yes, thank you. Are you the owner?"

"Right you are mate. Just call me JJ."

"Mr. JJ, my name is Arlen. I am with John, who is hiding out over there in the shoes department. He is the man with the money."

"Right, got you. You try on anything you like," said JJ, and then he walked over to me and said, "G'Day mate. You must be John."

"Yes, John Parker."

"Sorry I wasn't here when you guys showed up. We have all been glued to the tele over at the boozer last couple of days."

"I understand," I said. Boozer, was that Australian for bar?

"Didn't hear you guys drive into town."

"No, we parked just outside of town."

"Any problems with the car?"

"No, just needed a leg stretcher."

Then JJ drew close and whispered to me, and in the deepest Aussie accent I had ever heard, "The tall guy, cancer right?" My lightning-fast wit figured it, our cover story,

"Yes, you noticed? What gave it away?"

"The chemo, y'know, not a stick of hair on his head, and that pasty white color of his skin. Poor fellow. … So, John, anything I can help you mates with?"

"Certainly, Jim, we would like to set up some sort of account with your store. That's if you can deliver to our island."

"Island? You mates live on an island?"

So that he'd know I was telling the truth, I sat up straight and looked him in the eye, and explained, "Yes, we are setting up a retreat for cancer survivors."

"Oh, I got it. Hey, anything you mates want, I can deliver. That's a picture of Betsy, my plane, over there on the wall. Fly her anywhere. She can handle up to six people, with a ton of cargo. You just say who and what, and I'll git it there. We 'ave just one rule. No tab, cash or pre-approved credit only."

Straining my eyes and catch a quick view of Betsy, I noticed something else next to her. Something I'd been thinking of, but couldn't get into my consciousness. Unexpectedly, I yelled out, "That's it." I walked over to the wall where the pictures were hanging. JJ, with a curious look on his face followed me, "That's it," I repeated. "That is what I have been trying to conger up." I unpinned the picture off the wall to have a closer look.

"You like that, John? That is a picture of my honeymoon trip to Tahiti. We stayed in one of those beach side cabañas."

"JJ, you are a charm, would it be possible to make a photo copy of this, so I can take it with me?"

"Sure thing, mate."

"I can't wait to show this to Dr. Who." Now, back to the business at hand, "Well, Jim, I think you have a paying customer. If you get me a purchase and sales agreement, I will fill it out. As treasurer of the island I can authorize up to one million American dollars transferred into your account to be drawn on. That's if we can set up a delivery schedule of, say, three times a week?"

"You mates sure mean business. So where's this island?"

Before I could answer Hippee ambled over with his arms full of clothes saying, "John, there is a lot of stuff we want to take back with us."

"Krykie, there's two of 'em." said JJ. He just stared at Hipp and chewing on his cigar. Then I heard him mumble something like, "Oh my," and after a brief pause, "You sure have some tall mates, John." Not catching on to the fact that our cover was blown, I whispered, "JJ, please just act normal in front of them." Then I told Hippee to go and pick out whatever he wanted while I finish up with Mr. Johnson. "Those boys don't get out much JJ, and when they do, they are just like kids in a toy store."

"I see what you mean, John."

I was beginning to suspect that our ruse was compromised, but Jungle Jim took it well, money talks even in the outback. Plane service arranged. I gave JJ the coordinates of Harry's island, and mentioned that there was a runway, but no tower yet. "We do have satellite phone coverage, so you can call us," and gave him my number. Our job was almost complete when Arlen and Hippee came rushing back with more arms full of clothes and stuff.

"Arlen, how are we going to get all of this back to the shii-ipp'n car?" Quick to catch myself, then whipping out his car keys, JJ said, "Here, just load them into the back of old Nellie. That's my '52 Chevy pickup parked across the street, and don't you boys need to pick up some groceries this trip?"

"Why, yes," I said, "when we are done here, then we will need to hit the grocery store."

"A little shy about being seen in public are you?"

"Huh?"

"That is Haddie's Grocery store across the street. She is off ill today, and she asked me to look in on it for her. So if you guys need anything I'd be happy to walk you over."

"You really are a godsend, Jungle Jim."
He tallied up all our purchases, and I flashed him my AmEx-Black fantasy card which I received compliments of the US Government.

"My, that is a fancy card. That's that James Bond card. I've only heard of them until now. Unlimited credit right?"

"So far it hasn't been refused anywhere I have used it." Which is interesting? General Bradley is a detail-oriented person. As he hasn't canceled my credit card, he must be cooking up some plan, but to do what? JJ ran the card without a problem.

Finished at the trading post we tossed our full bags in the back of JJ's truck, and walked into Haddie's Grocery.

"You mates have a list?" he asked.

Hippee was first to talk up, "Well, what we want most is some beer and some popcorn."

I have an idea," I said, "let's break up into two teams, JJ, why don't you go with me. We will each grab a shopping cart, fill it with whatever you want, and then meet back here at the cash register in say, five minutes.

"That's a good idea, John," said JJ, "Here I'll grab a cart too, and you can toss in whatever."

"Thanks for being helpful, JJ. Alright, you two, have at it, remember we are on a tight schedule."

I was not sure if these two aliens had ever been in a grocery store before, but they must sell stuff to eat on other planets? Let's just see if their superior alien brains can handle it? JJ and I headed off down the aisles. I am not going to be particular about what I grab, what I needed was mostly staples, and a lot of them. So far, we had eaten well, but it has been only synthfood. Certainly better than tang and astronaut rations, to be sure, but I would prefer a real steak tonight. Which reminded me, "JJ, we are going to need to hire some local help for the island? For instance, cooks for the restaurant, wait staff, and maids for the hotel. Have you any thoughts?"

"Nah, sorry, John, not many people live around here in Brawley. Why don't you put out some ads? Where I can help is with shuttling people and supplies to your island. You say you have a hotel already?"

"The Towers, yes, and the restaurant will be done very soon."

"How many people can this island handle?"

"Well, we have facilities for up to fifty."

"Krykie, I can't wait to see it."

Needing meat for over sixteen people, I managed to clear out the meat case. Cart full and hard to push, we made our way back to the check stand where Arlen and Hippee are waiting.

"God sake's, boys," said JJ. "That's an awful lot of popcorn and beer. Is it OK to drink beer in your condition?" They just stood there quiet and emotionless, and didn't have an answer to his question. The rough corners to our interstellar communications showed as little misunderstandings. Trying not to dwell too long on conundrums, I quickly mentioned, "It's OK, JJ. This is their first-time shopping for food. I'll see to it that they get proper nutrition."

"Well, alright, let's get you totaled up."

We help bag the groceries and tote them out to the truck, when JJ hits me with, "John, with as much stuff as you mates bought, why don't you give me the keys back, and I will drive you three to your vehicle, and help you unload?" Suddenly my mind raced. Drive us back to our spaceship? Shit! There is a hitch in every plan. I have never been a devious or cunning type. I'm a scientist damn it. Not a politician. My brain doesn't think that way so on such short notice the best I can squeak out is, "I am not sure that would be best, JJ?" Then he opened up and admitted that he was on to us,

"Y'know John, I like you mates, and I want to help you out any way I can, but if we are going to be in business, I think we should be up front with each other. Now, I haven't seen these two before today, but your mug has been plastered all over every channel for the past week. You're John Parker, the one who first saw the aliens. The newscasters speculated that their spaceship disappeared somewhere out in the south pacific. Guess it's true."

"You're right, JJ. We weren't sure how we would be received. So I thought up a ruse, but we still need your help."

"Ah, don't worry about me. As long as your money is good, I'll fly your supplies to your island, but I am going to have to have a look at that spaceship."

"Well, there is one like it only half a mile outside of town."

"Fine, why don't you take shotgun and I'll drive, but I think Arlen here and his friend are going to have to ride in the back."

I think we parted as friends with Jungle Jim. The truth now exposed, he didn't say a word when we arrived at the skiff. Speechless, and his mouth agape, his stub of a cigar fell to the ground. I felt pretty much the same way the first time I saw it.

"This went better than I had expected John." mentioned Arlen.

"Yes, and boy will the others be jealous of all these clothes."

"This is an interesting world John, what I have seen of it."

"Yeah, we need to get out more," said Hippee.

"We will, once we get accepted."

"It will happen soon." Then a fear crept in— crap, we don't have passports. If we get busted, we could spend years in jail. I told my two alien friends that we should hurry. The skiff quickly loaded, we waved goodbye to JJ and made tracks. We won't know for sure if JJ is on our side until Sunday, March 6th, when we see if he makes his first delivery.

* * * * * *

The flight back to the island wasn't going to be a long one. Once in the air we relaxed, leveled off, and put the skiff on autopilot. That gave me some time to ask Arlen explain a few things to me.

"Arlen, I know you have said that the Breen have very long lives. To me, you all look to be the same age, about thirty-five years of age for a human; however, you seem to be able to distinguish who among you is older or younger than you. How do you do that?"

He gave me an odd and disbelieving look, and then said, "Huh, we all look the same to you John? I didn't know that. The Breen all look different to me. Perhaps it is just a sixth sense we have developed." Not an answer, I sensed that he was truly confused by the question, and he apparently didn't have a better one. Then I was confused. Enough with the inquiries, we had some cold beers on board, and there weren't be going to be any sobriety checkpoints so we cracked some open.

We made it back to the island a little past one. There was sparse activity. No one was in the mood to whoop it up. In our absence, Dr. Who had the restaurant and café built, or grown I should say, with the use of his nanites. I made a quick inspection tour and found the facilities great, yet lacking in furnishings, and more importantly, employees. Without the bustling of workers and patrons, they were just cold empty buildings, and this island playground felt the same way. I expected better of sixteen shipwrecked space sailors. So far they lacked a spark. That changed as we unloaded the groceries and handed out six-packs of beer. I suggested a beach barbeque that night to help get things rolling.

It worked. With fresh supplies—real food for a change—moods improved, and with full bellies, we eagerly waited for the lighting ceremony which signaled party time.

18:

The Days of Hedonism

Day Twelve

Sunday, March 6th, my fifth day in captivity. The aliens have been here on Earth for twelve days now, and were no closer to escaping the confines of their island home. Harry was the only one among us who fretted over the Sub incident. He had hoped for deeper contact with our leaders and scientists. That possibility still seemed remote. The Breen had flexed their technological muscle, and at the same time shamed the United States' government in front of the world. It was a shock and awe moment, but the Breen hadn't traveled over seventy light-years just to make a mockery of our military, or of the world's for that matter. They had two main hopes in coming to planet Earth, and at the moment, neither of them was doing well.

The Breen took their cues mostly from news headlines gleaned over the internet. Fear and uncertainty were the norm right then. The world hadn't yet gotten over the shock of the survey, and then the submarine incident showed us what we were truly up against—Aliens with a power beyond our comprehension. Harry hoped that in the ensuing weeks anxieties would calm down, and some heads of state would attempt to make in-roads to establish talks, but his desire to have a friendship with the greater human populace would have to wait. For, currently, a more urgent danger loomed, one which threatened not just relations with the humans, but his control and captaincy of the crew.

Hope two, shore leave, was in jeopardy. It has been two days since our trip to Australia. The supplies we procured there were already gone. Rumblings of mutiny were quietly voiced, and then echoed more loudly across the sandy beach beside the lagoon. With the Breen's command structure what it was, the possibilities of an overthrow were all to real. If conditions didn't improve, Harry would no doubt be replaced as leader. Examples of breakdowns in authority are well chronicled, and the results of which rarely lead but to anarchy.

As I sat lagoon side and conversed with my castaways I sensed their growing discord. Pained looks bordering on anger were shot silently from one captive to another. No words were needed to voice what was being felt silently by my shipwrecked friends. Harry was curiously absent—holed up in the ICC, I heard mention. He was no doubt well aware of his predicament. Then, come late morning, we all heard the drone of a small twin engine plane approaching the island from the south. We listened and watched it through openings in the weather dome as it circled our tiny island twice. Once the pilot got his bearings he swung around and down to the east and flew in under the huge domes opening.

The half-mile long tarmac where the Val sat made a great runway.

Many of us hurried to meet this stranger who braved to land here. Who was he, what had he brought? No other human dared set foot on Harry's Island, and how this alien creature appeared was of great interest. My brain flashed the idea of a zoo, only in reverse with the animals coming to visit. We quickly lined up outside the antique flying machine.

Shortly the engine's propellers stopped spinning. Next the hatch cracked open and swung down and out to meet the pavement. After a pause that seemed an eternity the scruffy Aussie inside peeked out of his cage. With his eyes bulging wide in expectant fear, and still halfway hiding behind a bulkhead, he simply said, "Goodday." The Breen didn't wait for an obligatory handshake and stormed the plane.

JJ was suddenly mobbed by a ravenous horde of seven foot tall beings. It must have been rather scary. At first I wasn't sure if they were more interested in the food, or in just meeting another human. Aside from me, he was the only person most of the Breen had ever seen in the flesh. Inside the cramped confines of the plane, five of the crew gathered around him. Right away he was ushered to the door, and quickly guided off his plane. I watched as many hands on his shoulders escorted him away from the landing strip, and out towards the lagoon. I heard later that they gave him a royal tour of the island, and then talked his ears off. The rest of the crew and I worked together to unload the ton of provisions. Dr. Who had a bodega, complete with cold storage, grown off to the side of the runway, and we promptly loaded it up with our new supplies.

Provisions stowed away, and it was now time to

celebrate. A guest had come for dinner, and that night we feasted. Over his initial shock, JJ warmed to the Breen. Well, they do have a way of growing on you. Later that evening, after dinner, we sat on the beach sand beside the lagoon, and cracked open some cold ones, then sat back and waited for the lighting ceremony. The improvement in morale was wondrous to witness.

The island's main attraction, the water slide, was turned on. A thunderous roar of water crashing into the lagoon drowned out conversation. Red lights simulating the glow of hot lava lit up, and a stream of natural-gas exploded from the hills top simulating a magma eruption. Fires began to erupt up and down the slopes to illuminate the night. Then a rhythmic rumbling shook the entire island. Dr. Who had replicated an authentic eruption down to every detail—volcano ablaze, it was party time.

The warm weather here is very conducive to late-night frivolities. Located just below the equator, it stayed cozy all night long. The wise addition of the weather dome protected us from tropical winds, cooling night air, and the prying eyes of brooding Generals alike. We partied on until the wee hours. JJ was ensconced by the engineering crowd. They were all sitting in a circle on the sand by the bottom of the volcano. He was spinning yarns of the outback for his new Breen friends, while they all enjoyed an abundance of drink. With the roar of the flames above, and near-constant traffic coming down the slide and splashing into the waters of the lagoon, it was a wonder they could hear anything. But there they sat and talked well into the next day. We invited JJ to sleep it off by spending the night at our hotel.

Day Thirteen,
Monday, March 7th
The Help Arrives

Suffering the effects of too much cheer, JJ awoke late the next morning; in fact we all slept in. I was unusually slow to stir. Somehow last night I found my way back to my beach cabaña, which is a marvel in itself. Two days earlier, after returning from Australia, that afternoon we were all crewed up in the lanai, or patio area, which is sited between the lagoon and the Towers. There, Dr. Who, with the use of his bugs, as he calls them, had manufactured two of what us earth people call barbeque tables. They were heavy, hard, and appeared to be made out of nothing more than beach sand. Not that I was complaining, this was one of the most upscale of informal patio areas I ever had the pleasure to sit in. The level floor was nicely tiled with pavers, the spacious area was open at the top, but enclosed on four corners by a framework of lattice and beams, all decorated with tropical shrubs and flowers. The Breen do little by hand, and I know the entire patio had been grown, and probably from one of his virtual catalogue pages, but how they manufactured the living plants complete with flowers is still a mystery beyond my knowledge.

We had cases of beer close by sitting in a chiller, and with an assortment of snack foods laid out in front of us we quickly reveled in our recent good fortune. My Breen friends, even the engineering staff, loosened up and celebrated.

Then, Arlen, in a moment of alien ineptitude, decided to roughhouse a bit, and shoved Hippee over and into me. Hippee in an attempt to catch his balance flung his arms upwards hitting me in the chest and knocking me backwards. I was able to catch myself, but the picture I had folded neatly in my pocket came flying out and landed on the table.

Ever playful, Arlen wasn't done yet. He then grabbed for the picture and said, "What's this, John?"

"That's a copy of something I heard him ask JJ for back at the store," said Hippee.

Dr. Who, sitting across from me, asked, "May I have a look at it, John?" Now here you must appreciate the calm formal respect given by an engineer. Though he never bust a gut in playful laugh, nor engaged in spirited mischief, unlike Arlen and Hippee, neither was I in fear of being pummeled to death by him. Bending to his polite request, Arlen handed him my copy of JJ's honeymoon cabaña.

"Is this something you want built, John," asked Dr. Who.

"What is it," demanded Hippee.

"It is a beach house. Nothing unusual. We have many of them on Pleasure Planet, and Genera Prime," said Dr. Who.

"What, are you tired of sleeping with us, John," asked Hippee.

"He doesn't sleep with us, Hipp. He sleeps alone in the Towers," argued Arlen.

"Well, it is a romantic thought, perhaps he has some future ideas in mind," shot Hippee. Trying to ignore their buzzed drivel, I answered, "Yes, I have always wanted to stay in a cabaña just off shore in shallow tropical waters."

"Very well," said Who, "just show me where to put it."

"Well, how about two hundred yards down the

beach and beyond the reach of the weather dome."

"I have buildings like this one on file. I can show you what it will look like exactly where you want it on the beach." I have never known engineers not to have a front shirt pocket full of pens and other devices. No small amount due to their need to show off. Dr. Who, was no different. Reaching to his pocket he brought out a fat pencil looking device about half an inch in diameter. He held it in a manner so that it came apart at the seams exposing a thin film which was coiled up inside. As he pulled, it stretched wide apart into an interactive computer screen. He spent a few moments purposefully touching icons which appeared on its screen. "Here, John, have a look at this." Immediately a holograph of a cabaña appeared above his device. It was interposed on a section of the surf south of us where I suggested. This was no static picture as we are accustomed to viewing. This was, for lack of better words, a real time video of the beach area as it would look in the here and now with a cabaña on it. OK, everything else on this island aside, that was impressive.

I took a long look at my new home hovering in the air before me. All of us did. "It is very impressive," I said, "but after seeing it for real, how am I going to get in and out without getting wet?"

"Ah, let's move it closer to the shore, and add a walkway." after making some adjustments, Dr. Who had the design of my dream house wafting in 3D right under my nose. "I can't think of a more perfect design," I said.

"Then let's build it," said Who. "Come on, John. Let's walk down the beach where you can see it all happen." Flabbergasted, I strolled along with a small band of Breen out from under the sky dome, and down the beach. We all stopped just up-shore of where my new home was to be built. "This might impress you, John," said Who.

Five of us were standing well up on the sandy beach with the palm orchard at our backs. Dr. Who, was standing in ankle deep water about twenty feet away from us. As he stared intently down at his computer screen, Lilliputian waves slowly rolled past him then foamed up the wet sands and disappeared. You would never know our island was stuck in the middle of a vast ocean. The weather was calm, and the seas flat. The water was bathtub hot, crystal clear, and what passed for waves gently lapped at the shore.

Dr. Who made what appeared to be a few minor adjustments, then tapped an icon on his screen, and said, "OK, here it comes." Like an impatient child I expected to see fireworks blast off, but nothing happened. For a long moment I neither saw, nor heard, nor felt anything. Then, out in the shallow surf, three of four feet down, some stirring commotion bubbled up and clouded the water. Something was taking shape below. Then, as if to catch up, this stirring began closer in. I was witnessing the rise of support posts. They were growing out of the corrals. We watched for five minutes as this process continued and seemed to be speeding up. Soon the posts broke through the water's surface and up above sea level several feet. The sub-structure took shape and beams crossed and connected.

Wanting fireworks, I wasn't to be dissatisfied. Once the foundation had formed the speed with which those little bugs grew increased dramatically. Now the side walls rose up, and as they met the ceiling, they rounded over and down, and fell from the top to form the siding. They were producing an exact replica of a grass hut. The roof then proceeded in like fashion. If you listened closely you could hear a slight hiss as the army trillions upon trillions of nanites mobilized to create the structure. Their precision, down to the molecular scale, was perfection to watch. Within fifteen minutes it was over. My beach hut, complete with quay way, was ready for occupancy. If mankind could ever conquer this technology, what wonders we could achieve. Dr. Who, with a smile on his face said, "That's it, John, you can move in today if you like." Then he and a contingent left. Arlen and Hippee stayed with me as I marveled at the creation I had just witnessed.

We walked the short gangway and entered the hut. It was perfect. I reached out and grasped a handful of the siding material. Its structure seemed a cross between palm frond and a thick switch grass, "But it looks and feels so real," I exclaimed to my friends.

I did move in that night. The rustic simplicity of my surf shack took getting used to, however, I had overlooked its relaxing effect its blank nothingness would create, that, and the constant lapping of the waves all about was hypnotic. Inside, lying on my cot, I easily slacked off into dreamland. This morning I struggle to remember that today is a crucial test of my solution to our problem of getting hired help to run the restaurant and hotel. JJ was on a special mission to bring in prospects from Vanuatu Island. I must see him off.

Finding the strength to get up, I splashed some cold water on my face, and ran off in the direction of the tarmac half a mile away. He must have as stronger constitution than me, and was already making his preflight check, and soon to leave. I had only time to quickly board and wish him well.

JJ's plane spun around, and then he powered up and raced down the runway. In less than a minute his small plane was gone from my view and I wondered if I would ever see him again. As he left I felt a piece of my humanity go with him. Deep inside I knew I didn't belong to this group of beings. That my true home bided with my own species. Yet, I wasn't done here. No, there was still much to learn and experience from these space aliens. They were thoughtful and friendly, but something nagged at me about them, and I was only beginning to suspect what it was. I never thought of my help for the Breen as a form of contamination, but that is the way our military saw it. That any aid, from either side, would lead to more, and as contact between our two species grew, came the inevitably of alien technology falling into someone's, anyone's, hands, creating as imbalance and probably world war.

None of us stop to think that technological advance is a bad thing. Our pedestrian beliefs lead us to think a jump to the future would not come with a cost. As an economist I should have known this was wrong. General Bradley and his ARC group, whether you agreed with their methods or not, had stumbled upon this hidden truth sixty years earlier. Too bad he didn't put it in a book and share it with the world. For now we were, and with my help, forming alliances with an enemy, an enemy who, as far as can be seen, looked and felt so friendly, but in reality, posed as great a threat to humankind as any plague, any natural disaster, or any demonical tyrant ever could.

* * * * * *

To my surprise, four hours later the glimmering silver plane returned, and my spirits lifted again. As before he flew in under the dome and landed on the tarmac coming to a stop behind the alien's spaceship. This trip, his plane was full of prospective employees. They were given no advanced warning of what to expect, and I worried they may be ready to piss in their pants. I gave JJ no prep spiel either. "Just fly them in, and we will wait for their reaction," I said. If I were they, what would I be thinking right now? Well, let's see, first there was the sight of the weather dome over the island, that was unusual. Then there is the giant spaceship parked only two hundred meters away, not to mention the sight of eight very tall extra-terrestrials standing in a line on the runway, all peering into the plane's windows smiling hungrily. Yes, I would be about to piss my pants too.

The plane's hatch cracked open, but no one appeared at the doorway. After a moment, I decide it best if I walk up and into the cabin. Perhaps the reassuring face of a local earthling would ease tensions. I popped inside and let it rip, "Ladies and Gentlemen, my name is John Parker. I am the one you spoke with on the phone a day ago," then silence. As I looked up and down the aisle some mouths were gaped open, but not a word could be heard. They just sat. I was primed for screams of mortal fear, or at least a look of terror. There cold indifference seemed insular.

JJ walked past me and exited the plane without saying a word, then ambled over to the Breen who were still standing in a line. They hugged and greeting each other as if old friends. This did not go unnoticed by my guests. That simple act of friendship between man and Breen helped break the ice and our guests livened up. It was time to speak the truth. "Yes," I said, "these are the aliens you all have been hearing so much about on your televisions the past two weeks. I would have told you about them when we talked the other day, but I had no idea what to say. The jobs we are willing to hire you to do are real, and the pay is above average. The amenities here on this island are quite nice. Any of you are invited to stay, to visit, and to talk, whatever you like. Those who would rather not stay can fly home again in twenty minutes. If any of you want a tour first you can join me now."

No hands went up to ask a question. Had my speech missed the mark? These were all islander people. It was all quite odd. I will call later and cancel my conferences as a motivational speaker. Before I reached to shake some life into these people, JJ stuck his head in and in a rather loud tone said that he, Booh'raan, and Hippee were going to hit the bar. Well, he said boozer, but I knew what he meant. As if snapping out of a trance, to a person, they rose up and said they wanted to join him in the bar. This was a clear demonstration of the superiority of action over words.

I lead them out of the plane, and off on the short walk to the restaurant, where they all sat and relaxed. The restaurant windows provided a great view of the lagoon and water slide. Judging from the loud splashes, the slide was getting a lot of action. Four of the engineering staff were sitting in lawn chairs on the shore watching on. It was just a normal day in paradise.

The group of ten hires chatted amongst themselves for half an hour after which time JJ approached them and said it was time for him to leave. He had to get back to Australia, and said, "Any you folk not wanting to stay the night, better come on. I got a five-hour trip back home, and it is getting late." To a person they all stated they would stay and work. "Well then, John here's your man. You blokes get that restaurant up and running. I'll be back tomorrow to try it out," and with a thumbs up, JJ signaled he was leaving. It was that easy.

Now, with Jungle Jim's help, our supply pipeline was up and running. We had help to run the restaurant. In addition we had wait staff, a concierge, and several maids for the Towers Hotel. Food and drink were piling up, we were living the dream, and slipped into a shore leave stupor which could only be called hedonism. …

Later that evening
We gathered beside the lagoon to await the nightly lighting ceremony. This was becoming a ritual. It all started on the night of day one when I made the remark that the lagoon and the beach lacked decoration. I suggested that some tiki torches be installed all around the beach area. Tiki torches are sort of a paradise staple, and every backyard barbeque should have them. Dr. Who and his engineers searched the internet for the specifics, and then cooked some up. The following night we planted them all about and turned them on. They weren't the big improvement I had hoped, and did little to raise spirits. Our play area still looked a stark and uninviting.

The next day the engineers got together to devise some improvements. Lighting was added to the bottom of the lagoon, and all along the waterslides length. That evening my torches were outclassed. When the new lights were turned on they enlivened our little playground, and activity jumped and spirits improved.

After the lighting ceremony that night, Dr. Who, while sitting beside me, asked what I thought. "It's really nice," I said, "but I have seen better." Then, being an engineer, he pulled his pencil looking computer device from his shirt pocket, and opened it up. I was impressed with it, but had to mention, "Oh, I've already seen that, our scientists are working on the very same thing." He smirked then asked me to show him what I meant regarding his volcano lighting. I asked if he had internet access on his device and was greeted with that, "you can't be serious," look.

"Alright," I said, "On the internet, look up Las Vegas." A Vegas hospitality page opened up. "No, that's not it," I said. "Let's see, put in the Mirage Volcano." Then a short movie clip of the Volcano erupting in front of the Mirage Casino played on his screen. "Right there, there it is. See the flames? See how they sort of flow down with the waters?" With that, and still with a smirk on his face, Dr. Who disappeared for the rest for the night.

The following morning, as I was heading out to the tarmac, I crossed paths with Dr. Who,

"John," he said, "I have planned something special just for you at tonight's lighting ceremony."

"Oh, something for me? ... Can't hardly wait." Then I asked, "Dr. Who, JJ is due to arrive in a few minutes, would you like to walk over with me and meet him?"

"Why yes, John, I have heard a lot about Mr. Johnson, and would like to meet with him."

Jungle Jim was supposed to be bringing in some

vital supplies today—fresh meats; beef, chicken, lamb, etc. Plus some more hired hands. Spot on time, JJ again circled the island, and then swooped down and in under the dome, his plane stopped right next to the bodega. There was a crew of anxious Breen waiting to meet with him, and to help offload the supplies. JJ has made fast friends with several of the engineering techs, which I thought odd considering their vastly different attitudes. JJ was a braggadocios, beer swilling bloke, and he was socializing with total computer nerds. However, it worked, and on days when he had time the six of them would sit beside the lagoon, share stories, and get rather buzzed.

The planes hatch swung open, and as before we flooded inside. A quick look about showed crates of supplies, his two large ice chests were full to the brim, but no employees.

"Sorry, John, couldn't bring the hired help this trip. All that ice added too much weight. I will make a special trip tomorrow, and bring those people out here then."

"Why did you need so much ice, JJ?"

"It's just over three hours out here, depending where I start from. Had to keep all the fresh meat cold so it wouldn't spoil. These are just ice boxes, not refrigeration units."

"So, why don't you get some refrigerated units, I'll pay for them?"

"Why thanks mate, but you wind up with the same weight problem. Refrigeration motors are heavy. Just so much this old plane can carry." Dr. Who was standing next to me the whole while, "Oh, I am sorry, Dr. Who, let me introduce you. JJ this is Dr. Who, head of the Terranomics division."

"Good-day, sir. A pleasure to finally meet you."

"Mr. Johnson, I want to thank you for spending time with my technical crew. We Breen looked forward to these cultural exchanges, trying as they might be at times. We had hoped earth's population would be friendlier."

"I think I am beginning to understand what you mean," mentioned JJ, "It was wrong what the Americans did to you. We Australians are a friendlier lot, and I am hoping to have more cultural exchanges with your crew mates this afternoon."

"They will like that," he said. "May I have a look at your icebox?" The boxes appeared to be built into the plane's skin. We opened the tops. Inside they were filled to overflowing with a foot of melting ice.

"They're great boxes," said JJ, "had them custom made to fit snugly against the hull. They pop right out for easy loading and unloading, a bit heavy though"

"Mr. Johnson," said Dr. Who, "what if I could build you an icebox that would keep your provisions frozen without the need of ice, or refrigeration units, and yet weigh a tenth as much?"

"We'll, I'd be eternally grateful, I would."

"Mind if I take a picture of them?" With that,, Dr. Who held up the same type of device Arlen had back in my residence in DC. The one he used to copy my house plan. "Mr. Johnson, this device will take an accurate facsimile of your box's dimensions. Here let me show you." He held the device over the iceboxes. Instantly a holograph of the iceboxes appeared and floated in the air above his device. "There," he said, "now I can transmit this data to my engineering staff, and they will have two new boxes made in the exact shape of these two."

"And you say they will weigh a lot less?"

"They will be quite strong, and almost

weightless. Further, I can add in a meta-material. It has an energy wicking ability. By that I mean, it can be designed to move heat from one side to the other. On some planets it is used as an insulator and for static refrigeration. If I have a panel of this material built into the lids of each box, they will keep your goods frozen without the need of ice, or heavy refrigeration units. What temperature would you like the inside of the boxes to be?"

Flabbergasted, JJ stumbled to say, "Cold enough to keep stuff frozen, I guess?"

"How about we shoot for ten degrees below zero Celsius? There, done, I just sent the information to my technicians. They will have it ready for installation in thirty minutes."

I couldn't believe what I was hearing, and by the look on JJ's face, neither could he. Dr. Who being instrumental and cooperative. Not the ogre he had been made out to be. For me, curiosity over this interchange between Dr. Who and JJ was worth its weight in gold. Unloading the supplies took us about thirty minute's time. Just as we were finishing I noticed Booh'raan walking across the tarmac. He was carrying something really big over his head. It was one of the new iceboxes.

"Well, JJ, should we install them right now?" I asked. We spent a few minutes unshackling the old boxes which were hauled off and discarded beside the bodega. The new iceboxes fit perfectly.

"Notice the slight warmth on the top of each box," said Dr. Who. "That is the heat wicking effect. These new boxes, and the insulating panels, will be of great advantage to you Mr. Johnson, and don't worry; they are not Breen technology so you are free to do with them as you will. Gentlemen, thank you for letting me be of assistance, I have some last-minute details to see to," and like that, Dr. Who walked off. The Breen may all look to be only thirty-five years of age, but they certainly are as different personality wise as any mix of humans could ever be. Booh'raan had to break JJ and I out of a state of bewilderment. Our work for the day now done, it was high time for some cold beers…

"JJ, would you be spending the night?"

"Thought you would never ask, mate. Y'know, that Dr. Who ain't the raw prawn he is made out to be." Then Booh'raan added, "Well, wait until you get to know him better. Not to change the subject, but perhaps we will get to see John use the waterslide today?"

"What, he hasn't taken the plunge yet?"

"As I recall, neither have you, JJ."

"OK, Booh'raan, OK. Maybe after a little beer-fortification, I'll give it a burl." And the three of us walked over to the lagoon shoulder to shoulder—as close as any friends could be.

The night of day fourteen led to one of our wildest parties yet, and you have to understand that the Breen are composite beings. Their blood streams are full of several types of nanobots; tiny machines constantly on the prowl for tissue injuries, harmful pathogens, toxins, and genetic damage. Imagine trying to get drunk when you have billions of little robots continually mopping up the alcohol. The Breen like to party, and they like to drink adult beverages. To be able to enjoy the effects of booze, they would need to slow down the speed at which their nanobots normally respond. An insurmountable problem? Certainly not. These party goers have invented a substance you chew and eat that helps retard the bots, plus it has a mild psycho-active or hallucinogenic effect. It works perfectly for a short while, that is if you are a Breen.

Late that evening, we all are gathered around the lagoon. As with each night prior, the lights got turned on. My tiki torches come on, the lagoon water floods light up. Heenon's water-fall volcano lights begin to simulate a red flow. Then Dr. Who steals the show with his surprise. The entire beach began to shake. We hear this deep rumbling noise, and then with a roar, flames erupted out of the top of the hill. The flame continued to grow, and began to flow down the hill atop the waters. All eyes were on the eruption, as, what appear to be flaming waters, ran down and poured into the lagoon. Then we felt another large rumble, and an even loud roar, and several more volcanic vents on the hill's side began to erupt with hot red-white flame. I was taken aback. Dr. Who didn't have to ask, the smile on my face said it all. The sensation was really wild, as we now had a true Hollywood scene of erupting lava flowing into the waters of the lagoon. Our very own theme park ride to rival anything Universal Studios could produce and I had a head of the line pass. Over the days of the Breen's stay on the island, this volcano waterslide became the island's biggest attraction. A truly over-the-top ride, and it would continue to evolve almost daily. Mentally, spiritually, I became lost to this Disney Land of Disney Lands...

The island now lighted up, the party began. The festivities this night seemed more intense, what with the roars, and flaming waters, and all. I know I was excited. God knows what spectators on neighboring islands were thinking? As for us, the drink began flowing. There was near continual use of the water slide. I even saw Harry come down and do a cannon ball into the lagoon.

As the night grew on, someone suggested we drink mai tais, a fatal weakness of mine. On towards eleven, as my Breen friends we just getting warmed up, Arlen and Ge'eenna walked over to where I am sitting, and offer me a piece of some substance they were chewing on. I asked what it was.

"It's what you might call a fun enhancer," said Arlen "We call it retard. It helps retard the action of our microscopic nanobots from cleansing the alcohol out of our system, plus it has a mild hallucinogenic effect. Here try just a quarter of one wafer." I agreed, and began to chew on some of the gummy substance, which didn't taste bad—like spearmint gum. Thirty minutes later, all three of us were holding hands and dancing in a ring around the bon fire like children in some storybook tale. As though on some wild drug induced trip, and began to act crazy. The sights and sounds of volcano began to play on my senses. As the night wore on, more drinks and more retard were consumed. At one point, I yelled out something like, "This stuff really makes one feel euphoric." And so much so that I forgot how much I was drinking. It got away from me, and sometime in the wee hours, it all came to an end, my mental faculties ceased. The puking started right after and continued for hours.

At early morning, I was lying across a patio bench with my head hanging down the end; seems to hurt less that way. Note to self, next time you are abducted by aliens remember to bring aspirin. I've had hangovers before, but this one was a doozie. My friends hadn't abandoned me, and were sitting nearby watching as I suffered. At about eight A.M. Dr. Sa'aarron happened by, and Arlen asked him to have a look at me?

"What did you fools give him?"

"A piece of retard," Ge'eenna said.

"What? You idiots! Didn't you stop to think that that would have the opposite effect on him? You were all too high on retard to think properly, weren't you? Your friends tried to kill you last night, John."

I mumble something like, "Uh huh."

"He just has a nasty hangover. Give him a few hours and he'll be alright."

"Couldn't you give him some Cleanse? It's sold over the counter on pleasure planets?"

"Cleanse, but that is for … Ah, yes, alcohol toxicity is a listed symptom. Yes, you can give him a dose of One Shot, as it's called, but no more retard for humans."

"I'll go and get it for him," said Ge'eenna.

Shortly Ge'eenna returns with something in her hand,

"John, here drink this. It will cure your aches."

Careful not to talk too loudly, I managed to slur out, "Sure, anything. What is it?"

"It's a product called One Shot. It will cleanse your body of the alcohol you imbibed."

"Yes, John, think of it as a morning-after pill," said Arlen.

"Morning after, what, did I miss something last night, am I in danger of becoming pregnant?"

"Pregnant? … No, this is a mixture of anti-toxins and specially designed nanites which have been programmed to cleanse the body after, say, hard play. We approved it for use on pleasure planets. Its use will remove the alcohol and any other toxins, or diseases, you may have contracted. Also, the nanites will perform minor repairs to ease muscle strains and tensions." The way these people party, I'm beginning to get the point. The Breen brew goes down. It was not bad tasting.

"It will take about twenty minutes to work," said Arlen.

"I'm not going anywhere. Not going to move from the comfort of my bench." With my head hung down over the end of the bench, drool oozing from my open mouth, I wondered how many brain cells I killed? Shortly the albatross that had been spinning me round released its grip. Ten minutes in, and some clarity of thought returning, I felt good enough to sit up. Things were still twirling about some, but my head ache was gone. I sat silent for another ten minutes then, opening my eyes, I said, "Wow, this stuff really works," then, "I have to run, Arlen. I have an urgent need to piss."

Analyzing my experiences with my captors so far proves one thing, the Breen are not perfect. No, they are subject to exuberance and mistake just like any of us. Was I to expect pious solemn behavior? Not from these brigands. Sure, the Breen loomed over us technologically, but individually they were no gods. How fortunate for the universe then that they religiously held to a set of rules to temper and contain themselves—above all else, a god must show respect. Man exercises no such Theocorporalism in his affairs. We pillage, we plunder, without a care, yet in grandeur of dreams, we visualize the godhead, ever taunting us to strive on—man becoming god— and God laughs. For he knows we are not ready. The gulf between the two of us is too great. Yet, I sensed a hope, a lesson, if you will, one taken from my otherworldly friends who had survived to explore the stars, might they teach us the way? And I began to understand that our journey to touch His face, was not of one through space or time, nor advancement in mysteries of atom or energy, but that the rungs of heaven's ladder are wrought of acceptance and respect—something that lies only within. But I would like to visit to that pleasure planet.

Tuesday, March 8th
It is 8:00 AM in Washington DC

General Bradley is in an update meeting regarding the Breen. An aide brings in the most recent satellite photos of the island. These photos were taken at midnight island time.

"So gentlemen, what has happened in the last twenty-four hours?"

"This General, sir. Our satellites caught this plane landing on the island, and then departing the next morning."

"Do we know whose plane it is?"

"Actually, we do. We got lucky and were able to track it back to its point of origin. A small town in Northeastern Australia called Brawley. We were then able to determine the plane belongs to an Australian citizen who goes by the name Jungle Jim Johnson. He runs a small store, and a cargo delivery service."

"Yes, we know about Mr. Johnson's store. That is where Parker used his credit card. We are keeping his card active, so we can track his purchases. So they are making contact with certain humans. Hmm, cargo delivery. So that is how they are getting food and supplies out to their island. Better get the CIA onto this and right away, and let's alert the Australian authorities. We may need to put a quick end to those deliveries."

"We aren't the only ones with satellites up there, General. The Chinese have also tasked a spy satellite to peer down on them."

"Well, we can't bother with that now. So what

are these?"

"Last night's photos, sir."

"What the F'in hell is going on down there?"

"Those are flames, sir."

"Flames, it looks like the whole damn hill is on fire."

"It is, sir."

"And what does your analysis make of this?"

"Best we can tell, sir, is that it is simply that."

"Simply what?"

"Fire, sir. Fire for decoration and excitement like that fake volcano in Vegas, sir.

"First a waterslide and now you are telling me they have a fake fucking volcano? Bloody damn unusual. … That airplane man, what was his name?"

"A Mr. Johnson, sir."

"Well, Mr. Johnson spent last night on that island, and must have seen what these damn aliens are doing. You call the Australian authorities, and you tell them to sweat him. I need answers."

"What about Dr. Parker, sir?"

"Parker, we haven't heard word one from Parker. For all we know they could have taken over his body. Damn it, we need better intell. Let's try some fly overs with our new stealth UAV. We've got to get someone in there."

Of course, every word of these proceedings were being recorded by the Breen. Harry and his cadets knew ahead of time about the meetings, and made certain to listen in on them. There is an eight-hour time difference between DC and the island.

"The General seems truly upset about our using a waterslide for recreation. I find that very odd. … So they want to fly some type of spy plane into our space? Go ahead, and let it through, but let me know when it arrives at the 200-mile security line."

"What can we do to help JJ, Captain?"

"He's a good man. We haven't put any surveillance on him have we?"

"No sir, not yet."

"We need to protect our supply line, and I don't want JJ to suffer any trouble on our account. Let's get a stealth spy pod over Brawley, and keep tabs on who approaches him."

"We'll do it now, sir," said Heenon.

Day Sixteen,
Wednesday, March 16th
The Fight

The days dragged on, blending one into another. In the mornings here gentle breezes, warmed and with the perfume of the South Seas, wash over this island to drown away any care. This island casts her hypnotic spell to quell our senses, any thought of the outside world lays hidden. Castaway and captive, we are, and there is no escape. We've been shunned by Earth's suspicious populations, our senses by satiety dulled, our souls by womb whelmed, neither pitied nor exulted, alone, in a bleary dream we now live.

Today I woke in the late morning; it had been another long night of partying. Groggy, I try to rub the sleepiness from my eyes. All around the island seemed strangely quiet. Was I all alone? Had my hosts packed up and left? Had they been snatched up in some military coup? Curious, I leave my water born home and stroll up the beach where my drowsy gaze turned east and out over the ocean whose calm beauty belied the true perspective of our jailor. Her even seas may as well be walls unassailable. Hotter today, she stretched horizon round, and flat to eternity, you could not get farther away from anywhere. I thought, "This would be a lonely place to be alone, but would that be all that bad?"

Walking up the beach toward the lagoon I notice Booh'raan and two other Breen sitting in lawn chairs, they were wearing what looked to be heavy black sunglasses. They are just staring blankly out into empty space—it's an odd sight. Were they now the Blues Brothers? I think not. (I found out later that their dark glasses were actually wireless mini-TV screens, which allowed them to take whatever they were watching, wherever they wanted.) No one else was around. There was no splashing in the lagoon, no yahoos or yippees could be heard being yelled by someone coming down the waterslide—all was quiet, strangely quiet.

As I walked up to the trio,

"Another hard night of partying, John?" asked Booh'raan.

"Yes, it was another wild night."

"Heard you crashed early."

"Passed out is more like it. So what is up, it's awful quiet out here?"

"Everyone is watching the fight."

"Fight?"

"Well, grudge match actually. Oh, you went to bed early, and missed it. Hippee may have had a bit too much retard, and said the wrong thing to Ge'eenna. They have been going at it ever since."

"You mean they are actually fighting each other?" All of a sudden, I get three heads turn towards me, all with a quizzical look on their faces. "We aren't sure how to answer that, John. They are playing a game we call war, but, well, here, come with me, and have a look." Booh'raan led me away from the lagoon, and over toward the Val. Apparently, the fight, or war, was going on below decks in the exercise room.

I visited the exercise room my second day here, but as we enter, this was not the same room I remember it to be. All the equipment is gone. This huge room is empty except for what looks to be a basketball court, and a set of bleachers off to the side. It reminded me of my high school gymnasium. Most all of the crew are here watching the event. The court, as with any full-size basketball court, has two ends, each with what must be a 15 foot tall post. Atop the post is a 3 foot wide net which sort of looks like soccer net.

"Come on, John, let's sit in the bleachers." I followed Booh'raan and joined the others. Out on center court were Hippee and Ge'eenna. At the moment, they were wrestling over control of a ball somewhat smaller than a regulation basketball. Interestingly enough, they were both in the nude. I spied what used to be their clothes, now just a torn heap of rags, tossed along the far side of the court.

"What are the rules of this game?" I asked?

"Rules? ...No rules. Usually a number of goals are agreed upon beforehand. In this case, they agreed on no set number, the winner is the one who first gets to ten more points than the other player. They have been going at it for nine hours now."

"That's a big scoring net for such a small ball; couldn't he just throw it from behind the center court line to make a goal?"

"Yes, but that only scores one point. You have to be in the red zone to score three points."

"I notice they are making full body contact."

"Yes, that is what it is all about. Preventing your opponent from scoring, anyway you can. You can steal the ball, hit your opponent and take the ball, slam him, wrestle him. No rules."

This was all out warfare; it was like a combination of rugby, basketball, and soccer. The crowd was really into the action, so I hushed up and watched along with them. So this is the Breen's idea of sports, I can't believe the physicality of it.

"You say they have been at it for nine hours?"

"Well, it all started on the trip over here to your planet, when Hippee made some slur about Breen women and Ge'eenna overheard it. That sparked the original match which lasted two days."

"Oh, who won?"

"Ge'eenna won." … "And last night in a retard induced stupor Hippee again made a remark about Breen women. Hence the grudge match."

Hippee was not considered tall for a Breen. He is only six foot eleven, and Ge'eenna who was of average height for a female was just as tall. They each had the look of supreme fitness about them; I would say they were equally matched. How they could go at it that hard for hours on end though is beyond me.

The two Breen sexes are similar in appearance, that is, aside from the slight and most obvious differences. The women were slightly shorter, and I gather from my talks with the men, that they all varied from Earth women in that their breasts were small to barely noticeable, and having an undeveloped look, and apparently were not thought of as objects of sexual attraction. Well, if you intend to only have a child every thousand years, or so, your parts might suffer. Breen males do not have external genitals like ours—they are hidden internally. Having no sensitive spots made for an evener battle between the sexes, and the women never backed down from a challenge.

Back to the fight: I see Hippee with the ball, he

breaks free, and make a run for the end zone, when Ge'eenna throws out a leg and trips him. They both fall to the floor again, and wrestle for the ball. Ge'eenna grabs one of his legs and twists it. Hippee yells in pain. They exchange some heated words. Unfazed by his verbal assault, she jumps right in on top of him, they struggle, and the ball squirts free.

"John, if a loose ball crosses the court boundary, the last person to touch it gets possession, and must bring it in from the far end." Thank you, Booh'raan.

Ge'eenna manages to break free of Hippee's grasp. She stands, and runs at the ball, grabs it and moves to the middle of the court. Hippee is up, and moves to block her goal run. She is dribbling the ball back and forth, tries to circle around. She breaks hard right. The swiftness of their moves is amazing. Hipp, just a bit late to block her goal run, jumps forward to grab her leg, and misses. Ge'eenna is off, and makes an easy goal.

The crowd of spectator's clapped loudly. Possibly sensing blood, I hear a couple of, "Go get him Ge'eennas." At this point, Ge'eenna is up in the contest by seven points. One more netter and she wins. Hippee gets to bring the ball in. He must control the ball and score this time, or it is over. He runs the ball in dribbling; Ge'eenna moves to tackle him and misses, and gets thrown to the floor. Hipp had an open lane to the goal, but gets a hand to his ankle, and goes down hard. After a long struggle, he gets back up, but Ge'eenna is right on him. He turns and holds the ball over his head. Ge'eenna moves closer thinking to engage him in wrestling holds and steal the ball, when Hipp smashes the ball off her forehead hard. No rules! This stunning maneuver doesn't faze her. Then she and Hipp go down to the floor, and begin fighting again for control. Hippee, now desperate, and in possession of the ball, tries a rock and roll maneuver—some back and forth elbows to Ge'eenna's torso which temporarily stuns her, and Hip finally gains a free ball. He's up, but standing at the wrong end to make a goal run past her. Ge'eenna, not wanting to let him have an easy goal, and with un-human strength manages to pop straight up from the floor to snatch the ball from his arms. Fantastic!

Hippee then, using blocking maneuvers, legs and arms spread wide, manages to back her up, and across the center court line. Just then, to the far side of the court, and to the aft ward end of the exercise room, a door opens, and Harry walks through. I hear him yell something like, "Hippee, over here!" Hipp falls for it, and turns to face him. Ge'eenna makes the most of Hipp's moment of confusion, and throws the ball hard right at him. I see it smash against his head and then rebound back into her arms. Momentarily stunned, Hippee falls back. That was her break, she is free of his grasping hands, and is off and running. Her speed to the end court was blinding, she jumped up, made a three pointer, and won the game ten up. Roars erupted in the bleachers.

Out in mid court, Ge'eenna does a victory flex, thumbing it to the men folk, then heads off to the showers. I was not sure if the roars were for Ge'eenna winning, or for Harry's dastardly ruse.

What better way for immortal beings to settle a dispute. Rough and tumble, but no harm, no foul. I found the event exhilarating. It was all so brutally honest, just Breen on Breen fun, and the only thing harmed was Hippee's ego, but he will get over it—or perhaps we will be entertained with another grudge match…

Later, that day at dinner I saw the four of them sitting together enjoying a fine meal and sharing each other's company. They were friends again, acting as if nothing had ever happened. These are truly remarkable people, and yet something about them keeps nagging at me. Booh'raan said that Ge'eenna and Hippee had last fought for two days straight. How could any organism exhibit such endurance? I can't help but feel some dark secret is being kept from me.

Day Seventeen, Gone Divin'

Last night had been another long night of partying here on the island, and I fear I have succumbed to the temptations once again. Somehow I managed to make it back to my cabaña. There is a patio bench just inside my bungalow which I am lying on. I find the cot won't stay still, my head swirling about. Better to just lay here on something solid. Benched, is this how that term came about? I sense it is morning now. There is a smell here in the tropics at dawn, and it is unmistakable. In the morning, there is no breeze, and that gentle hint of tropical flowers wafts back from the hill and mixes with the smell of the beach sands, and the continual ooze which bubbles up from the sea to create a vaporous cologne that infuses the senses. At the moment the ocean is calm, and I am listening to the gentle lap of the waves upon the shore, and even in my diminished state I find it entrancing.

As my delirium is clearing, I sense someone trying to talk to me. Head still spinning, I manage to turn slowly to the side. I see what appear to be four apparitions standing in my doorway. Careful not to shake my head, for fear of sudden rush of pain, I rub my eyes open. Seeing clearer now, I make a second look at my apparition, and am startled by what I see. Four seven foot tall aliens buck naked, except for their tattered Bermuda shorts. They are standing near me with sharp-pointed spears in their hands. Confused, and startled, I make a sudden jerk of my head.

"Oh, dear god!" I yelled out. Suddenly, my head was again spinning, and nearly splits from the pain. "No more sudden moves," I tell myself. Opening my eyes, and trying to look up and over to the doorway, "What the... Booh'raan? Shit. Is that you?"

"Yes, good morning, Dr. John Parker, have we woken you?"

"Have you woken me? Well, I guess you have. You four gave me quite a start. What is this, 'lord of the flies' day?"

"Lord of the Flies,' accessing, ah, yes, a reference to a movie about shipwrecked children who are all alone on an island, and without adult supervision, run amuck. Yes, that would be fairly accurate Dr. Parker, and let me guess, another late night for you? That Arlen and his buddies will be the death of you, Dr. Parker."

"Yes, a couple more hours of death here alone wouldn't be so bad either."

"That is a curious affectation."

"Huh? What? My god. Just look at you four, your Bermudas are not more than a week old. What happened to them?

"It's the waterslide, John. Just tears this cheap fabric to shreds, but we like the look."

"For engineers you guys are really stepping out on it."

"Yes, to borrow a phrase, we have gone native."

"I see. So that's what it is. Well, we will have to do something to get you more clothes. What is with the spears and snorkeling gear?"

"In talking with the chef about tonight's dinner, he said he needed something called a lobster, and he mentioned we could find plenty of them out here in the ocean. We thought it might be fun to go diving for these lobsters, but we need a guide."

"You want me to lead you on a dive for lobster?"

"Please."

Engineering types are the same no matter where in the universe they are from. They are like lost rabbits outside of their labs, but always so formal in their address. How could I say no? Besides what a great Polaroid moment, me standing next to a group of nearly naked aliens with our catch of lobster in hand.

"Did you bring some gear for me?"

"Yes, and here, Arlen said you could have this."

"Oh, what have we here?"

"It is a small bottle of Cleanse pills; he said you might have need of some."

"What a guy that Arlen." I take a long moment to clean up and pop a pill. Then the five of us walk down and out into the ocean.

Even though it is morning, the water here is hot like taking a bath. We walked out through the sandy shallows which extend out about one hundred yards. Then the sand gives way to deeper water and coral reef. Not sure about sharks, I mention it best if we stay near to the island. We were in water about fifteen feet deep, all of a sudden, a question pops into my head, Can Breen swim? I have seen them playing around in the lagoon, but out here in open water? Snorkeling for me was easy as I have done it in Hawaii several times, but I had no idea if my friends could, and forget about sharks, what about the strong currents dragging us out to sea? In a panic, I turn to see my friends all lined up behind me. I stop swimming, point a finger to the sky, and make a circle, which means huddle up, I guess. Booh'raan and his tech friends managed to swim over to me.

"Dr. Parker, you look a little consternated?"

"Just worried about you guys. Sorry, I don't know all of your names yet, and can you guys swim OK? I mean, there are currents out here. We need to be careful."

"Interesting thoughts again, Dr. Parker. You humans do exhibit some curious behaviors. We Breen find it odd how you care about certain people and not others. …We swim fine. Our ancestors were ocean dwellers, remember?"

"Ah, well, maybe I was just concerned for myself. We are a bit far out. I would feel better if we all swam side by side, and kept an eye out for each other, use the buddy system."

"You're the Captain, Dr. Parker. So where are these lobsters?"

"They live on the bottom among the rocks. Let's dive down and check it out." We all dove below the surface, and swam to the bottom. Snorkeling in Hawaii was great, but these tropical waters are ten times as beautiful. It is like diving inside an aquarium. There are corals and fishes, in colors and shapes, I hadn't even dreamt of. You see something like it on the discovery channel, but nothing compares to seeing them in real life. It was all so enthralling it was easy to forget about time. We must have been diving down and searching for lobster for thirty minutes before we saw one. Booh'raan was on top of it. It was a big spiny feeler'ed thing with a long tail. I motioned to him to spear it. Like a pro, he drew his spear back on his wrist, and put stress into his spear's arm band, aimed, and let go. The crustacean didn't struggle, pierced through the head. The other Breen gathered around us at the bottom to see the catch. I motioned for us to go top side to talk. At the surface, Booh'raan held the bug up in the air. I was shocked at how large it was. Not the size of the lobster in tanks at your local food mart. No, this bug was huge. It later weighed in at ten pounds.

We hadn't figured on where to put our catch. We had no nets, no floats, so Booh'raan had to swim in with his lobster, while the rest of us eagerly searched for more. We must have spent another hour scouring the sea floor for our food. Life was so easy here. I think back on my time spent in Washington DC, how impossibly cold it was to survive there in winter. Not here, this place is perfection, and it is so easy to get lost in body and soul.

We each caught a bug that day. What a fun time, we had dived the deep and survived the sharks. More than that, we caught enough lobster to feed everyone for dinner. I thanked my friends for the experience, and I even got my Polaroid—albeit alien style.

That same day, down in Australia
Australian authorities were alerted to JJs many flights to Island Breen by the US and Chinese governments. Being close by, and their relations not tainted murderous by deeds, they were asked to approach JJ, and squeeze him for information, but their Ministry had another idea in mind. The CIA has been wise to the Breen's hacked bank charge account, but are allowing it to remain open to track

the alien's activities. Aware that their account could be canceled at any time, the Breen began to worry. The original five million dollar balance had dwindled anyway. They will need to find another source of funds soon—Australians to the rescue. The Aussie's decide to make the aliens an offer they can't refuse.

In Brawley, Australia

"Mr. Johnson, Mr. Jim Johnson?" Two tall men dressed in dark suits, approached JJ, who was ensconced in his store.

"Yes."

"I am Agent Jim Foster, and this is my partner, Agent Mike Jackson. We are with the Australian National Security Department. We need to talk to you about your recent trips to deliver supplies to an island out in the Pacific."

"What, I haven't broken any laws, have I?"

"Depends, we may well determine that you have, but for now we just want to talk with you about what is going on out there. And we know about the aliens, so no need to concoct some story."

"You know about Dr. Parker, and the aliens you say?"

"Of course, the Americans have spy satellites following their, and your, every move. We just want to know what you know."

"Guys, I just deliver the goods, and y'know, when I am there, we party a bit. Other than that, what could I know?"

"These are some recon photos from the other night. Can you explain what this is?"

"Oh, yeah, that's the volcano waterslide, all lit up for night play. That's a really great ride. You two ought at give it a burl."

"So they have built a water slide? For what

purpose?"

"Just for fun, these aliens just come here to visit and have fun. If you guys would lighten up, there's a lot they can teach us."

"Have you seen this alien craft?" Showing him a picture of the skiff taken at first meeting in America.

"Yes, that's the sporty craft they came here in. It sits on the runway behind the larger spaceship."

"Then you have seen the spaceship."

"Seen her! They gave me a tour of the beastly thing."

"Excuse us a minute, Mr. Johnson."... "Mike, come over here, and let's talk about this. I am getting the feeling we aren't going to get anything useful from JJ. Like he says, he is just a delivery boy. What we need most is to get onto that island, and see first-hand what the hell is going on there."

"What about the Ministers plan?"

"We can't have Mr. Johnson asking them to help us out. He has no idea what we want of them, plus it needs to come through official channels." Of course, back on the island, Heenon was listening in on all of this conversation. His ears pricked up at hearing about a new plan that involved the Breen.

"And the American's man Parker, seems he's gone all troppo. No, we need one of our own in there, and we had better do it before the Chinese get involved."

"Well, we better ask to be invited. We don't want to piss them off in any way."

"Alright, Mr. Johnson. You want to do your country a favor?"

"I've always been a stand up mate. Just tell me what you want?"

"When is your next delivery to be?"

"Going in tomorrow in the morn."

"Here is what I want you to do, Mr. Johnson. Call you contact on the island. Explain to Mr. Parker, and the aliens, that the U.S. CIA is on to their credit card scam. The only reason they haven't closed it down is that they are using it to track the alien's activities, but any day now their bank account will be seized, Parker's Black Fantasy credit card will be canceled, and they will be without any means of paying for your services. Those are the facts."…"But our government is willing to help out the aliens. We have an idea to sort of work out a form of trade with them. Our Minister has a favor to ask of the aliens for which he is willing to pay millions. We can give them a real bank account, with real dollars. One which won't get closed. You tell them that, and that Mike, and I, want to come and talk with them in person tomorrow, to explain the details."

Heenon uses his quantcomm, level two, to inform Harry about the interesting turn of affairs, "Harry, it is Heenon; our surveillance on JJ has paid off. I have recorded an interesting conversation he just had with the Australian authorities. I think they plan to make us an offer we can't refuse."

An hour later Harry has called me into a meeting in the ICC,

"So John, you say JJ called, and wants to bring in some visitors tomorrow? This could be why. We have had surveillance on General Bradley since his attempt to alien-nap Arlen and Hippee. We intercepted a plan of his to have the Australian government put the squeeze on our friend Jungle Jim. Heenon, go ahead and play the surveillance tape for John."

After listening to a replay, "Sounds like we have been made. If they cancel our bank accounts, we will be isolated again. We better talk with these Australian feds. Any idea what they want help with?"

"Not yet. Go ahead and arrange for their visit. Sounds like they need help and you know what they say about a friend in need?"

Day Nineteen, The Feds Arrive

It was eleven in the morning on March 13th and JJ was just arriving. Today, he is bringing in more food and supplies, and two self-invited visitors. Waiting for them along with me is only Harry. Everyone else is enjoying the morning sunshine out on the south beach, or hunting for more lobster. As before, JJ opens his planes hatch. We decided to wait outside for the three of them to exit.

JJ walks out of his plane with the two men in tow, "Harry, these are Agents Foster and Jackson. Guys, this is Harry Breen, and John Parker, the American." In my so many days here with constant exposure to the non-indigenous life forms I may have become used to seeing them, so much so that I, at times, forget that the ordinary man is still in for a shock. It was painted all over the Agents faces, but as I have found the best way to get them over it is to press forward like nothing has happened.

We all shook hands, and then I suggested, "Gentlemen, welcome to our island. According to our friend JJ, you want to talk with us. Perhaps it would be best if we walked over to the boozer, have some drinks, and relax." Harry was being unusually quiet. He has slipped back into his command mode— pensive, yet direct. I lead our guests while Harry and JJ followed behind some. Once at the restaurant, we sat by the front window for the view effect. The lagoon beach is vacant at the moment, and aside from the restaurant staff we are alone.

Agent Foster opened up first, "So it is true. Up until now, we have only seen TV clips from the day of first contact. I am sorry, but you look and talk so much like us. I never thought we would be so much alike. This truly is a remarkable event."

"Agents, I was told you represent the Australian government, how may I be of service?"

"We came to offer our help to you, Harry. That is, if you want it? We know the Americans didn't show you much respect. Damn shame what they did, and now our intelligence network suggests that they will soon pull the plug on your bank accounts leaving you without a medium of exchange."

"Our internet account, can they close that also?"

"Your internet account was approved by accident. In the Cyber world, these things happen. They discovered the fraud the next day, but the CIA wanted the account left open to track your actions."

"You came here to tell us this?"

"We came here to tell you that we can help with your money problems."

"You Australians would side against the Americans?" said Harry.

"There is no agreement with them to destroy you, and there is no planet-wide conspiracy against you either. Each country has its own separate ideas on extra-terrestrial affairs. Frankly, we don't share the paranoia of the Americans, and we look at this as an opportunity to help each other."

"If all your people are as friendly and straight forward as JJ has been, then we welcome your help."

The Plan

"As a separate and sovereign country we can act by ourselves. We offer you a free port, so to speak. I can't say that all of our people will openly accept you, or how they will react if and when you visit, but we promise, we will take no military action against you. Further, we could use your help with a problem we have. Specifically, our land of Australia is under changing stresses from nature. Ours is a harsh land, full of challenges, and our survival depends on understanding these challenges, and adapting to changes. We have three weather satellites needing to be put into orbit, which will assist us with future analysis of our changing weather patterns. We are a small country with no real-space program. So we have to buy a ride on someone else's rocket to get a satellite up. Right now, putting just one satellite into orbit costs on the order of fifty million dollars, a cost above what we can afford to pay. If you can help us put our satellites into orbit, we, as a show of appreciation, will provide you with an account drawn on our national bank with a balance to start at thirty million dollars."... Wham! ... Just then there was a loud and startling sound.

"Great Maker! John, are you alright?" asked Harry. I just fell over backwards in my chair.

"I'm OK; here let me pick myself up off the floor. ... Agent Foster, I don't think I need to explain Earth type economics to my friend here from another world, but if I understand the deal you are offering, it would be a great saving to your country, and a huge windfall for the Breen as well."

"Something mutually benefiting we hope. After all, it was cooperation that won the war."

Harry took over, "I really must say, Agent Foster, and your proposal is quite tempting. Let me mention that my crew and I are eager to make wider contact with Earth's people. We have made quite a home here on this island, but we originally came to Earth in search of friends, and it looks like we may have found that in you Aussies."

The Answer
After more talk, "Agents, I accept your proposal. We will put your satellites up in orbit around your planet, but in addition to the bank account, I want your promise that you will contact other world leaders. Tell them what we have here. Tell them who we are, and invite them to come and speak with us."

Note…A glimmer of hope develops for Harry's desire to be accepted by the larger human population, and at hearing that the Australians have brokered a deal with the aliens the frustration of General Bradley continues to grow. We accepted their help, and they ours. With the Australians now chewing on a piece of alien pie, others were certain to follow. The contamination will grow. Who will get the biggest slice? Does it matter anyway? As a truism, the first to get their slices are the winners. With a limited number of pieces to go around, there are going to be winners and losers. The losers, well, might they not fight for a slice too? Such things are wars made from…JP

* * * * * *

The offices of Dr. Chas Chaswick, OBGYN
Dr. Chaswick sees over a local free clinic in lower Queens, New York. In finishing with his morning exams he calls to his secretary, Janis,
	"Janis, the boys just texted me, and they need a fourth for this afternoon. Could you call and

reschedule my afternoon appointments?"

"Sorry, I forgot to tell you, both of your patients called just this morning and canceled. Apparently they got their periods."

What? That is the third time this week. We noticed a drop off at the hospital also. We are in the middle of a worldwide baby boom, and Queens is experiencing a rise in spontaneous miscarriages? Just doesn't make sense. I better make some phone calls, is there any mention of this on the web?"

"No, I haven't heard of anything yet."

The Breen virus has been at work for over a week. Pregnancies, which up to now, have been on the rise, are showing a marked drop off.

Day Twenty

All thanks to our joint venture with Jungle Jim, the Australian government has made an offer to help make us flush with cash. No doubt, when people from other parts of the world hear of our alliance with the Australians, more will ask to be our friend. Harry has hopes that this will lead to an Open Island policy offering acceptance, and provide discourse between both of our species, Breen and human. About this, only time will tell, yet deep down inside I have some doubts. As a child I had a friend whom I played with exclusively for months. Then, one day, a new boy moved in next door, and I began to play with him. My old buddy, at seeing this, got angry and never spoke to me again. Are nations as petty as little boys? Yeah, well, there is a new boy in town, and he has some of the best toys I have ever played with. Fights on the playground of world politics don't result in bloody noses. These fights are for keeps, and people's lives will be at stake.

"Harry, it is time to leave. We said we would put the satellites up this morning."

"OK, Arlen, just give me a minute. You are going to drop me off at the minister's building before you go to their space port. Has Heenon given you the directions?"

"Yes Harry."

"I'm just being thorough. Everyone check to make sure you are wearing your threat detection devices. That means you to John. If they shoot at us, they might miss and hit you. So buckle up."

"Harry, you are going to be alone all day while we play in space?"

"Yes, I want to spend time talking with their leaders. I think we are making in-roads boys." Plus we now have a legitimate money account. John, let's think about setting up another pipeline. Any thoughts?"

"Yes Harry, I have been thinking about my time spent in Rio, a really beautiful and fun place to visit. I have some connections there, and will contact them right away."

"John, would you like to pilot us today?" asked Arlen.

"What, me fly this contraption?"

"Sure, come on. You can use any interactive device you like. Joy stick, steering wheel—whatever. It's easier than flying a plane."

"OK, give me a setup just like a small plane." Thus began my first lesson in piloting a spaceship. I was going up into space today. I was going to pilot the spacecraft—hold me down. We were going to place the three satellites into Earth's orbit for the Australians. Two delegates of their fledgling space agency were going to accompany us on this flight. Being lowly engineers, I am sure they were excited beyond words.

We would fly Harry to a government building in Sydney, there he was to meet with the Australian Prime Minister, and select others, while we were left to do the hard work. Harry seemed oddly preoccupied this morning. If he weren't Breen, I would say he was nervous.

When we were all aboard, I piloted the skiff out from under the weather dome, heading straight east. I had my bearings, like a compass built right into cranium. The controls I plied maneuvered the craft just as if it were a plane. Once clear of the dome, I pulled back on the stick and turned right to the north. I wanted to make a loop of the island first. One loop around, and then I shifted our course to south by southwest—a heading direct for Sydney. Flying the skiff was fun, but way too easy. Getting used to the 3D navigation screen in front of me was my biggest concern. Arlen assured me that safeguards were built-in to the crafts computer, and that I was never in danger of hitting anything—how comforting.

After we dropped off Harry, we flew to Sheffield Field, just outside of Sydney, which is where the satellites were put together. With us were Dr. Sa'anntee of Solar and his assistant Be'nnee. The placement of the satellites into orbit could have been done remotely back on the island, but Sa'anntee and Be'nnee wanted to get off island, and this was a perfect opportunity for them. An external device was attached to the hull of the skiff which is where the three satellites were to be loaded for the flight out into space. Once in space, each one in turn would be let loose, and then sent on to its orbital track by a Breen power probe. Dr. Sa'anntee would handle this alone with a laptop looking device he brought along.

The idea of it couldn't be simpler.

Placing the satellites into their holder took quite a while. The technicians handling the task were way over cautious, at least in my opinion. In absolute boredom, Arlen and I watched as they made a simple stupid process tedious. As we fumed, we hadn't noticed, but Dr. Sa'anntee and Be'nnee managed to slip off to snoop around. Arlen threatened to leave them behind if they weren't back by launch.

Two hours later, we finally got the go-ahead to take off. This event was not publicized for many reasons, so there was no media present to record it, yet word did manage to leak out, and a growing number of spectators had gathered round to take pictures. All I need is more publicity, and shit, just wait until General Bradley hears about this.

The six of us took off shortly after 2 PM Sydney time. Arlen again let me drive; I was really getting the hang of it. Just move or turn the stick in the direction I wanted to go. Pull back, to angle up, push forward and down, to go down. Slight bend to the right for right, and left for left, all relative to up in the skiff of course. Several screens on the dash showed our position relative to Earth, as well as other pertinent data. For speed, I chose to have a gas pedal type device. Forward velocity was determined by how far I depressed in the pedal, exactly like in a car—push it in to go, let off to slow down. I was cautioned not to make sudden maneuvers, or to gun it. For safety, the skiffs flight computer automatically programmed the position of all other orbiting satellites, and space debris, and would adjust our vector to avoid hitting them. We didn't want to run into anything, not at these speeds.

The trip up, about 220 vertical miles, took only

five minutes. Sa'anntee, watching his computer screen, spoke up,

"You can stop anytime, John. The power pods are programmed to set each satellite into its own orbit, so all you need to do is to hover." We came to all stop directly over the continent of Australia. What a beautiful sight. Sa'anntee still fiddling with his computer was preparing to launch the first satellite. The two Aussie engineers who came along to supervise the procedure were at that moment peering out a small window. This was the first time in space for them, and they were rather giddy with it. Then I got this devilish idea,

"Psst, Arlen, want to have some fun?"

Arlen turned to me, ponders for a second, and then gets this wide grin on his face. "I think I am reading your mind, John."

"Well, why not do it now?" I said.
And with that Arlen reached to the front console, tapped several icons on the control panel, and turned on the windows, so to speak. Instantly, the entire ship's hull became invisible. It appeared and felt like we had been suddenly, and explosively, ejected out into space, which had the desired effect. I won't relay their exact words, their screams said enough. The Australian's horror was so great I had Arlen turn the hull back on.

"Sorry guys, we just thought you might enjoy the view." Holly Crap! Now that's what I call a scare. One of the engineers calmed down right away, and saw the humor in it. The other wasn't so forgiving. He was still visibly shaking. After a couple more minutes he was able to compose himself, and shortly, they asked to turn the windows on again, and we all enjoyed the fantastic view.

Arlen leaning toward me, whispered in my ear,

"John, you might become a Breen yet." I did enjoy the moment, yet couldn't shake this pang of guilt that I may have really hurt their feelings. It was a mean thing to do.

"Good one, John," added Sa'anntee. "OK guys, just another moment and I will have the first one sent on its way. Are either of you two in contact with your ground control station?"

"Yes, we have our COMM unit turned on. Space Command is tracking us, and will give us a heads-up on the satellite's tracks."

"Alright, satellite one is away. There, we should wait five minutes before it settles into a stable orbit before launching number two," said Sa'anntee. "How do you guys like the view up here in space?"

"Practical jokes aside, this is where we want to be, and I can't express strongly enough how much we appreciate what you are doing for us, and for Australia."

"There, number two is off and running. You know, John, we need to stay in space at least ten minutes after all of the satellites are launched, to make sure they are all on track, but that doesn't mean we have to park it here," said Dr. Sa'anntee.

"Doctor, are you suggesting a pass around the moon?" I asked.

"What do you think, Arlen?" asked Dr. Sa'anntee. I noticed Arlen sort of scan all around inside the skiff. He had a rather blank, yet quizzical, look on his face. I knew that look, I had seen it before. I hope he doesn't suggest another deadfall when we return to Earth. "What? The moon? That is a great idea, Sa'anntee. John, let's go ahead and make a loop around the moon for our guests. Tell me; do you two guys like roller-coaster rides?"

Back in Washington, upon hearing that the Australians had brokered a deal with the Breen, General Bradley feeling stabbed in back, started pounding his fist on a desk, he yelled, "Damn, damn, damn! Do we have any idea what the aliens got in return for lifting the satellites into space?"

"No, not yet sir, but at current costs, I am sure it is huge."

"So we can't attack them monetarily anymore. Well, that's it gentlemen, the contamination we feared has been turned loose. No doubt it will continue to grow. Intell suggests that the Chinese will be next. I tell you, we are doomed."

Day Twenty One, March 15th
Island side, the daily routine played out as a continuous daze of blissful, yet monotonous events. The perfection of morning soon to give way to endless contented play beside the lagoon. The waterside, once so spectacular, had now become familiar; we knew every turn, every scary bump, and the thrill of every death defying plunge at the end soon failed to charm our souls. At night we ate and we partied, on the morrow, again, we ate and we partied. A sublime uneventful pall had fallen over our Eden. We were rich, flush with Australian cash, and eager to burn every cent of it. The Breen longed to venture out on day trips, off and away, from the jaded safety of this confining island home. Our newfound friendship with the Australians was slow to pay dividends. It was high time to open up new avenues for cultural experiences, and find new allies. We had fooled ourselves into thinking getting accepted somewhere, anywhere, would be difficult. The American's militaries' tendrils were not as pervasive as they hoped, and held no sway over

sovereign nations, not when access to alien tech was possible. But still we proceeded cautiously.

While working with my International Economic Research Team, the job I reported to General Bradley about, we often met in Rio at the United Nations offices. Thanks to that endeavor I grew to made friends with several high-ranking officials in the Brazilian government, and also some of the fine people connected with the U.N. To my surprise when I contacted them, they were already quite aware of what was happening over Australia way. "Somebody was talking, but who and for what purpose?" I didn't know.

"Have I been taken out of the loop?" I wondered. "Has my name been added to some kill on sight list?" My old friends seemed quite friendly and receptive to a visit from us when I talked to them on the phone, but that could all have been some ruse on their part. Some trick to lure us into their trap. Our Republic of Breenistan doesn't even have a press secretary, let alone ambassadors and cultural attachés. We are not members of any earthly
fraternity, and our only friends so far were the Australians. Though we had big sticks, fantastical otherworldly batons, I suggested we still walk softly when off island.

My thinking in the arena of world affairs was somewhat pedestrian. Not surprising considering that my training as a twenty-first century American taught me to believe that all I need to do is drive to a nearby store, and I can pick up whatever I want. This is not so in other countries. Flying into Rio the first time a fear crept over me. After all, we don't have visas, no passports, and we don't have diplomatic status. The idea of being arrested and put

into some South American prison raised my
existential red flags. Adding to our worries, this skiff
stands out like a sore thumb. Why didn't we ask JJ to
fly us here in his vintage plane? Nothing odd looking
'bout that.

For most earthlings, fear and hope still ruled the
day. Fear of pissing off the aliens, and hope that
they might offer up something valuable to trade on.
We were instructed to land beside the airport at the
Brazilian Naval Academy School grounds. What
better place to bushwhack aliens, a small soccer field
surrounded on all sides with tall buildings.

For this trip, only Arlen and Hippee accompanied
me. This was, in essence, a pre-visit. A short, face to
face, meeting used to set up for a longer visit if
agreeable rules of conduct could be reached.
Whether fortunate of not, Arlen's appetite got in the
way. He had been talking with Heenon, and they got
on the internet and researched the local customs and
culinary treats of Brazil. What particularly caught
Arlen's eye was what is called a Churrascaria, or
Brazilian steak house. It is an eatery where you can
sample many types of barbequed meat, and it is an
all you can eat buffet style eatery. Don't mention an
all you can eat to a Breen—ever.

We landed in Rio at about six in the evening in
their time. My friends in the Brazilian government
were there to meet us. The usual small talk ensued,
then, without waiting for the relationship to develop,
Arlen blurted out that he was tired of being
constrained to island fare, that is; beer, popcorn,
steak, and lobster, etc., we had the best chefs on the
island, but he had to try Brazilian food, and
demanded to be taken to a local eatery where he
could sample some peasant fare.

My friends suggested that going into town would

not be a good idea, but Arlen in his obstinate and demanding way made it clear we were all going there to have dinner. Well, he has a point. I mean, what the fuck, you travel through space for two weeks to get to Earth. You squat on some small island for another three weeks, waiting to be treated like a guest, and invited out, just to be told you are restricted to some military's mess for dinner. Not the treatment due visiting worker aliens. Anyway, the fear of not wanting to piss off the tall alien worked, and we were off to downtown. Downtown Rio is not for the faint of heart, there an overabundance of humanity has created desperate poverty, and people dying to escape from it. Fortunately for us we had a military escort.

Commander Sanchez listened to the alien's pleas, and ordered a jeep escort to lead the way. He said he knew of just the place where we all could have a wonderful Churrascaria dinner. The building he took us to was not in Dr. Who's catalogue of intragalactic restaurants, but it should be. It was South-American charm, romance, and gluttony all in one. Numerous flat open topped fireplaces, which doubled as barbeques, were situated all around, and close by every table. Flaming meats, on long skewers, lay atop charcoal embers on each. The smell of searing beef was heavy in the air, and more than I could resist. It was time to eat.

We sat, then gorged and drank, and talked of nothing important. Some discussion of what has been termed the Australian affair cropped up, but Arlen and Hippee were too busy stuffing their Breen gullets with Brazilian cow to talk, and I was starting to feel the effects of drink on my lips. Getting a bit buzzed, and the sight of a dozen or more armed guards outside the restaurant, made for uneasy conversation. I suggested we can the serious talk for later, much later.

It took a lot to sate my alien friends' appetites. Someday I'll have to ask Dr. Who to explain Breen anatomy to me. How can they eat so much? Well, anyway, with dinner over, and Arlen now full as a stygian blood bug, his words, he was again in a more playful mood. I called for a huddle to talk, saying, "I think we should ask to be taken back to the skiff. If they need that many military police, perhaps our being here isn't totally safe."

"I'm cool with that John, and I have had more than enough to eat, so we can go anytime." That left no doubt where Arlen's loyalties lie, somewhere below the belt.

"John, our mission was to establish a rapport with them, we really haven't talked much yet." said Hippee. "Harry will be pissed if we come back without some positive news."

"I'm not in much shape to do serious talking right now Hippee," I said, "and do we really want to spend the night here?"

The Arlen added, "Why don't we invite them to come back to the island with us? Then Harry can do the talking, and they, I am sure, would enjoy the water slide."

"That is your first-best idea Arlen. I might make an earthling of you yet."

He laughed and said, "S'pose I deserved that one, John. Go ahead and call your friend Commander Sanchez over here, and we can detail it out for him." Oddly, it didn't take any amount of persuasion to get Sanchez to join us on the trip back. Almost like he was expecting it, in fact, he insisted we take along four other members of his group. This, I felt was a positive sign.

"John, before we leave, could you tell your friends that I want to have a talk with the Chef."

"What is it now, Arlen?"

"Just ask him over." I don't speak Portuguese, and my Spanish wasn't much better. Fortunately my friends spoke enough English, and we managed with the translations. The chef was invited over, and Arlen thanked him for the great meal. Then he said he wanted me to hire the chef to cook for us back on the island. Shocked at the prospect, the man asked to have a day or two to think about it. Commander Sanchez gave him a number to call if he wanted to accept the offer. About to wrap it up, Arlen then decides to take a Breen picture of the restaurant. I knew where this was going to lead.

We left downtown and followed our convoy back to the Naval Academy. Our Brazilian guests were excited to return with us, and eagerly boarded the skiff. It was eleven in the morning, island time, when we got home. Harry was waiting for us, and our guests. They visited and interacted with us that day and into the night, then asked to be taken back home to Rio. Their overall reactions to the Breen and the island I thought were generally positive, but only time will tell.

Note—If someone, new to my land, had made the demands in the way they were made that night, then made a pig of themselves at diner, in my house, and then tried to steal away one of my best cooks, I might feel slightly affronted. Obviously, manners and attitudes are not universal. Some slack was cut for my extra-terrestrial friends, but at what cost later on. No doubt the Brazilians will want to be friends, and equally sure, they will soon ask for some favor which we will feel obliged to obey. And the contamination will mount…

Day 24, I'm Rich, the Holoroom

Several days had passed since our trip to Rio. It was midmorning of day 24 here on Earth for the Breen. I had been held captive on the island for eighteen days. I'm in an island stupor, locals call it, gone all troppo, and am unaware that I am falling ever deeper into the abyss, and in danger of succumbing to the crazies,

"Am I lost to this island? By day its hot languor numbs me with perfection, its nights pass to sated hungers. This island my universe, there is nothing more, its comfort steals my every wont. I am powerless before it, in its majesty, it even commands the sky above, to bow down and kiss this vast ocean round and round. So to it demands the night, where stars sparkle in reflection, not to reveal where heaven end and earth begin. Heed the warning of the Ancient mariner, all who hear, for here who has not heard the siren's call? To her song I could not help but listen, beguiled and entranced, this ship now, my soul, lured, then dashed upon these shores. A passing sailors doom, whether near, or from afar, your serene beaches lull me to sleep, I lie now, on your sand, to waken nevermore?"

Like they say, time flies when you party hard every night. These have been some crazy and fun days. I wouldn't trade them for anything. This living only for today is a far cry from life back in Washington DC. I am living in the here and now. I don't know what the date is, I don't care. I now measure time by the shadows thrown by the palm trees. Preciseness doesn't seem to matter here. This lifestyle to a modern man is more intoxicating than the drugs and booze.

Leaving my little beach side cabaña, I walk up to have a bite to eat in the restaurant.

Oh good, there are Harry and Arlen. Looks like they just got here also?

"Mind if I join you two?"

"No John, go ahead and sit down. You are just the person we wanted to talk to."

"Oh, sorry, did we have a meeting I missed, or isn't JJ due in this morning, or?"

"No, and not today, John," said Arlen.

"John, I worry you might be getting a little too much island in your blood," said Harry. "You have a lost look. What was that term JJ used the other day?"

"It was, Gone all troppo," said Arlen.

"Yes, that's it. Gone troppo. We've been having a lot of fun, haven't we? This lifestyle is very addictive. You must be careful though, John, Arlen here and his friends will party your ass off. Being a scientist and all, I thought you might have found Dr. Who's company more enjoyable?"

"Ah ha, this is beginning to sound like an assignment speech."

"Possibly, I just want to make sure you don't get too lost. This nightly madness will end someday soon, and we will all have to get on with other tasks. We are transitioning now, and I expect us to have more and more visitors daily. I am passing the word on to my crew to be more respective of our Island when our guests are here. Just look at this place. It looks like drunken sailors are in charge. Do you want our esteemed guests thinking we aliens are nothing more than drunken sots out of some old sea farer novel?"

"As usual, your remarks are spot on Harry. We

have been on a drunken binge, and I for one, am tired of trying to keep up with these guys. As party animals they are a bunch of cheats. With their tiny machines help, they could drink any human under the table. … Yes, it is time to sober up—some." I had to throw in a little caveat just in case my twelve-step program fails later tonight, plus I heard in a success seminar once that spontaneity is a key secret to being popular.

"I am glad you agree, John, but enough of that for now. Arlen and I have some good news for you. Heenon was hacking around on the internet, and found out that you are rich."

"Huh?"

"You're an author, you wrote a book, and now you are rich."

"Rich, Harry, I don't think my book even made it to the shelves? If it sold more than two hundred copies I'd be surprised?"

"That was before we showed up. Now, with the entire world knowing who you are, and the help you are giving us, people took notice. They heard of your book, Tipping Points, and began buying it. Apparently, it has become a best seller. Nice read by the way. Kind'a corresponds with our survey data."

"You should contact your publisher, John." said Arlen.

"Yes, and with that said, there is something else we want to show you this morning. When we are done eating let's head over to the Val. I have a movie of sorts to show you." So some good finally came of all that media coverage I so desperately tried to avoid. Hmm, me, rich? Well, I'll just have to take a vacation—when I get back home.

After eating breakfast, Arlen, Harry, and I walked over to the Val, and went below decks to enter the exercise room. This was where the fight was held some days prior. The three of us entered one of drab looking partitioned rooms I had noticed when I first toured the ship. Harry said, "John, one form of entertainment we use when stuck out on long space flights are holograms we have created. They cover a myriad of subjects. What we are going to be viewing today are holograms, or movies, of other planets. They can be viewed in a room such as this one, you can call it a holoroom, similar to the holo-deck on the star ship enterprise. Though ours is not nearly as interactive, and we cannot create matter, still I think you will find it exciting."

Then Harry went on to say, "What I want to show you first is your own planet. This is a holo made by a survey taken by a deep-space probe we sent through this area of the galaxy one-thousand centuries ago. Long before man rose to prominence here on earth." Harry dons this game controller looking device on his forearm. "Ready? Here we go." The holograph came alive, and we appeared as if stuck right in the middle of it. My senses told me the three of us were standing on the ground, out in the middle of a grassy savannah. As I looked around, besides Harry and Arlen, who were standing next to me, off in the distance I could see dozens of unfamiliar looking animals grazing all about. Then, suddenly, the floor, or ground, beneath my feet just disappeared. The Earth's surface was now two hundred feet straight down. As if I were falling from a great distance up in the sky, I yelled out, "Whoa," and frightened, I instinctively splayed my arms and hands, preparing to protect my head from crashing into something. But in reality, I only fell the short distance to my feet, where I now lay fretting like a scared child. Harry had purposely re-set the holo view to two hundred feet in the air. Though I had never stopped standing on a firm deck, my brain told me I was in midair, and forced me to act like I was going to fall to my death.

"Nice one, Harry, really nice."

"Well, I think our Australian friends owed you that one," he said. "Now, if you can stand up? … OK, let's begin. We are going to do a fly over of planet Earth as it was long ago." We took off, or it seemed like we had taken off, as the holograph moved through us we became part of the scenery. And what scenery it was. The Breen probes were able to capture Earth as it was, and in lifelike clarity. This was no Google Earth flyover using pictures taken in space; no, we were right down in it, and speeding like a jet plane flying at tree top level. Talk about addicting, a guy could get lost in here for days, or even months.

"John, this older style recording of Earth only presents a static picture of the environment, unlike the newer surveys which offer some video with sounds and smells. However, it still is a remarkable testament to how much man has changed his planet." Harry took us on a guided tour of old Earth. Even though I knew it was my planet, you could not recognize it as such. The mountains, oceans, and lakes were pretty much the same, but this planet was covered with lush forests, wooded lands, prairies, and jungles where none exist today. I could make out herds of strange animals carpeting the plains areas. Animals in number and species I had never seen before. Could this strange place truly be Earth of the past, has man actually caused that much change? Have we caused that many animals to go extinct? My heart sank to think that we, in a mere geologic tic of time, so totally and possibly irrevocably changed our planet. How could one species in less than ten thousand years have done so much damage?

We must have spent thirty minutes touring old Earth, then Harry said, "We will not spend any more time on old Earth. I just wanted you to get an overview of how it looked back then. John, you can view any of these holos whenever you like. Arlen will show you how to use this portable interactive controller, and how to access the holo cubes. You can use it wherever, but these cubicles produce a more realistic feel, and are semi-private. I hope these will be of use to you when making your chronicles of our vacation here. Now let's take a look at the Breen planet of Leanarus-3."

Harry pops a new holo cube into the controller device. Instantly, I am treated to a view of a most beautiful planet. In many respects, it was similar to Earth, yet different somehow.

"This is a modern holographic recording with full video. These newer surveys show a totality of data, and in my opinion, way too much data. Notice the symbols on the upper right. That is a list of the collected data being displayed. Arlen can help you to narrow the parameters of data to display. The language is in Breen, but you can have it transcribed into English, if you like. I chose Leanarus as it is a typical Breen inhabited planet. You will notice how we manage to live in complete unison with the environment. There is no runaway development anywhere. The total population of the planet has been stable at about 500 million people, and has been at that level for millennia. Here, let me show you this one continent." We sped across an ocean to arrive at a large continent. "There, this whole continent is forever set aside from development and

Breen habitation. It is similar in size to your African continent, only here all the animals and vegetation are left alone to live, to evolve, and exist without impact from any prime species. As you know, the runaway population on your African continent is decimating all plants and animals living there. Once the animals are gone, they, and Africa are changed forever." As we flew over this Breen style Africa, I was totally amazed by the sights, and wondered if perhaps, in the recent past, our Africa had such a flourish of plants and animals.

"There is another continent in the south hemisphere of Leanarus which is much like your Australian continent, and it has been set aside for a population of aboriginal Breen. Some of us choose not to live as enhanced beings. The Breen living on this continent prefer to live a natural life; to be born, live a short life, and then die, and have chosen to live free of much of our advanced technology. This whole continent has been set aside for them. The point here is that we are not all the same, with the one exception that we have all agreed to live within sustainable ecological standards. As you mentioned in your book, John, man has grown beyond the natural controls nature puts on life, and is now in danger of ending his own existence, and that of thousands of other life forms on this planet. We can talk about what sustainable ecological standards are some other time."

"Next, I want to show you your planet today, as our survey found it." Harry takes a new holo cube and puts it into the controller device. I recognize this planet. It looks quite familiar. No need to belabor it, this is Earth of today. "Watch now as I overlay the two holograms. Now you can see Earth of yesterday and today, side by side, to gain a contrast of man's impact on the environment." As I watched the holo movies superimposed, one on the other, I am saddened by the changes we have made. It is rather troubling when you see the way it was next to the way it is today.

"Furthermore, John, you can slip into status mode. This mode of use highlights data, such as natural resources, areas that are in trouble due to pollution, or areas already in an environmental collapse. Take a look. Further, you talk about trends in your book. We can have the computer trend out these changes in, say, ten-year increments. Here, watch, as I change to trend lines. There, this is present day Earth. Now, I'll run it forward ten years so you can see the changer. There, and now another ten years, and then another. As you see, the trend over the next forty years is not good for man or Earth."

"You are the first human to see this data. We plan to make the results of our survey public, and hopefully soon. The reason I am showing you this today, is that man needs to be told the harsh truth about the danger he faces. So far, we haven't shared this data with anyone here on Earth. I am hoping you will study these holos. Become aware of what the data show, and somehow convince your fellow man, that this is not a problem he can run away from. We are able to offer only minimal help to mankind. We cannot solve Earth's problems for you. However, there is still time to save mankind from oblivion, but as each day passes, you come closer to that precipice you mentioned...."

I got Harry's point, and if the Breen data are correct, and I already suspect they are—we haven't much time. Certainly don't need encouragement to view and study these holographic videos—as captivating as they are. Looks like I am going to have to shave my face, soap up, and rinse off island life. Time to cram the books once again...Was this to be the end of Hedonism? No way....

Day 25, March 19th

On the Breen's twenty-fifth day here on planet Earth, Harry was invited to fly to Rio. This offer came as a result of my visit back on day 21. Government officials of Brazil, together with my former friends in the U.N. had gotten together, and decided to talk with regarding the Breen's future exposure to Earth's many countries. Some sort of protocol needed to be addressed. This meeting was also an appeasement to the many nations who were citing the Australian affair, and demanding equal access to the aliens, a step taken to avoid infighting and war. No one should be left out or barred from gaining access to what might be considered game-changing technology—or, in General Bradley's mind, the contamination.

Harry was sensitive to the wants and needs of Earth's leaders. He understood the geo-politics involved. Stating, that the Breen had no intention of excluding anyone, but further, would appreciate the opportunity to tell the world who they were, why they had come to Earth, and how they can help us.

As a result of this meeting, the U.N. officials agreed to set up a televised speech, just so Harry could make his address to the world. This speech, to be held in Rio, was scheduled for the night of Tuesday, March 22cd.

19:

Harry's UN Speech

Day 28
Harry's First UN Speech, Tuesday, March 22nd.
Location: Brazil Naval Academy, Rio de Janeiro,
Brazil

The offering to Harry to make this speech grew out of our visit to Rio only three days earlier. To say it was a rush is an understatement. Typical Harry, take any opportunity that comes along. As news of his speech circulated around the island, questions arose about what he should say, or even if. Interestingly enough the Breen political process is to debate an issue to reach a consensus. However, it is an amorphous process with tenuous rules. What is interesting about that process is that they typically split 50/50 down the lines, and a true consensus is never reached. Gridlock is broken by fiat by the Captain, but they seem OK with this system. Having long life lends itself to greater patients I guess. Their tepid approach to conflict resolution, almost a relegation to an authority figure, is what many human populations have eternally fought against. Yet this advanced alien civilization relies on it—most curious.

The location for the speech was set up at the Brazilian Naval Academy grounds, which is on a secure island just off to the side of the airport in Rio. Tall buildings edge the island making for a central field which is hidden from casual view, a perfect place to land an alien craft safe from prying eyes. This field would become a favorite stopping spot for our many visits to Rio in the future.

Considering the subject to be discussed, I was surprised there wasn't more fanfare, but this meeting was quickly arranged, and I doubt if more than a handful of nations even know it is taking place. Much could change tonight. Harry's hope for calling this meeting is to generate goodwill, and establish a dialogue with earth's people. I hate to be cliché, but there is that old tried statement, "Be careful what you hope for."

Present for the meeting are: Captain Harry. Also present are Dr. John Parker, Dr. Sa'aarron, Arlen, and the three Cadets. Those chosen to attend the audience were selected by the U.N.; we had no input into the selection of participants for this meeting. There were several television stations airing the speech live, and piping the feed out to the satellites, for the entire world to see.

Harry takes the dais, the rest of us are sitting on a small stage off to the right of the auditorium. The beginning of his speech is not introduced.

"Ladies and Gentlemen of Earth, thank you for coming here. I have looked forward to this meeting since we first arrived here weeks ago.

Misunderstandings at first contacts are common. Let us tonight put all past misconceptions and belligerence aside, and start anew.

Please excuse me if I get some of your salutations wrong. We have just recently learned your language, and though we know your basic words, many parts of your speech usage are still unknown to us. You are a diverse people with many different languages, and though I will be speaking in English, you should all feel equally welcome.

My name, spoken in your voice range, would sound something like, Here'eee. I would appreciate it if you simply called me, Harry. Our race is known as the Breen. I would talk to you in my own language, but I am sure you would find it alien and unintelligible. About half of our speech is in a range far above what you normally can hear. We have the ability to adjust our vocal cords so that we could speak in a manner that you can understand. We do not expect you to learn Breen, but I have put our language equivalents on a computer file, and listed it on your internet. Any of you can download this file, and hear our true spoken language if you desire.

My intention tonight is to convey to you some perspective on who we are. Our first contact with you, and the few days that followed, did not set a proper stage for two potential friends to come together. We Breen truly wish we could have met under better circumstances. Hopefully, it is not too late not to plot a more peaceful course for our two peoples. Contrary to what you may have read in your print, and other news media, we have not come here to colonize or conquer. We have not come to take anything, or hurt anyone, and I guarantee that your planet will always be yours.

We originally entered this quadrant of space

some 54 days ago. Our job, if you will, was to terraform a planet some 70 light-years distant from earth. While there we picked up on some of your old radio transmissions. We recognized them as coming from an intelligent species, and we eagerly wanted to meet fellow beings like ourselves. Naturally occurring life in the cosmos is rare, and finding new and intelligent life is always very exciting. So when our work on planet Ga'alle'een was at a point where we could break away for a visit, well, here we are. We still have over two of your months left to spend here on your lovely planet before we must get back.

Let me briefly say a word or two about who we are. We Breen are an ancient race. By that I mean we have existed as you see us today for several hundred thousand of your years. Earth by comparison has only recently entered its technological age. So, are we more advanced technologically? Yes. Have we been around for a much longer time? Yes. However, in many ways we are not so different from you. Both our species have two legs, two arms with hands and fingers, and sadly, only one head apiece. Yes, astonishingly, we look much alike, our two species. Though there is a technological gap between us, we hope to develop ways to bring our two species together. Can we not celebrate our differences, and yet still become friends and neighbors? In the end, I hope for you to see that we are not so vastly different after all.

We know from past first contacts, that species at your stage of development often feel as though you are alone in the universe. You are not. There are thousands of planets between Earth and our home planet of Be'eerreen Prime which are inhabited, and by just about as many species. We are members of a consortium of planets. Our race alone now inhabits over 1,578 worlds, most of which were terraformed. Once your science has solved the current problems that face mankind, and decide to move out into space, we and all these other races will be waiting there to join hands with you.

There is one last thing I wish to bring up tonight, before I answer some questions. I would not bring it up now, but that our time here on earth is short. As you are aware, upon our arrival on earth, we made a survey of your planet. That was the purpose of the spheres you saw crossing your oceans and land areas. As ecologists and world builders it is a common practice of ours to make such surveys. Sorry, if some of you were frightened. Many took this as a prelude to an invasion. No, we do not invade other worlds. We do not need to. Our task is to help and guide evolving species.

The purpose of the survey was to gather data on your planet, such as: size, land masses, catalogue plant and animal species, analyzed population size and growth patterns, locate natural resources, and estimate their use rates, and to determine the overall health of the planet. The results of our survey will be put up on the internet later tonight for all to see. I encourage earth's scientists and citizens alike to read this survey. Study it. Learn from it.

Those results should alarm you. The conclusions reached point to serious problems facing mankind in the very near future. At the top of the list of major problems facing you are global warming and resource depletion. The survey data, analyzed by our computers, makes predictions about Earth's future. I will not discuss them with you tonight. We can discuss them together later, if you like. Let me just say that in our long experience, and we have catalogued hundreds of civilizations, most will rise to your current level of development, just to collapse back into a stone age. The plain truth is that 68.5 % of all advancing civilizations do not make it past their technological age.

I know that most of you here tonight and many more living in cities across the planet know of this impending peril. Deep down, you sense it is true, yet none of you will act together to make the changes needed to prevent this catastrophe. It can be prevented if you act now.

That being said, I would be willing to answer of few questions."

While Harry fielded questions, conversation broke out between the five Breen and me. We felt that for him to make that type of speech at this juncture was wrong; it was too short and confusing. In the future, we will get him a speech writer. His details may be correct, but was this the venue to tell the Earth's populace that they are in dire straits? I think not. We were already aware of our long and deepening economic slump, did we need to be slapped in the face with it? The tenor of the audience changed from one of listening in awe, to one of a grumbling discourse. I grew worried that the audience could turn hostile, and that we would be the focus of it? I wasn't the only one with a sense of foreboding. The cadets were fidgeting, and Arlen appeared dour, and was looking down at the floor, and shuffling his feet. This would be a good time to beat a quick retreat.

Some of the questions asked that night:

Q. "What you have said is truly more than a person can digest in one evening, Harry. Yes, I would say that many of us have known, or felt, for a long while now, that we are headed for disaster, but like you say, there isn't much we can do about it. There are just too many different countries and peoples, and even if we were only one country, I still doubt, given what I know about how governments work, that any consensus could be reached to change our ways. Are we doomed?"

A.   Harry stood still for quite a while pondering that question. Perhaps he realized he had opened up a can of worms. Did he really need to tell us about our pending doom, or tell us in this manner? Further, he knew from experience that it was doubtful mankind would do anything about its situation. That the Breen virus was the only true short term hope for mankind. And here I think it shows Harry's lack of experience as a diplomat, but as one intrepid Captain, he was never afraid to go boldly ahead, and he did.
   "I tell you, and I tell all those listening tonight, and everyone else on this planet that we will not let the human race die out. We will find a way to help Earth survive."

Q.   Guest in audience— "I find it remarkable that you Breen look so much like us humans. Are all advanced civilization's humanoid?"

A. "Yes, with very few exceptions all prime species appear as you say, Humanoid. I would say they have a Breenoid appearance. However, you are correct, there seems to be a direction on every planet, and whether you call it co-evolution, a galactic anthropic principle, or something more divinely directed, life on each and every planet shares very similar forms."

Guest—"And you know this for a fact?"
Harry—"Through the millennia we have met over 1586 different sentient species on as many planets, and the one thing they all have in common, with very few and limited exceptions, is that they all have what you call a humanoid appearance. It is a universal and primary evolutionary principle. It is an 'a priory' necessity that a species have this form or something like it to evolve to where we, or you, are now."

Q.   Guest—"You mean that there are 1,586 planets with people on them like us?"

A. "Probably many more. The Breen have only explored about 5% of the galaxy. There is a lot more space left out there to explore."

Guest—"Remarkable."

Q.   Guest—"What technologies can you share with us?"

A. "We have a strict code regarding sharing advanced technology with what I might call junior species. It is generally not an accepted practice. Although there is no law against it, it is a rare occurrence. I would leave that at that. At some time in the near future if a delegation of your leaders comes to us with a request for our help, we will discuss it further with you, then."

Q.   Guest—"Do you have any pets on your ship?"
(Laughs were heard in the audience)

A. "Pets, accessing—Ah, you mean cats and dogs. No, but it is an interesting question."

Q.　Guest—"What can you tell us about your ship's mode of propulsion?"

A.　"We use what we call pulsed quantum wave technology for our main drive. It is a type of propulsion which uses positive and negative energies to create waves in space on which one can travel, much like a surfer riding an ocean wave. This may be ahead of your science right now, but some day your scientists will unravel its mysteries."

Q.　Guest—"What is the top velocity you have achieved?"

A. "I do not know if a top velocity has been reached yet? Our scientists, like yours, are continually working on new stuff. Who knows what they may come up with? As far as the Val goes, well, we got here from over 70 light years away in just under two weeks." (Rumble in the audience)

Guest—"That's impossible. Nothing can go faster than the speed of light."

Harry—"Is that a question?"

Guest—"Our mathematics and experimentation has shown us that it is fundamentally impossible to go faster than the speed of light. That barrier cannot be breached."

Harry—"Oh, perhaps your math is wrong. Once, long ago, our scientists thought the same as you do now.

That faster than light travel was impossible. Yet think for a minute, you once thought air flight impossible until your Wright Brothers built their first airplane. As we moved out into space its vast reaches forced us to find ways to travel faster and faster. Each time we needed to go farther, and get there faster, we did. And driven, as you are, we sought ways to travel faster still, until one day our scientists found a way to exceed the light speed barrier. We did find a way to do it, as I am sure you will one day too."

The occupations of the participants in the audience covered a wide spectrum of human interests; scientists, statesmen, media personnel, military and the like. With each Q and A the tenor of the crowd changed. Not surprising considering what they have heard. The Breen sensed this unrest mounting in the audience and began to talk quietly amongst themselves on their quantcomms. Little was offered in the way of security for this meeting, and no one wanted the situation to degrade any further. Harry was urged by his crew mates to bring it to a quick close.

"Gentlemen, tonight we have had a good first introduction. Our two species started out as strangers. After tonight, and in meetings to follow I hope we can become friends. Certainly, we have much more to discuss, but for tonight we should let it come to a close. Let's not end a good start here. I invite any of you to come and visit with us out on our island. We will make time and arrangements for you through your internet and other channels. Our go-between, Doctor John Parker, is also available to help with facilitating your visits."

As the meeting came to a close the clamor in the crowd became deafening. Guests were shouting at us, and at each other. Several stood up, hands in the air, to ask further questions. The media blitzed the stage where the Breen, and I, were now standing. What security there was, three armed officers, held the mob of reporters at bay long enough for Harry, and the rest of us, to exit out the back of the meeting hall, and entered the skiff. We all, of course, were wearing safety devices, yet my fear was palpable. This was more confrontation than I was used to, and my adrenaline level peaked. How I yearned once more for the apparent safety of the skies, and of my new island home.

* * * * * *

The United States military was alerted to Harry's speech days before, thanks to the spies General Bradley had in place in Rio. General Rudy was watching the speech in the comfort of his office. He had invited several close friends to watch with him, though no popcorn was allowed. This could signal the submission of Rudy to the inevitability of alien contamination of planet Earth. His mood that night was quite somber.

General Bradley commenting on the speech, "Damn, the contamination will spread faster now. We are doomed, I tell you." ... "That Parker, no, he's not a traitor; he's just caught up in it. Who wouldn't be? That was the whole point made by the ARC group. Advanced alien technology is just too seductive to pass up." Some mention of formulating a Committee to analyze the Breen survey was bandied about.

* * * * * *

We all sat quietly on the journey back to the island—odd, because the Breen are such a talkative lot. I hadn't yet seen Arlen brood. It had an ugly distaste to it. Once on the ground we were greeted by Hippee and several others. Their mood was a one eighty from ours, all smiles they were. They had been watching the meeting on internet hookups, and by a growing number of spy devices they have placed in very high places. Apparently, watching the event from a distance evoked a different response than actually being thrown directly into it.

Once home, our mood picked up a little. Hippee remarked that I was going to be quite busy now. To that I had Harry to thank. "I think you are going to become quite busy, John," he said.

"Yes John, you are going to be very popular," added Dr. Sa'aarron.

"Swell," I replied," and I am thinking to myself, "Does a resignation from a pentagon job need to be in person? The General is not going to take this kindly."

Then Harry popped back to his practical self, "They will need to set up some committee. We can't have 7 billion people contacting us directly. Yes, some U.N. directed committee, I should think."

I heard Dr. Sa'aarron lament, "Great Maker, What is the common sense to this all? I thought we were supposed to be here on shore leave?" It had been a long day. We all headed off for some sleep.

* * * * * *

Day 28
Office of Dr. Chaswick, OBGYN
Lower Queens, New York

In a twist of irony, he was listening to Harry's 'We came in peace' speech. Ten days earlier he began to notice a marked drop off in pregnancies. The last few days his office has been nearly empty of patients. For the first time in years, there are no new pregnancies for him to examine. He made note that his only remaining patients who are still pregnant are well into their second trimester. Chaswick isn't alone in noticing this startling trend, thanks to the internet, and an ever more connected medical network, he is alerted to the fact that this phenomenon is being noticed throughout the civilized world. Amid growing concern a day ago he placed a call into the CDC.

Easton Bio-Medical School
Chicago, Ill.

A thousand miles away in Chicago, students at a specialty college have just made a startling discovery.

"Prof. Henderson, would you have a look at this?"

"What have you got, Mr. Lehman?"

"Take a look at these orange spheres, sir."

"Orange spheres? I thought you were researching a new technique to investigate sequestered venereal diseases in female reproductive tissues?"

"Yes, sir. Many of these virus types remain latent for years by hiding inside the cell wall. We are working on a method to section out individual cell walls and examine them with an electron-microscope in an effort to determine how they hide. We were just through cutting into an ovary cell wall, when we saw these orange globules."

"Well, let's have a look. … Yes, I see them, must be a contaminant."

"Why would you think that?"

"It's the color. I don't know of any natural occurring disease, viral or bacterial, to have color. Those little guys stand out like sore thumbs. See if you can localize one of them, and let's shoot some high energy photons at it."

Thirty minutes later

"Professor, we have some samples set up, and are going to x-ray them now. As you can see, they are circled there on my monitor."

"Very well, let's see what is inside of them." They then hit the spheres with a burst of x-rays. "What just happened?"

"They just disappeared. Just like that, they, I want to say, melted, sir."

"How very odd. I have never seen a sample do that. This is very perplexing. ... Tell you what, re-set, and let's analyze the tissue behind them. Perhaps that will tell us what type of contaminant we are dealing with."

Besides their best efforts, Prof. Henderson's team was unable to select and analyze the spheres. Further, their analysis of what was left of the spheres after they melted, showed to be nothing more than common and medically benign chemicals.

* * * * * *

The following day, true to his word, Harry had the Breen survey, translated into English equivalents, of course, posted to their web site. From there it went viral. The conclusions could be debated, but the thoroughness and accuracy of it could not be denied. World scientists would spend days analyzing the data, and their conclusions; bottom line, we all knew the Breen were right in their assessment of man and Earth. Unlike crackpot predictions of doom, this prediction came complete with supporting data. What's more, the source of the report added certainty, and a major WOW factor. Could we any longer deny we have a serious problem? And yet, if we do accept these findings as true and correct what then? I mean, it is not like we could do anything to stop this runaway train, is there?

A Consortium from the UN Requests a Meeting

It took two days of worldwide rumblings. We, I mean, myself, and the crew of sixteen Breen I have been imprisoned with on this most beautiful of tropical Isle, continued to enjoy our island retreat. We had beaches, plenty of sunshine, a mountainous high waterslide falling into the crystal clear waters of a lagoon, movies every night, tons of popcorn, never-ending conversation—man these beings can talk. I felt as though I have been cast down from the world of man, where I served an evil General, but now, in a strange twist, I rule in exile. If I had time, I might have scratched an outline for a book titled, well, Paradise Found. And did I mention that these aliens partied like drunken sailors on shore leave. My new job, to see to their earthly comforts. Was it servile? Sure, but the perks were simply out of this world. Anyway, after two more days of hedonism, reality rang and wanted to meet. Harry was right, world leaders, prompted by a populace in near revolt, decided to utilize the United Nations as moderator between the aliens and the humans. A delegation was asking for permission to visit our island tomorrow, and I suspect it had something other to do with than sunbathing.

Well, why not open up the island to visitors; the Towers Hotel was ready. My first days on the island I had suggested a fine-dining restaurant, and Dr. Who had it built. With Jungle Jim's help, we have hired a large staff of helpers. Supplies were being flown in several times a week. Mañana, I was headed to Rio anyway to exchange out some chefs. Some of our work staff have asked for rotated shifts, with time enough to go home to their families. (I never would have suspected that a Chef could be a spy. We learned later, that we did have spies among the help. Fortunately for us, no harm was caused, plus the Breen spy-bots were watching and listening.)

On the morrow, I arranged to meet with the U.N. delegates, and fly them to Harry's Island. They were members of a quickly thrown together UN committee, as part of an experiment, to attempt to broker relations between Earth's many nations and people, and Harry. I had become adept at flying a skiff, and none of my captors seemed to care that I was running off to places unknown with one of their most advanced spaceships, in fact, they preferred that it were I who ran these menial errands. The authorities in Rio were quite supportive of my frequent visits next to their airport. I never went into town. That was suggested by all not to be a good idea. We had no problem getting the supplies asked for, my requests were sent ahead, and would be there waiting for me at the academy grounds. Amazing what you can do with a thirty million dollar bank account.

As I approached Rio, I flew the skiff in almost straight down, leveled off and hovered a sec partly to impress the UN delegates, then landed on the soccer field where a reception committee was waiting. Before I exited the skiff, I peered through the cockpit window to get a feel for their mood. Yep, I remember that look. That was the same look that was on my face only 29 days ago, when I first met the Breen, it was a look of horrified surprise.

They had expected to be greeted with the visage of some over seven foot tall alien beings, only problem, I had no Breen on board. I hit the hatch, and manage to stumble out to greet them. One of the five delegates first to approach me was a man of medium build, bearded, not dressed in formal attire, more old school; brown pants, gray tweed sports coat, button-down shirt, green stripped tie, and loafers for shoes—my first thought, "Oh god, not a school teacher." I was expecting more of a military or politico type as the leader, but they send me a teacher? I had more than enough of that mentality in my college days. He walks up, we shake, and he introduces himself as a Professor Tynan—how did I know?

"John Parker, My name is Professor Tynan. I have been selected to head up the new U.N. Counsel on Alien Affairs."

I took a second to correct him, "Please, it's Doctor Parker," I said. There are enough titles going around, but I earned mine. Though I look the part, I am tired of being treated like some surfer dude limo driver.

"Sorry, then, Doctor Parker, it is." The Professor introduced the rest of his small group; representatives all of the larger human population areas of the world. I've heard the term BRIC used, it is pretty accurate. I explain that I am waiting for two more people, but if they like, they can begin to board the alien craft and have a look. Professor Tynan then asked if the aliens were waiting inside.

"Sorry," I said, "No aliens yet, just a disheveled

economist slash naturalist. Harry and the others are waiting for you back on the island." There look of tense anticipation turned immediately to one of disappointment. I ushered the delegates inside.

"So, Doctor Parker is the only access to the island going to be by this Breen craft?" asked the Professor. An intelligent question, but hadn't they heard of Jungle Jim's cargo delivery service?

"I hadn't thought of that, Professor," I replied, "actually, it would be helpful if we could set up a regular daily visit by some other aircraft, perhaps a medium sized prop driven airplane."

"If you make that a request, I can get someone to work on it right away," he said.

"Our island is very remote. Closest continent is Australia."

"Yes, I saw that on the map."
Thinking to test him, or catch him in a lie, I mention, "We already have a building set up in Australia, as a warehouse."

"Oh, we have heard about the Australian affair, but our facts on it are sketchy. Would you fill us in on it later?" Well, that didn't work. I'm not totally ignorant as to how governments and people work. That perfidy to most is as practiced as taking a dump. Perhaps I am a little paranoid, not surprising considering these strange events, so I keep an ear open in case to catch any small inconsistencies in their statements or behavior that might signal that I am being played.

"May I ask what the Breen like to eat?" he said. Not intending to be flippant, I reply, "Just about anything you put in front of them."

"So they have no particular dietary concerns, or problem eating Earth food."

"None that I have seen, just true hedonists.

They are partial to popcorn though."

"Popcorn?—huh?"

"There, I see my chefs, Please make yourselves comfortable while I have a talk with them."

After a brief talk with the two returning chefs, I escorted them on board, and with everyone strapped in, so too speak, we took off, and headed back to the island. I have been cautioned not to rip holes in the atmosphere, the loud sonic booms startled people on the ground. So the slow trip home would take about two hours, plenty of time to talk some with these U.N. delegates.

"So Doctor Parker, with the many high level visitors who are requesting access to Harry, we will need to address some security concerns."

"Are you concerned for the Breen's safety?" I asked.

"Not only that, but world politicians will need to be protected." The depth and scope of this conversation could quickly get out of bounds of my training and experiences so I had to think quickly. Let's see, who is in charge of security on the Val? Stop dribbling, and pass the ball stupid ..."I will explain your concerns to Harry," I said, "and you two can work out whatever."

"I must say, Dr. Parker, I am surprised that none of the aliens came to meet us today."
Not being the one to give up secrets to the enemy, I fabricate a small white lie, "So far they seem content to stay where they are."

"Interesting, don't they like Earth cultures?"

"Oh, they eat it up, but before they venture off the island, I sense that they are waiting for something to happen, but I don't know what."

"You have been living with them for what, about three weeks now, what can you tell us about the

Breen?"

"Well, they are playful to the extreme, at times almost bordering on the sinister." I saw the Professor's head jump back at hearing that, as though he were squirming in his seat chair.

Then he said, "Not quite sure I follow you, Dr. Parker."

I took a moment to think before I answered, "You see, the Breen are what I would call an extremely active species, and they have developed a physical strength to match. Their bodies are engineered to be able to endure hardships which would make any human cringe. Further, any injuries they incur self-heal and rapidly. These abilities coupled with their native exuberance can get the better of them. So it is not that they intend to be cruel, or sinister, as I mentioned, it is that at times, they forget we humans are not nearly as tuff as they are."

That seemed to do it. For the rest of the trip my guest sat quietly and let me drive in silence. Not that I wanted to be cruel, just wanted not to get drawn into meaningless partisan drivel. As they sat for the rest of the trip, they each showed on their faces the look of a man contemplating his past life as he walked that last stretch to the gallows. And yes, I was beginning to enjoy this. … So much so that I feared that Arlen's baleful playfulness might be rubbing off on me.

Upon returning to the island, I circled slowly above the crystal sky dome, and pointed out some of the new amenities we've added to it. I mention the mountain water slide and lagoon. Must sound like a sales pitch. What, am I selling swamp land in Florida? Flying at two thousand feet our guests have a good first look. Then we went down and under the dome and landed on the tarmac behind the much larger Val. All the while my guests were all catching flies with the mouths?

As we disembarked Harry and three crewmen come over to greet the delegates.

"Harry, it is wonderful to finally meet with you."

"Professor Tynan, nice to meet you also. What may we help you with today?"

"I have been selected to head up a U.N. committee to oversee and act a mediator for people and groups seeking access to you and your crew. That is if this is acceptable to you?"

"This U.N., is it a worldwide representation? I mean, will you represent all of Earth's peoples?"

"The U.N. represents all those people of Earth who want to be represented; not everyone, but most."

"Good, then let's talk."

It was early in the morning, warm and sunny, we decide to move over to the patio area which affords a great central view of the island and it's improvements. This was perhaps a bit informal of a venue considering the nature of the discussions to take place, however, Harry, and his crew, were all dressed in casual island attire. Which isn't much, shorts and Hawaiian shirts, which were the rage this past week, but I have seen my Breen friend's wardrobes. They don't have business suits; they are just your common, every day, blue-collar, worker type aliens.

Professor Tynan led off the discussion by mentioning, "Many of Earth's leaders have expressed a desire to meet with all of you, Harry. They have several concerns regarding access though, and I can't stress strongly enough how delicate of a mater this is. Few of Earths governments trust one another, and would prefer to have some control on who is allowed to come here. Another concern is regarding Breen technology. I have been asked to express to you how serious they believe this issue is. What if someone were to take a small object, a part off the skiff for example? Possibly, they could analyze it, have it reverse engineered, and learn your secrets. Consider how disruptive such knowledge could be in the wrong hands?"

"We do understand the paranoid nature of your peoples and governments, Professor Tynan. Your concerns are valid, and worth taking into consideration. Let me assure you we are not cavalier with our technology. You can tell the United States and other governments that we will not be giving out any technology, nor let anyone have access to it, without first obtaining major consensus of approval from your world's leaders. We know Earth's scientists have made great technological strides, yet the discoveries which make our technology work are still several centuries ahead of Earth's best scientists, and without them, there is no way anything taken from here will aid anyone. Plus, we have in place security measures, and watch everyone like a hawk (That was not exactly correct. Aside from the scans upon boarding the plane, security here was lax to the extreme.) No one will be stealing into some area, and running off with our stuff, as you say."

"Yes, I believe you Harry, yet you let Parker fly your alien craft unsupervised? He is here with you 24/7, and has private access to you and your technology."

"And he is American, and this bothers some world leaders."

"Yes, but it is more than that. This type of unfettered access is the kind of thing which can lead to the perception of favoritism."

"Yes, well, I suppose some may not trust this situation. I further suspect they don't much trust us Breen either. That is fine. Mention to Earth's peoples and governments that we are here. We eagerly want to visit with them. Hopefully, their trust of us will grow through these meetings. However, we selected Doctor Parker to live with us here for the term of our visit, and to chronicle these events for you, and for Earth's future reference. In the short time he has been with us, we have grown to think of him as a close friend. There is nothing nefarious about him being here, and you will just have to accept that." I always found a sense of finality in Harry's dictates. That said, the delegates were taken on a tour. Nothing was going to be settled today anyway.

In the following days Professor Tynan set up his headquarters in Rio. The United States was overlooked as a possible headquarters for the Alien affairs' committee. No doubt this was a result of the attempted assassination of the Breen. A direct phone line, or bat phone, was installed between the U.N. offices in Rio, and here on the island. The Hot line was tied in to Heenon's ICC console, and through that into his quantcomm device in his head. Not having to carry a cell phone around with you— priceless.

Many curious ears were eavesdropping in on the discussions between Harry and the UN delegates. Some of the crew, and the senior doctors, expressed concerns they had over having so many humans invading their sanctuary. Harry had asked for no consensus regarding this imposition, and had no choice but to bend to their concerns. A decision was made to limit the number of invitees to no more than ten at any one time, and to limit visitations to just four days each week. This trip was to be part vacation, was it not? Further, the limitations of being isolated away out in the pacific, and beyond the reach of most Earth type aircraft added another level of difficulty. The larger jet planes can't land here, just isn't room, and JJ is already stressed, and making almost daily runs. He is quite happy about visiting, and spends several nights here each week, but one man can fly only one plane. One solution rumored about last night was to simply boot Harry off the island. I hear mutiny is common in the south pacific.

Frankly, neither I, nor any of the Breen crew, wanted more people on the island. Quite to the contrary, we felt if we were to survive, we had to escape this tiny dot of solace. This invasion of earthlings was not viewed as rescue, just further punishment for sins not committed. We wanted our island paradise preserved as a place of refuge to return to, not have it tainted with gawking masses and political stink. Earth has many treasures to be tasted first hand, places far and beckoning to all space tourists. What we desired was a raft ride together down the Grand Canyon. Arlen, Hippee, and a few others wanted to go to a dude ranch and ride horses. A rather large contingent wanted to break free and go to Bombay, or Mumbai, just to eat Indian food. Oh, we had entertainment and the holo cubes, but they paled next the real show, and the one sided cultural visits planed by the U.N. would not sooth the hunger of a mutinous hoard.

In consideration of restrictions put in place, and with the promise of future freedom from their manufactured Eden, the visitations were agreed to by all island-mates. A do's and don'ts list for guests was drawn up and posted on the web site. The U.N. had the authority within the agreed-upon rules to schedule visitors, and on Friday, the 27th of March, Harry's Island Resort was open for business. But to the rue of many,

Thus died Hedonism,
       "Oh, what sadness I now endure; change and progress, have worked their lure.
       Our paradise, by hoard besieged; the walls so high they need not heed.
       The gate to the east, loosed it was; and then came in a fiend despicable.
       Where there I roamed, high and esteemed, free and to frolic; now trod
       With cloven hoof, a creature less perfect, whose presence thus marked,
       As stone over grave, where died my beloved Eden."

The number of spoilers allowed in Eden at any one time was limited to only ten, and then for only four days a week. To placate other nations and governments, the names of all visitors were posted to the internet. Only pre-selected airplanes would be allowed to enter to within 200 miles of the island. For security, the cadets had, and secretly of course, inserted stealth probes inside each approved airplane. Each and every passenger was surreptitiously scanned, including all luggage and cargo. The thoroughness and detection capabilities of these probes were unbelievable. I witnessed several of the scans, and I must say that it is a good thing that our guests had no idea their privacy was exposed, especially for the female guests. Let's just say the scans were revealing to the extreme. We had no problem with explosives, but several hand weapons, thought to be for personal protection, and were confiscated. It is remarkable what you can hide in a garter belt.

It is of note, that the Breen don't, at least in any of my experiences with them, exhibit the slightest amount of personal shame, or hint of need for privacy. Had they evolved beyond being embarrassed over subjugation to body probes, or having private musings aired for all too see, be that possible, perhaps so. From what I have seen their take on privacy was a one eighty of ours. And aren't we headed in that same direction—to wit—social media.

Truth and Consequences

After the first week of open visitations, I began to sense the futility in what Harry had so hopefully wanted to accomplish, and I further sensed he knew it too. Chalk one up to his lack of experience in interplanetary relations. Openness and mutual respect simply cannot be forced, or maneuvered into being. If meaningful relationships are going to occur, they crucially need time to blossom and mature. Given the intellectual and technological gulf between man, the organism, and Breen psyche, that could be a long, long time.

Each day more new people would arrive, and each the day the same old questions would be asked. The repetitiveness of it all came to hurt. The scientists always wanted to know how do you do this, or how do you do that. The politicians only wanted to know when, and if, the Breen would help their country. In short, they all wanted something. None came just to visit and talk, that is with the exception of several Australians, including JJ. Harry wanted to share cultures, not technological secrets. We earthlings wanted only to see what we could steal away with. Was the gulf between us just too great to span? Was there no place on which common ground could be found between us? Was there to be no altar on which our two species could kneel and take communion?

However, Harry's endeavor would not be without some reward. I had occasion to discuss with him the pros and cons of the visits. I suggested he look past our pettiness, and focus only on the possibilities of future relations. That we are a young naïve race, and need time. We need time to gain insight into interplanetary relations. We may stub our toes many times; we also may fail in this quest. That those were the perils we had to face on our own. He thanked me, and in his sober-sided manner related to me that he appreciated that not all human's lacked wisdom. At that moment I think he and I made some kind of breakthrough. Some form of a deeper cosmic connection took seed between us, and that perhaps someday, someday far into the future, man and Breen will stand together, hand in hand, out in the cosmos….

* * * * * *

Day 38
April 1st, or April Fool's Day
The Breen virus has been running loose in and spreading through our populations for a month now. Designed to prevent pregnancy, its effects were quick, but that result would not be immediately obvious to a couple trying to conceive. The phenomenon presented itself as a statistical aberration. It was healthcare practitioners who were

the first to notice the drop in pregnancies, and within two weeks were making startled calls to government officials.

Notice of this sudden and complete cessation in conception was then brought to the attention of the Center for Disease Control, or CDC. A Dr. Dorothy Weis was the official put in charge of the government's investigation. One of her first tasks was to reach out to the medical community for answers. Among the questions she sought answers to were, *What*?, *When*?, and then *How*? So far they had no idea of the *What*. The sudden drop in conception, thought astonishing in scope, was only a symptom, but of what? To help decide the *What* she was forced to turn to the *Where*.

Modern medicine is not without means of investigating emergent diseases. Chief among the determiners they have in their arsenal are data. As time and place data rolled in, it became immediately clear that the initial outbreak started worldwide. Which was a problem in and of itself—there would be no patient zero to home in on. Correlating the reports showed that the phenomenon started in every major city first, from there its time lines stretched out into small towns, and then into rural areas. With this data the statisticians were able to backtrack and estimate that the first occurrences were circa March first, but the question of the *What* still remained. These were highly trained scientists not fond of making assumptions. They would speculate, but relied on solid data to support their theories, and then to build a case. The outbreak timeline, coinciding with the arrival of the Breen here on Earth, led many of them to speculate; but as yet there was no solid evidence, not even a clue, that hinted at the alien's involvement.

In a search for the *What*? Today the CDC investigative team had a meeting scheduled with Professor Henderson, of Chicago's Easton Bio-Medical School. Ten days earlier his students had made a baffling discovery, which on top of hearing about a drop in pregnancies; he thought it necessary to contact the CDC with a possible cause.

He arrived at the Chicago headquarters of the CDC, and was immediately led into a small auditorium where Dr. Weis and her team were waiting.

"Welcome to our forum, Dr. Henderson. Thank you for meeting with us." After some introductions, "Let me first mention that everyone here has at the minimum an MD, so there is no need to candy coat it for us. Feel free to talk to us just as you would the students in your classes. I will stop you if there is a need for clarification."

"Thank you, I appreciate that," he said.

"Could you bring us up to speed on the type of research you and your students do?"

"Our research covers a wide range of endeavors; however, the lab making the discovery was primarily investigating virus latency in reproductive tissues. In specific, they were using recently aborted fetuses, and searching for the syphilis virus. Ten days ago our students noticed what we have come to label the Orange virus. Here, I have some stills taken of it insitu." He passes around the enlarged photos.

"The resolution of these photos is remarkable. I see that you have your scale bar set at 200 nanometers, and these are light photos?"

"Yes, we have the most powerful light microscope available today."

"I can see quite a number of those tiny orange spheres. You say those are what you suspect to be a virus?"

"That is the question. They are on the one hand most obvious, and on the other they have managed to resist most of our investigative techniques. Here, let me show you what we are up against. This is a video we took of one as we bombarded it with X-rays. As you can see, it simply dissolved into a mush. Regardless of how many times we tried, all we got was mush. They appear to be sensitive to high energy photons. Further, when we attempted to sequester them from their tissue bed, the same results occurred. This prevents us from analyzing their internal structure, and without that?"

"That is most curious," she said. "Have you been able to determine anything else about them?"

"We have determined that its host range is limited to humans, and has so far been found only in our reproductive tissues. How they got there, or where they came from, is anybody's guess. What we do know is that they don't act like a naturally occurring virus. Their method of reproduction appears to be through binary fission as opposed to using the cell's machinery to reproduce. We have made DNA analysis of the infected cells, and couldn't find any viral anomalies. So it doesn't appear that this little bugger inserts itself into our genome. In fact, at this time, we have no idea what the orange spheres do, or if they do anything at all. It was just their sudden emergence and positioning in reproductive tissues, coincident with a worldwide interruption in pregnancies, which caused us to ask the question whether or not the two are related?"

"Have you made an analysis of the mush, as you call it?"

"Yes, that was one of the first things we did. All results show it to be a combination of simple ordinary compounds. They are all listed here in this report which I handed you. There is nothing that has been shown to be toxic or harmful in any way by either compound alone, or in combination with the others."

"You have set quite a mystery in front of us," she said. "Dr. Henderson, if you were to speculate about this Orange virus, what would it be?"

"If my imagination were to run wild, I would suggest that we are dealing with something that has been engineered, possibly from the atomic scale on up. Consider this; if I was a mad scientist from the future, bent on sterilizing a species, I might look to its epigenetic code, something we at present are only beginning to suspect exists. Then I might engineer a micro-factory, these small orange spheres, to produce molecular sized particles that search out reproductive cells, sperm and ova. I would instruct them to insinuate themselves along our DNA beside the epigenetic molecules. There, perhaps by means of ionic and anionic properties, they would prevent these cells from performing reproduction, but, that for us is a science light-years away." On hearing his recitation, Dr. Weis, and the twenty of her research assistants, took a moment to converse among themselves. Then,

"Dr. Henderson, are you and your students going to continue to investigate this discovery?"

"Yes, I have one lab working on it 24/7. The spherules disintegrate rapidly upon examination, but we noticed some back scattering before they did. What we are doing now is to X-ray as many of them as possible. We are putting the results from each in a computer hoping to build a model of their interior piece by piece."

"The arrival and character of these orange spheres certainly suggests they have some responsibility in this current epidemic of abortions," said Dr. Weis. "And we must investigate them. I wonder, Dr. Henderson, if you wouldn't mind allowing me to place several of our research scientists in your lab, and let them work right alongside of your students?"

"Yes, I think my students would find that very exciting."

20: Survey Results

April 3rd
Day 40

It has been twelve days since Harry's U.N. speech was aired worldwide. What followed was global tumult. Tumult not caused by his speech which was considered rather mundane, but by the published results of the Breen survey which showed planet Earth in the midst of global collapse. This knowledge coupled with our perennially poor economy put our world's populace in near revolt. Groups of people were gathering en mass to protest. Their immediate and unreasonable demands not met, they resorted to violence. Casts of people, used to plenty, now starved, beseeched their leaders to grant them added welfare. But nations, already bankrupt, sought ever greater austerity measures, The flames of defiance and rebellion thus fanned, unthinking mobs set fire to their towns, further putting their countries assets to ruin.

        This was a negative reaction Harry hadn't hoped for, and world leaders were neutered in options to quell the masses. The cause of the long and worsening economic down turn, now made obvious, this, coupled with the realization that we have set mankind on a course to destruction, was more then we could endure. We needed answers, but not only answers; we also needed actions and reassurance that our leaders would be able to find painless ways to save us. When you can't help yourself, who do you look to? The government of course—we now affectionately call it entitlements. When a government can no longer help itself, who do they look to? That's right, a higher authority. One from outer space, for instance; if one happens to be in town.

Today, Professor Tynan, and four other representatives from the U.N. returned to our little island. They requested a meeting with Harry, specifically. The U.N. contingent was led into the Val where Harry, sequestered inside of the ICC, was waiting.

"Gentlemen, how may I help you today?" Harry was standing with his back turned to the group; his hands were hanging at his side while he stared into a blank holo screen. His voice had a harsh and dry tone to it. His hoped-for contact with Earths finest has left him in a mood these past few days. It was not going well, these visits that is, and he realized it. Sure, we have made inroads with Earth's governments. The Breen crew were now able to set up some day trips, and have started to venture out, but the visits to the island were of themselves a cause of stress on all. Just last night Dr. Sa'aarron was heard mumbling, "These pesky little humans, all they ever want is give, give, give. I told you so Harry, this experiment of yours will come to no good end." There is even serious talk of simply ending all visits to the island for the remainder of their shore leave.

"Harry, Earth's leaders are in a quandary," said Professor Tynan. "Ever since the publication of your survey and its prediction of Earth's pending doom became common knowledge, people have been rioting in the streets. They are demanding we do something about it. But what can we do? This problem is bigger than any of us together can deal with."

"It was Earth's massive population explosion which caused these problems, why don't you start there?" said Harry.

"What? We just can't rid ourselves of billions of people overnight. Plus there isn't the will among our people to control their future reproduction. It just isn't in our nature."

"If it is your nature that is at the heart of the problem, then why ask us for help?"

"It was your survey, which caused this problem."

"No, it was man's ridiculous and stupid misuse of Earth's natural resources, and his inability or unwillingness to control his own population growth, which caused these problems. The survey only brought them to light."

"Harry, we didn't come here to ask for help. We came here to plead for help. The tragedy would be to let our governing processes and control of our people to fail, and then could anarchy be but a quick slip away? I suspect we aren't more than a few weeks away from a total civil collapse. When the rioting turns violent, millions could die. All they need right now is a sliver of hope, or a token of help. Something to believe in order to stave off their fears long enough so we can begin talking about changing our ways. I plead with you not to let it end this way."

"Professor, thank you for your heartfelt plea, just give me a day or two to discuss it with my crew. Perhaps there is something we can do to help. Now if you don't mind, I want to be alone to think." They left it at that. Harry was not in a mood to talk or entertain today. Professor Tynan and his group were flown back to Brazil almost as soon as they had arrived. Harry remained somber for the rest of that day and into the night. What would happen next?

Early the following morning a dreadful dream woke me from my sleep. These unusual thoughts scared me, and I couldn't shake this feeling of forlornness which caused my body to shudder. Where did this come from? It was just dawn, but there would be little sunshine today. Looking to the east through the wide open window of my cabaña, the rising sun ribboned a horizon wide bank of dark-gray clouds with a crimson glow. A storm was on the way. Feeling a chill, the first since coming to this island, I threw on a sweatshirt and walked off to the cafeteria for some breakfast and hopefully a stimulant to elevate my mood.

Later that morning Harry called everyone together for a briefing. We all gathered below decks in the exercise room, and took seats in the bleachers. He stood out in the middle of the Warball court and began to address us,

"Crew mates, you are all aware of what the UN delegates asked for yesterday. They reached out for our help. Professor Tynan is right; we can't let it end this way. Senseless rioting will not teach them the lessons they need to learn, or help our cause in any way. Our virus has been working its magic for about a month now, but that is a very long term fix, and right now time is of the essence. What I am asking you for are ideas on what we can do as terraformers to help give these people hope and more time." As with all debates I witnessed between the Breen, the desire to help, and the desire to let nature take its course was a 50/50 split. Those favoring letting nature win out didn't offer up suggestions though, and from those willing to help some rather bold ideas came forth. They ranged from giving us new energy forms to food production advice. Booh'raan even suggested they terraform the moon. Engineering minds are never practical. In the end, the idea Harry grasp a hold of was building atmosphere purifiers.

"Alright, if we build these air purifiers, remember we can't leave active Breen technology on a non-Breen world. I want division heads to have a look at this plan. Let me know if we can work within the rules, and show me a plan to make it so." With that I heard some laughs, and then crew got up and started to leave. The meeting was over. So what was so funny, and virus? What virus?

I cornered Harry before he could leave the room, "Yes John. You have questions about the virus I mentioned? Sorry we haven't said anything about it to you until now, the timing just wasn't right."

"This virus affects us humans somehow?" I asked.

"Well, obviously, now that the whole world is aware of the fix they are in, it is somewhat a moot point, isn't it? We haven't told you until now, as we didn't know you well enough to take you into our full confidence, and we didn't know how you would react. You have viewed the surveys we made of Earth. Part of my reasoning for showing you the holos of Breen worlds was to make you aware of how we live. You should have noticed the population size on all of those worlds was very small."

"Yes, but Harry, a population of only 500 million people here on Earth is ridiculous. Why there were more than that back in the dark ages."

"Well, perhaps not exactly, but to your point, back then they didn't live as energy and resource heavy as you do today. You are living at a higher level of use of natural resources, and you know as well as I that this planet can't support its population of seven billion people with the same standard of living that you Americans enjoy. You are part of the twenty percent who live in relative luxury, while the eighty percent starve amid horrid poverty. You know this John, you wrote the very same thing in your book *Tipping Points*."

"So what does this virus do to us?"

"If you were us, and you truly wanted to find a way to save this planet and its prime species, how would you go about it?"

"I have thought about that, and you know that the results I came up with are in my book. There is probably nothing we can do, or will do, to save ourselves."

"At least you are honest. If more of Earth's people were that honest, the situations which led up to this problem would have been averted. And you are right John; all of our experience tells us the same thing. And to quote you, "but given our penchant for denial, I suspect it will be instead a head long race into collapse." To say that your technology is advanced beyond your ability to use it properly is obvious. Which is why most species die out at this stage of development? Naturally evolved life is rare in the cosmos, and well worth giving it a chance to survive. Our only desire was to prevent Earth's and humankind's collapse, but we aren't babysitters, and we can't and won't be around to mop up your messes. That just is not how it is done. So we engineered a virus which will infect every human. The effect of this virus is to render your species sterile, but only for a short period of time. Then it mutates, and over time you will again be able to sire children."

"So you're killing us off?"

"No, John, you are not listening. No one has to die. You and they can and will live a normal life. This is simply population reduction by attrition."

I got the beauty of Harry's plan, but I was irate that he took this action without our help or knowledge. So angry that I couldn't stand in his presence any longer, and had to go off and hide for a while. How dare they? Feeling betrayed, my heart throb crushed, my eyes teared up as I walked out of the Val, and with my head hanging down I broodingly stomped off in the direction of my cabaña. I had soon left the safety and shade of the sky dome. I strode past my seaside abode and just kept on walking down the beach until I had reached the islands southern tip. There two narrowing strips of land meet, and what was terra firma dissolves into a thin line of broken reef tops that slowly disappear down and out into the Coral Sea.

As I stood on that last patch of sand a feeling of horrid sadness overcame me. For humanity's sake I cried, and racked with guilt for my part in its soon demise I watched my essence continue on out into the breakers. I walked then swam out farther and deeper, until I found that last vestige of solid land to place my feet upon. There, half sunken, I turned around to glimpse back for safe ground. Afar in the distance it stood. The entirety of the ocean was now broken by only the narrowest sliver of land. I was awash in vast stormy waters. Then waves whipped by fierce winds came crashing against the bulwark of my soul. They knocked me off my fading throne and swept me away. Where I once stood soundly, I now foundered against the majesty of this foamy maelstrom. Its hands grabbed for me and pulled me down beneath the surface. There the roiling surf dashed and broke my body against the mighty spine of the island I thought my home: my corpse, our corpse, rapidly consigned to the benthic deeps. For man's sins, death was due as payment, and extinction an apt punishment, and what more fitting grave could a sinner hope for. Mankind's burial place to be left unmarked, no words would be spoken, nor monument erected, and for all his timeless glories, man is abandoned and ever forgotten, for the world weeps not for her lost children.

The sand beneath me felt cold and wet. Didn't matter. I sat down to wail. A single man weeping, a thousand miles of empty ocean circle me around. I the only person now who knew the dark secret of humanities end. Nor comfort could I draw from my nearby friends. One cannot describe how utterly alone I felt just then, at that moment, at that place. There, diminished for me time and space, and giddily I began to relish in my feelings of anger—how strange—farewell fairest of races.

For hours I sat, till he sun was to set on my worst day in paradise. I have had no alcoholic bracers today, and looked reality soberly in the face. My consternation was, after more careful thought, perplexing, as I wrote the book on overpopulation problems. I knew full well the trouble Earth was in, yet I still hated having the solution forced on me. Strange, these commixed feelings were, and if I hated it, and found them confusing, how would the other seven billion souls on Earth react?

Staring out across the ocean wide, her allures seem inconsequential now. I am left with two metaphorical options: one, a Jesus moment, as I cautiously walk on the waters, and try to escape to Australia. The other, also a deferment to extra-worldly powers, was a walk back to the sanctum sanctorum, and genuflect before god-Breen, and subject myself to his prefecture.

It was near dark now and my anger had abated, or more precisely, mutated into a terrifying amusement for things to come. Curious, we humans are, singularly, caring and thoughtful, yet together, as a race, we become oblivious. Short of any concerted action planet Earth and its resident human population will face staggering environmental collapse caused by global warming and resource depletion. A disruption of the oil supply alone is enough to throw the entire planet into an inescapable death spiral. Few think about it, but no oil; food production will plummet. No food, mass starvation will occur leading to the horrid deaths of billions as unruly, scared, and starving mobs battle each other for any scrap. Putting it all in a balance: with certain collapse in one hand, and reducing our population to a manageable level slowly over time, in the other, and offering at least the potential that mankind will survive, any sane person would choose the latter.

As I walked back, the Breen contingent were sitting in the restaurant eating dinner. This was an off day for visitations, and judging by the loud echoing conversations, looks like they are all in there together. Fine, I will deal with them one by one. I entered the dining room and looked over and past the others; Harry was sitting, having his meal in the far corner and still in a funk from the recent failure of his open island program, he is eating alone. Once I started walking over to him the place came dead silent. They all knew now that I knew, and the focus of my attention would be on Harry.

No one tried to stop my approach. This was to be settled between us alone.

Standing before him, by height alone he towered over me by nearly a foot and a half, I said, "Harry, I understand the reasoning behind your plan to use the virus." … "Given the complexities of global human populations and the potential for loss of life if nothing is done, I agree that you are doing the right thing." Then I stretched out my arm, and we shook hands. For the first time in days his stern look thawed.

"John, you look hungry, please join me, and have something to eat."
That said, I looked back at the crowd of onlookers, still not a sound could be heard. I still ruled the room, and as any Breen, this was a perfect moment, one not to be wasted. There was Arlen sitting just a table away and keenly eavesdropping in on what we were saying.

"Harry, I accept your offer, but just give me a moment." I then walked over to Arlen and put my hand on his shoulder, and said, "Arlen, you have been my protagonist and best friend, and the one who has been at my side all these weeks." And the one who was responsible for more pranks at my expense than I care to count, "Arlen, I want to," then I bent forward slightly and do a fake sniff, sniff, then say, "Arlen... you stink." The room burst out in laughter once again. Proud of my redo of an old movie scene, I joined Harry for dinner. Arlen, with a smile, decides to join us.

"Nice one, John."
"Thanks, Arlen."

We continued our talk the next day, "John it is a terrible thing we are doing to the people of Earth. I wish there had been another way."

"It is a partial solution, Harry, deep, deep, down in our collective psyche; we all realize things can't continue as is. There is an endpoint to our folly; I just hope Earth's population will allow for the saner reaction to your solution. You are going to tell them aren't you?"

"If you were me, what would you do, John?" I had to think on that one....

Note..."I talked at more length with Harry that day. We discussed the Breen classification system for civilizations, and the many civilizations on other planets within the Breen auspices. Their numbers for sustainable and healthy populations are very low judged by Earth standards, but the numbers all boil down to economics, my specialty. What we fail to consider here on Earth is that the economics of having long life change the game dramatically. The possibility exists that we will conquer aging in my lifetime. What happens when we all begin to live to be hundreds of years old? Even a small population of humans with a life span of say four hundred years, and an average worldwide birthrate of 2.4 per cent, would shortly overrun the planet, and you are right back to where we are today. The Breen have remarkable control when it comes to managing their desires to reproduce. That awareness does not exist in the human population. Just something to think about."...JP

21:

The Great Machines

April 7th
Day 44

Since the impassioned plea by Professor Tynan and his representatives from the United Nations just days ago the Breen have been tormenting over whether to aide human kind with their advanced technology, or not. Other than the basic rules of conduct, no clear rule of law exists in Lex Breenica on the subject of helping junior species. There was no non-interference directive. Each instance of intervention was left up to the Breen involved. There is no oversight committee to appeal to, no board of governors to formulate and administer rules, no judicial system to mete out punishment if it all went wrong. However, it was generally accepted as poor form to interfere with more primitive civilization's development.

There have been communications going back and forth between the island and Rio for three days now. The UN delegates have been led to believe that Harry was putting together a plan to help us. Worldwide, the riots and demonstrations have grown, and in many cases become violent. Clearly, someone needed to say or do something, and soon.

By now, because of Harry's open island policy, major players on the world scene have been able to insert spies just about everywhere. The U.N. group in Rio has been infiltrated. One of the cooks on the island has close ties to the Brazilian office of Internal Affairs. All communications from and to the island have been tapped, and several countries have spy drones making routine flyovers of our domain from high up, so it was not surprising that news of potential alien help leaked out.

Certain factions were dead set against any alien interference. General Bradley and his Alien Response committee, or ARC, were alarmed that the Breen were offering to give advanced technology to anyone. Their worst nightmares were coming true. The ARC committee was originally formed back in the 1950s, what with all the hubbub surrounding UFO encounters, the Roswell Incident(s), and the like. Our government wanted to know what to do if aliens actually showed up one day. The group's recommendation—get ahead of it immediately. Deny any visitation had occurred, abduct the aliens if possible, destroy them and erase any trace of the encounter at the earliest possible time. Was this paranoia? No, actually it was quite a sensible plan. True, it was an 'if you can't control it, kill it' mentality however; part of their thinking surrounded the hypothesis that there is an order to things. The 'what ifs' that an alien visit, whether an invasion or not, would create, scared them into thinking any alien influence would be disruptive and potentially detrimental to America and mankind. True, the ideas which formed their theories germinated in a vacuum of ignorance, none of the committee members actually thought aliens even existed, let alone could visit Earth. However, now, we had alien influence spreading uncontrollably all around the world—this was totally unacceptable, but after three failed attempts to repel the aliens, all the ARC committee could do was to sit by and watch.

The Decision
The decision to help us or not would fall on Harry's shoulders, but Harry was a torn man with conflicting considerations. In his thoughts, "Our sterility virus is taking something away from the humans. It would be much easier for them to accept the changes they were about to face if we offer them some help in exchange." Or, it could be surmised that Harry wanted merely to save his own face. Yes, the Breen were light-years ahead of us humans technologically and even physiologically, yet they still managed to burden themselves with many of our emotions, and guilt is not a many splendored thing. In dealing with his daemons Harry sought out the vote of the Val's crew, but as usual Breen, the vote was an even split, and no consensus could be drawn. So the final decision would rest with Harry himself. How would he vote?

It was early morning on the island. Harry was having a meal with several crew members when a discussion of the request by the U.N. Counsel on Alien Affairs came up. The U.N. found it necessary to form this new counsel which was designed to deal with the flood of requests for access and for help from the Breen. Many factions of worldwide diversity were asking for Breen help and intervention with everything from the monumental to the mundane. The counsel was designed to act as a buffer between the Breen and us, seems Santa Clause was in town. Most requests were dismissed out of hand; that is all but one, help with global warming. Harry sensed here a way to solve two problems at once. One, he could offer to help and cleanse Earth's atmosphere of dangerous greenhouse gas build-up. I mean after all they are terraformers for god's sake. Secondly, it would give Earth a renewable, or reusable, fuel, that being carbon rock. Alleviating Harry's guilt over using a virus to sterilize all humankind would make it three problems solved.

"Well, Harry, have you come to any decision yet?" asked Arlen.

"Yes, Harry," asked Dr. Sa'aarron. "Great Maker. Let us build the contraptions."

"We haven't even told them about the possibility of using the great machines yet Doctor; perhaps they won't even want it?"

"Nonsense, they will. Even these primitives can sense their planet is being choked to death. These machines solve half of this planet's problems—Global warming and a reusable fuel. You have already dealt with the other half of the problem."

"Thank you, Doctor, I am well aware of what I have caused to happen," Harry snapped back.

Arlen, a member of the contra voter's, breaks in, "I don't like it. Rarely does butting into another planet's affairs work out to the better. Just too many ways it can go wrong."

"A bit too late not to interfere," said Harry, "Culling their numbers alone won't change how they treat life on this planet, or themselves. Neither will more speeches help. We can berate them; point out how they are headed over a cliff if they don't change their ways, yell, scream, rant. None of that will work with this species. They just won't listen. However, the act of giving them the machines, of showing them that change is possible, would demonstrate sincerely that our actions were intended to help them, not eradicate them. Remember the virus has been at work here for over a month now. Their pregnancies are in decline, and I think they are starting to become suspicious that we are involved."

"The decision rests with you Harry. I like the idea of helping them out, and it would give us something to do. I and some of the planetary boys are itching for some action," said Dr. Sa'aarron.

"Not so fast," yells out Dr. Who upon entering the room.

"Crawling out of your cave doctor, is it Spring already?" chided Arlen, who was always eager to badger the sometimes petulant doctor. "Now hold on Harry. I have reviewed the plans for these machines, and they don't apply in this instance," argued Dr. Who.

"We have built and used the same exact machines on numerous planets' doctor, what is so different here?"

"You forget rule 5 Harry. No active Breen technology may be left on a non-Breen world. These Great Machines require active power pods to keep them in the air, and an array of nanobots to service them. As the senior scientist on board I cannot and will not sign off on it."

"Well, that is that," said Harry, with a heavy sigh.

"No, perhaps not," now Doctor Sa'aarron speaks up. "We can scale down. Why not use the smaller atmospheric modifiers? It's a primitive technology by today's standards, but they are stand alone, ground anchored devices, which will run indefinitely, and without the use of our technology, or continued help."

"Excellent idea, Dr. Sa'aarron. Is this an idea you can sign off on, Dr. Who?"
Now a bit gruff at being upstaged, Dr. Who responds, "Yes, but they are too small to totally cleanse Earth's air of excess CO2 build-up."

"Perhaps that is even better, I have been troubled that the great machines may have offered too much help, and given the Earthlings no reason to change their ways. These smaller air modifiers while still removing greenhouse gasses yet won't completely alleviate the problems facing the humans. We still need them to face up to their self-created problems, or they won't learn anything. Let's call for a meeting with the U.N. counsel, we can outline our plan to them, and see where it leads. Parker is due back to the island tomorrow. I would like him to accompany us, and to be in on the meeting. Besides he needs to chronicle all of this for future reference," said Harry.

"Yes, and where is John anyway?" asked Hipp.

"I think he is on Vanuatu Island," said Arlen. "He flew a skiff there to swap out some hired help."

"Perhaps tomorrow he can reconnect with his lady friend, Sherry," said Heenon. "The General had her hired as secretary to Professor Tynan, and she is staying in Rio."

"Yes, it would be a good thing for him to reunite with humankind. Remember we will be leaving soon, and John will need to let us go," said Harry.

"He has become a good friend, and I will miss him. Unless we take him with us?" said Arlen.

"Now, how would that work?" asked Hippee.

"No, his place is here, and he needs to finish his

work on the chronicles, and his race will need him in the future," added Harry.

April 8th
 In Rio...Office of the United Nations Secretary to Alien Affairs: A new department recently created to act as a go between of the Breen and others—public, private, and governmental. Some control was deemed necessary, and demanded by the United States and Russia. You just can't have anyone gaining access to the Aliens and their technology.

"Excuse me, sir, it is Harry Breen calling, and he wants to meet with the World Technology Counsel. He said it has something to do with a plan to help us."

"Thank you, Sherry, I'll take it in my office."

"Yes Harry, this is Professor Tynan, What's on your mind?"...

The Plan
Each day man puts about 13 million metric tons of carbon dioxide, a potent greenhouse gas, into the atmosphere—this is a staggering amount. That is man's contribution to the carbon cycle. This monumental increase leads to a buildup in the atmosphere and is causing to global climate change, or what is commonly called the green-house effect. Worldwide increase in the average annual temperature is a leading cause of melting of icecaps and rising sea levels. Rising temperatures have also caused changing weather patterns, and worsening annual storms, all leading to planet-wide destruction and increasing the potential for catastrophic loss of human life. With our addiction to fossil fuels, this trend in CO2 buildup is not about to change. Green-house heating will continue to grow, and at some

point it will get too hot for man, or just about anything else, to live on the surface of the planet. Currently, there are about 390 PPM of CO_2 in the atmosphere. The amount in the atmosphere in the nineteen fifties was only 350 PPM. This trend in the growth of atmospheric carbon dioxide will continue each year. It has been estimated that a count of 450 PPM would increase temperatures enough to cause dead zones to appear in the oceans, and at 550 PPM, we could see a rise in temperatures beyond human tolerances.

Yes, we are at deaths door, and sowing the seeds of our own demise. Just can't seem to stop it. This was the scenario derived from a planetary analysis made following the Breen Survey of Earth, which showed mankind reaching an untimely demise in the year 2058. Of course, if the trend of putting tons of carbon dioxide and other green-house gasses into the atmosphere were to end, then we could extend this end-date—a little. This was Harry's plan. Build and install atmosphere modifying machines to remove these excess green-house gasses from the air.

The following day I flew Harry and his small contingent to Rio. After landing at the academy soccer field, we were immediately ushered away to the U.N. offices, which are located nearby in a building used by the Brazilian Naval School. Conditions were such in downtown Rio at the present that we could not visit there anymore. Aside from Harry and me, we were attended by Arlen, Hippee, and Dr. Sa'aarron. We were to meet with Professor Tynan and the members of his committee who had been eagerly waiting.

We walked up the tall wooden steps of the

academy building and went inside. The boxy old building has a single long corridor running straight down the middle with a row of offices to each side. Immediately upon entering I noticed a familiar smell, something I hadn't detected in weeks, the ever so slight waft of a woman's perfume. "I know that smell," I thought. Harry led us, and in single file we walked to Prof. Tynan's office which is at the end of the long central hallway. I was taking up the rear. As the Breen entered Prof. Tynan's office, suddenly I hear a faint but sharp and too fast, as if hurried, click, click, click of high heels stuck on the end of what my senses told me were long and slender legs confined too tightly inside a long skirt. "I know that sound." I stopped dead in my tacks. Blocking her entry to the office, I swung around, our eyes met. As my eyes feasted on this gorgeous young thing, all I could think to react with was a wolf whistle.

"Well, hello there stranger. All these weeks and not one phone call?"

"Well, I have been held captive."

"Captive?" With a soft sly laugh she said, "I don't think so. I have credit card receipts of yours from several towns across Australia, as well as Vanuatu Island, and also for a very pricy dinner hear in downtown Rio. And just look at you, boy do you look scraggly."

"Scraggly ... don't you mean swarthy?"

"No, I mean scraggly. What, don't you have a barber on that island of yours?"

"Oh, I thought you would like the surfer dude look."

"Surfer dude, perhaps, but beach bum, no way. I've heard that you went native. Guess it's so."

"You're just jealous of my tan."

"Think again, mister. Now if you please, you're

standing in my way."

"So that's the way it's going to always be, Huh? There will always be something or someone coming between us?"

"No, I just haven't been properly asked out by a clean cut gentleman."

"Well, then maybe I'll simply show up at your door one day with my spaceship and take you for a ride to the moon?"

"Well, if you could manage to wash that island smell out of you, you just might get lucky." With that she pushed by me. Smell, what smell? Feeling rebuked, I joined the others to listen to Harry's plan.

Presiding over the meeting was Professor Tynan, the liaison to the world scientific community; also present was a representative from World Governments, a Hindi named Sanji Ranjipur; and a British Ambassador, Sir Charles May (unknown at the time, May was a CIA and British Secret Service plant—a spy.) Also present and taking notes was Mr. Tynan's secretary, Sherry Lawson.

"Gentlemen, thank you for meeting with us on such short notice," said Harry, who has mastered our language, word wise, yet no Breen has yet conquered the nuances—I'm sure his clichéd mannerisms were overlooked. "We have considered your requests for our help in various areas. Please note that it is rare that we choose to interfere in another plants evolution. For this reason, few of the requests that have been made of us will be honored. However, there is one area we are willing to help you with, and it is this I want to talk with you about today. As I have stated before, our ecological survey shows your planet is headed for total collapse in few short decades. A large part of the problem is your using the atmosphere as a dump for every noxious chemical you create, causing a run-away green-house effect. Cleansing excess carbon dioxide from your atmosphere would help to ameliorate the problem. We have put together a plan to do just that."

We have in mind to use our terraforming technology to cleanse your atmosphere. The plan is to build several air processing machines, which will take the carbon dioxide directly from the air, compact it down, and release it to the ground as ordinary carbon rock. Here, I have a movie of an actual air modifier in action. Harry pulls out a portable holographic device and turns it on. It is showing the air modifying device, a large apparatus sitting atop seven tubular towers. The overall device stands eight thousand feet tall. "This is one of many devices employed on one of our planets to adjust the atmosphere. In this case we were removing environmental toxins caused by a period of excessive volcanism, but the principle is the same."

"That is remarkable," said Tynan, "if I understand the perspective here, this is a massive machine. These seven towers look to be about two hundred yards in diameter each, and about hundreds of yards apart from each other. The whole device must stand over a mile high."

"They are nearly two miles tall. And yes, they need to be huge. Your atmosphere is equally huge. This is not going to be a small job."

"You can do all this with just one machine?" he asked.

"No, in order to appreciably lessen the amount of carbon you put into the air each day, there will need to be at least seven of them built, and placed strategically around the planet."

"Atmospheric correction, by only seven giant machines—the scope and scale of these machines is beyond my ability to comprehend. Can this actually be done?"

"Yes, with our help, they can be built easily. And once built, these machines would have a dual benefit to your people. Obviously, a reduction in greenhouse gasses will help prevent further atmospheric degradation, and lessen future climate change. Second, it will give you a carbon neutral fuel you can process, and re-use for energy purposes."

"This would be a real game changer for some nations. We will need to consider that. Also a consensus will need to be gotten from the world scientific committee and world governments before any building may commence. But, I will take your proposal to them, and right away."

"We understand your concerns Professor, but please keep in mind; our time here on Earth is running short. It would be best to get started soon."

"It would take us decades to plan and build something of this scale, Harry, and you have said you are going to be leaving Earth soon. How is it possible to get anything done in such a short amount of time?"

"Professor, take our plan to your world governments. Gain their approval. Once agreement has been reached, and suitable sites have been selected, Dr. Who, our chief Terraformer will start the building process. He has assured me that the actual construction of the machines should take no more than half a day."

"Half a day? Incredible, just incredible."

Path to Consensus
Professor Tynan took the Breen's offer to the world

communities. As is typical, the pros and cons were split for a myriad of reasons; few of any sagacity—if the machines were to be built it first appeared it would have to be without a majority consensus. Then the nations in favor of the project got together among themselves, and decided to have a straw vote to decide who would win, stating that only the pro country's names would be put into a hat. Seven names were to be drawn in all, with three additional as alternates. The offer to have a machine in their country was too good to pass up, so they said, "Damn those who want to stand in the way."

The pro group's decision to go ahead was made clear to all. The usual detractors were irate about this, but with the US, and Russia all giving the go ahead, the detractors had no choice left but to cry out in assent. There was only one snag, China would only go along if they could have one additional machine built just outside Beijing, but that was good enough to proceed. A couple of belligerencies, once they heard that their names would not be put in the hat, were quick demand entry into the contest. And it was done. The names were drawn. Knowledge that we had reached agreement was conveyed to the Breen. There were just two caveats. One, that at least one machine is built in China. The other, a small group of Earth's scientists and engineers must be included in the planning, and allowed to help out with the construction.

April 13th
World news headlines once again reached six inch type. ALIENS TO BUILD SKY MACHINES, ALIEN'S PLAN A TRICK, WORLD TO BE TERRA-FORMED, THE END IS NOW. The headlines ran the gamut. There really was no consensus among Earth's inhabitants.

Quite a few in horror, planned for the worst by building bomb shelters, and raiding stores for supplies. Others hailed this collaboration as a godsend. Everyone waited now, and watched.

The Breen crew were still split 50/50 on whether to help us, or not, but would stand behind their fearless leader regardless. Harry, hearing the news seemed happy, and was eager to hear what locations had been chosen. He even agreed to build the first modifier outside of Beijing. This elated the Chinese. As far as letting a group of Earth's best work alongside of Dr. Who? That was not going to go over without some ruffled feathers.

The short list; China, Argentina, Japan, the Gulf coast of Mexico, Egypt, South Africa, and one in Indonesia, and Australia. Now that the list had been set, it was time to start the next battle. That would be between Earth's scientists and engineers, and Dr. Who, the penultimate terraformer with an attitude. Dr. Who didn't hide his feelings of disdain toward of us humans. In an attempt to smooth over any rough feelings, Harry mentioned to our scientists and engineers that Dr. Who hated just about everyone, Breen too. Plus when they heard of Arlen's usual bellicosity towards Dr. Who, well that helped some. Remaining problem, how to you win over an ego-mad terraformer? Easy, just put him to work.

Nothing could have been more alien to our way of thinking of construction methods than Breen technology. We typically start out with a set of plans, of course, then go on to clear off the job site, and erect foundations, cement pylons, steel or wood members nailed, welded, or riveted together, all of this, of course, done by hand—human hand. Sure we use machines; tractors, cranes, and the like, but the process is always guided by hand. Not so with the

Breen. They employ the use of machines to construct other machines, and not machines as you or I would recognize. No, their usual builders of choice are nanites, which are microscopic, even atomic sized machines. Nanites minuscule in size, yet potent builder's en-mass; programmable, self-replicating, self-repairing, and self-fueling.

The Terranomics department, and Planetary genomics, would be working together on this project. Planetary Genomics would be working with each nominee to choose the best site where each of the machines would be placed, and to offer advice and help to us humans with handling the huge piles of rock carbon that will be building up. Terranomics was simply charged with the actual construction.

The machines would operate autonomously once built and required no crew of maintenance workers, only periodic inspections, a remarkable achievement considering their immense size. This, build and forget, style didn't sit well with the human oversight committee. A machine which never required maintenance or repair, and never broke down, this was not something human experience can handle, and we demanded modifications to the machine's design to allow for occasional inspections. One modification to the design, requested the machines be capable of being turned off, to control the rate of carbon output. Of course, any control room would have a sterile empty look; there would be no dials to watch, no controls or levers to pull. Dr. Who did offer a compromise and had access doors and walkways built into the behemoth, so the skittish engineers could walk the length to make observations. An airstrip was located on top where a small plane or helicopter could land. These accommodations were deemed nonsense by Dr. Who. The machines were designed to be autonomous.

A potentially fatal drawback—The Breen hadn't used this type of purifier in centuries. They preferred more recent designs. One problem in using them was overlooked by all including Dr. Who. The modern designs required active maintenance bots, which use, Dr. Who overruled. No active Breen technology can be left on a non-Breen world. Problem—the older design of purifier, the style we were going to get, though autonomous and did not need active maintenance, did require nanobots to be on hand for periodic maintenance and repair. The carbon collectors would work, and work superbly, but if a problem did arise, there would be no alien technology to fix it, and any repair by us was out of the question. We simply did not have the technology of scale to be useful.

Another problem—how to control the carbon output—a requirement made by Earth's oversight group. It was Dr. Sa'aarron who suggested a workaround. The inner workings of the collector itself were only long hanging strands of a porous material only yards wide and only half an inch thick. How they worked was simplicity itself. Air would flow in one side of the upper part of the machine, making contact with the sheets, where a chemical reaction took place scrubbing the carbon atoms from the air. The sheets themselves were infused with a catalyst, which through a short process, removed carbon atoms from oxygen atoms. The oxygen would be released back into the air and exit the apparatus. The carbon would get trapped inside small tubes built into the sheets; there it would fall down to a lower area of the collector where it would combine electrostatically with other carbon atoms, until a soot size formed. This soot sized carbon fell to another level, where it was mechanically compressed into bricks, which were then simply ejected out of the bottom, and down to the ground below. That was the design, simple, elegant, and continuous. How to control something so basic? Easy, if you are an advanced super intelligence, enter Dr. Sa'aarron,

"Harry, I have a workaround that complies with the humans request to control the collector's output."

"What do you have doctor?"

"It's really quite a simple thing to do. We modify the chemical reaction sheets; in essence, we cover them with an electro-reactive film. The film will only allow for air to pass through them when a voltage is applied to the sheets, otherwise they just hang inert."

"That would work. What do you propose for power?"

"Wind power, Harry, we use wind power to generate electricity and store it in batteries. Problem solved."

"Excellent, that should suit everyone. Do you want me to give the details to Dr. Who."

"I don't make command decisions Harry. I'm just a problem solver. Handle it however you want."

The Earth oversight committee of five scientists and five engineers were permitted to work closely with the Breen on this project. Doctor Who, group leader in Terranomics, and his technicians, were not happy with this arrangement. To them, the primitive human process of putting everything down on paper was anathema. "Primitives, primitives all," they barked. Dr. Who wore an arrogance, but it was an arrogance born or his experience and abilities, and the primitive humans would just have to deal with that.

Humans, ever suspicious, needed reassurance at every step. The engineers argued the scope was impossible. The scientists looked at the chemistry involved and scoffed—"No way can this work." This disbelief chaffed the Breen even more. At one-point, Dr. Who threatened to vaporize two of the engineers, a threat which actually drew kudos from the scientists. I mean, who hasn't wanted to see an engineer get vaporized? That different disciplines don't work well together was not lost on the Breen either. Terranomics and Planetary Ecology seemed at constant odds with each other—petty squabbles over jurisdiction. It was Dr. Who's ego, which won out.

Planetary Ecology put together some paper work for us humans to look at, but didn't bother to wait for approval before they got started with the construction. The whole world was abuzz. Still no coordinated agreement existed to give the go ahead and build the machines. A couple of nations even threatened war for various reasons. Finally, Harry went forth and gave a speech which was aired worldwide, and in just about every language. He simply said, "Enough. This stupid infighting has got to stop, and I am not talking to just the people of Earth, but also to my crew. Shut up, and work together. In less than two months' time we will be leaving Earth. All of you decide now if you want these machines to be built, or not." That alien bitch slapping actually worked. For once the big three, China, Russia, and the US acted as one in pushing for the other nations to get in line. Those nations who were chosen to have a machine in their back yard, readily agreed. There was much too much potential profit in it not to. There were still minor squabbles, but since the host nations, and the big three, were in agreement, a consensus was given to go ahead. That, and a promise, that 50 percent of the carbon rock are to be put into a pot to be shared equally with every nation. And the Breen, those of the crew involved in the project, temporarily put aside their differences. For the Breen, the payback for their effort was in getting the project done— nothing else mattered now.

April 18th, The China Machine Goes Up...
On the morning of the day the first air processor was to be built, Dr. Who, was locked away in his lab with his technicians. The festivities were not scheduled to begin until 8:00 A.M. Beijing time. China being several hours behind island time, there was still time for Dr. Who, and his build team, to finalize loose ends and make it to the site. The oversight committees were already at the site. I was on the island making preparations to fly the skiff to China, with the esteemed doctor aboard. Harry took a moment to eat a meal in the Val's mess alone with his command staff—Arlen and Hippee.

"Harry, I don't know how you do it. You managed to get them all together, and in only five days—congrats," said Arlen.

"Yes, and with all of those bloated egos, it's just a miracle. How did you do it?"

"Oh, I just step aside, and get out of the way. You know, just let each party do what they do best."

"What a load, Harry."

"Yes, you just got lucky."

"Didn't either of you ever consider that luck is the biggest part of command?"

"No."

"Well there, I have let you in on the big secret," he said. "I was surprised though to see the senior doctors tolerate the humans."

"I actually think Dr. Who is warming up to the humans."

"Sure Hippee," scoffed Arlen, "like master to his pet dog."

"Perhaps there is hope we can overcome petty differences?" said Harry.

"Petty differences yes, but egos, those go on forever. Just wait a week; they will all be back to their usual nasty selves." Hippee was always the philosophical type.
Just then over the intercom, "Harry, it is Dr. Who, we are off now."

"Alright doctor, we will be watching your progress."

I Can See For Miles and Miles...
Building the great machines would start as any usual construction project, from the ground up. But there it took a distinctively Breen turn. Each of the seven sites where a machine was to be erected had to be chosen carefully. At about one million tons of carbon rock per day, a monumental pile of rubble would begin to accumulate. Further, the process would produce a carbon dust foot-print reaching for many miles. The Japanese actually decided to have their machine placed at the eastern edge of their island where the bricks and dust would be scattered into the ocean. How they were going to collect it was as yet not considered.

Once a site was selected and Okayed by Dr. Who and Dr. Sa'aarron, a production control site was set up. The control site would need to be at least two miles distant to be considered safe. To accommodate the humans, Dr. Who agreed to allow for a mobile room to be hauled to the site. He scoffed that it was another needless step, and that he required nothing from us.

The entire machine was going to be built, or rather, grown, at the site. The first phase of construction was to build the collector pod. Raw materials for phase one of the construction would come from the earth itself, or dirt, I mean. The nanobots took ordinary mater, and somehow processed it into a building medium. Talk about a marvel to watch. We set up a control camp several miles away from the China building site. Dr. Who put the programmed bots, which were sealed in a clear vial, out on a table. He had a small iPad sized device setup on a tripod in front of him. After he fiddled with it for a minute, I saw a small, maybe two-inch wide sphere grow from it. The sphere hovered in midair a second, then moved over the jar of bots, engulfed them, and then rose up and flew off towards the middle of the building site.

Once at the site, the probe released the bots by dissolving the jar. Right away, the bots took to replicating themselves—doubling, doubling, and doubling again and again. Who knows how many they became? Quadrillions. The rapidity with which they multiplied was staggering to watch. There must have been about one hundred people at the control site, all with spy glasses fixed on the happenings three miles away. In less than ten minutes we could see the outline of the concentrator unit appear. A perfect hexagon of forest a half a mile wide seemed to dissolve, and in its place grew the great contraption. Fascinating!

We all watched from afar in utter astonishment as the machine took shape, and rose up through the clouds. The collector pod itself was two thousand feet tall. Astoundingly, the initial growth phase took just two short hours. However, Dr. Who was not done yet. I heard him call out to Heenon. Heenon had four large power pods waiting. Just hovering in the sky, the blue white shimmering light they emitted almost burnt your eyes to look at. The collector pod now done, the power pods were moved over to the collector and attached themselves at the upper sides. Once attached, Dr. Who worked his control pad again. This time, what he was attempting to do, was to lift the collector into the sky, slowly. The collector would be turned on, and carbon would start to be processed, and fall out of the bottom. This falling carbon was to be used a feed for the nanobots which were now instructed to build the seven support towers. The collector would be raised just ahead of the rise of the towers. This process would continue until the entire structure stood eight thousand feet tall. At which time, the two structures would be fused together. The scientists, to a man, the whole time were catching flies with their mouths. It was an engineer, of course, who calculated the overall weight of the atmosphere processor at thirty seven million metric tons. Just as the construction phase was coming to an end, I noted a thin grey mist falling down and from the towering machine. I asked Doctor Who what this could be. "Apoptosis," he said. "The bots are programmed to destroy themselves when no longer needed." Huh, I did not know this. They all simply dissolved back into basic materials.

A Monster Comes Alive
It was a little before noon in the foot hills outside of Beijing, China. The morning mists had not yet burnt off. Doctor Who had his control panel in front of him the whole while the building process was going on. All I could see or understand on the little device were

the changing icons, and blinking lights of various colors. His device, and pardon the pun, was alien to me, but the smile on his face said he was pleased with this historic accomplishment. Then I noticed several icons move and line up along the upper left-hand corner of his screen. They started to flash white, and then, a beeping noise was heard coming from the control pad. With very little pomp due his arrogance, Doctor Who called out, "Grab onto your under-drawers boys." With that said, he touched one of the icons. The lights turned green. Seconds passed, I sensed nothing new happening, OK—why the drama? Just then, I felt a deep rumble come up beneath my feet. "An earthquake—good god, what bad timing," I thought. No, it was just the thunderous roar of all that carbon rock hitting the ground some three miles away. Almost immediately the rock began to pile up—this was truly amazing! We stayed on-site for another hour, and used our spyglasses to watch the miracle happening miles away. Then it hit me like a ton of carbon bricks, and in wonderment, I thought to myself, "Dear god, I had no idea we used that much carbon each and every day, and this was just one of the machines."

After successful completion of the China machine, teams located at each of the other sites were given the go-ahead to begin their construction processes as well. Within a day all of the machines were completed, and came on-line turning CO2 in the atmosphere into a useable form carbon.

Aftermath
It was too soon to judge the longer term effects of this free form of energy, but as kilotons of carbon amassed, nations and people wasted no time in processing it. In the short term, what the aliens gave

us was now viewed as a gift of great value, and it was our time to return the favor. Their help was a game changer, and Earth's populace as a whole took a moment to relax. We now viewed the Breen more as friends than enemies, and they were invited to venture out from the safety of their island. This gained the chagrin of General Bradley, but what could one begrudged General do by himself?

My friends were now invited to visit the many faraway places they had heard of. There were trips to Paris for breakfast, and dinners in Bombay. We all enjoyed river rafting down the Grand Canyon. Hippee and Arlen, ford of surfing, dragged us to Australia for a surfing competition. We partied by day, we partied by night. They stuffed their mouths full of local ethnic foods until their alien guts burst. Everywhere they went, it was always 'all they could eat,' and always 'on the house.'

The next four weeks went well for us, and we enjoyed them to the fullest. Visitations to the island were cut down to only one day a week, and then by appointment only. Harry had tired of the visits anyway, only thirty days of shore leave remained and he wanted to partake of it. The Breen preferred cultural exchanges anyway, and going off-island to meet, one-on-one, with the common folk, was much more enjoyable than sitting around to listen to the litany of requests from visiting guests; their greedy wanting pleas, always asking for Harry's help, which he had no intention of providing.

To the Breen's many tales, their exploits during their last month here on Earth, read like a globe trotters dream. Our planet was now their own private playground, but I chose not to catalogue these exploits. Though exciting, they did not fit the parameters for insertion into the chronicles, nor did they provide insight with regard to the calamities to follow.

Of course, I did accompany my friends almost daily to wherever they wanted to go. We had wonderful times; however, I began to tire of the constant parties. I needed a break from alien friends and longed for a different form of companionship, and secretly I pined, "My dearest Sherry. How the world had impinged upon us. We haven't had a moment alone in many weeks." She accompanied us on many an escapade, yet I found it impossible to cheat her away from the grasp of her tall and inquisitive chaperones. I didn't voice my displeasure openly, but there were many opportunities for them to pick up on my body language. Arlen was particularly clueless in this regard.

In the arena of world politics rumors ran that the carbon rock was not the panacea many thought it would be. Furthermore, oil exports from the Middle East curiously started to wane. Contrary to our being told that all was well below the desert, many suspected the opposite. Gas prices at the pump shot up to a price not easy to pay, few could shoulder this terrible cost increase. I didn't trouble my other-worldly friends with these happenings. Their time here was limited, and they made it clear that our problems required our attention. So be it, I decided to ignore the growing unrest in the world and filled my hours with sensual pleasures.

Karma—A Universal Constant
Whether of alien intent, or of human design, every endeavor has an inherent possibility for tragedy. And even here, amidst the great benefit and hope for mankind brought by the machines, tragedy could not

be avoided. Three weeks into operation, during a storm, rare multiple lightning strikes hit one of the support legs of the Argentina machine. Being made of primarily carbon, the lightning strike caused a crack to form along the upper attachment, where the leg attaches to the modifier module. The crack, aided by the powerful winds, spread through part of the structure causing a large piece of it to fail and fall to the ground. The mechanism, not having active Breen technology, could not self-repair. Fortunately, it fell onto a sparsely populated region.

One farmer's ranch came under fire from debris which was flung up to five miles by the fallen machine part. Witnesses said it was a scene from hell. Curtains of carbon rock came raining down. Several cows were pummeled to death, but sadder yet; a large piece of carbon hit and killed the farmer's daughter.

22:

Conquest Earth

For over a month now doctors and research scientists have been troubled by an epidemic of spontaneous abortions and the nearly complete cessation of pregnancies across the globe. Their efforts have led them to suspect that tiny orange spheres, now infamously named the orange virus, are to blame. Yet, for all of their advanced investigative techniques and tools, they have been unable to determine what the spheres are, much less how they could possible cause abortive sterility.

Amid the clamor over the building of the Great Machines, it was easy to overlook the work of Dr. Dorothy Weis, and Professor Henderson. The world was blinded by the help offered by the Breen. So blinded, we failed to consider the dubious long-range benefit of the carbon rock. We also neglected the immediate effects of a shocking trend in pregnancies, or lack thereof.

Our scientists have been alerted to the fact that something anomalous was going on in our reproductive tissues. Over the decades, our technological prowess in the biological sciences has outpaced any other field of science. Our new toys, if you will, can peer right into the heart of a living cell. Our, state of the art, investigative machines and techniques are now light-years beyond where we were only a decade ago. We were quick to notice the 'orange spheres,' inside our bodies, but knowing something is there, and being able to do something about it are two different things. This new virus proved to be hideously difficult to examine.

Tuesday, May 10th, Day 77
A Little Slip

Doctor Dorothy Weis was sitting at home. It is very late and had been another sixteen-hour day, and she just wanted to relax on the couch. She has been heading up a team of researchers studying the strange orange spheres which have been dubbed the *Orange Virus*, recently found to infect human reproductive tissue. She turned on the television, a news broadcast was just finishing up, and the late shows would be on in only a few minutes.

"Nothing I have found helps me fall asleep faster than watching the late news," she mumbled to herself, "especially of late; all you hear about is Breen stuff, Breen, Breen, Breen, nothing but Breen." The news channel began to air an interview with Dr. Herman Katz; he was the head of the Earth Oversight Committee. His committee supervised the design and construction of the giant air purifiers. He was relating some of the work he had done in conjunction with Dr. Who, while assisting in the build-out of the Great Machines three weeks earlier.

News Anchor: "Dr. Katz, Many people and governments have voiced concerns over the safety of the use of the nanobots. For instance, what would happen if some of them got loose in the environment?"

Dr. Katz replied: "We worked closely with the Breen, and I must say their technology is beyond anything I could understand. Particularly, those little bots, they are programmable to do just about anything, but safe as could be. Dr. Who even showed us how safe they were. He took a sample of them out of their containment field, and put them onto a workstation table. I watched them with the aid of a microscope as they immediately self-destructed, I mean, *"they just turned to mush, right in front of my eyes."*

"Oh, my God!" Dorothy yelled out. This was a clue her team had been looking for. It now became clear what the origin of the spheres was. As to their purpose? …

The following day, Dr. Weis, called her research team together. Once they were all assembled in the auditorium, she played a copy of last night's news clip of Dr. Katz for them.

"Gentlemen, it has now become clear, at least to me, that this orange virus was created and disseminated by the Breen. All of our investigations point to them. Further, we must assume that since everyone infected with this virus has shown to be sterile, that the intent is to put an end to the human population."

"Good-god! How can we be sure?"

"Let's look at the facts; the virus infects only humans, it appears to amass in the reproductive tissues of both sexes. This virus, if it is that, appeared only days after the Breen arrived here on Earth. Lastly, we now know those other Breen technologies; specifically their nanites, self-destruct in a similar manner. This is probably a built-in safety measure. To me these are more than coincidences. All indicators point as arrows straight toward the aliens. Can any of you think of a more facile yet sinister way to conquer a planet? Without being able to procreate, within a few short decades, our enfeebled populations will simply wither away. Then the Breen step in and take over without a fight. They would suffer no loss, there would be no lingering radiation from nuclear war, there would be no destruction of our infrastructure; our roads and buildings still intact, our dams and water delivery systems unblemished, they would have an entire world ready for them to populate."

"But what do we do now?"

"There is nothing we can do. We haven't a clue as to how to combat this invader. Nothing we have tried has worked. It's checkmate. This is now a matter for national-security experts, and world governments to deal with. We need to pass this information on to someone at the Pentagon."

"Let's call and talk with that General Bradley. He has been the one who has been heading up efforts to fight the aliens."

General Bradley was contacted that afternoon and brought into the loop. His conversation with Dr. Weis went as follows,

"I don't understand, Doctor Weis, how can you be sure the aliens are involved? I thought it took three months to determine pregnancy, and they have only been here for a little over two?"

"No, that isn't true anymore, General Bradley, you are living in the past. We can determine within days now, if a woman has conceived. Further, aside from the lack of conception, the epidemic of first trimester aborted pregnancies from across the globe cannot be denied."

"Yes, that is startling. Do you have data showing the Breen are involved?"

"Well, it might be all circumstantial, but we have five sets of data, and they all point straight to the aliens. For instance, using conception data as a benchmark, our research has been able to determine that the initial infection took place within three days of March 6th, less than two weeks after the Breen arrived."

"This is all very troubling, Doctor Weis. If your data are correct, they could be trying to let us go extinct, and you say we have nothing with which to combat this virus?"

"As yet, sir, we haven't a clue. Maybe with a decade of more research we might come up with a treatment—until then, no woman will bear a child. That is why we came to you sir. There must be something our military can do to stop them."

"I tried that, and you know what happened. And if everyone is already infected, then it is too late to stop them anyway."

"You mean all of Earth's mighty armies can do nothing to stop them?"

"Not likely, most of our world's nations love the Breen for the help they have given us."… "Second, even if I believe what you are telling me is true. You still have no concrete proof, only circumstantial data. Third, the Breen say they will be leaving in only two weeks, much too short a time to plan and do anything militarily."

"So what you are telling me is that we are doomed?" …..

23:

The Price of Change

Harry's Second Speech to the United Nations
It came on May 16th, or Day 83

The behemoth structures built to help cleanse Earth's atmosphere of excess carbon dioxide have been in operation for twenty-eight days. The Breen were scheduled to leave us in one week, and world governments were intent on making a formal show of thanks to the Breen for their great gift. In Rio the naval academy auditorium was turned into a convention hall, and a huge gathering was arranged to this momentous event.

Captain Harry and his contingent arrived as usual aboard an elongated skiff. He was accompanied by Arlen, Dr. Sa'aarron, Dr. Who, Heenon, and of course me. A handful of Breen, most of the engineering staff, were already in Rio to partake of an earlier comparative cultures program arranged by Professor Tynan, and the UN. Of course, the Breen, not being fond of perceived government formality, would not share much. Frustrated at the lack of results, Prof. Tynan called a quick end to the failed concept. The Breen engineers were more interested in interplanetary eating and drinking, and decided to go bar hoping. Professor Tynan, tired of their constant frat boy antics, was heard commenting that he found the Breen's near total lack of seriousness troubling. To him, an educator, superior beings should act more, well, serious.

These last few weeks my relationship with Sherry, even amid constant interference by others, has blossomed into love. Upon our arrival in Rio I dismissed myself from the festivities, and rushed off to meet with her. She has been in Rio this past week, but has to head back to the US in just three short hours. We have plans to meet in her hotel room for a quick tryst.

"Well stranger, come on in," she beckoned.

"It's been five days—feels like it's been an eternity, Sherry love."

"Yes, sometimes I fear I might lose you to your surfing buddies."

"Nah, I'm not into making love with tall pale blue men." She smiled and gave me a little laugh.

"Aren't you always the comedian." ... "Oh, enough banter, come and take me you fool." I rushed over to embrace her, and accidentally scratched her arm with my PPD.

"Ouch, damn, must you wear that alien thing in here?"

"Sorry, love, I'll take it off. I don't think I'll be needing it in here—will I?"

"Mmm'hmm, maybe I am the one who will be needing protection from you? She quipped coyly as I took off my PPD and packed it in my travel bag.

"We haven't time to be cautious," I stated,

throwing my arms around the small of her back.

"Aren't you afraid you'll miss the meeting?" she asked.

"No, I live the meeting every day. Now, where were we?"

* * * * * *

 Meanwhile, back at the assemblage it is a full house—Harry is trying to make his way to the dais to begin his speech, but has to wade through a sea of humanity. He is shaking hands, and receives thanks from many world leaders and scientists, as he slowly moves ahead. Arlen and ten more of the Breen crew are seated up on the left side of the stage facing the audience. Several of the scientists and engineers who participated in the great undertaking were seated off to the other side of the dais. Harry finally manages to make his way to the dais. He moves to the microphone to begin his speech. Before he can start, the audience breaks-out in a huge round of applauds. Stoically, Harry holds his hands up high and says, "Thanks to all of you."

The ovation went on for some time. Though the Breen love to have their egos stroked, they to a man avoid adulation. Harry was no different, and his speeches showed this distain for hero worship in their lack of political wetness. This, and then there is the Breen's unwritten rule on making speeches to lesser species, or the 'Less is More' rule.

His speech begins
"We were happy to be of help. This is a great first step you have undertaken. We managed to overcome a shaky start, and learned how to work together. That's what was important. To the accident

in Argentina, and to the tragic death of the little girl, we sadly apologize. But through all of this, the machines did get built, and are now functioning and stable. They will continue their removal of harmful gasses from your atmosphere, and at the same time provide you with a re-usable supply of carbon rock for energy. And so it is to hope of a better future for Earth, and to all of mankind, that I symbolically raise my glass.

Gentlemen, we now turn over control of the machines to the governments of Earth. We have given you the knowledge and means to use and maintain them. Over time, they will reduce earth's atmospheric carbon dioxide to a level low enough to prevent further greenhouse warming. Yet, I cannot stress hard enough that this is only a first step. One of many more that will be needed to be taken if you are to avert the catastrophe predicted by our survey.

Sadly, these next steps you will have to take alone. In too short of time we will have to leave earth and return to space. Our job awaits us. You will again be on your own. We encourage you to take these further steps. Be a good Sheppard to planet Earth. We further encourage you to develop and use alternative energies. Give up your selfish and unsustainable use of your natural resources. What took nature millions of years to create cannot be sucked from the ground in such a massive fashion and be expected to last?

But enough on that, this is supposed to be a momentous and festive evening. So let's move on and open it up to questions."

Q: "It seems obvious that you Breen have developed a type of energy light-years beyond crude oil. You have access to a form of energy that can supply all of earths needs for now and into eternity. Would you share this knowledge with us? Save us from certain energy depletion in the years to come."

A: "We have learned to manipulate the forces of nature, and to extract energies from them. These energies and the processes that control them are currently beyond the ability of your science and technology. Giving you access to this knowledge is not the answer to the problems before you. In building the Great Machines, we did share with you some of our technology. We showed you how to clean up your skies so you could breathe again. The decision to share that technology was not easy. Trust me, I struggled over it for many days, and now you see why. The struggles that lay in front of you, the paths you must walk to find their solution, must be taken by you. We cannot walk them for you. I needn't tell you that anything of value must be earned. More to the point, you are not ready for such advanced technology?"

Q: "So you feel we are not ready to handle such knowledge?"

A: "We are talking about the energy and the power to reach the stars and beyond, and for that; no you are not ready yet. Your people still have much to learn. We cannot let you as a species expand out into space until you learn to conquer the daemons that still plague the Human race."

Q: "What Daemons are you talking about?"

A: "I hadn't wanted to talk about this tonight, but you brought it up…. It isn't the vast galactic distances which will forbid man access to the universe. It is your own malicious and hateful ways. There is still a madness running loose on this planet. It is an evil that has spanned millennia, an evil which even now inhabits every corner of this globe where man touches. Giving you the power of space flight, it would, I am sure, threaten to spread with you everywhere you go. We will not let that happen. Until man learns to cast off his skin of vicious and aggressive intents he will not be allowed to spread out into space. The many planetary systems around you all share one common law, that is that no race, no planet, is allowed to disturb the peace and welfare of the others. To do so brings harsh and swift judgment."

Q: "You talk as though we are all a murderous horde. We are not. We want nothing but peace."

A: "I understand what you have to say, but we have to consider your civilizations as a whole. Admit it, you are a violent species, just look at today's headlines—bombings, murders, rapes. You celebrate the actions of your best, but you will be judged by the actions of your worst. You may not see this as fair, but it is the way it is."

Q: "Could you be more specific about these evil intents, Harry?"

A: "You want me to explain to you about the evils of mankind? Your literature has spoken of them in countless books. Writings which you have revered and studied for centuries, yet you would still feign ignorance of man's inhumanity to his fellow man.
       For one example, how about you're many wars

or your hatred for others; even of your own kind. What about the destruction of your environment on a planet-wide scale—for another. You treat your planet the way you treat each other—poorly. Simply being given greater power will not solve these issues. What you need to do is change your inner-man. Gain better knowledge of your common souls. You already have all the answers you need—they can be found throughout history in your literary works. What you lack is the resolve to make these changes happen. Earth can be an Eden to all, but it is up to each of you to make it one."

Q: "What you are describing is a Utopia scenario. Utopias don't exist."

A: "No, a perfect place, and perfect people do not exist. What I am suggesting is that there are better ways to live. Imagine an Earth where all humans live equally well, and in harmony with each other and their environment. We Breen have a planet called Leanarus-3, a planet not unlike Earth in size and makeup. Leanarus has had a stable population of 500 million Breen for over one hundred thousand years. They all live in harmony with themselves and their environment. There have been no population explosions or environment losses. What is more, no wars have ever been fought on this planet. No one has died there from criminal intent, and no one is in jail. By contrast, here on Earth today there were five hundred murders in America alone. Worldwide, war has eliminated three hundred souls this very day. This month, starvation has taken over fifty thousand humans, and millions more live in poverty beyond my imagination. As for wars, this decade has seen the death of two million, and in the last century over one hundred million souls were taken. Is this what you want for your future—more killing, more starvation and death? Is this what you wish spread with you out into space?"

Q: "We aren't perfect, but is that a reason to not help us to survive and grow."

Harry paused on that question. His Hoosenine Plan has been in effect for ten weeks, was now the time to tell all?

A: "What you want, what you ask for, is reassurance that we will not let Earth, or the human race die out. It is my promise to you that we will not let that happen. We will not leave Earth without having first given you access to the information and inspiration you will need to advance; to help you create a better world. We will build, on our island, a library into which we will put information about your peers on other planets. We will show you how they live. We will share with you their languages, their customs, and their literature. You are not alone in the galaxy. Take comfort from this knowledge."

"In closing, our time here on your planet will soon come to an end. In seven short days, we will be gone. Earth is a remarkably beautiful planet. Keep it that way. Help your scientists find ways for all of you to enjoy equally the plenty this planet has to offer. Most of all, we hope for, and look toward meeting you some day out among the stars."

"Gentlemen, Thank you."

There were some closing salutations and a loud

round of applauds.

Harry didn't like being placed in the position of being a diplomat. He was a ship's Captain, and Captains make quick decisions, and bark orders. It's a diplomat's job to make long oratories, review options, and negotiate details. Not ship's Captains. Captains ruled swiftly and supremely, and his speeches showed this in their trend toward brevity. Short and to the point—it was classic Harry.

   The Breen virus has been working its sinister magic for months, yet few earthlings are as yet aware of it, and Harry was not ready yet to tell the world that the Breen have been toying with our genetics.

Half an hour earlier, after our tryst in her hotel room, we left for the airport. Sherry was about to board her plane back to the US.

   "OK, John, I have to board now, or I'll be stranded here."

   "Oh, just one more kiss."

   "You're insatiable."

   Whining, "I couldn't think of a worse place or person to be stranded with."

   "I'll miss you too," she said, as she turned away to hurry and make the plane.

   "Sherry, wait. I have something I need to tell you."

   "John, there isn't time lover, I must go, bye love."

   "But the Breen," I was trying to yell above the din of the plane's engines. "The Breen have a plan to."

   "John, tell me about it when I see you next in a couple of days," she then turned and ran to board

the plane head back to America.
   "Damn, she has a right to know."

After seeing Sherry off, I made my way to the
assembly room just as the meeting was adjourning,
but in time to gather and leave with my friends. We
were to head back to our island sanctuary.
   After an interminable amount of applauds and
afterglow, the meeting now over, we prepared to
leave. Once gathered we walked out of the main
conference room, then entered the annex building
whose rear door leads out to the central grounds
where the skiff was parked and waiting. Just as we
entered the annex, a bomb was detonated. The
Breen's protective devices sensed the blast and in
microseconds enclosed them in a protective energy
bubble. I had taken my PPD off in Sherry's room,
and absentmindedly, forgot to put it back on.
Unprotected, I received the full brunt of the
explosion. Though not a huge bomb, it was more
than enough to have killed all of us. My body was
blown across the annex hall. There, my charred
remains lay on the floor, wedged up against a wall.
   Curiously, I didn't feel the explosion, neither the
force of it flinging me through the air, nor the
slamming of my body into the far wall. The event
was recorded in all its gory detail by the Breen's
PPD's. Heat from the explosion instantly seared my
skin. I had numerous broken bones, and massive
internal injuries; least of all a broken neck.
Curiously, there wasn't much bleeding, my heart had
stopped, my body functions ceased: I was dead.
   Harry and his cadre rushed over and surround
my crumpled body. Arlen, in near tears, wailed,
   "Oh, John, Great Maker, No!"
   Harry, visibly angry, wasn't so kind and in a

harsh tone said, "Damn it, these bloody bastards."
No one knew as yet who or why the bomb had been
placed. This was a meeting signaling hope for a
better future for mankind. No one was supposed to
die—least of all me.

"We must help him," said Harry. Dr. Sa'aarron,
trying to show some calm objectivity argued, "No
Harry, you can't do that."

"We can't let our friend die doctor, not like this."

"Do you know what that will mean?" barked Dr.
Sa'aarron. Of course Harry knew what using Breen
technology to save me would mean. But this
question was more than just rhetorical. It was a
warning, admonishing Harry not to mess with
nature. A death, tragic as it may be, but messing
with Mother Nature, that's another thing indeed.

"We'll take that chance, Doctor," said Harry.
"There is too much at stake, the future of this planet
could all revolve around this one man." Arlen,
kneeling down beside of my crumpled body, visible
shaken, and in tears, said, "Let me do it, after all the
hard times I have given him, I owe him this."

"Hurry then Arlen, do it before his mental
structures fail."

"I will need to give him some of my master
controllers," said Arlen. "They will concentrate on his
vital areas first."

"Harry, for Maker's sake." Dr. Sa'aarron tried
one last warning, but to no avail. Harry was strident
on this. Dr. John Parker must be saved, but at what
cost? And to whom?

What Arlen was going to do was, by force of will
send an army of his native nanites from his body and
into my broken and dying mass. Once there, they
would sense the damage, then reproduce en mass.
Nearly instantly, they would multiply, and multiply

again, and again, in numbers too vast to calculate. This army of trillions would then hastily be able to effect repairs necessary to return life. The Problem— the nanites are Breen technology. Master controller nanites, the ones necessary to make the emergency repairs, were just that, masters. They were not specialists designed to make controlled specific repairs, but masters designed to orchestrate and maintain system-wide functions—Breen Functions. These master nanites would not sense my humanness as natural, but as alien, and undesirable. My, now perceived Alienness, would be erased, and supplanted with Breenness. I would now, and for evermore, be part Breen. That is the price I will have to pay to live again.

Arlen's nanites entered my body as planned, and began their miracle. Their first course of business would be to make emergent repairs to prevent brain and organ death, and memory loss. Further repairs, and the major changes to my body would ensue shortly thereafter. Now time was of the essence. Only moments had passed since the explosion, but people were already starting to gather around to assess the damage—who had been hurt? Were any of the aliens killed? What had caused the explosion, and how could something like this have taken place at the UN? However, the investigation would have to be done by someone else. Now time was an enemy as a war was being waged inside my body. Harry and his crew had to get me back to the island as quickly as possible. The nanites wouldn't wait. Their course of repairs would surge forward, and without reprogramming would completely remake me into the likeness of my Breen donor. The only architect capable of reprogramming and directing nanites this side of the galaxy was Dr. Who.

The energy fields generated by their protective devices worked to keep on-lookers away. Many came over to watch and see the Breen lift my body and hurry it away. What the Breen were doing was still a mystery to many. Several doctors were present at the meeting, and asked if they could be of any assistance. The Breen did not respond. Not that earth medicine could have done anything for me now. If I were to survive it would have to be a Breen show now. However, many prying eyes looked on. The condition of my body was apparent. Further, pictures were taken of its lifeless mass. The state of our media being what it is, news of this bombing and the pictures hit the wires instantly.

"Harry, I have activated a med-surg table on board the skiff," said Dr. Who.

"Will its use allow you to control the nanites?"

"No, we will need to get back to my lab for that, but I can slow them down, and its use will allow us to keep John alive. He will need to be hooked up to it so I can infuse him with a synthetic blood. This will keep his body tissues oxygenated." He then said, "Heenon, if you care anything about John this will have to be the fastest trip you have ever flown."

No one interfered with Harry and his fellow Breen as they lifted my body and carried it off to the skiff. Once all were on board they sped back to the safety of the island. There, my still lifeless body was taken aboard the space-ship. The Val had no sickbay; there was just never a need for one; no one ever got sick. Any Injuries the Breen suffered healed by themselves, and major injuries were rare to the extreme. They took me into the Terranomics department. It was Dr. Who, Who alone, with the knowledge, machinery, and experience to control the nanites. If I were to live again as a human, it would be by the grace of his hands.

"Doctor, can you save him?" asked Harry.

"Save him, save him from what? His body functions are already stabilized. Now the true fight will begin."

"Explain please?"

"Harry, he is infected with our master controller nanobots, and an ever increasing army of them. An army so small and vast in number no power can stop their plunder of his body. In that sense they are doing exactly what we designed them to do, wage war against injury, age, and disease; that war, I fear, is already lost. I only hope we can win at least one battle. They have already begun to convert him into one of us. There is no way to stop that now. You should have let him die, Harry. It might have been kinder for him in the long run."

"No, this planet needs him. For our plan to succeed we need him. So what can be done?"

"I will have to work fast if we are to save any of his Humanness. I can retain his outside appearance, but I won't speculate on anything else."

"Arlen, would you and Hippee hurry and bring me that old-style med-scanner over here, and quickly?"

My body was lying on a med-surg table. In essence, it was a tall flat hospital bed, but instead of a mattress top, it was fitted with a full form body outline. I was lying down inside of this pre-form. Below the table were an array of medical and surgical tools, but I wouldn't need surgery. No human medical process could help. What I desperately needed was a nanite programmer. Dr. Who was going to convert an old and rarely used medical scanner into a control unit. The scanner was wheeled over and placed on top of my body. The device looked like a large MRI unit cut in half.

"Now let's get this device powered on. … Dear Maker, look?"

"What is it doctor?"

"I was afraid of that; they have already started to build the DNA-comb organ. Once completed, it will start changing his human DNA into Breen DNA. We need to stop that immediately. Here is what we will do" …

While Dr. Who worked to prevent me from becoming a copy of Arlen, my love, Sherry Lawson, is still unaware of the explosion. Her plane has been in the air for a couple of hours now, but won't touch down for several more. Sergeant Mike Streblow, one of General Bradley's aides, goes running into the General's office. He has just received a security update through CIA channels,

"General, there has been an explosion in Rio at the conference. Dr. John Crater has been reported killed."

"Good God, not Parker? Crap! And what about the Breen?"

"My source says that the Breen's protective devices saved them."

"No doubt." … the General rose up out of his chair and was showing some actual concern for me. After some thought, "Sherry Lawson is due in at the airport soon, have a car brought up, we are going to meet her at the plane."

"Yes Sir, I'm on it."

"Oh, and Streblow, get me Mr. Tynan, the Secretary of Alien Affairs, on the line, I want to have a talk with him."

After a long talk with Prof. Tynan, General

Bradley and his aide rushed off to meet Sherry Lawson at the airport. He has made plans for her to be flown immediately to be at my side. Heenon, as a result of Gen. Bradley's call, has flown a skiff to Washington, and is already waiting on the tarmac at Ronald Reagan National airport, ready to shuttle her to the island. General Bradley, through Prof Tynan's bat line, called and personally talked with Harry about this mishap—perhaps some new hope could be generated here?

The war going on inside my body was still being waged, and would be for several days. My deathly injuries have put Harry's entire plan in jeopardy. While I lay in Terranomics I would be tended to and visited by many. I was more than an acquaintance to the crew of the Val. They had come to think of me as a dear friend, and understandably the mood on the island had turned somber, it was as though this act of violence had happened to one of their own. Nightly festivities were stopped. Visits, except for a select few were cut off. This incident came at the most inopportune time. The Breen were scheduled to leave earth in just seven days, and were in the process of shutting down the island anyway. Excess help were thanked for their service, paid a hansom bonus, and flown home.

Heenon arrived with his passengers some thirty minutes after they left the Reagan National airport. They immediately swooped in and under the dome, and landed on the tarmac behind the Val. It was a speedy trip. Several Breen were there to meet the skiff, and to console and escort Sherry. Her mood was sullen. Heenon was first to exit the skiff. He was followed by Sherry, who was followed by a surprise guest. It was General B. himself.

They didn't stop to admire the surroundings, but

were ushered right into my makeshift hospital room. Already at my side, perhaps just to torment Dr. Who, and to make sure he worked as hard as he could to save me, were Arlen and Hippee. I was unconscious, and would remain so for another day. My body, lying reposed inside the Breen style hospital bed, had to be encased to control the environment as Dr. Who battled with the nanites. Asleep and within a large clear plastic cover, no communication was possible, not even a simple human caress. At my side Sherry wept. She knew Arlen and Hippee well through our shared exploits, yet the three of them did not share words, or a comforting moment. She just stood before my healing body and stared and cried.

The duo had no idea that General Bradley was coming to the island, and were star struck, if that term applies, when he walked in. The two Breen, standing side by side, simply turned their heads, unaware and unforgiving, they stared directly into his eyes. I would have enjoyed seeing their startled looks just then. Bradley was a warrior, trained for and by confrontation throughout his whole career. Arlen and Hippee, though officers in the Breen's Terraformer Corps, have led what a human soldier might consider sheltered lives; they have never known war or even hostile intent. Now face to face with an admitted enemy, their reactions to this stressful situation differed. While Bradley stood stoic and unconcerned, Arlen and Hippee showed a curious contempt for him by an almost humorous openmouthed stare. Although they towered over their foe, I think it was Bradley's bold appearance that caught them off guard. Heenon, following orders from Harry, approached the group and told Sherry she could stay as long as she wanted. She managed to cry out a reply, "Thank you." Then Heenon told

General Bradley that Harry would meet with him in the ICC, and escorted him out of Terranomics. A historic confrontation was but a moment away.

As Bradley exited Terra, Arlen and Hippee turned and gave each other a knowing look. This wasn't an event they were going to miss, and in unison mentioned,

"Sherry, we are going to leave you in Dr. Who's company until we get back." A groaned look formed on his face; the last thing he wanted was to be left alone with a sobbing human female. They both drew comfort in his pained look, but with curiosity killing them; they nearly tripped over each other as they rushed to find a secretive place to watch this extraordinary encounter. The duo left terra and headed up-decks for the observation lounge.

"Hurry Hipp or we will miss it."

In the ICC, Harry was waiting for General Bradley to be shown in. At seven foot four, Harry cut quite a figure next to Bradley, who is only six feet tall. Harry was standing mid-room with his hands clasp behind his back, his facial expression—a slight smirk. As Bradley approached his footfalls echoed inside this huge room. Alone, the two foes faced off in front of each other. Then Harry said,

"General Bradley, I believe it is a custom of your people for strangers to shake hands when they meet for the first time." And with that he once again extended an alien hand out to humanity. How would humanity react this time?

One can't imagine the conflict going on inside of General Bradley's mind. He never trusted the Breen, and nothing about the current situation changed that. Bradley wasn't a diplomat. His mind is not convoluted that way. He was a warrior, plain and simple, and would not be going down without a fight. But for now, formality called out, and he met the alien's hand with his.

"It is a pleasure to finally meet with you Mr. Harry."

"Please, just call me Harry."

"Yes, I have been apprised of your tendency toward informality."

"General, I am pleased you have come to be at John Parker's side."

"Well, he is a bit of an arrogant intellectual ass, but in spite of that I have grown to like the man. That and I know how much Sherry loves him. For that I am thankful you could save his life."

"Is there anything else I can help you with, General?" Harry didn't waste time and got right to the point.

"We know about the virus Harry. My analysts tell me that your past actions suggest that you want to help mankind, not kill us off, but then you infect us with a virus causing sterility. If your intent is to kill us all off, then I am here to beg you to reconsider. I will get on my knees if that is what it takes."

"Now sweat him a little Harry," said Arlen. Arlen and Hippee, and all of the crew were watching this encounter on a viewer somewhere. The Breen have a thirst for drama, and this little skit playing out in ICC could have made the whole trip worthwhile.

"Yes, well, we did not get off on the best foot now did we?" said Harry. "I could have overlooked the attack on our ship on first contact. But you tried to kidnap two of my crew. Then without warning, or any declaration of war, you tried to nuke us. An act which I understand is against your laws?"

"Our protocols may be out-of-date, Harry, and were devised in an era of fear. This truly is our first rodeo, so to speak. The original architects of our Alien Contact Plan never contemplated the possibility that aliens even existed, let alone would show up at our door step someday. That we reacted poorly, for that I apologize."

"It must be difficult for a hard-nosed military man like yourself to debase himself in this manner? ... General Bradley, I appreciate your forthrightness in coming here. I wish we could have had a conversation like this when we first came to your planet. Perhaps we all could have made different choices."

"Then there is still time to discuss alternatives? This virus can be fought off?"

"Let me assure you General, we have no intention of, killing off, all of mankind. The virus is designed to save your species from dying off. It will reduce your populations to sustainable levels only. In time, it will mutate, and then, within a span of years, disappear entirely. By then, we hope Earth's people will have learned the benefits of living within sustainable bounds. Sadly, the use of the virus will be to no avail if humankind does not change the way it views the world around it. Once the virus has mutated, and your women begin bearing children again, your population can and will explode once more, and in only a few short decades you will again be facing the same problems. We have seen this happen on countless other planets."

From up in the observation lounge,

"Damn it, Harry. You should have sweated him some more. You see Hipp, Harry is too much of an appeaser. He had the man right where he wanted him."

"This time I agree with you Arlen. This dress down is a bust. Not Breen like at all."

"Yeah, let's get out of here. I need to give some thought as to what and how to tell Sherry about John's changes. Let's go and sit in one of the high pools of the water slide."

Back in the ICC the discussion was still proceeding,

"Cause sterility in everyone for any amount of years, few people are going to be happy with that one, Harry. No right is considered more sacred by humans, or more taboo to talk about. To be sure, when the masses learn that they cannot have children, there is going to be rioting all across the globe. This is going to cause a war, one that you have started."

"Yes, there are going to be riots, and possibly a war, but this war should be against your inner selves. The battles must be fought against your ignorance, your stupidity, and greed. I explain this to you, as you are a military man. You are going to need to get down into the trenches with them. Fight for these changes General. Be the man who leads your people to victory. For this is a fight not just for the survival of Earth, but for mankind's very soul."

"Our best people have poured over your survey. Many dispute the findings that we are doomed, and whether stubborn or right, few people will agree to change. They believe they have a right to live as they want."

"What, that they have the right to overpopulate themselves out of existence. That they have the right to cause the extermination of millions of other life forms, to pollute without regard, to cause environmental destruction on a planetary scale. You and your peers live in a self-imposed state of denial about the conditions on this planet. It is a fact that only twenty percent of Earth's population enjoys a twenty-first century lifestyle. The other eighty percent live in abject poverty. Is this a fair situation? You delude yourselves into thinking that you have some manifest destiny, or divine right to exploit this world's resources, at the expense of the less fortunate. When these resources run out, no god is going to come down from above and thank you for wasting the treasure put there for all. In your future hour of need, only the poor and the suffering will be left to hear your wails of penance, yet I doubt they will feel much sorrow for you. No General, there has to be a better way. Education and change, if man is to survive the next one hundred years, this is where your new war must be waged."

"I see that you have a good grasp of the human condition, Harry. I am not arguing against your plan. I understand your reasoning in using the virus perfectly well. But, to say the least, we humans are not all of one mind. This new collective way of thinking will be hard for many to swallow. It will be a very difficult fight, and I am just one tired old general without the resources needed to fight such a battle. I fear we will not be able to rise to this challenge. We suspected a worsening of world crises even before you arrived here. That is why we hired Parker. He was supposed to investigate his theories on global collapse for us."

"Yes, it is interesting that John became the nexus we both need. I selected him to chronicle the events surrounding our visit. It appears the universe has an even greater job in store for him. Earth's salvation lies with him. It lies in what he has learned from us, and in where he can lead your civilization.

Parker, together with the testimonials we will put into the library, those are the resources you need for your new war."

"And this brings us to a problem we need your help with," said Harry. "In order to save John's life, we had to use some of our most advanced technology, and because of that, from this day forward, and for the rest of his life, John Parker will be a changed man. He will not be completely human nor Breen, but a mixture of both. The problem is we are leaving in a few days, and he cannot go with us where we are going. I fear that would be too much of a change for him to endure. The human psyche is geared for a short life. What John will need is time to inure to his new being, to see if he can mentally withstand living for hundreds of years. It would be best if he did that surrounded by people he associates with. We can't totally abandon him here on Earth either, that could become cruel."

"Poor boy. If there is anything I can do to help him, just tell me?"

"He has a job to finish here. I want you to take care of him. Protect him from those who would do him harm. We will watch him for, say, a century of so. If his pain of living among short lifers becomes too great, we will return and offer to take him to live on one of our planets, while Earth's population matures. Then, someday, as mankind advances and learns to live in peace, he can, if he chooses, return to you."

"I will discuss it with my President, but you have my word that I will give him sanctuary in any way I can. And then there is Sherry. She is like a daughter to me. She needs to be told about his changes."

"We have been wondering about how to tell her and John both. How would you like to approach it,

General Bradley?"

"If you don't mind, let me tell Sherry about John, but I think he would like to hear about his ordeal from her and a small group of his Breen friends together. I think he would like that the best." Harry and General B. continued their talks on into the evening. Bradley toured the Val and enjoyed the sights of the island. He was invited to stay for as many days as he liked, and said he would stay until I regained consciousness.

My full recovery no longer hinged upon the healing of wounds, it was a balancing act between two distinct forms of life. Dr. Who struggled to minimize my Breenification. Some of the changes he could minimize; others, already changed, could be altered or reversed. My height would remain, and my appearance would still be me, and human, but inside, there was no way to prevent or reverse the major changes and upgrades. The nanites had already insinuated themselves too deeply into my every being where they would remain as long as I breathed.

Sherry while at my side remained speechless. From her silence, it was clear how much she loved me. Hippee, later that day, in a show of compassion, said,

"John will be alright, Sherry. It will take another day or two, but he is going to be just fine." I think she intuited by the complex alien processes taking place, that I would be altered. No one had as yet mentioned to her how much of me was going to be lost.

The Following Day in Terranomics,

"Doctor, I thought his body was healed, but I

see you are keeping him sedated," mentioned Arlen.

"Yes, the transformative process is still going on, and would be quite painful to him. No reason for him to experience it just now."

"He looks just like he did before the explosion. You were able to keep his human appearance quite well. How much of me is there going to be in him?"

"Just look at the scanner. I'll turn it on. I had it turned off while Sherry was here."

"Huh, my, that's a lot. He is nearly full Breen. I will need to talk to Harry about this. How much longer will his regeneration process take?" asked Arlen.

"There is no exact time frame, just an estimate. Should be sometime tomorrow towards noon. I can wake him up then."

"Wake him up? … Wake him up? … Should not Sherry be here when you waken him?"

"You're asking me, do I look human to you?"

"No, and I am sure he would rather see her face than yours when he wakens." Doctor Who, steaming from Arlen's sleight said, "I actually like Parker, he is one of the few humans whose company I enjoyed, so I will do it for him. Sherry will need to be told first you know?"

"Yes, Doctor, I know. I am headed to talk with Harry now to figure out how to broach the subject. He says he has reasoned out some plan for John with that General." Arlen then left the room.

Time to wake up

It was agreed that anyone who wanted to could be at my side when I woke up. That of course was everyone. They were all standing beside the bed when Dr. Who brought me out of the induced coma.

"There," he said, "he should wake up any

moment now." The clear plastic cover I was under had been removed. Someone had the courtesy to have my naked body dressed. It was just Bermuda shorts and a T-shirt. Sherry took my hand and rubbed it.

"John, honey, it's time to wake up." A little groggy at first, I began to move. Shortly I rose up in bed, and my eyes opened for this first time in many days. Sadly, I think the first face I saw was that of Dr. Who. As typical of late upon rising I closed my eyes again, and fell back down in bed. Then, trying to speak, I cleared my throat, and with eyes still closed, said, "Wow that must have been some party last night."

"John, I think you are dreaming honey." I heard Sherry's voice, huh, where did she come from? Shaking off the grog form my head, my eyes opened wide. "Huh. Uh, well hello. Hello to all of you. What? Have I been out of it?"

"John dear, do you remember anything from the UN meeting?"

"Meeting? ... No."

Then I heard Arlen ask, "Is his mind OK doctor."

"His brain is fine; I gave him a memory scan the other day. He may not recall the blast, but the rest will return to him soon."

"Wait, the UN meeting, I remember. ... Sherry, love, why is everyone here?"

"Oh, John, there was an explosion after the meeting. You were injured."

"Injured, I do feel funny." Apprehensive, I immediately sat up and lifted my legs. I counted my toes, checked out my arms and hands. "Well, that is a load off, so I wasn't injured. I mean I see no bandages. I still have ten," ... and then a fear crept across my mind, "Oh No!" and with a quick look down below, "Whew—for a sec I thought."

"Yes dear, you are perfectly healthy," reassured Sherry.

"So what happened?" Her eyes began to tear up.

Arlen spoke up, "John, you were severely injured in the explosion, and would have died, but I decided you would want to live, so I used some of my master nanobots to heal your broken body."

"Must have worked, I feel fine."

"John, I suggest you stand up and try walking a little," said Dr. Who.

Twisting to the side I slid off the bed and stood up and took some steps around the room, "Yes, I feel fine, a little lighter and springier in the feet, but all together, I feel just fine. Did I lose some weight?"

"Doctor, is he OK to go?" asked Arlen.

"Yes, he is completely healed, and none too soon either. Now, if you would all leave my lab?"

"John, how about we take a short walk on the beach, just you, me, and Sherry?"

The three of us exited Terra and then the Val. We strolled south out past the Towers Hotel, past the lagoon beach, and soon left the gentle protection of the sky dome. It was a perfect afternoon in paradise. The ocean today a protective womb, its gently lapping waves infused our senses. A soft breeze mixed the salty sweet scent of the surf with the musty smell of the coconut grove. The sun warmed hot our skin as we sauntered past the quay way to my cabaña, and on down the sandy beach. Ensconced between my two best friends I listened quietly while Arlen explained to me the facts of the life, Breen life....

24:

Dominion

My resurrection came on Wednesday, May 18th. I spent that afternoon walking the shores of the island getting used to my new legs. Arlen had explained to me the Breen facts of life. Whether in denial, or shock, I took the knowledge of the changes well. No outward appearances descried my having any discomfort. With their human friend well again, festivities Island side returned. The waterslide was again in full use. The lagoon beach was alive with activity. That night, as usual, a party broke out around the lagoon, and I socialized the evening away with his close friends. All seemed as usual, and no one suspected any different, but inside of my mind a battle was still being waged, and at risk was my sanity.

We partied late. Sherry over celebrated a bit and I relented and let her sleep it off in my Oceanside cabaña. General Bradley spent most of the day in conversations with Harry. They were going over Breen culture. After a tour of the ship, he was treated to a holo tour of several Breen worlds. He also did a flyover of Earth of the past. He said that that was one of the most remarkable things that he had ever seen. The General was put up in the Towers Hotel, but would be leaving early the next morning.

Thursday morning, May 19th

After spending three days here on the island General Bradley is about to leave. Most of his stay was spent in conversations with Harry. They examined in detail earth's plight, and that new found knowledge he has convinced him more than ever that our civilization is standing on a precipice and only one short step away from doom. This realization has taken a toll on him. Where before, inside of his gruff exterior, a method he used for command, had shown the bright light of a very positive man, whereas now, his generally upbeat mood has turned dark, and this worries me. Just before he boarded the skiff for a ride back to DC,

"Parker, you look good. It is nice to have you back."

"Thank you, General." He continues to drop my title, but I don't care anymore. It doesn't seem to matter now. Just look at me anyway? I look like some feral mongrel. Island life, Breen life, is changing me. Who Am I?

"Sherry, you have a good man there. Take care of him. I want you two to be happy. Enjoy life, or what we earth people have left of it."

"Good-bye Uncle Rudy," said Sherry. "You have a nice trip back to Washington."

"Thank you Sherry. How about a hug for your old Uncle." They hugged, then Bradley boarded the skiff, and with no more ado they took off for America.

"John dear? Don't you think that was an odd thing for Rudy to say? He almost sounded apocalyptic. I have never seen him in such a dour mood."

"He did appear a bit sad. You are right. That is a side to General Bradley that I have never seen either. All of the times I have been around him he acted positive. Why, his mood was almost sobering."

"Almost sobering? Almost? Just listen to you. You are like a college boy on spring break." No soldier in a funk was going to intrude on our lover's plans.

"Yes, well, I need to have a little wiggle room. Just in case."

"Alright, you party animal. What are your plans for the rest of the day?"

"Well, as long as we are imprisoned here in paradise? C'mon, let's rush over and take a few runs down the water slide."

"What, I thought you were afraid of the twenty-foot plunge at the end?"

"Afraid? No way! That is the best part." And we hurried off toward the lagoon for a day of fun and frolic.

That evening at dinner,

"John, tonight we have prepared a surprise for you and Sherry," said Arlen, "With Dr. Who's help, we have made some improvements to your beach bungalow. Now, we know that Sherry is to leave tomorrow, so we wanted her last night here to be an enjoyable one. Word has also been put out for everyone to stay off the southern beach tonight."

I didn't feel like joining in the late night frivolities as before. I no longer found pleasure in alcoholic beverages, and I have begun to shy away from social situations. Even sherry, though I adored her, and enjoyed her company, (something sad was growing inside of me) and I at times just want to be alone. Shortly after eating, I asked if the two of us could be excused.

I wondered what sort of surprise those guys had in store for us? We retired early and walked hand in hand back to my ocean cabaña. It was late, but the sun still hung above the horizon. As we walked down the beach toward home we encountered some signs. Some of the guys put them together thinking to be funny. One read 'Any man who passes here abandon all hope of escape.' Sherry got a laugh out of that one. At my pier a sign with an arrow pointing toward the cabaña read 'Eden.' Over the entry door hung a sign reading 'Nuptial Bower.' "Perhaps a hidden message there," I said.

"What is it, John?"

"Oh, Nuptial Bower was the name that Adam and Eve gave to their home in Eden. That was just before they were evicted."

"Well, just listen to you. What, are you a literary professor now?"

"Yeah, that is funny. There is no reason I should know that. You know, it is as though I can recall everything I have learned or experienced in life. What's more, I can call up passages from books I have read, and see them. I mean, in my mind I can see them exactly as I first saw them. It's scary."

"That is scary."

"No, not really. Here, do you want to see something really scary?" I moved over to the open front window, reached up and gave a tug on the pull chord. The shade immediately lowered, and we were alone.

"Now why would you want to do that?" she

giggled. For the next twelve hours we shut out world, and it left us alone. Laying with her brought me comfort and then sweet sleep. Something I had missed. I will thank my friends tomorrow for the king sized bed, fresh linens, and many large pillows.

Friday, May 20ᵗʰ Day 87

Last night was enchanting, but I wanted it to end, and didn't know why. Sherry was leaving the island today. I was going to stay with the Breen to the last.

After enjoying the sunrise together, we walked hand in hand to the restaurant for breakfast; she would be leaving shortly thereafter. As we were eating a small crowd gathered around us. Everyone wanted to bid Sherry farewell. We ate leisurely and chatted for a while, and then it was time for her to go. JJ was on the island, and walked with us out to the skiff where Heenon was waiting,

"John, are you sure you will be alright?" she said.

"I feel fine, dear."

"What about that nightmare you woke form early in the morning?"

"Too much wine at dinner. Now, come on, and don't worry. All of my friends are here with me."

"Alright. And you JJ. I am leaving him in your custody. Might be the craziest mistake I ever made."

"Don't you worry none little Sherry," said the Aussie. "I'll see to your boy for you."

"And that is supposed to make we feel better?"

"Awh, come on now, mate. He couldn't be in better hands than mine."

"OK. John dear, give me a kiss before I go. And make it a good one, as it is going to have to last me for a couple days." We embraced, and then she gave me one last kiss. A tear welled up in the corner of her eye and ran down her cheek. She wiped it, then holding back a sniffle, boarded the skiff taking her back to her home in Washington D.C.

Later, during her flight back to Washington DC, she thought to herself, "John seems different after the explosion. No, it isn't the physical changes. There is something odd about the way he is acting. Before his injuries, I couldn't keep his paws off of me. Now, he seems almost indifferent when we part. And he is no longer afraid of going down the waterslide? Then there are the nightmares, and always in the early-morning hours. My poor lover." With a lover's insight, Sherry was keen to sense that something was amiss.

Back on the island,

"John mate. That is a good woman. I can tell she loves you very much."

"Yes, you are right about that JJ. Sherry is a lovely woman. I might have to marry her one day. But I am not ready for that just yet. … JJ, I'm headed over to the Val to have a talk with Harry. Have you any plans for later today?"

"I'm headed back to Brawley shortly. Got a few things to see to there, but I will be back before the departure on Sunday. Are you going to be alright till then?"

"I'll look for you on your return JJ." And then I walk off. Everyone is so damned concerned about my well-being. All of this attention is getting to me. I don't see JJ off. Just need some space. After I enter the Val, I go down into the exercise room. It is still divided up into little holo cubicles. That is how the Breen make it through those long boring space flights, they get lost in computer reality shows. At this moment, most of the Breen crew outside recreating. Well, there are just two days of hedonism left. They might as well make the most of it. No one was in the rec-room, so I decide to walk the halls of the ship. Hard to believe that it was only a little over two months ago that I first met the Breen and now I am one. I don't get lost in the maze of hallways like I did before my injuries. Although I can't explain why, but her layout seems quite intuitive now. Same way I know that Harry is in the ICC at this very moment, which is where I am going next,

"Welcome aboard the Val, John," said Harry. "How are you doing?"

"I am doing different, Harry."

"Different? You mean that you are no longer yourself? ... I'm sorry. That quip was just the Breen in me coming out. Let me say that I am not insensitive to your apprehensions."

"That's alright Harry. I almost laughed at that one myself."

"If you are having trouble with anything, we can pay a visit on Dr. Who?"

"No, it is nothing physical. That part of my reformation is fantastic. I don't even think it is the shock of being reborn so to speak."

"Ah, then if I may surmise, something doesn't feel right up top?"

"I am having nightmares, Harry. I have strange thoughts. They are especially disturbing late at night while I sleep. Occasionally strange places and sounds flash on my consciousness, things that I just can't explain or ignore."

"It could be transformation shock, or your brain not being used to thinking clearly for a change. Remember, you have little machines in your blood now mopping up any toxins. I saw you have several glasses of wine last night at dinner. Didn't manage to get drunk did you?"

"No, you are right about that one. Sobering up has been thrust upon me suddenly. Though, not to complain, but you all will be gone in a day. Then, all alone, here, will I be, and with no one to turn to for help."

"We could take you with us John. However, stay here on Earth. Help your planet through the upcoming changes. Give yourself time to adjust to having a very long life. It is going to be a difficult change for you. In ways you haven't even suspected yet."

"Then marooned, am I to be."

"John, we Breen live by a code just as those in your military do. 'Leave no man behind,' we say. So don't worry, we have put a sign post in orbit, and we will be watching. I promise you. We will check in to see how you are doing. Take these next one hundred years, or so, to adjust to your new life."

After our short talk, I leave Harry and the ICC, and head out for a walk alone on the beach. Troubling it is, being now no longer human, but something different. Harry is right, this is going to take time and experience to adjust to. Next one-hundred years? Sounds like a joke. I will have to learn to cope. It will be weird though; I will not change, in a world that is constantly changing. I did sense that Harry was either not being completely honest with me, or was just too busy at the moment making plans to leave, to consider my plight seriously. Or perhaps as I am the great experiment there are no protocols to follow. Yeah, probably a combination of them all.

Early that afternoon I was looking for a challenge.

Standing on the lagoon beach I saw the water slide was getting good use. The death plunge at the end no longer warned me off. Emboldened I now wanted to show it who was boss. Going up to the top of the volcano, I entered the slide and went straight down. I didn't bother to stop and chat in the hot pools. Passing right through the last of the endless bends and long traverses near the bottom the wide straight chute was just around the next bend. This time I was not going to spread my arms and legs, and bank high so as to slow down. No, I was going to stay down in the water stream, take the corner at highest speed, tuck my limbs in tight to my body, and barrel down the chute feet first.

At the bottom the cute has a slight curve upwards. The Breen love to hit this going fast. The contest was to see how much air you can get. I don't know how fast I was going when I hit the upslope. Fast! Fastest yet. My body shot up, and up. I had never been so high. Shooting like an arrow, my still stiff body started to arc over the top as I began the downward free-fall. As I arched over I looked down and saw that the end of the lagoon loomed. Fortunately I hadn't over done it. As I fell, I saw the water's surface. Suddenly I felt as though I detested it. It was now my enemy, an object that I hated, and I was intent on injuring it. I bent my legs, raised my arms, and splayed hands apart. As I entered the surface, instead of a neat cannon ball, or straight dive, I violently slapped at the water with my legs then my hands creating a huge splash. Deep into the lagoon pool my body drove and I felt relieved. Once back to the surface I noticed Booh'raan and a couple of the engineering staff had risen from their chairs and were clapping. I enjoyed it. I had punished the water. And then I thought, "This is addicting. What can I do next?"

Saturday, May 21st.
Day 88
Today I awoke quite early. Who can sleep anyway? The Breen will leave Earth in a day. The island has been cleared of all humans. I am not adjusting well. Last night, perhaps my worst yet, the nightmares returned. In a cold sweat I woke screaming. After waking I dove into the ocean to wash away last night's fear. I swam out to the breakers, but in no time. It was all too easy. I had never been a strong, let alone, good swimmer. Now, I don't tire, neither is there concern for my life. Without existential threats I ask myself, "How can this be fun?"

After a morning repast, I trod alone to south beach with a lawn chair. I planted it there at lands-end and just sat and looked out across the ocean, and thought of nothing great.

With his time here short, today was Harry's final speech to the world. Would he now divulge the dark secret he has been keeping from mankind? How do you tell a worldwide populace that their time is up? That business as usual is over? That for now and into the far future mankind's choices will have to bend to another worldly power's mould?

He chose to make his last speech on safe ground. I wonder why? We fed it up to a satellite, and then it was shared with any television network interested. All who cared to listen in were welcome, and that was just about everybody.

The Speech
Ladies and Gentlemen, here is Harry Breen,

"Thank you, peoples of Earth. Our time here on

earth is too soon at an end. We will all be leaving you in just a short stretch of days. For those of you who have been of help, many thanks. For those who have caused pain and suffering to us and to our many friends I say, so long. I will not dwell on any of the bad times. Parker, as you know, was injured in a bomb blast meant for us. Thanks to our technology he is well again, and will be hard at work writing to chronicle our visit with you, and all that has happened during our stay. He will gladly share all this with you, and even some of our private conversations and meaningful events."

"It has been a great pleasure to visit such a beautiful planet, full of such wonderful people. We will think of you often I'm sure, and parting will be painful for us as well. Parting, as friends, knowing that we will probably not be back here in your life time makes this leaving even more difficult. Even though we will be gone, we leave you with the knowledge that you are not alone in the universe. …" (And on he rambled for some twenty minutes. I did not bother to listen to the entire speech. I knew what he was going to say. And what do I care about Earth's human population anyway?)

"…On the island we will soon be leaving, we have erected what you might call a library. This library contains materials for all mankind to share, and to learn from. In this library, we have placed detailed accounts of many other civilizations living on scattered planets throughout this galaxy. There you will find other species with many and varied customs, each uniquely special and beautiful. They are your peers of the future, each of them beckoning you to come, to visit."

"So with that said I will close now, and say good-bye to all of you. In our leaving, we put forth a challenge to you to come and visit with us, share with us your stories, share with us all that which you call—your soul. On any of these faraway places, there, we will await until you are ready."

* * ** * * *

And that was it. The speech of speeches was over so quickly. No long good-byes. Possibly the most earthshaking event in recorded history, a visitation by people from another planet, and all we get is a short TV spot. Well, the fun is in the visit isn't it, and the visit is now over.

Harry tried to be succinct—he was. I think he even managed to insert a little mystery into his speech. Did they, or did they not infect us with a sterility virus? I knew the truth, but his speech left that particular detail a bit vague to just about everyone else. Was this an example of alien parsing of the truth? Messing with our ability to procreate is a touchy subject, and perhaps he just wanted to be out of town when the fog lifted and the truth was revealed. He further made no mention of exact timelines—no babies, for how long? Was that for us to discover?

His speech was, and was not, received well. Many found it irresponsible of the Breen to interfere in something most of us consider an ultimate birth right—the desire to procreate. Others felt as though a burden had been lifted from them. That this actually was "tant mieux," or best for us all. Still others were left confused. There were going to be holdouts that refused to accept change. All who took umbrage at this inhuman act looked to their respective abilities for revenge. Religious leaders wailed and rallied their congregations against the

Satin Breen. Military men clamored war to their leaders, and plotted secretly to do just that. Media headlines took a particularly nasty bent. One paper showed sixteen coffins rising on a mushroom cloud.

Of course they threatened war against the aliens. However, for all of their posturing our military men and their instruments of death were rendered impotent by the alien's defenses. Their island fortress has been shown to be impregnable, and in one day they would be leaving our planet anyway, all too short a time to plan and amass an army or deploy weapons systems.

That the Breen hovered over us in absolute dominion was hard to swallow. Was this a sick joke? Was it something we could discuss and possibly implement later? What? Not have children? For how long? Many questions remained, but we were going to be left to find the answers for ourselves. The age of 'blame it on someone else' was over. The time to grow up and accept a more worldwide view of our responsibilities was now thrust upon us.

Cooler heads were hard to find, but they were out there. Their voices started out low at first, and then grew in intensity. After the initial revenge mania died down, we all took pause to consider what these changes meant. We certainly will never get a majority consensus in favor of the Breen Plan. Not in this world, or any other. The Breen knew this, and in times of desperation, someone must act, and act they did, knowing full well the scorn they would earn. Could we get past this as a species? For that, we have only time to rely on. Harry said something in his speech about a library on the island. That he had put there testimonials from other civilizations on planets far and diverse. I hope an answer lies there....

* * * * * *

Early that afternoon, after Harry's speech, I was still sitting in my lawn chair at the islands southern tip. I listened as wave after wave rolled along the shore, and then broke gently into a sheet of water that fanned out and up the beach and hissed just as it disappeared into the sand below my feet. Lost in this hypnotic trance I turned my gaze out across the ocean and toward Australia. The sun was still high above. Weeks earlier, before the accident, the blinding glare at this time of day caused me to squint. Now oddly, it was as though my eyes had built-in filters. There was no glare. Questioning this new ability I opened them as wide as they could go. Then, wham! all of a sudden the sky opened up in a blaze of colors. Their intense beams shocked me and I fell backwards out of my chair. "What the ...?" As I peered around the world had changed. My eyes were now like piercing ray guns. Everything I looked at held a strange psychedelic pallet of color. I had never seen colors like this. I wasn't blind. Everything was still there, but with a new and intense glow to it.

It was difficult to stand and walk. My depth perception was affected. Alarmed, I decided to wander back to the Val and seek out Dr. Who. I inexplicably knew he was below decks in Terra. Into his sanctum I went.

"Come on over John. What's on your mind?"

"It's my eyesight. Strange color visions have nearly blinded me."

"Oh?" He then grabbed for his portable flat screen computer device. Making some adjustments to it he then said, "Here, can you see these shapes?" He showed me some simple floral patterns.

"Yes. The acid trippy colors. What does it mean?"

"Watch what happens now as I take the trippy colors away."

"They became just flowers as usual."

"Bingo, John. Your eyes are now capable of seeing in a fourth dimension. You just experienced it for the first time. What you are seeing is what many birds and insects see naturally. Your eyesight has been modified to detect wavelengths into the ultra-violet spectrum and deep into the infra-red spectrum as well. You will never get lost in the dark again. You could guide yourself out of the darkest of caves by your body's heat radiation alone." He went on to say, "This came on you suddenly, but so did your metamorphosis. It will take a little time, but you will learn to control these abilities, and then be able to use them only when you want."

Curios, I had to ask, "I've always been a perspective buff. It's about the improvements the Breen have made to their bodies. There must be some history as to how and why you did this to yourselves?"

"Yes, there is quite an extensive history about them. We have made vast improvements to our bodies over the millennia, but their genesis was early on just as we were emerging out into space. I think that is what you might find the most interesting to hear about.

Of course, the changes we made followed our technology. So at first there was only slight benefit. The story began with our extreme sports enthusiasts. We didn't chastise them the way your society does. We embraced their desire to improve. Some wanted extra strength, some wanted to recover faster after a hard workout, others wanted to run faster or obtain greater endurance. Initially there was a period of flirtatious steroid use, but the changes they made were odd and out of character with sustained Breen life. Then we discovered ways to alter our genetic code. This allowed us to increase muscle strength without massive bulk. We learned to improve our senses, and this research also taught us how to prevent disease and lengthen lifespan. Our quality of life improved dramatically during this era. The blind were given sight. The injured were healed. Our lifespan increased. Yet our athletes wanted more.

Then we discovered nanotechnology. The nanobots enabled us to enhance healing capabilities. We were now able to heal tissue and bone injuries almost immediately. From this followed the development of the DNA-comb organ, and then life immortal."

"From what I have seen and experienced with you and my other friends here is that these changes are just the natural extension of abilities by technological advances," I said. "I am sure that humans will also someday soon learn to make these very same changes."

"Yes, that is certainly quite possible." Then he went on to say, "The fantastical improvements came much later. They had to wait until we discovered micro energy generators. That is when it got really interesting."

"Fantastical improvements? What? There's more?"

"Why, yes, and thank you for asking." I had forgotten how Dr. Who liked to gloat. "No one has mentioned this to you, but your new body is capable of sustaining itself almost indefinitely."

"I'm not quite sure I understand what you are

getting at."

"Well, suppose that you are working in outer space, you are wearing a life suit, and somehow you get lost. This is not a hypothetical case, it actually happened. Centuries ago, a Breen did get lost in space. He was out floating about for six months. When we finally recovered him, he was found in perfect health."

"Six months without food or water? How is that possible?"

"Energy, John. With energy everything your body needs can be produced, and your body, together with its nanobots and specialized organs is designed to do just that. You can eat until your gut bursts, but you don't have to. If you stop eating your body will provide itself with the necessary sustenance. What's more, neither do you need to breath. Your system is designed to produce oxygen if it senses a need. This body that you have is the ultimate design, and all thanks to the fantastic atomic sized energy producing machines inside every one of your cells."

"Given how some of the crew eat, Arlen in particular, that claim is hard to believe."

"Yes, well, gluttony isn't lost on only you humans."

"Is there anything else I should be warned about?"

"I can't think of anything at this time. … You have some amazing abilities John, but you must be careful. You can live and enjoy a long life, seemingly forever. But remember, you and we are not gods, and neither are we immortal. It is true that you could survive a major trauma such as a stake through your heart or a bullet to your brain. You can also grow new limbs, and your nerves if damaged will always grow back, but if your head ever comes off at your neck you will die."

I left Dr. Who's side better informed, but confused. My sensory anomaly had gone away. Being able to see farther into the light spectrum was interesting and I can't wait to try it again. Yet, there was still something nagging at me, as though there was something more I needed to know. Something he forgot to mention, or was not ready to mention.

"Harry, it's Dr. Who." After my talk with him, Doctor Who contacted Harry on his quantcomm, level three (private).

"Yes, Doctor. What is it?"

"John was just here. He had some questions. He is beginning to experience some of his new abilities."

"We expected that."

"Yes, but I can't help but think we are making a mistake about leaving him here. So far he only knows about some of his physical and mental abilities. I fear that he may one day discover the others."

"How is that possible? We haven't told him about them; neither does he suspect that even we have such powers."

"Call it an idea whose time has come. His nanites will continue to modify his body. On their own they may be able to turn him full Breen, and with a signpost in orbit there would be no limit to the energy he could access. He could one day alter the destiny of this planet with it."

"Now that is a chilling thought," said Harry. "Well. That is something we can deal with when and if it happens. For now, let's just let it be."

25:

Bon farewells!

Sunday, May 22
Day 89

As world populations reeled in shock over news of the sterility virus, my Breen friends were in the process of closing down the island. They could have easily returned it back into a pristine tropical isle, but part of Harry's promise to us humans was to enshrine testimonials here from extra-earth civilizations in what he called a library. Imagine being able to select a holo cube of some other world, a world light-years distant. Pop its holograph into a projector and see this new world in perfect detail. To actually be able to step into this holograph and experience this world as though you were there. To view images of our peers who live, even now, on another planet. Imagine being able to visit their homes and cities; to hear their voices; to amaze at the different creatures, plant life, and scenery. What a remarkable gift this would be.

This library was to be a place where anyone could come and view the testimonials for free. What more of a spectacular demonstration that we are no longer alone in the universe, and that our future survival through change is possible? These would be blueprints of sorts, demonstrations on how other civilizations survived their own shortcomings.

With only a day to go, the island has been cleaned up, but some changes remain to be made. No active Breen technology can remain on earth, not even one nanite can be left behind. The mountainous water slide has to be shut off, and active repair processes in place in the other structures would be stopped.

"Harry, we can turn just about everything off, even the waterslide, and the basic structures will still remain, but my fears are once we are gone, nature will take over, and we could see failures. I estimate the dome to develop serious structural failures within two hundred years due to geologic forces. Time will take its toll, and without active repair, things will start to crumble," said Dr. Who.

"What, the waterslide won't work? That was our biggest attraction."

"Harry, please."

"Alright, I'll get serious. I want you to dissolve all our machinery, and end any active processes, but leave the machinery rooms open; empty, but open. If the humans want a water slide, then they will have to install power systems and water pumps, and the same for the rest of the island—except the library. We need to leave some type of power system to run the library and the hotel. Can't we figure into the dome a solar power system?"

"Yes, why that's brilliant Harry. A simple solar-energy system would produce more than enough power to keep it all running without the use of our electron power device. However, the dome, as well as everything else here will age and eventually fail."

"Not our problem doctor. We are not the universe's handymen. If the humans want it, let the humans fix it. … Now, in addition to the changes to the island, we will need a sign post up in orbit."

"You mean, spy post, Harry?"

"Monitoring, that is all part of the plan. We haven't gone through these tough steps, taken mankind's population to task, and shaken their civilizations to the core, just to let them revert back to their suicidal ways. And for John, one day he may discover how to use his quantcomm. Without a relay station close by it won't have the power to reach us if and when he needs help."

"You feel a responsibility toward him?"

"Much more than that Doctor, it is part of our service code, Leave no Breen Behind."

"Is he Breen? What is it that makes us Breen? Is it these physical parts, or something deeper inside, say our soul? He doesn't have a Breen soul Harry. He was born human."

"That is a typical response I would expect from an engineer. I should have thought Parker's soul might have touched yours Doctor? You did call him a friend the other day."

After some musing Dr. Who responded, "Yes, I did Harry, and I am not so stubborn as to not mention I will miss him, and his curt missives. Perhaps we all have grown some on this trip."

"I'll put building your sign post at the top of my list, and we will have the dome covered with a solar power generating polymer, but I must say Harry, at first I didn't think you could pull it off. This turned out to be a very difficult first contact. Looks like it will, in the end, workout for the better. Personally, I think you got too involved, but you learned from it, and I want to be first to tell you—congrats."

"Why, Doctor Who, that coming from you of all people really means a lot. Softening your attitude a little are you?"

"No, and no need to mention this to the others, I do have a reputation to uphold."

* * * * * *

On every planet the Breen have visited usually one or two foods really stand out. For earth, it became our use of the corn kernel to make popcorn, a simple, yet delicious food, not found on any other planet. Heenon has gathered with a small group of crewmen and they are determined to find a way to bring the un-popped corn with them on the trip.

"Guys, we still have several hundred pounds of the stuff. It makes for a great snack. I think we should put in storage, and take it with us."

"I don't know Heenon. It hasn't been tested; you know the rules about transporting foreign species."

"But it is such a basic little thing. Just a seed actually."

"Look Heenon, we all love this stuff, but it is a seed which if planted could become invasive, and destroy native life on some other planet."

"Well, we aren't going to settle this ourselves, let's appeal to a higher authority."
A coterie of Breen, headed by Heenon, rushed into the ICC to ask Harry's advice.

"Captain, this popcorn treat we all have been eating?"

"Yes, Mr. Heenon?"

"Well, sir, we all wish to take some of it back with us."

"What, so you can plant it on some other world, perhaps Breen Prime?"

"Well, yes."

"Rule sixteen, Mr. Heenon. No interplanetary transportation of a possibly harmful and invasive material of any kind is allowed without the minimum of a ten-year study." Seven heavy sighs could be heard. "Yes, sir, we understand."

"Or, as I was going to finish saying, unless it is certified safe by a licensed Planetary Ecologist." And of course Dr. Sa'aarron has multiple licenses. With that little nugget profuse muttering was heard as the seven Breen rushed off to find Sa'aarron, who was out pool side.

"He loves the stuff too. I just know he will sign off on it."

"Oh, and Mr. Heenon?"

"Yes, Captain?"

"Remember it has been three months since this behemoth of a ship has moved. We will need to do a quantum alignment test on the propulsion nodes inside of the hull, and run a test up to full power. We don't want to have any snags tomorrow at takeoff."

"Sorry Captain, I guess we should have told you, but it is already done. We came in here last night and ran all the tests, including a power up. We put it all in your log."

"My log? Huh, I haven't thought about my log let alone picked it up in over a month. Oh, very well then, carry on" … "Those boys a bucking for a promotion."

* * * * * *

Physically, I was doing well, in fact, quite well. As a Breen hybrid I will always be in perfect physical health. My newfound strength and abilities were phenomenal. I could exercise without tiring, before I couldn't jog half a block. Now I could burst off at full speed till days end and not see my heart rate rise. Likewise, mentally I had never experienced such clarity. I no longer stumbled for a word or thought. Thanks to the internal computer-brain interface I now enjoyed an eidetic memory. What's more, it is self-programming. Each day I find it had searched my mind for old and hidden memories. Now every page of every book I have ever read can be recalled in exact detail. But for all of my mental and physical prowess, emotionally, I am a mess. Wracked by nightmares I get little sleep. Day in and day out I hear a haunting whisper in my ears. Further, I no longer know what I am.

When the Breen leave tomorrow they will be taking a part of me with them—that part which we have shared for the past three months. At first I saw these beings as alien, but now I no longer consider them aliens, nor friends either—they have become much more. They are now truly as much a part of me as I of them. A sadness has been welling up in my gut. The thought of saying good-bye to them, perhaps forever, I sense as somehow tragic, and inside I feel terribly lonely. And what am I now? Part alien, still part human; to where does my allegiance lie? Do I still want to be human? Will the humans still want me? I can hide my abilities, but what of my desires? I am not human, I am something … superior.

Jungle Jim returned to the island this morning. He will miss the Breen also, and wanted to be present for their departure. These past two months we have become fast mates, and he has sworn to remain at my side for as long as I need him. With most of the crew busy packing, JJ, Arlen, and I decide to stay out of the way. Walking side by side we have left the cover of the sky dome, and slowly made our way down to south beach.

"John mate, how does it feel to be part Breen?"

"JJ, I feel different. It is not a thing I can put my finger on, but aside from the increase in physical strength, I feel changed. I feel happy about my new abilities, and I feel sad at the same time."

"Why do you feel sad John?" asked Arlen.

"Arlen, I do feel sad, perhaps at being different now. I am no longer human, nor am I Breen. I am stuck somewhere in the middle—separate and alone. I fear I will not be accepted by my human friends. And after hearing about the virus, they probably will hold me partly responsible. A man alone am I."

"You have Sherry, John. She is here for you, and she loves you. You two could get married."

"Yes, she is wonderful, and her friendship is important to me, but right now I am about to lose something very dear to me. These have been the best days of my life spent with the Breen. You have become my best friend Arlen, and I will miss you terribly."

"We will all miss you, John. We would take you with us if we could."

"JJ, you also have become a great friend, will you stand by me?"

"John, mate, I would go to war for you. Just say what you need, and I will be there for you."

"I think that after my friends leave tomorrow that I would like to go with you back to Australia. I just have this urge to be away from civilization for a while."

"What you need mate is what the aborigines call a walkabout. It is a time to walk and commune with nature and yourself. I know of some fine places, and even better, you will be utterly alone."

* * * * * *

General Bradley after spending days on the island has returned to Washington DC, and is in a video phone conference with the President of the United States,

"I must say Rudy it took some balls for you to go into that lion's den the way you did. After all of your attempts to destroy the aliens and they still accepted you. Perhaps you were wrong about them all along? Just wonder how things might have turned out if we had received them with more open arms in the beginning? And now with the economy hitting the fan, we could have used a friend like them. Too bad they are leaving so soon. I am looking at this virus thing as a future positive for mankind. You and I both know our population growth was out of control, and now we have a solution."

"As far as attacking the Breen I am still not convinced we did the wrong thing, sir, but for now it is what it is. As yet there does not appear to be any serious alien contamination, but I am not going to worry about that any more. Right now, we have enough home-grown problems to deal with. That is where we should focus." ….. "Before we move on sir, there is a little problem that needs to be cleaned up. My man Parker is going to need to have our protection, and probably for years to come. I am asking for your permission to allow me to provide him with sanctuary."

"This man Parker, you say he has Breen technology inside of him?"

"Yes sir, he is now a human/Breen hybrid. He looks the same, but can do some remarkable things, and supposedly will live forever."

"And we control him. Being part alien, in that way is he not in some way the contamination you were originally worried about Rudy?"

"Yes sir. I see what you are saying sir. However, I see what happened to Parker as more of a tragedy than an opportunity, and I think he would agree with us on that. Can't say if we will be able to use any of his specialness in the future or not. In talking with Harry Breen, the changes made to John's body, the new organs, and the nanites, are made with the use of a technology so far advanced beyond us as to be useless to us right now."

"Well, Rudy I authorize you to take care of Parker as you see fit. Pass on my sympathy for his suffering, and congratulate him for his service to his country."

"Thank you sir, thank you very much."

******

The cleanup work on the island, and the Val, is done. The Library is finished. My friends will be leaving bright and early the next morning. Many ships have amassed out beyond the two hundred-mile line. None will be allowed to approach the island until the Breen have left. They demanded this for security's sake. Once they are gone this island will be overrun by humans from all the world's countries. JJ and I have no desire to be a part of that, and will be leaving immediately after the departure of our extraterrestrial friends.

Monday, May 23rd.

That day, that time, had finally arrived. The Breen were all packed, and ready to leave for their next destination. Only one thing remained—teary good-byes.

To personalize their good-bye, all sixteen crew members passed by JJ and I, one at a time. First was Dr. Who, he smiled at us, and thanked us for our accommodating his techs. Booh'raan couldn't find the words, and we just hugged. Ge'eenna, who I partied with almost nightly, yet who I considered a strange girl, kissed me, and then gave me a package which contained a war ball. Hippee and Harry were next to last. They reminded me to always look to the stars. Harry had a private message which I am still trying to figure out. He said, "John, someday, if things get tough going for you, think hard on us, and we will be there for you."

Arlen was last to say bye. This was so much more than I could stand. As tears welled up and fell I had to bend my head down and look at the sand. More tears fell at that good-bye than any other time in my life. I even saw JJ mist up. We three did a group hug, and then the big guy said he had to go, saying, "John, I will remember you always, think on what Harry just said. JJ, I will miss you too, and take care of each other will you?" We were too teared up to respond. And with that the last Breen boarded the Val.

A moment later, and as silently as when I first saw it, the Val gently rose up and off of the tarmac. JJ and I stood shoulder to shoulder as we watched it float away to the east and out from under the sky dome, and then away from the island. Then finally, as if realizing too late its departure, we raised a hand to wave good-bye. The Val sailed away slowly at first, then gaining speed, it began to rise higher and higher, then faster and farther away, until at last all that was left was a patch of empty blue sky.

My head now lowered in sadness, the beach beneath my feet turned an ocean. Upon this ocean I reminisced of a place of solace where my friends and I had partied so often; was now but a barren waste. Sorrowful tears dissolved my memories and filtered them down into the warm soft sand. The island felt vacant, as though a strong wind had kicked up and blown away the playful voices, the laughter, and the splashes. All the joyous times that until recently echoed their splendor loudly to fill every moment. Now no remnants of Hedonism exist to fill my senses. Three months earlier the tides of the universe had washed the Breen upon our shores. Like shipwrecked sailors they made the most of it. Those same winds have now carried them away, but one lonely castaway persists to languish in bereaved solemnity.

The End.

26:

Postscript

On that warm tropical morning the crew of sixteen Breen, all packed-up, boarded their spaceship, and left planet Earth. They came, they partied, and then they left. Pretty much as they said they would. They enjoyed ninety days of shore leave, and then went back to work—wherever that may be.

Like a band of intergalactic thieves they had stolen our innocence and left us bereft. A hole in our collective soul had been filled, yet now another lonelier one has opened up. Our metaphorical gods had died, but on whom do we now rely? Is it time for us as a species to cast off the shackles of superstition and replace them with the freedom of rational thought?

The Breen did give us the knowledge that we are not alone, that we are part of a greater cosmos of civilizations, but still there seemed to be a lack of connectivity with our neighbors. Other than the testimonials in the library, we were not in contact with anything extraterrestrial. Oh, there was the sign post in orbit, a new star dimly visible in the northern sky, yet there still existed a vastness cold and dark between us and anyone beyond. It is doubtful the Breen would return, at least not in a normal human's lifetime. However for any wild animal there comes a time to be weaned, and to forage out for its own answers going forward.

Did we suffer loses? No one actually died as a result of the virus. That is unless you consider the loss of future generations of humans important? Watching our population shrink was hard for some. Worldwide reduction in numbers to a more sensible level is appealing only to the well-to-do, and the learned. To the poor and ignorant, to those who still cling to tribal and ethnic customs, religious tenets, or superstitious beliefs, this change was very difficult, however, isn't it our fault for not teaching them to procreate responsibly in the first place?

The probable loss of generations of young aside, our species survival cried out for something else. We needed an intangible quality found only inside man's heart. It is that better part of us, the part that separates us from the animals. It is something not alien and not Breen, a simple thing really, we call it— humanity. For without humanity we could not survive change, and without changing our ways we have little chance of forestalling perdition's come.

The circumstances that existed here on Earth when the Breen arrived they did not create. Neither are they responsible for our economic collapse which worsened during and right after their visit. The cause of these events rests squarely on our shoulders. It was the failure of a key oil field one week after their departure which sent the world into chaos. One deep and ancient reservoir we had been drawing from for over sixty years, an unprecedented amount of time for a natural resource to last, finally gave out. Our civilization had inattentively bet its future on one lake of crude located beneath an Arabian desert. Toward the end, this one field, this one ticking time bomb, was supplying only about six per cent of the world's daily crude oil usage. Not a huge percentage, but we were unable to recoup this loss. No other great oil fields remained to be developed, and production in existing fields was already at maximum capacity. This loss was enough to create an oil shock which precipitated harmful distribution perturbations across the globe, and sparked the oil wars that followed. We should look back in disbelief that we allowed so much to depend on so little.

Many will choose not to believe that we alone were the architects of our own destruction, but who remains to blame? The vast experiences of the Breen told them the world we knew was doomed. They knew we were tied into a death spiral from which it was doubtful we could recover. In retrospect, I think what they attempted with their virus was to give the human race another chance, but at some future time. Better ultimately to save a few, than to let all of humanity go extinct.

My task was to chronicle the Breen visit. To record not just their technological and scientific wonders, but also their experiences with extraterrestrial cultures transitioning into their own space-travel age in the hopes that such knowledge would be of benefit to all of mankind. To suffer a worldwide collapse is a tragedy, to not have learned from it would be a mistake.

As a child, I recall each story read to me at bedtime of having a moral at the end. We do not know yet if this is an ending, or a new beginning for man, but perhaps the Breen have shown us that no matter how man's story ends, the moral of his story is to always live within your means…..JP

www.ingramcontent.com/pod-product-compliance
Lightning Source LLC
Chambersburg PA
CBHW051430260626
47162CB00001B/26